Reviews of *At the Mouth of the River of Bees*

"Ursula Le Guin comes immediately to mind when you turn the pages of Kij Johnson's first book of short stories, her debut collection is that impressive. The title piece has that wonderful power we hope for in all fiction we read, the surprising imaginative leap that takes us to recognize the marvelous in the everyday."
—Alan Cheuse, NPR

"For all the distances traveled and the mysteries solved, those strange, inexplicable things remain. This is Johnson's fiction: the familiar combined with the inexplicable. The usual fantastic. The unknowable that undergirds the everyday."
—Sessily Watt, *Bookslut*

★ "In her first collection of short fiction, Johnson (*The Fox Woman*) covers strange, beautiful, and occasionally disturbing territory without ever missing a beat. . . . Johnson's language is beautiful, her descriptions of setting visceral, and her characters compellingly drawn. These 18 tales, most collected from Johnson's magazine publications, are sometimes off-putting, sometimes funny, and always thought provoking."
—*Publishers Weekly* (starred review)

★ "[The] stories are original, engaging, and hard to put down. . . . Johnson has a rare gift for pulling readers directly into the heart of a story and capturing their attention completely. Those who enjoy a touch of the other in their reading will love this collection."
—*Library Journal* (starred review)

"When she's at her best, the small emotional moments are as likely to linger in your memory as the fantastic imagery. Johnson would fit quite comfortably on a shelf with Karen Russell, Erin Morgenstern and others who hover in the simultaneous state of being both "literary" and "fantasy" writers."
—*Shelf Awareness*

"Kij Johnson has won short fiction Nebula awards in each of the last three years. All three winning stories are in this collection; when you read the book, you may wonder why all the others didn't win awards as well. "Ponies", to pick just one, is a shatteringly powerful fantasy about the least lovely aspects of human social behaviour. . . and also about small girls and their pet horses. Evocative, elegant, and alarmingly perceptive, Johnson reshapes your mental landscape with every story she writes."
—David Larsen, *New Zealand Herald*

AT THE MOUTH OF THE RIVER OF BEES

At the Mouth of the River of Bees

stories

Kij Johnson

Small Beer Press
Easthampton, MA

At the Mouth of the River of Bees: Stories copyright © 2012 by Kij Johnson. All rights reserved.
www.kijjohnson.com

Small Beer Press
150 Pleasant Street #306
Easthampton, MA 01027
www.smallbeerpress.com
www.weightlessbooks.com
info@smallbeerpress.com

Distributed to the trade by Consortium.

Library of Congress Cataloging-in-Publication Data

Johnson, Kij.
  At the mouth of the river of bees : stories / Kij Johnson. -- 1st ed.
      p. cm.
  ISBN 978-1-931520-80-5 (trade pbk. : alk. paper) -- ISBN 978-1-931520-81-2 (ebook)
  I. Title.
  PS3560.O3797I6A94 2012
  813'.54--DC23
                            2012020736
First edition   2 3 4 5 6 7 8 9

Text set in Centaur MT 11.5. Titles set in Didot.

Printed on 50# 30% PCR recycled Natures Natural paper by C-M Books in Ann Arbor, MI.
Cover illustrations by Jackie Morris (www.jackiemorris.co.uk).

Contents

for James Gunn

26 Monkeys,
Also the Abyss

1.

Aimee's big trick is that she makes 26 monkeys vanish onstage.

2.

She pushes out a claw-foot bathtub and asks audience members to come up and inspect it. The people climb in and look underneath, touch the white enamel, run their hands along the little lions' feet. When they're done, four chains are lowered from the stage's fly space. Aimee secures them to holes drilled along the tub's lip, gives a signal, and the bathtub is hoisted ten feet into the air.

She sets a stepladder next to it. She claps her hands and the 26 monkeys onstage run up the ladder one after the other and jump into the bathtub. The bathtub shakes as each monkey thuds in among the others. The audience can see heads, legs, tails; but eventually every monkey settles and the bathtub is still again. Zeb is always the last monkey up the ladder. As he climbs into the bathtub, he makes a humming boom deep in his chest. It fills the stage.

And then there's a flash of light, two of the chains fall off, and the bathtub swings down to expose its interior.

Empty.

3.

They turn up later, back at the tour bus. There's a smallish dog door, and in the hours before morning the monkeys let themselves in alone or in small groups, and get themselves glasses of water from the tap. If more than one returns at the same time, they murmur a bit among themselves like college students meeting in the dorm halls after bar time. A few sleep on the sofa and at least one likes to be on the bed, but most of them wander back to their cages. There's a little grunting as they rearrange their blankets and soft toys, and then sighs and snoring. Aimee doesn't really sleep until she hears them all come in.

Aimee has no idea what happens to them in the bathtub, or where they go, or what they do before the soft click of the dog door opening. This bothers her a lot.

4.

Aimee has had the act for three years now. She was living in a month-by-month furnished apartment under a flight path for the Salt Lake City airport. She was hollow, as though something had chewed a hole in her body and the hole had grown infected.

There was a monkey act at the Utah State Fair. She felt a sudden and totally out of character urge to see it. Afterward, with no idea why, she walked up to the owner and said, "I have to buy this."

He nodded. He sold it to her for a dollar, which he told her was the price he had paid four years before.

Later, when the paperwork was filled out, she asked him, "How can you leave them? Won't they miss you?"

"You'll see, they're pretty autonomous," he said. "Yeah, they'll miss me and I'll miss them. But it's time, they know that."

He smiled at his new wife, a small woman with laugh lines and a vervet hanging from one hand. "We're ready to have a garden," she said.

He was right. The monkeys missed him. But they also welcomed her, each monkey politely shaking her hand as she walked into what was now her bus.

5.

Aimee has: a 19-year-old tour bus packed with cages that range in size from parrot-sized (for the vervets) to something about the size of a pickup bed (for all the macaques); a stack of books on monkeys ranging from *All About Monkeys!* to *Evolution and Ecology of Baboon Societies*; some sequined show costumes, a sewing machine, and a bunch of Carhartts and tees; a stack of show posters from a few years back that say 24 MONKEYS! FACE

THE ABYSS; a battered sofa in a virulent green plaid; and a boyfriend who helps with the monkeys.

She cannot tell you why she has any of these, not even the boyfriend, whose name is Geof, whom she met in Billings seven months ago. Aimee has no idea where anything comes from anymore. She no longer believes that anything makes sense, even though she can't stop hoping.

The bus smells about as you'd expect a bus full of monkeys to smell, though after a show, after the bathtub trick but before the monkeys all return, it also smells of cinnamon, which is the tea Aimee sometimes drinks.

6.

For the act, the monkeys do tricks or dress up in outfits and act out hit movies—*The Matrix* is very popular, as is anything where the monkeys dress up like little orcs. The maned monkeys, the lion-tails and the colobuses, have a lion-tamer act with the old capuchin female, Pango, dressed in a red jacket and carrying a whip and a small chair. The chimpanzee (whose name is Mimi, and no, she is not a monkey) can do actual sleight of hand; she's not very good, but she's the best Chimp Pulling A Coin From Someone's Ear in the world.

The monkeys can also build a suspension bridge from wooden chairs and rope, make a four-tier champagne fountain, and write their names on a whiteboard.

The monkey show is very popular, with a schedule of 127 shows this year at fairs and festivals across the Midwest and Great Plains. Aimee could do more, but she likes to let everyone have a couple months off at Christmas.

7.

This is the bathtub act:

Aimee wears a glittering purple-black dress designed to look like a scanty magician's robe. She stands in front of a scrim lit deep blue and scattered with stars. The monkeys are ranged in front of her. As she speaks they undress and fold their clothes into neat piles. Zeb sits on his stool to one side, a white spotlight shining straight down to give him a shadowed look.

She raises her hands.

"These monkeys have made you laugh, and made you gasp. They have created wonders for you and performed mysteries. But there is a final mystery they offer you—the strangest, the greatest of all."

She parts her hands suddenly, and the scrim goes transparent and is lifted away, revealing the bathtub on a raised dais. She walks around it, running her hand along the tub's curves.

"It's a simple thing, this bathtub. Ordinary in every way, mundane as breakfast. In a moment I will invite members of the audience up to let you see this for yourselves.

"But for the monkeys it is also a magical object. It allows them to travel—no one can say where. Not even I—" she pauses; "—can tell you this. Only the monkeys know, and they share no secrets.

"Where do they go? Into heaven, foreign lands, other worlds—or some dark abyss? We cannot follow. They will vanish before our eyes, vanish from this most ordinary of things."

And after the bathtub is inspected and she has told the audience that there will be no final spectacle in the show—"It will be hours before they return from their secret travels"—and called for applause for them, she gives the cue.

8.

Aimee's monkeys:
- 2 siamangs, a mated couple.
- 2 squirrel monkeys, though they're so active they might as well be twice as many.
- 2 vervets.
- a guenon, who is probably pregnant though it's still too early to tell for sure. Aimee has no idea how this happened.
- 3 rhesus monkeys. They juggle a little.
- an older capuchin female named Pango.
- a crested macaque, 3 Japanese snow monkeys (one quite young), and a Java macaque. Despite the differences, they have formed a small troop and like to sleep together.
- a chimpanzee, who is not actually a monkey.

- a surly gibbon.
- 2 marmosets.
- a golden tamarin; a cotton-top tamarin.
- a proboscis monkey.
- red and black colobuses.
- Zeb.

9.

Aimee thinks Zeb might be a de Brazza's guenon, except that he's so old that he's lost almost all his hair. She worries about his health but he insists on staying in the act. By now all he's really up for is the final rush to the bathtub, and for him it is more of a stroll. The rest of the time, he sits on a stool that is painted orange and silver and watches the other monkeys, looking like an aging impresario viewing his *Swan Lake* from the wings. Sometimes she gives him things to hold, such as a silver hoop through which the squirrel monkeys jump.

10.

No one seems to know how the monkeys vanish or where they go. Sometimes they return holding foreign coins or durian fruit, or wearing pointed Moroccan slippers. Every so often one returns pregnant or leading an unfamiliar monkey by the hand. The number of monkeys is not constant.

"I just don't get it," Aimee keeps asking Geof, as if he has any idea. Aimee never knows anything anymore. She's been living without any certainties, and this one thing—well, the whole thing, the fact the monkeys get along so well and know how to do card tricks and just turned up in her life and vanish from the bathtub; *everything*—she coasts with that most of the time, but every so often, when she feels her life is wheeling without brakes down a long hill, she starts poking at this again.

Geof trusts the universe a lot more than Aimee does. "You could ask them," he says.

———

Kij Johnson

11.

Aimee's boyfriend:

Geof is not at all what Aimee expected from a boyfriend. For one thing, he's fifteen years younger than Aimee, 28 to her 43. For another, he's sort of quiet. For a third, he's gorgeous, silky thick hair pulled into a shoulder-length ponytail, shaved sides showing off his strong jaw line. He smiles a lot, but he doesn't laugh very often.

Geof has a degree in creative writing, which means that he was working in a bike-repair shop when she met him at the Montana Fair. Aimee never has much to do right after the show, so when he offered to buy her a beer she said yes. And then it was four a.m. and they were kissing in the bus, monkeys letting themselves in and getting ready for bed; and Aimee and Geof made love.

In the morning over breakfast, the monkeys came up one by one and shook his hand solemnly, and then he was with the band, so to speak. She helped him pick up his cameras and clothes and the surfboard his sister had painted for him one year as a Christmas present. There's no room for the surfboard so it's suspended from the ceiling. Sometimes the squirrel monkeys hang out there and peek over the side.

Aimee and Geof never talk about love.

Geof has a Class C driver's license, but this is just lagniappe.

12.

Zeb is dying.

Generally speaking, the monkeys are remarkably healthy and Aimee can handle their occasional sinus infections and gastrointestinal ailments. For anything more difficult, she's found a couple of communities online and some helpful specialists.

But Zeb's coughing some, and the last of his fur is falling out. He moves very slowly and sometimes has trouble remembering simple tasks. When the show was up in St. Paul six months ago, a Como Zoo zoologist came to visit the monkeys, complimented her on their general health and well-being, and at her request looked Zeb over.

"How old is he?" the zoologist, Gina, asked.

"I don't know," Aimee said. The man she bought the show from hadn't known either.

"*I'll* tell you then," Gina said. "He's old. I mean, seriously old."

Senile dementia, arthritis, a heart murmur. No telling when, Gina said. "He's a happy monkey," she said. "He'll go when he goes."

13.

Aimee thinks a lot about this. What happens to the act when Zeb's dead? Through each show he sits calm and poised on his bright stool. She feels he is somehow at the heart of the monkeys' amiability and cleverness. She keeps thinking that he is the reason the monkeys all vanish and return.

Because there's always a reason for everything, isn't there? Because if there isn't a reason for even *one* thing, like how you can get sick, or your husband stop loving you, or people you love die—then there's no reason for anything. So there must be reasons. Zeb's as good a guess as any.

14.

What Aimee likes about this life:

It doesn't mean anything. She doesn't live anywhere. Her world is 38 feet and 127 shows long and currently 26 monkeys deep. This is manageable.

Fairs don't mean anything, either. Her tiny world travels within a slightly larger world, the identical, interchangeable fairs. Sometimes the only things that cue Aimee to the town she's in are the nighttime temperatures and the shape of the horizon: badlands, mountains, plains, or skyline.

Fairs are as artificial as titanium knees: the carnival, the animal barns, the stock-car races, the concerts, the smell of burnt sugar and funnel cakes and animal bedding. Everything is an overly bright symbol for something real, food or pets or hanging out with friends. None of this has anything to do with the world Aimee used to live in, the world from which these people visit.

She has decided that Geof is like the rest of it: temporary, meaningless. Not for loving.

15.

These are some ways Aimee's life might have come apart:

   a.   She might have broken her ankle a few years ago, and gotten a bone infection that left her on crutches for ten months and in pain for longer.

b. Her husband might have fallen in love with his admin and left her.

c. She might have been fired from her job in the same week she found out her sister had colon cancer.

d. She might have gone insane for a time and made a series of questionable choices that left her alone in a furnished apartment in a city she picked out of the atlas.

Nothing is certain. You can lose everything. Eventually, even at your luckiest, you will die and then you *will* lose it all. When you are a certain age or when you have lost certain things and people, Aimee's crippling grief will make a terrible poisoned dark sense.

16.

Aimee has read up a lot, so she knows how strange all this is.

There aren't any locks on the cages. The monkeys use them as bedrooms, places to store their special possessions and get away from the others when they want some privacy. Much of the time, however, they are loose in the bus or poking around in the worn grass around it.

Right now, three monkeys are sitting on the bed playing a game where they match colored balls. Others are pulling at skeins of woolen yarn, or rolling around on the floor, or poking at a piece of wood with a screwdriver, or climbing on Aimee and Geof and the sofa. Some of the monkeys are crowded around the computer watching kitten videos on YouTube.

The black colobus is stacking children's wooden blocks on the kitchenette table. He brought them back one night a couple of weeks ago, and since then he's been trying to make an arch. After two weeks and Aimee's showing him repeatedly how a keystone works, he still hasn't figured it out, but he keeps trying.

Geof's reading a novel aloud to the capuchin Pango, who watches the pages as though she's reading along. Sometimes she points to a word and looks up at him with her bright eyes, and he repeats it to her, smiling, and then spells it out.

Zeb is sleeping in his cage. He crept in there at dusk, fluffed up his toys and his blanket, and pulled the door closed behind him. He does this a lot lately.

17.

Aimee's going to lose Zeb and then what? What happens to the other monkeys? 26 monkeys are a lot of monkeys, but they all like each other. No one except maybe a zoo or a circus can keep that many, and she doesn't think anyone else will let them sleep wherever they like or watch kitten videos. And if Zeb's not there, where will they go, those nights when they can no longer drop through the bathtub and into their mystery? And she doesn't even know whether it *is* Zeb, whether he is the cause of this or that's just her flailing for reasons again.

And Aimee? She'll lose her safe artificial world: the bus, the identical fairs, the meaningless boyfriend. The monkeys. And then what?

18.

A few months after she bought the show, she followed the monkeys up the ladder in the closing act. Zeb raced up the ladder, stepped into the bathtub and stood, lungs filling for his great call. And she ran up after him. She glimpsed the bathtub's interior, the monkeys tidily sardined in, scrambling to get out of her way as they realized what she was doing. She hopped into the hole they made for her, curled up tight.

This only took an instant. Zeb finished his breath, boomed it out. There was a flash of light, she heard the chains release and felt the bathtub swing down, monkeys shifting around her.

She fell the ten feet alone. Her ankle twisted when she hit the stage but she managed to stay upright. The monkeys were gone.

There was an awkward silence. It wasn't one of her successful performances.

19.

Aimee and Geof walk through the midway at the Salina Fair. She's hungry and they don't want to cook, so they're looking for somewhere that sells $4.50 hotdogs and $3.25 Cokes, and Geof turns to Aimee and says,

"This is bullshit. Why don't we go into town? Have real food. Act like normal people."

So they do, pasta and wine at a place called Irina's Villa. "You're always asking why they go," Geof says, a bottle and a half in. His eyes are a cloudy blue-gray, but in this light they look black and very warm. "See, I don't think we're ever going to find out what happens. But I don't think that's the real question anyway. Maybe the question is, why do they come back?"

Aimee thinks about the foreign coins, the wood blocks, the wonderful things they return with. "I don't know," she says. "Why *do* they come back?"

Later that night, back at the bus, Geof says, "Wherever they go, yeah, it's cool. But see, here's my theory." He gestures to the crowded bus with its clutter of toys and tools. The two tamarins have just come in and they're sitting on the kitchenette table, heads close as they examine some new small thing. "They like visiting wherever it is, sure. But this is their home. Everyone likes to come home sooner or later."

"If they have a home," Aimee says.

"Everyone has a home, even if they don't believe it," Geof says.

20.

That night, when Geof's asleep curled up around one of the macaques, Aimee kneels by Zeb's cage. "Can you at least show me?" she asks. "Please? Before you go?"

Zeb is an indeterminate lump under his baby-blue blanket, but he gives a little sigh and climbs slowly from his cage. He takes her hand with his own hot leathery paw, and they walk out the door into the night.

The back lot where all the trailers and buses are parked is quiet, only the buzz of the generators, a few voices still audible from behind curtained windows. The sky is blue-black and scattered with stars. The moon shines straight down on them, leaving Zeb's face shadowed. His eyes when he looks up seem bottomless.

The bathtub is backstage, already on its wheeled dais waiting for the next show. The space is nearly pitch-dark, lit by some red EXIT signs and a single sodium-vapor lamp off to one side. Zeb walks her up to the tub, lets her run her hands along its cold curves and the lions' paws, and shows her the dimly lit interior.

And then he heaves himself onto the dais and over the tub lip. She stands beside him, looking down. He lifts himself upright and gives his great boom. And then he drops flat and the bathtub is empty.

She saw it, him vanishing. He was there and then he was gone. But there was nothing to see, no gate, no flickering reality or soft pop as air snapped in to fill the vacated space. It still doesn't make sense, but it's the answer that Zeb has.

He's already back at the bus when she gets there, already buried under his blanket and wheezing in his sleep.

21.

Then one day:

Everyone is backstage. Aimee is finishing her makeup and Geof is double-checking everything. The monkeys are sitting neatly in a circle in the dressing room, as if trying to keep their bright vests and skirts from creasing. Zeb sits in the middle, beside Pango in her little green sequined outfit. They grunt a bit, then lean back. One after the other, the rest of the monkeys crawl forward and shake his hand and then hers. She nods, like a small queen at a flower show.

That night, Zeb doesn't run up the ladder. He stays on his stool and it's Pango who is the last monkey up the ladder, who climbs into the bathtub and gives a screech. Aimee has been wrong that it is Zeb who is the heart of what is happening with the monkeys, but she was so sure of it that she missed all the cues. But Geof didn't miss a thing, so when Pango screeches, he hits the flash powder. The flash, the empty bathtub.

Afterward, Zeb stands on his stool, bowing like an impresario called onstage for the curtain call. When the curtain drops for the last time, he reaches up to be lifted. Aimee cuddles him as they walk back to the bus. Geof's arm is around them both.

Zeb falls asleep with them that night, between them in the bed. When she gets up in the morning, he's back in his cage with his favorite toys. He doesn't wake up. The monkeys cluster at the bars peeking in.

Aimee cries all day. "It's okay," Geof says.

"It's not about Zeb," she sobs.

"I know," he says.

22.

Here's the trick to the bathtub trick. There is no trick. The monkeys pour across the stage and up the ladder and into the bathtub and they settle in and then they vanish. The world is full of strange things, things that make no sense, and maybe this is one of them. Maybe the monkeys choose not to share, that's cool, who can blame them.

Maybe this is the monkeys' mystery, how they found other monkeys that ask questions and try things, and figured out a way to all be together to share it. Maybe Aimee and Geof are really just houseguests in the monkeys' world: they are there for a while and then they leave.

23.

Six weeks later, a man walks up to Aimee as she and Geof kiss after a show. He's short, pale, balding. He has the shell-shocked look of a man eaten hollow from the inside. "I need to buy this," he says.

Aimee nods. "I know you do." She sells it to him for a dollar.

24.

Three months later, Aimee and Geof get their first houseguest in their new apartment in Bellingham. They hear the refrigerator close and come out to the kitchen to find Pango pouring orange juice from a carton. They send her home with a pinochle deck.

Fox Magic

Diaries are kept by men: strong brush strokes on smooth rice paper, gathered into sheaves and tied with ribbon and placed in a lacquered box. I know this, for I have seen one such diary. It's said that there are also noble ladies who keep diaries, in the capital or on their journeys in the provinces. These diaries (it is said) are often filled with grief, for a woman's life is filled with sadness and waiting.

Men and women write their various diaries: I shall see if a fox-maiden cannot also write one.

I saw him and loved him, my master Kaya no Yoshifuji. I say this and it is short and sharp and without elegance, like a bark; and yet I have no idea how else to start. I am only a fox; I have no elegancies of language. I need to start before that, I think.

I was raised with a single sibling, a male, by my mother and grandfather in the narrow space beneath Yoshifuji's storehouse in the kitchen garden. The storeroom's floor above our heads was of smoothed boxwood planks; there was dry, powdery dirt between our toes. We had dug a hole by one of the corner supports, a small scrape hardly big enough for the four of us.

It was summer. We sneaked from the garden and ran in the woods behind Yoshifuji's house, looking for mice and birds and rabbits. But they were clever and we were hungry all the time. It was easier to steal food, so we crouched in the shadow of the storehouse and watched everything that went on in the garden, waiting.

The cook, a huge man with eyes lost in rolls of fat, came out some days and pulled roots from the dirt. Sometimes he would drop one, and I would wait until his back was turned and run out, exposed to the world, and snatch it. Often the cook came to the storehouse. We eased farther back, listened to the latch open, and the man's heavy footsteps over our heads, one board creaking; and then the sounds of his leaving, the latch being secured and sounds of his footsteps scuffing up the walk to the house.

One day we listened, and there were the noises, just as there should be, but—The latch was not twisted shut. I looked at my brother, who crouched beside me. We said nothing, for we were just foxes, but we knew what we wanted. No one was in the garden. We crawled out and ducked into the open storehouse door. There were the foods, just as we had smelled them: a hanging pheasant and dried fish, pickled radishes, sake and vinegar. We knocked over jars and chewed open boxes and ate and ate.

The shout at the door took us completely by surprise. The cook was back: he was cursing at us, at the damage we'd done. I spun around, but there was nowhere to hide; I backed into a corner and bared my teeth. The cook slammed the door shut. This time we heard the latch.

Panicked, I scrabbled at the walls, at the tiny cracks in the floor through which I could smell my patch of dirt. I cracked my claw and smelled the thread of fresh blood.

There were voices outside the door again, and it was suddenly thrown wide. The cook was howling, yelling with rage. A woman stood behind him in rich robes, with a huge red fan concealing her face. I'd seen her before: I knew she was the mistress of the house, Shikibu. She tilted the fan slightly to stare in at us. Light through the fan colored her skin, but she was very beautiful. I growled; she screamed and jumped back. "Foxes!"

The third person looking in was Kaya no Yoshifuji. He was in hunting dress, blue and gray, with silver medallions woven into the pattern of his outer robe. In one hand he held a short bow; arrows stuck over one shoulder from a quiver on his back. His hair was oiled and arranged in a loop over his head. His eyes were deepest black; his voice when he spoke was low and humorous. "Hush, both of you! You are making it worse."

"Oh, Husband!" the woman cried. She was shaking. "They are evil spirits. We must destroy them!"

"They are only animals—foxes, young foxes. Quiet, you are frightening them."

Her fingers knotted on the fan's sticks, "No! Foxes are all evil. Everyone knows this. They will destroy our house. Kill them—please!"

"Go." Yoshifuji made a gesture at the cook staring open-mouthed at Shikibu. The man ran up the path and into the house. My lord turned to Shikibu. "You must not stay out here where everyone can see you. You are being foolish. I will not kill them. If we just give them a chance, they may run off on their own." Yoshifuji turned his back on her. "Please go inside."

She looked in at us again. I felt my ears flatten again, my back prickle with lifting hairs. "I will leave, Husband, because you order it. Please come to me later?"

Shikibu left us. Yoshifuji knelt in the dirt of the garden for a long moment with his hand over his eyes. "Ah, well, little foxes, so it goes, neh?—

> "'Foxes half-seen in the darkness;
> I have courted knowing less of my lady.'"

I recognize now that what he said was a poem, even though I wasn't sure what a poem was. It is a human thing; I don't know how well a fox can ever understand it.

He stood and brushed at his knees. "I will be back in a bit. It would be wise to be gone before then." He paused a minute. "Run, little foxes. Be free while you can."

I couldn't stop watching him as he walked up to the house. It wasn't until my brother bit me on the shoulder and barked that I followed him through the door and down into our hole.

I learned to cry that night. Crouched together in the scrape, my family listened in silence. After a time, Grandfather laid his muzzle against mine. "You have magic in you, Granddaughter: that is why you can cry."

"All foxes have magic, Grandfather," I said. "They don't all cry."

"Not this magic," he said.

After that I crept often to the house's formal gardens. The carefully shaped trees were cover to me as I approached the house itself, which was of cedar and blackened wood, with great eaves. In the shadow of a half-moon bridge I leapt a narrow stream; I slid past an ornamental rock covered with lichens and into a small willow tree that slumped down to brush the short grasses that grew near the house. Lost in the green and silver leaves, I crouched there and watched. Or I hid in a patch of glossy rhododendron. Or under the floor of the house itself; there were many places for a fox to conceal herself.

I watched whenever I could, longing for glimpses of my lord or the sound of his voice; but he was often gone, hunting with his friends or traveling in the course of his duties. There were times, even, when he stayed out all night and returned just before dawn with a foreign scent clinging to his clothes and a strange woman's fan or comb in his hand. It was his right and his responsibility, to live a man's life—I understood that.

Still, I felt a little sorry for his wife. Her rooms were the innermost of the north wing, with layers of shoji screens and bamboo blinds and curtains-of-state between us, but it was the seventh month, and she left as many of these open as she decently could, and sometimes I saw her, almost lost in the shadows of the dark-eaved house. She had a handful of women: they played children's games with tops and hoops; they practiced their calligraphy; they wrote poems; they called out the plaited-palm carriages and went to the monastery and listened to the sutras being read. It seemed clear that all these things were merely to fill her time until Yoshifuji came to her. Her life was full of twilight and waiting, but I envied her for the moments he did spend with her.

And then Shikibu left to visit her father's family in the capital. She took her women and many servants, including the fat cook. The house was very still and empty. Yoshifuji was home even less often, but when he was there, he was almost always alone. He spent a lot of time writing, taking great care with his brushwork. Most evenings at twilight, he walked through the formal garden and into the woods, to follow a sharp-smelling cedar path that led between two shrines. I paced his walks in the woods and tried to see his expression in the dusk.

There was one night when I crouched under the willow. My lord sat alone in a room with the screen walls pushed back. I think he was just looking at the garden in the moonlight; maybe he was drinking *sake* as well. His face was lit by the red coals of a brazier and by the reflected blue light of the full moon. My heart hurt, a sad heavy weight in my breast. Tears matted my cheek fur.

A shadow slid past the ornamental rock and settled next to me. Grandfather touched his nose to the tears and to my ribs, which belled out without flesh to soften them.

"You will die," he said. "Without food, you'll waste away."

"I don't care. I love this man."

He was silent for a while. "Nevertheless," he finally said.

"Grandfather. We are foxes and we have magic. Can we bring him to us?"

"Is this what you want?"

"Yes. Or I *will* die."

"If you want this, we will do what we must," Grandfather said, and left me.

The magic was hard to make. We worked a long time on it. I am a fox, but my grandfather and mother made me a maiden, too. My hair was as black and smooth as water over slate, and fell past my layered silk robes. One night I looked at myself in a puddle of water. My face was as round and pale as the moon, which delighted me.

My grandfather made me a small white ball, which glowed in the shadows. I looked at him curiously.

"For playing," he said. "You're a maiden. You can't just wrestle with your brother anymore. A ball like that is traditional for a fox maiden."

"I don't like playing with a ball."

"You don't know yet if you do or not. Put it in your sleeve. You will want it sooner or later. It will pass the time."

We made the space beneath the storehouse a many-roomed house, with floors and beams worn to a glow from servants' constant rubbing; and trunks and lacquered boxes filled with silk robes and tortoiseshell combs, porcelain bowls and silver chopsticks, Michinoka paper and bamboo-handled brushes and cakes of ink, a ceremonial tea set glazed to look like pebbles seen underwater. No, we did not make these things, exactly: it was still just bare dirt and a dry little hole. But we made it seem as if it were so. I can't explain.

We filled the house with many beautiful things, and then we made a garden around the place filled with stones and ponds and thick bushes. It would have been a fox's dream had I still been a fox. We placed a sun, a moon, stars, just like the real ones. We made many servants, all quick and quiet and clever.

And we made my family human. My brother became small and exquisite, with narrow poet's hands. We made my mother slender with a single streak of silver in the black hair that fell to her knees. And Grandfather was very handsome. He wore russet robes with small medallions on each sleeve; when I bent close to see what they represented, he smiled and pulled away. "Fox paws," he said.

I sat in a billow of skirts and sleeves behind a red and green curtain-of-state. I had a fan painted with a poem I didn't understand in one hand; I kept staring with wonder at the way the fan snapped open and then shut, and at the quick gestures of my human fingers that made this happen. My family was arranged around me: my mother behind the curtain with me, Brother and Grandfather decently on the other side. Mother had a flea; I saw fox-her lift a hind leg and scratch behind one ear, and, like a reflection on water over a passing fish, I saw woman-her raise one long hand and discreetly ease herself.

"Mother," I said, shocked. "What if he sees both?"

She looked ashamed and Grandfather asked what was going on. I explained and he laughed. "He won't. He is a man; he'll see what he wants to see. Are you happy, Granddaughter?"

"It is all beautiful, I think. But my lord does not love me."

"Yet." Grandfather cackled. "I'm enjoying this. It's too long since I got into mischief—not since I was a kit, and my brothers and I used to lure travelers into the marshes with fire in our tails."

I heard Brother sigh. I longed to see his expression, but the curtain separated us. Grandfather said: "Be respectful, Grandson. Be as human as you can, for your sister's sake."

Brother replied, "Why can't she be happy as a fox? We played and ran and I thought we were happy."

"Because she loves a man," Mother said. "We are doing this for her."

"I know," Brother said. "I will try to be a good brother to her, and a good son and grandson to yourselves."

"This man will help us all," Grandfather said. "He will be a good provider, and perhaps he will find you a position in the government somewhere."

"I will try to be dutiful and satisfy all your expectations," my brother said. He didn't sound dutiful, only melancholy.

"Well," said Grandfather. "Granddaughter, are you ready for the next step?"

"Grandfather, I will do anything."

"Then go tonight. Walk in the woods, and when Yoshifuji comes out, let things happen as they may."

I left the beautiful house—which meant I crawled from our dusty little hole—in the company of several ladies-in-waiting. There was a fox-path that appeared to lead through gardens and over a stream to the cedar forest-path, but it was really just passage through some thick weeds behind the storehouse. We moved down to the cedar path and walked there in the twilight.

He came. My fox-eyes saw him before he saw me. He was in house-dress, simple silk robes without elaborate dyed patterns. He wore no hat but his queue was arranged just as it should be. His face was sad—missing his wife, I imagined, as well he might, she was so pretty and gentle. What was I doing, stealing him like this? Now she would wait in her dark halls forever, with no one to break the dim monotony of her life. I wondered if I should just shed this maiden's body and ease back into the ferns that fringed the path.

But I am a fox, whatever else I have become: I steeled myself easily, and said aloud, "I would rather she were alone than me."

Perhaps he heard me, or saw the ladies-in-waiting, who were dressed in bright colors that glowed even in the gathering dark. At any rate, he walked toward us. My women squeaked and averted their faces, hiding behind their fans. They were magical so of course they did just as they ought; I, who was only mortal (and a fox), stared bare-faced, with no maidenly reticence. He met my eyes. I have given that hunting stare; I know it well. I responded as the animal I am. I turned to run.

He was beside me before I could gather my skirts, and laid his hand on my sleeve. "Wait!"

I felt trapped like a mouse in his killing gaze. My women fluttered up, making meaningless noises of concern. "Please let me go," I said.

"No. A pretty thing like you?" I remembered my fan and brought it up to hide my face. He caught my wrist to prevent me; the touch of his skin against mine made me dizzy. "Who are you?"

"Nobody," I stammered. Of all the things we had remembered, all the unfamiliar things we had been so clever about—the tea set, the stones in the gardens—we had given ourselves no names! But he seemed to accept this.

"I am Kaya no Yoshifuji. Why are you walking in my woods with no men to protect you?"

I groped, thinking desperately. "It is a—a contest. We write poems to the dusk, my women and I." The ladies chirruped in agreement.

"Do you live near here?" he asked.

"Oh, yes. Just on the other side of the woods."

He nodded. Fox magic made him accept this, even though the woods are a day's hard travel deep and he has made this journey himself. "Still, it is very unsafe, and it is really too dark for you to walk home. Would you and your ladies honor me by coming as guests to my house, to wait there until your relatives can be sent for?"

I thought of those rooms, and thought suddenly of Shikibu drifting aimlessly, waiting as she so often did for Yoshifuji. She would be a ghost there even in her absence. I shrank back. "No, I couldn't possibly!"

He looked relieved. Perhaps he felt her, as well. "Then where do you live? I'll escort you home."

"That would be very nice," I said with relief. "I live just over there."

Maybe he would have seen the falseness that first time when he stepped from the true path onto the fox-path, but he was looking at me, his head bent to try to see past the fan I had managed to raise. It was hard walking in my many robes, but he mistook my inexperience for blindness in the dark and he was very solicitous.

The fox-path was long and wandering. We walked along it until we saw lights. "Home," I said, and took his hand and led him the last few steps. He was lost in the magic then and didn't notice that he entered my beautiful house by lying belly-down in the dirt and wriggling under the storehouse. We stood on the veranda. Servants clustered around, shielding me from his gaze and exclaiming.

"You are the daughter of this house?" Yoshifuji asked.

"I am," I said.

He looked around at the many torches and stone lanterns that lit the garden, and the quality of the bamboo blinds edged with braid and tied up with red and black ribbons. "Your family must be a fine one."

He followed me into my reception room, where servants had set up a curtain-of-state; they would preserve my womanly modesty here, even after I had committed the solecism of allowing a man to see me walk and to see my face unshielded. I sank to the mat behind the panels of fabric.

My lord still stood. "Perhaps I should go, having seen you home," he said.

"Oh, please wait! My family will wish to thank you for your kindness. Please sit." I heard servants bring a mat for him.

A door slid open with a snap, by which I knew it must be one of us foxes, as the servants were all perfectly silent when they moved around the house. My brother's voice spoke. "I have only just heard of your presence in our house. Forgive me that my sister was your only welcome."

I think Yoshifuji gestured, but I couldn't see this. After a moment, my brother went on, "I am the grandson of Miyoshi no Kiyoyuki, and in his name I welcome you." I sighed with relief. Someone had remembered! "Please accept our hospitality for the night."

"Thank you. I am Kaya no Yoshifuji."

"There will be food brought to you. Let me inform my grandfather. He is in seclusion tonight, but he will be deeply honored by your presence when his taboo has been lifted and he may socialize again. Please excuse me, so that I can arrange to have a message sent to him." The screen snapped shut and I heard my brother's narrow fox feet pad away from us.

He did not come back that night. Nor did my mother or my grandfather appear. Our only company was my women, silent and efficient. We talked and Yoshifuji teased a little. After a bit, I dropped my fan in such a way that one of the panels of the curtain-of-state was pushed aside and I could watch his face in the dim light of a single oil lamp.

My women brought my lord a lacquered tray with dried fish and seaweed and quail eggs arranged on it, a heaping pot of white rice, and a little cracked-glaze teapot with green-leaf tea brewing in it. There were also carved ivory chopsticks and a small shallow bowl for the rice and then the tea. I sniffed the air and smelled perfume and these delicate little foods; and at the same time I smelled the single dead mouse my brother had been able to catch and save. My lord lifted bits of the mouse with scraps of straw held between his fingers, and drank rainwater from a dead leaf, and thought nothing of it.

We talked and talked. He said:

> "'A mountain seen through shredding clouds;
> a pretty woman glimpsed through a gap of the curtains.'"

"I would be glad of a clearer view."

I knew the appropriate response was another poem, but I had no idea what to say. The silence was stretching. If I said nothing, he would know something was strange. He would look around and see that he was not in this house, but crouched in the dirt, hung with cobwebs—"Please sit beside me," I said.

This was forward of me, but I could think of no other way to distract him. At any rate, it worked. He barely blinked, just stood and moved behind the curtains with me.

A woman of rank is hardly ever alone, so my ladies-in-waiting were present; but they slept, discreet little piles of robes in the darkness. One even snored, a tiny undignified sound. I was grateful for that snore. It must make the women seem real, and our privacy seem absolutely convincing to my lord.

I hid my face with my fan, which he took away from me; with my sleeve, which he gently brushed aside; with my hands, which he captured in his own and held against his face.

From there things progressed. I had mated before with my brother but I think we were too young for it to take, for I had no cubs. Mating with a man was not so different from that—though cleaner and more polite—and yet I found it completely different. Yoshifuji was very handsome even with his hair in disarray and his robes kilted aside. I wept at his beauty, at the touch of his hand on my human breast, at the feel of him in my fingers, at the heavenly shower of his consummation. He brushed at my tears with a fingertip and I sobbed more helplessly and hid my face in my hair.

"What is wrong, my love?" he whispered.

"How she will mourn," I said to myself.

"Who?" he asked.

"Your wife," I said.

He shrugged. "It is you I love."

And that's how I knew that the fox magic had taken him.

Dawn came and Yoshifuji did not leave as he would have had I been a mere flirt. He stayed beside me, and played with my hair as my women rearranged my dress and scented my robes.

One of the shojis slid open, and my grandfather stood there in his red-orange robes. I squeaked with embarrassment—the evidence of our earlier occupation was clear around us, and even the curtain around the bed platform was in considerable disorder, its panels flipped out of our way in the night—but Grandfather said nothing of this.

"Ah, you're the lad," he said. "I'm Miyoshi no Kiyoyuki. It's good to meet you."

Yoshifuji bowed. "I am—"

"I know who you are; my grandson came to tell me about you last night. Please forgive me for there being no one but my graceless granddaughter to entertain you."

My lord bowed his head. "Your granddaughter is a woman of rare beauty and intelligence."

"Yes, well," Grandfather said. "I hope you mean that."

"I do," said Yoshifuji. "And your home, so elegant—"

"Well. You were always meant to come here, and now you must stay."

23

"It will be the delight and honor of my life," my lord said.

"Come drink with me," my grandfather said. "We have a lot to arrange."

Light-headed with happiness, I watched Yoshifuji and my grandfather leave the room. When my love returned, it was settled. We were to be married.

We slept together the three nights it takes to formalize a marriage and ate the third-night cakes, and drank *sake* together in the presence of a priest. I saw the wedding as my lord saw it: our bright robes and the priest's hands gesturing at us, my family watching, wisteria in my mother's hair; but when I cried, the wedding blurred into patches of color over the truth of the thing: four foxes and a dirty madman crouched in the filth and dust and darkness. I loved Yoshifuji. Didn't I want the best for him? Could this be better than his lovely house and his beautiful waiting wife?

No. I didn't care what was best for him. I wanted what I wanted. I am only a fox, after all.

We settled easily into a life together. At first Yoshifuji spent every night and most of each day with me. We mated often, most often when he quoted poetry to me. What else was I to do? When we were not pillowed together, he lounged in my rooms, twiddling with the soft-bristled brushes and ink. He sat many times writing quickly on a lacquered lap desk, the ink black and shiny as wet slate in the snow. I looked over his shoulder once and read, in large, strong characters:

> "The bowl's dark glaze reflects the sky:
>   Which color is the bowl? Blue or black?"

"What does that mean?" I asked and then I realized: poetry again. He looked at me strangely, and I blushed and blurted, "What are you writing, all the time?"

"I keep a diary," he said. "I always have. My wife . . ." His voice trailed off. I held my breath, for I knew he hadn't meant me. After a moment, he shook his head and laughed. "I had a thought but it escaped me. Perhaps it will come again."

"Come to bed," I whispered, and he left that thought and did not return to it.

After a time, Yoshifuji began to leave me alone more, to be with Grandfather and Brother. I sighed but I knew it was appropriate: men will seek out the company of men. The fox magic was such that my lord had responsibilities as he had in his other life. There was a constant stream of people in our house, with messages and problems. There were even envoys from Edo. He had many contacts. He found a position in the neighborhood for my brother as a secretary for an official of some sort.

This sounds so strange, even to me. We were foxes, what kind of work could we do? And there really was no job for Brother and no messengers, no reports to be sent to Edo. It was all just dreams. But our family felt benefits from this influential life Yoshifuji lived, as though it had been real and we had been human. Hunting was better than it had been and the weather was good. I can't explain. Fox magic.

One day, my husband was hunting with Grandfather. I drifted through my rooms looking for things to do. I played with my fan and tucked it into my sleeve; when I reached for it, I found instead the small white ball my grandfather had given me. I was looking at it when my brother ran in.

"Sister!" he said, out of breath. "Something terrible is happening up at the house."

"What? What?" I said, knowing he meant my husband's other house, terrified that somehow Yoshifuji had slipped from the magical world we had made for him back into the real world and found his way home.

"They're searching everywhere for him. They have the servants out everywhere. You have to see." He pulled at my sleeve, dragging me outside.

I held back. "Is she there?"

He shook his head. "I don't think so. It's just all the servants and his son—"

"He has a son?" I said, and let myself be taken out.

It was hard easing out of the woman's shape to become just fox again. I felt as though I had stumbled on a stone and wrenched my muscles falling. I crouched in the dirt under the storehouse with my brother, watching all the activity.

There was a boy with Yoshifuji's features. How could I have missed him all those days I had watched my husband? He was still young but he gave orders with an assurance that seemed very familiar. Servants ran in all directions. A priest walked in the gardens, calling the Buddha's Name and reading sutras for Yoshifuji's return. I saw the priest's feet slow as he passed us and I tensed; but he didn't stop. I had to laugh: the mighty Buddha, confounded by mere foxes? We watched all this for a time but no one looked under the storehouse. No doubt it seemed too humble a place to find a man.

When I slipped back into my woman's body, I made a discovery.

Mother shrieked when I told her. "Pregnant?"

"I could feel it. When I made myself a woman again, I could feel it, a little male."

"A son! Oh, such news! You will bring such honor to the house!"

"How can it? I am a fox. My child will be a fox. He will see and leave me."

Mother laughed at me. "You have lived all this time with a man and you have not learned the first thing yet. He will see a son because that is what he wants. He will be so happy! I'm going to go tell your grandfather. A son!"

It was just as she said. Yoshifuji was thrilled. I grew heavy with the child and after a time I could hardly lift myself to walk from room to room. My husband's responsibilities kept him often away. Though he spent every spare moment with me, I found myself often bored. I took out the little white ball from time to time and amused myself by tossing it in the air and catching it, and when it rolled from my grasp, my women retrieved it for me.

My delivery of my child was easy, comparatively painless as these things go. Yoshifuji rushed into the room as soon as Mother would allow him, and brushed through the curtain to my side.

"My son, let me see him!" he said. "You marvelous wife of mine!"

I gestured for the nurse to show my husband the child. He peeled away the tight cloths. "What a child! Wife, you are extraordinary. A beautiful healthy boy."

I said nothing, seeing for a moment the shadow of a man in filthy, ragged robes crouching in the dark to kiss a fox kit on its closed eyes.

Time was strange in the fox-world. Years passed for us and for Yoshifuji. Our son grew rapidly until he hunted birds with toy arrows and began to ride a fat gold and black spotted pony. Years passed but they were only days in the outer world. My brother, who brought us much of our food, said that my husband's other wife had returned.

"What is she like now?" I asked. I watched my son practice his brush strokes, tilting his head to see the shine of the fresh ink over the matte black of dried ink from earlier lessons; all our magic, and paper was still too scarce to allow a child to destroy more than the absolute minimum number of sheets.

"Sad," Brother said. "What do you expect?"

I shook my head, then remembered he couldn't see me. I was behind my curtain-of-state. As always. "I hoped she would feel better in time."

"How can she?" he said. "It is years you have had Yoshifuji beside you. Out there he's only been missing for a few days."

I dropped my ball and it rolled across the floor. "How can that be?"

Brother's sigh was impatient. "When were you out last, Sister?"

"I don't know. Before the boy was born, anyway."

"Why not?" He sounded shocked. "Why aren't you going out? Are you sick? I know you were nursing but the kit's weaned."

"I like to be here when my husband is around."

"We used to play, Sister, just you and me. Remember? We would run in the woods, and at night we'd hunt mice in the formal garden and play Pounce in the Shadows. What happened to you?"

"Nothing," I said, but I lied when I said this. So much had happened to me, how could I start?

"Then come outside with me. Now." Brother jumped up and knocked the curtain over. I looked up at him, too shocked to hide my face with my sleeve. He caught my hand and pulled me to my feet. My son looked up at us. I gestured to his nurse, who picked him up and took him from the room.

"Very well," I said. "We'll be foxes together."

Crawling out of my woman's form this time was excruciating, as though it were my own skin I pulled off. My brother's muzzle pressed against mine, I hunched over until the sense of loss eased. When I felt a little better, I lifted my head and left the space under the storehouse.

It was early evening. The moon was nearly full and the stars were washed out with its brightness in the east and the dying colors in the west. We traveled across the formal garden, moving in the trees' shadows. When I leapt across the stream beside the half-moon bridge, I caught a glimpse of my reflection in the moving water, and it startled me enough that I stumbled when I landed and rolled into a ball.

Brother stopped and nosed at me. "What's wrong?" he whispered. I shook my head, the gesture coming uneasily to my fox's body. I did not tell him that I had seen a woman in my reflection.

There were already lights in the house: torches set along the verandas, and braziers and lamps in the rooms despite the night's summer heat. Many of the sliding walls were open. I watched moths fly in and die in the house's many flames.

The north suite of rooms, Shikibu's rooms, were dimly lit. I crept up almost to the veranda and looked in. I couldn't see her, but I saw her sleeve half exposed beneath her curtain-of-state. A priest knelt before the curtain chanting a sutra. The night's breeze pushed aside one of the curtains; before one of her women could pull it back in place, I saw Shikibu, listless and sad in the gloom.

The house's main rooms were full of light. My husband's other son stood with two older men in traveling clothes, men who looked like brothers to Shikibu. They had brought a tree-trunk segment as tall as a man, and they clustered around it, with a Buddhist priest and many servants crowded in the garden watching. Everyone was dressed strangely; in mourning, I realized. It surprised me—no one was dead—until I realized it must be my lord they were mourning. I found that funny but something hurt quite incredibly in my chest at the thought.

The boy chipped at the tree trunk with a chisel and mallet.

"What can they be doing?" my brother whispered. "How eccentric humans are."

"I don't like this, whatever it is," I said.

"Come up closer. Let's see at least what it is." My brother crawled forward on his belly.

"Brother!" I hissed but he didn't turn around, so I followed him.

The boy in the hall passed the chisel and mallet to one of Shikibu's brothers.

"Finished, Tadasada?" the man said.

I squinted at the wood: close like this, I could see that it had been carved with an image of some sort, but I couldn't tell what the carving was. The priest stepped forward with two assistants who threw incense on the braziers in the room. Everyone else lay down and began to pray softly. The priest fell forward and began chanting in a loud voice.

He was praying to the Eleven-Headed Kannon—when I squinted, the carving made sense this time: there was the cluster of heads, and the arms and the crossed legs. My fur rose on my shoulders until my skin prickled with the strain. "I hate this," I hissed at my brother; he just nuzzled me and went back to listening.

There was no reason to worry. I remembered the priest who had called on Buddha and walked past us anyway. How could this one fare better? His voice went on and on, asking to know where Yoshifuji's body lay. Smoke from the incense snaked from the braziers and out onto the still air of the garden. One tendril seemed to move toward us as though questing. The tiniest breeze lifted its tip, so like a snake's head that my courage broke and I bolted, my heart so hot and heavy with panic that I could hardly see the garden I ran through.

I ran under the storehouse and rushed back into my woman's shape and stood there, shivering. "Husband?" I called. "Husband? Where are you?"

I ran through the rooms and hallways, careless of being seen by the men of the household, calling my husband's name. I was on one of the verandas when Yoshifuji emerged quickly from a brightly lit room, dropping the blinds behind him.

"Wife?" he said. His face was wrinkled with a frown. "I have emissaries. We could hear you all over—"

"Husband!" I panted. "I am so sorry—I know this is most unseemly—it's just that—I was so afraid...."

His face softened and he moved forward quickly to hold me. "What happened? The child? It is all right now, whatever it is. I am here."

I swallowed, tried to control my breathing. "No, not our son, he's fine." What could I tell him? "A snake of smoke, and it was looking for you. I—must have had a bad dream. I woke up and I was all alone and I felt so afraid."

"Alone? Where were your women?"

"They were there. I just meant—lonely for you." I threw myself against him, my arms tight around his neck and sobbed against his cheek. He held me and made soothing noises. After a while, he loosened my hands and passed me to one of my women, who stood waiting in the shadows.

"Better?"

I sniffed.

He took my hands. "I'll take care of this little bit of business and then I'll come and sit with you, all night if you like."

"Yes," I said. "Hurry."

I waited in my rooms. I sat in the near-dark, and tossed my ball and cried with the horror of that snake of smoke, and longing for Yoshifuji. My son was sleeping but my nurse carried him in to me, and I watched him for a time, curled up in a nest of quilts. "See, my husband must love me," I said to myself. "Here is the evidence. No Buddha can take this away. No Buddha can threaten his love for me." Then I would think of the snake of smoke and I would jump up and pace and stare out at our pretty fox-gardens again. And Yoshifuji did not come.

But the Eleven-Headed Kannon came. He came as an old man with only one head and holding a stick; but I knew it was he: he was not made of fox magic in a place where everything and everyone was. He smelled of the priest's incense. Who else could he be? He walked across the gardens stepping through the carefully placed trees, our rocks, and the ornamental lake; and he left a path in his wake, like a man raising mud as he fords a stream. The magic tore and shredded where he passed, leaving bare dirt and the shadow of the storehouse overhead. The magic eddied and sealed the break a few steps behind him but he carried the gash of reality with him like a Court train.

He walked straight through all our creatings, toward the house.

"No," I shrieked and ran out onto the veranda. "Leave him here!"

The man walked forward. I ran to the room where my husband was, burst in to where he sat with an emissary from the capital and his secretary. "Husband! Run!"

"Wife?—" he said as I felt the veranda beside me shiver and dissolve. I fell to my knees. Yoshifuji jumped up, his sword sheath in his hands. I clawed at the Kannon's robe as he passed me, locked my hands in his sword belt until he was pulling me forward with him. He did not even slow.

"What are you—" my husband bellowed as the man prodded him with the stick in his hand. Yoshifuji jumped backward and pulled his sword free.

I screamed. The sword shivered into a handful of dirty straw. My husband looked at it in disgust and threw it to the ground. The man prodded him again and Yoshifuji moved backward, through the house.

"Leave him, please leave him, they mean nothing to him, I love him—" I begged and prayed as the man dragged me through our house, out into the gardens. My hands bled from the hard edge of the belt. If nothing else around us was real, I knew this was, this hot blood in my palms. Yoshifuji kept turning back, trying to help me. The man just jabbed at him again, and forced him stumbling on.

The belt leather was slick with blood. My fingers slipped and I fell behind the man onto the dirt below the storehouse beside one of the support posts. The Kannon gave my husband one more jab, and he crawled out from our home and stood upright in his kitchen garden. I crawled after him but I knew it was too late already. I lay by the storehouse in my robes, blood on my hands, my long hair trailing on the ground.

It was still dusk there, the thirteenth evening after Yoshifuji had come to me, his thirteenth year in my fox-world. Nearly everyone was in the garden huddled in little clumps and talking among themselves. Yoshifuji was two things in my eyes, like something seen and distorted through water: handsome in his dress robes, a little dusty now, still carrying an empty sword sheath; and covered with filth, casual robes stained and torn, holding a little worm-eaten stick: a man who had lived in the dirt with foxes.

The boy was the first to see my husband looking around him.

"Father!" he shouted and ran to Yoshifuji. "Is this you?"

"Son?" my husband said hesitantly. "Tadasada?" I saw memory coming back to him, but the fox magic was strong enough to shape his understanding of things. "How have you not grown more while I was gone?"

The boy threw his arms around the man. "Father, what has happened to you? You look so old!"

Yoshifuji pushed the boy away. "It doesn't matter. I am only here to send your mother back to her family. She is here, I presume? I was so desperate after your mother left to visit her relatives, and she was gone so long. But I met someone, a wonderful woman, and married her. We have had a lovely little boy. He's growing much handsomer than you, I must admit. He's my heir, you know. You're no longer my first son, Tadasada: I love his mother so."

The boy looked up at a darkened room of the house. I saw a form there, robes shifting softly, and I realized it was Shikibu watching but too aware of the proprieties to come down and greet her husband in front of so many people. The boy straightened. "Where is this son of yours?"

"Over there," my husband said, pointing at the storehouse.

They saw me then. "A fox!" one man shouted, and they all took up the cry: "A fox! A fox!" Men ran toward me and the storehouse, carrying sticks and torches.

"Husband!" I screamed. "Stop them!"

He hesitated, obviously confused. "Wife?" he asked unsteadily.

"A fox!" the people yelled.

"Please stay with me!" I held out my arms to him. He stepped toward me. The boy threw himself into Yoshifuji's arms, overbalancing him.

I looked up at the house again in the instant before the men caught up to me, and for the first time I saw her face clearly, where she stood on the veranda. I saw tears on her face. I knew that she, alone of everyone here save my lord, saw me for a woman.

They chased us, the men. They stuck their torches down so they could see under the storehouse floor and poked around with their sticks, and my family fled in all directions: even my son, who was only half-grown. They followed me until I threw off even the seeming of my woman's body in blind panic. The pain drove me out of consciousness, but my fox's body ran anyway on its bloody pads.

I came back to my woman's shape much later, when I was sick from the fear that had choked me. My house was empty save for the servants, who brought me clean robes and food.

I have waited since then. My family has not returned. My grandfather was old, and I don't know if he could have lived through the heart-bursting panic of the chase. My mother, my brother, and my son are all gone. I hope they are together but I fear they are scattered.

Yoshifuji wept for many days. I heard him when I crawled through the darkness to his door, calling my name and the name of our son. The household summoned priests and a yin-yang diviner to purge my husband of his "enchantment," but they say its hold has been strong. Recently, I heard him say that he is over his sickness, but I don't know what to believe. It didn't seem like a sickness to me and he does not sound over it.

Without my family, it's hard to maintain the house and the servants. The garden is already gone, faded like mist. The house dissolves room by room. I don't leave my wing much, not wanting to see how far it has come, this melting of my home. My servants are fewer now and they are even more silent than they were before. I have thought of leaving, stripping off the humanness one more time and running in the woods again. I know I can't. I am no longer simply a fox.

But I am not simply a woman, either. I know it is a woman's role to wait, always lost in the shadows, patient for her lord. I know the old tales would have me wait until my death after such a thing as this. But I have waited so long already, alone, tossing my ball, puzzling over Yoshifuji's diary. I am so tired of this.

I have a plan, if a simple one. It was summer, the thirteen days he spent with me. Now it is winter. The first snow has fallen today, a cold cloud as deep as my wooden clogs. I know him so well. He will come out into the garden tonight to write about the snow and the moon. And I will roll my white ball across his path. If he still misses me, he will see it for what it is and find me, and we will be happy: no false lives this time, no waiting in the darkness, no magic but that which will keep us either human or fox together, according to our choice. And if he truly is content there with Shikibu and the boy, it will only seem another piece of the snow.

I think he will see the ball.

I have just thought of something:

> Fox magic:
>> Priests, you can cure him of everything
>> but love.

I think this is a poem.

Names for Water

Hala is running for class when her cell phone rings. She slows to take it from her pocket, glances at the screen: UNKNOWN CALLER. It rings again. She does not pick up calls when she doesn't know who it is, but this time she hits TALK, not sure what's different except that she is late for a class she dreads, and this call delays the moment when she must sit down and be overwhelmed.

"Hello," she says.

No one speaks. There is only the white noise that is always in the background of cell phone calls. It could be the result of a flaw in the tiny cheap speaker but is probably microwaves, though she likes to imagine it is the whisper of air molecules across all the thousands of miles between two people talking.

The hiss in her ear: she walks across the commons of the Engineering building, a high-ceilinged room crowded with students shaking water from their jackets and umbrellas as they run to class. Some look as overwhelmed as she feels. It is nearly finals and they are probably not sleeping any more than she is.

Beyond the glass wall it is raining. Across the wet quad, cars pass on Loughlin Street. Water sprays from their wheels.

Her schoolwork is not going well. It is her third year toward an engineering degree, but just now that seems an unreachable goal. The science is simple enough, but the mathematics has been hard and she is losing herself in the tricky mazes of Complex Variables. She thinks of dropping the class and switching her major to something simpler, but if she doesn't become an engineer what will she do instead?

"This is Hala," she says, her voice sharper. "Who is this?" It is the last thing she needs right now: a forgotten phone in a backpack, crushed against a text book and accidentally speed-dialing her; or worse, someone's idea of a prank. She listens for breathing but hears only the constant hiss. No, it is not quite steady, or perhaps she has never before listened carefully. It changes, grows louder and softer like traffic passing, as though someone has dropped a phone onto the sidewalk of a busy street.

She wonders about the street, if it is a street—where in the city it is, what cars and buses and bicycles travel it. Or it might be in another city, even somewhere distant and fabulous. Mumbai. Tokyo. Wellington. Santiago. The names are like charms that summon unknown places, unfamiliar smells, the tastes of new foods.

Class time. Students pool in the doorways and pour through. She should join them, find a seat, turn on her laptop, but she is reluctant to let go of this strange moment for something so prosaic. She puts down her bag and holds the phone closer.

The sound in her ear ebbs and flows. No, it is not a street. The cell phone is a shell held to her ear, and she knows with the logic of dreams or exhaustion that it is water she hears: surf rolling against a beach, an ocean perhaps. No one talks or breathes into the phone because it is the water itself that speaks to her.

She says aloud, "The Pacific Ocean." It is the ocean closest to her, the one she knows best. It pounds against the coast an hour from the university. On weekends back when school was not so hard, she walked through the thick-leaved plants that grew on its cliffs. The waves threw themselves against the rocks and burst into spray that made the air taste of salt and ozone. Looking west at dusk, the Pacific seemed endless but it was not: six thousand miles to the nearest land, ninety million miles to the sun where it dropped below the horizon, and beyond that, to the first star, a vast—but measurable—distance.

Hala likes the sudden idea that if she calls the water by its right name, it will reply in more than this hiss. "The Atlantic Ocean," she says. She imagines waters deep with fish, floored with eyeless crabs and abandoned telecommunication cables. "The Arctic. The Indian Ocean." Blue ice; tunnies in shoals.

The waves keep their counsel. She has not named them properly.

She speaks the names of seas: the Mediterranean, the Baltic, the Great Bight of Australia, the Red and Black and Dead Seas. They form an incantation filled with the rumble of great ships and the silence of corals and anemones.

When these do not work, she speaks the words for such lakes as she remembers. "Superior. Victoria. Titicaca." They have waves, as well. Water brushes their shores, pushed by winds more than the moon's inconstant face. Birds rise at dusk from the rushes along shoreline marshes and return at dawn. Eagles ride the thermals above basalt cliffs and watch for fish. "Baikal. The Great Bear. Malawi."

The halls are empty now. Perhaps she is wrong about what sort of water it is, and so she tries other words. Streams, brooks, kills, runs, rills: water summoned by gravity, coaxed or seduced or forced from one place to the next. Estuaries. Dew ponds and pools. Snow and steam. "Cumulus," she says, and thinks of the clouds mounding over Kansas on summer afternoons. "Stratus. Altostratus." Typhoons, waterspouts. There is so much water, so many possibilities, but even if she knew the names of each raindrop and every word in every language for ice, she would be wrong. It is not these things.

She remembers the sleet that cakes on her car's windshield when she visits her parents in Wisconsin in winter. A stream she remembers from when she was a child, minnows shining uncatchable just under the surface. The Mississippi, broad as a lake where it passes St. Louis; in August, it is the color of *café au lait* and smells of mud and diesel exhaust. Hoarfrost coats a century-old window in starbursts. Bathtubs fill with blue-tinted bubbles that smell of lavender. These are real things, but they are wrong. They are not names but memories.

It is not the water of the world, she thinks. It is perhaps the water of dreams. "Memory," she says, naming a hidden ocean of the heart. "Longing, death, joy." The sound in her ear changes a little, as though the wind in that distant place has grown stronger or the tide has turned, but it is still not enough. "The womb. Love. Hope." She repeats, "Hope, hope," until it becomes a sound without meaning.

It is not the water of this *world,* she thinks.

This is the truth. It is water rolling against an ocean's sandy shore, but it is alien sand on another world, impossibly distant. It is unknown, unknowable, a riddle she will never answer in a foreign tongue she will never hear.

It is also an illusion brought on by exhaustion. She knows the sound is just white noise. She's known that all along. But she wanted it to mean something, enough so that she was willing to pretend to herself, because just now she needs a charm against the sense that she is drowning in schoolwork and uncertainty about her future.

Tears burn her eyes. "Fine," she says, like a hurt child; "You're not even there." She presses END and the phone goes silent, a shell of dead plastic filled with circuit boards. It is empty.

Complex Variables. She'll never understand today's lesson after coming in ten minutes late. She shoulders her bag to leave the building. She forgot her umbrella so she'll be soaked before she gets to the bus. She leans forward hoping her hair will shield her face and steps out into the rain.

The bus she just misses drives through a puddle, and the splash is an elegant complex shape, a high-order Bézier curve. The rain whispers on the lawn, chatters in the gutters and drains.

The oceans of the heart.

She finds UNKNOWN CALLER in her call history and presses TALK. The phone rings once, twice. Someone—something—picks up.

"Hala," she says to the hiss of cosmic microwaves, of space. "Your name is Hala."

"Hala," a voice says very loud and close. It is the unsuppressed echo common to local calls. She knows this. But she also knows that it is real, a voice from a place unimaginably distant, but attainable. It is the future.

She will pass Complex Variables with a C+. She will change her major to physics, graduate, and go to grad school to study astrophysics. Seven years from now, as part of her dissertation she will write a program that searches the data that will come from the Webb telescope, which will have been launched in 2014. Eleven years and six months from now, her team of five will discover water's fingerprint splashed across the results matrix from a planet circling Beta Leonis, fifty light-years away: a star ignored for decades because of its type. The presence of phyllosilicates will indicate that the water is liquid. Eighteen months later, their results will be verified.

One hundred and forty-six years from now, the first men and women will stand beneath the bright white sun of Beta Leonis, and they will name the ocean Hala.

Hala doesn't know this. But she snaps the phone shut and runs for class.

The Bitey Cat

Sarah has a cat. She's only three but it's just hers. Everyone agrees. No one else even likes the cat. Everyone just calls her the bitey cat even though Sarah knows she's not really a cat. She's a monster.

Mom and dad are mad at each other all the time. Sarah never cries but it makes her scream and run and kick things. If she doesn't she feels sick and then she throws up and then mom and dad get mad at her too even though they act like they don't.

Mom and dad yell at each other at night when Sarah and Paul are supposed to be asleep. Sarah's supposed to stay in bed but sometimes when they yell she gets out of bed with her pooh bear and her blanket and she lies in her doorway where the hall light shines. Sometimes she goes all the way down the stairs and into the back hall because they won't notice anyway but she wishes they would.

They're getting a divorce Paul says one night. She's sitting in her doorway punching pooh and then feeling bad about it and hugging him. Paul's standing in his door across the hall from her. He's wearing his spiderman pajamas and he's holding his neopet. *That's why they fight all the time.* Paul's six and he thinks he knows everything but Sarah already knows about divorce because of Jeff A from daycare. His parents are divorced and that means his mom picks him up some days and his dad on other days. She thinks it's going to be like that.

Sarah wants a cat for her birthday. They ask what she wants and she says a cat because it seems like something someone would want. She's patted cats before at other people's houses and at daycare once when a little girl's mom brought a box that had a towel and four kittens inside. They were so little their eyes weren't open. Their mouths were very pink. Sarah held one but she was scared she would drop it so she put it back right away.

Her mom doesn't want a cat. She says *Who's going to* and then she says other stuff. And then dad says something and then there's more of the yelling that makes Sarah throw pooh at the wall.

A few days later they get a cat but dad doesn't come with them. Paul's mad he doesn't get a cat too so he complains and mom has to drag him along the sidewalk. The shelter is on owl trail road which is out in the country. She doesn't see any owls. There are big trees everywhere. The driveway is dirt. There's a big metal fence with a black dog behind it. The shelter is made from blocks painted to be shiny like daycare.

Sarah wants a kitten but her mom says no kittens. *They're too small* she says. *You'll hold it too tight and hurt it.* So they go to the big cat room in the back where the walls are painted green. She looks in all the shiny cages. There are two or three cats in each cage with a cardboard box with dirt and little bowls for food and water and towels to sleep on. There's poop in some of the little boxes and it's very interesting because it's so small and neat. Sarah imagines what it would be like to live in a little cage like that with a towel and some other cats. *Meow* she says trying it out. *Meow* the cats say back.

Sarah stops in front of a cage with one cat all by itself. The cat is the biggest of all and has orange and black and white spots all over and gray stripes on her tail and her feet have white toes. The cat and Sarah look at each other for a long time. The cat's eyes are yellow under the buzzing lights. She looks fierce.

This one Sarah says.

They open the cage door and mom picks the cat up but it wiggles a lot. Sarah touches the cat's fur which is soft like a bunny. The cat turns her head and takes Sarah's hand in her mouth.

She's biting you! mom says. *Not this one, Sarah. Get a nicer cat.*

This one Sarah says again. *She's not either biting me.* But she feels little sharp teeth pressing into her finger.

The cat comes home with them but Sarah has to scream a little bit first. Mom asks what her name is and Sarah says Penny because of the spots.

Sarah knows that Penny is not really a cat. That's why she didn't say about the bite. She sees something mad and bad looking out of the bitey cat's yellow eyes and she understands because she's mad and bad sometimes, too.

Sarah's the only person who likes Penny. Mom tries to pat her when they get home and Penny just bites her. *I'll let her settle in* mom says but Penny bites mom two days later and a day after that and then mom stays away and only feeds her is all. She doesn't bite dad even once but he keeps his hands away and just talks. Sarah thinks Penny likes how his voice is so low. Paul is still mad Penny isn't his cat and when he tries to play she bites him too.

Sometimes mom or someone else pats the bitey cat for a few seconds before she bites them but there are times she bites people even when they're not doing anything or she even follows them from room to room when they're doing something else and she bites at their feet. The bites don't make anyone bleed but sometimes they leave little white holes.

The bitey cat makes mom cry one day. *I just don't know what to do* mom says. *She bites everyone.*

She never bites me Sarah says but this is a lie.

Cats do lots of interesting things and Sarah follows her around. Penny makes little mouth noises when she eats crunchy food from a bowl on the floor. Penny pees in a box. Penny looks out windows. Penny jumps up on things.

Penny goes outside whenever she wants out of a special door made just for cats. Sarah can hear the door click from anywhere in the house and she runs to the back hall and looks out the little flap to watch Penny walk across the backyard around the corner of the garage.

Sometimes in the afternoon Penny sleeps on the floor in the sun and Sarah tries it too. She curls up right next to her with her face inches from Penny's. She can smell her breath and see how pretty her fur is in the sun. When Penny's eyes are open Sarah can see stripes in them.

Sarah knows that Penny is really a monster. She is huge and fierce and could kill you any time she wanted except now she's a cat with spots and stripes and white toes. But Penny remembers. That's why she's mad all the time. That's why she bites everyone. That's why she even bites Sarah sometimes when Sarah's not even doing anything to her.

At night she lies on the foot of Sarah's bed like a little spotty lion. Her eyes are yellow in the hall light. Sometimes she comes up next to Sarah and lies down so close that Sarah can feel her warmness. Sometimes Sarah can't stand it anymore and she puts her hand on Penny's soft fur and then the cat bites her. But gently and her sharp teeth are like a good night kiss.

Sarah thinks she knows what divorce is going to be like but she doesn't. Dad's not there very much. Mom cries a lot and is busy on the phone. Sometimes she forgets to take Sarah's pooh in the car when they're going somewhere. It always takes Sarah a long time to brush her teeth and mom gets mad. When they are at home Paul stays in his room playing neopets. Sarah and Paul have to be with Kara next door or in daycare a lot.

Sarah pees in her bed one night. She's scared to wake mom up, so she sleeps on the floor in her doorway with her blanket and pooh for a pillow. Penny sleeps next to her. And in the morning mom comes and Sarah knows she's mad even though she doesn't say anything. Sarah starts to scream and then she starts thrashing. Mom tries to hold her but Sarah bites her on the arm even though she hasn't bitten anyone since Tim G in daycare. Mom snatches her arm back. There's a look on her face like being scared.

This makes Sarah want to bite people more. At least they notice her then. At least then she knows why they don't love her even if she wishes they did anyway.

Sarah and Paul and the bitey cat are in the family room. Paul's got his neopet and she wants to look at it. They start rolling around and fighting but quiet because they don't want mom to come in from the kitchen. He accidentally kicks Penny and she howls and runs away. So Sarah bites him and when he tries to get away she bites him harder.

Then there's blood all over Paul's arm. Sarah can feel skin in her mouth. Paul's screaming. Mom runs in from the kitchen still holding the phone. Mom grabs Paul up and grabs Sarah by the hand. *You just wait* mom says. *I'm taking Paul to the hospital and* you *are going over to Kara's house.* And she starts crying. *How could you do this?* Mom has never used that tone of voice before. Sarah starts to scream but this time it doesn't work. Mom doesn't even bring pooh when they go next door and Penny isn't anywhere.

Kara is nice. She gets pooh when she sees Sarah doesn't have him and wraps her in a blanket and puts her on the red couch where she can hear the TV. So Sarah feels okay asking if she can go pee.

Do you need any help? Kara asks. Sarah shakes her head. *Okay then* Kara says. Sarah tiptoes into the hall to where she knows the little bathroom is right by the back door. There's a big window in the door. She can see yellow eyes shining in the backyard. Sarah knows about not going outside alone but this isn't her back door and it's not locked and mom is mad and Paul is all covered with blood and Penny's walking away.

She opens it and goes outside.

The only times Sarah has ever been outside at night she's always been in mom's or dad's arms or in the car seat watching the lights.

The alley is different than that. The light is only in places where the poles are. The little rocks are cold and sharp and hurt her feet. Penny walks way off to one side by the bushes which are full of black. She stops to smell things and Sarah does the same thing. Even though Sarah knows she's not supposed to go into the street she follows Penny because Penny shouldn't either and Sarah's a monster now. They're going to be fierce together and bite things and kill them. They can protect each other.

Penny is suddenly lit bright from one side and there's a car right there.

This is what happens next. Mom says she was coming home from the hospital and she saw Sarah in the street and slammed on the brakes and skidded into a utility pole. But Sarah knows what really happened. She and Penny see the headlights like giant eyes. And Penny arches her back and hisses and gets very big. Bigger than the car. Bigger than a house. And the car squeals and jumps out of Penny's way and then it hits a pole and dies.

And mom and Paul get out of the car and Paul's arm is wrapped in white stuff. And mom's crying really hard only it's okay because mom isn't holding a phone or yelling at dad. She's holding Sarah and Paul. Sarah starts to cry.

They can't find Penny anywhere even though mom and then dad look for her but Sarah wakes up one night and there's Penny so close that Sarah can smell her breath. Sarah puts her hand on the bitey cat's soft fur. Penny holds her hand in her mouth for a moment but it doesn't hurt at all.

Dad doesn't come back to live with them but Sarah and Paul stay with him sometimes and Sarah has her own room there. After a while mom stops crying all the time and even takes Sarah to the park. The big ragged bite on Paul's arm turns into a scar.

No one else ever sees Penny again. But Sarah does sometimes at night, until she grows too old and forgets to look for her.

The Horse Raiders

We were deep in Morning when the barbarians came, far from n'dau, our right place: n'dau, where the sun hung at the proper angle in the sky and our shadows were their correct shape and height. At n'dau, a cloth tape cut to my height would exactly stretch the length of my shadow. My shadow and myself would be matched: n'dau.

N'dau is the correct length of my shadow, and it is the sun's perfect position in the sky, and it is one's correct location on Ping's slow-moving surface. We travel as we need while Ping moves under us. It does this slowly, taking a lifetime to move from Night so far to the west, past Dawn and n'dau into Noon, where it is said that stones explode from the heat, and the air can melt flesh from bones. If we stopped traveling, we would move into Noon with the ground we stood on, but to do this would be absurd. To stay still is to slip from n'dau.

We were far from n'dau. The sun rode too high in the sky. The shadow that dogged my heels was too short. We had wandered so far from n'dau because we had found a broad ribbon of Earth grasses and shrubs rooted into the soil left over from a Dawn meltwater river, dried now to a marshy trickle. The horses could eat the native vegetation of Ping, but the grass from ancient Earth was best for them and so we let the herd graze noonward.

We wanted colts so we set up the estrus tents; using a water clock, we placed the mares in darkness for one emptying of the water clock, then out in the light for another, then back in the dark tents. After we had done this for a while, the mares went into heat. Our stallion went mad with lust and after fertilizing many of them ran amok, in the end killing himself by falling into a ravine on his way to the gelding herd, which was several leagues to the north.

It did not matter. We had fifty mares in the mare's herd and thirty-five foals, fourteen of them male. It would be simple enough to trade for another stallion when we came back to our people. The horses of my family's herds were famed for their beauty and small sturdiness; these would be worth a lot back at one of the traveling trading fairs or at Moot.

But we had not traveled much during the mares' pregnancy, and the planet did not stop its eternal creeping toward Noon. And now we snarled at one another, sick of the food we had, sick of each other, cranky with the wrongness of it all. Time to return to n'dau.

My brother Ricard finally agreed. When the sleep time was over we would turn dawnward again. But I was too hot to sleep, too impatient, so I walked among the mare herd.

Foals and their dams scattered at my passing. They seemed listless and irritable from the heat and the stagnating water, but they were fat and healthy, and their coats gleamed through a thin sheen of dust. I checked several horses for things I had recently treated. The blazed black mare's right flank, ripped by tearthorn bushes, showed a dark shiny scar that was already blending into her hide. The small gray mare's newborn foal had been attacked by feral dogs before I had found them and returned them to the herd; the filly's shoulder was deformed by a bite but she moved easily. She would probably never sell. Still, her blood was good and as long as she could keep up, she should be a good broodmare.

The sorrel mare's was the last foal not yet born, and due very soon. Her belly was a huge copper-colored bloat. She shifted awkwardly from foot to foot but she let me handle her without resisting, too heavy and hot to care. Her mouth membranes were pink and healthy-looking, and her eyes were clear. When I thumped her abdomen, I felt movement, a sharp thump back.

I heard a distant bark: one of my dogs, no doubt chasing birds far from camp. A second dog took up the sound. I looked out toward them, toward Dawn, and saw dark shapes.

My uncle's wife Brida and I started shouting at the same time. "Riders!" We ran toward the camp. "Strangers dawnward!"

The tents had been quiet, dogs sleeping in the short shadows. Now my family ran to the central work area, and the dogs danced nervously about them. The three children in the family clung to their parents. Ricard had been sleeping in one of the tents; bare-chested and squinting in the light, he gestured and we all armed ourselves with knives and swords and spears.

"The dogs," he said to me.

I nodded and pulled my whistles from my sash. They were a handful of silver tubes bound together with silk cords, each a different note to make the different commands. They were not as convenient as whistling the notes between my teeth but they carried. I whistled *everyone out* and *alert*, and *dawnward*. The dogs loped off, dark shapes galloping through the pale grass to meet the handful of man-shapes coming.

The foremost rode under a banner but we could not see the color. I fingered my whistles, watching Ricard for direction. We had twenty dogs and eight adults. I would lose some dogs but we could stop these men in the unlikely event we needed to.

"White," my brother's wife Jena said.

Trading color: barter and news. Ricard relaxed and smiled and the armed ones lowered their weapons. My brother was new to his role and still likely to take the hard road to any decision. There are not many people on Ping; in the time it took for my sister Meg to get pregnant and bear her daughter Mara, I never saw strangers. This was our first contact since before our father had died and Ricard had assumed the family's leadership: better that this be an easy meeting.

"Peace," he said.

Jena nodded. "I'll make the tea for the greetings." She walked to the cooking fires, my nephews complaining beside her.

"They might not be peaceful," my uncle Den said.

Ricard turned. "Why not? They ride under white."

"Still, better to—"

Ricard laughed, "Den, we are nine and they're six. They ride under white and no one would betray that. We're not fighters but we'll defend ourselves if we have to. What could they do?"

"Ricard—" Den said sourly.

"All right." Ricard gestured impatiently. "Katia, send one of the dogs out to bring in Lara and Willem from the gelding herd. The geldings won't wander far before they return. Satisfied?"

I nodded and whistled for the young black bitch, and *other herd*. She loped away to the north. She did not know enough yet to be useful here, but my cousin and her husband would see her and know she was sent to summon them.

"Let's get the children out of the way," my sister Meg said. "Rob, Mara, Stivan, into the sleep tent." But no one moved. The children clung to their parents: tiny Stivan and Rob clutching Jena's skirts, Mara holding Meg's hand tightly. We stood there as though trapped out of time, flies hanging in honey.

And then—the trick grassland plays on us—they were suddenly present. Time began again: the camp was flooded with noise and motion. The dogs whirled around the horsemen, jumping and barking. The strange horses flinched away from them. Several of the riders looked no more happy. One man had a whip with which he flailed around his horse's flanks. The dogs thought this was a game, and danced away, grinning as dogs do.

I whistled *everyone* and *back*. Obediently the dogs moved away. When they were far enough away not to make the strange horses nervous, I whistled *drop*, and they collapsed panting in the trampled grass.

I had never seen such large horses. They stood so tall that I could barely see over their backs, with long rangy legs and rough coats. They all looked sick and exhausted, as though they had been ridden harder than they should. I recognized prayer flags, scraps of fabric and paper and hide that had been woven into tight little patterns and hung from their bridles.

And I had never seen strangers like these: no surprise on Ping, where one might never see members of the same group twice in a lifetime. The barbarians—for so I thought them—were gold-skinned and flat-faced. The four men had shaved heads; the two women had long black braids that fell to their heels as they rode. They were dressed identically in knee-length dark quilted tunics split front and back for riding. The tunics would fold closed and secure with plain gold buttons close to the throat, but it was too hot for that; they wore them gaping open to show sweat-darkened shirts and trousers of undyed Pingworm silk.

They were all warriors. Hung from their belts were knives and embroidered bow cases made of oiled cloth, covers flipped back. Block quivers nestled in the small of their backs. Their felted boots had toes that pointed up and notches in their shaped soles. The stirrups nestled in the notches: very sensible, worth trying to imitate.

One of the riders said, "I am Huer, bodyguard to the emperor Erchua of the Tien, and the leader of this group." Nonsense words to us, for all their being in the Trade language. He swung from his saddle and stood beside his blood-colored mare: a man just my height—and I am short for my people—and a dog's lifetime older than me, with papery wrinkles seaming his face. A bright beetle's wing and a strand of sky-blue beads hung from his dark brimless cap, his only ornamentation.

"I am Ricard," my brother said. "We are the Winden clan of the Moot people." These would be nonsense words to them as well, but necessary for all that. "Greetings."

"Foals!" One of the barbarian women called out in Trade, then said something in a different tongue, pointing at the herd. Several dismounted.

"Wait—" Ricard started; but exclaiming they walked into the herd.

I whistled softly through my teeth, the tones for the two smartest dogs, the lead bitch and the gray-faced male, and *look around* and *be wary*. They rose and loped toward the herd.

"Who made the noise?" the leader asked Ricard. "Why do the dogs go?"

"Katia told them to." Ricard gestured toward me. "She is our handler."

The stranger looked at me until I flushed and ducked my head. "She wastes her time training curs."

We had run into other barbarians who despised dogs as unclean. Ricard did not defend but only said, "She works medicine with the horses, too."

One of the barbarian women trotted toward us from the herd. "They are small but they are well," she called to Huer. Her accent was thick but even through it I heard her excitement. "And all the foals. Completely healthy."

"Are you here to trade for horses?" Ricard asked.

"Your horses are not sick?"

"No." Ricard said. "They're the best horses on Ping. We have—"

"You know horses?" the leader interrupted, staring at me. "What makes them ill? You have medicines?"

"Why?" I asked warily. "Do you seek help?"

"Are any of the others healers?"

"I am teaching one of the children, but—"

"Which one?"

I said nothing, but Mara huddled in Meg's arms and hid her face in her mother's sleeve.

He turned away to look at Ricard. "I have important news. Are you all present?"

"No," Ricard said—too young to lead, I know now, to know better than to say this. "Lara and Willem are out with the geldings."

"Good," the barbarian said and shouted a word. It seemed impossibly fast. The strangers pulled their short bows free of the cases at their hips and shot.

The leader struck the metal whistles from my hand before I could get them to my lips. I dove for them, but he caught me as I dropped. I fought to free my hands from the folds of his tunic, to pull my knife.

Three rounds of arrows had hissed through the air in the moment I had fought. Ricard was down, an arrow sprouting from his breastbone. Jena was fallen, Stivan beside her; I could not see the arrows. Den, Mikel, Brida, Meg, Daved: arrows and blood blooming from throats and breasts and backs. And the children.

Several dogs broke the *drop* command. Silently my lead male launched himself at the leader's throat. An arrow threw him sideways before he hit, but the young male dog behind him struck the man as he raised an arm to protect his face.

My knife pulled free. I jabbed for the leader's side as he shoved the male aside; whistled *attack* with my mouth, too soft and too late. I heard the dogs scream as they were shot.

I howled with them and slashed again at the barbarian. Although I was good with a knife, he threw up his quilted bow case to snag the blade and disarmed me.

My family and my dogs were down, but my lead bitch still crawled toward the man who held me, her hind legs dragging uselessly behind her. An arrow struck, and a second. She was dead before her head touched the ground.

I screamed with rage. Insane with it, I fought my captor, snarling and biting like a dog myself, mad for killing. In the end, he crushed my face against his tunic until I hung in his hands, trying not to faint for lack of air. I heard whimpers and sighs and over them my niece Mara's constant screaming, as though she had no need for breath.

After a time, he loosed me. I fell to my knees, gasping for breath, heaving helplessly. The barbarians moved through the clearing with bloody knives. We had killed one of the strangers, and a woman knelt beside him and sang foreign words in a steady drone. The rest were injured in one way or another, from bites or knife wounds. One of the women held Mara off the ground with the child's head pressed into her tunic to stifle her screams. She seemed unhurt.

"You have your horse medicines?" I looked up. My captor was a dark silhouette against the high sun.

When I was a girl, I had a fever once and nearly died. I saw everything around me as though through smoke then: things happened but they meant nothing. This was like that. I saw the light, the darkness; saw blood dripping from his arm where my dog had hurt him; heard his voice and a woman's shouts giving orders to gather the mare herd which had scattered from the fight. But none of this was real.

"Medicines?" he repeated more slowly, as though he were not certain I could understand his words.

I stared at him.

"They are mine now. And you," he said and walked away.

They were slicing the walls of the tents and pulling free the bundles and packets inside. I heard one calling from my open-roofed work tent. I knew that he had found my parfleches of tanned painted horsehide, and inside, all the boxes and jars and bottles and packets. Everything packed as I always kept them.

My sister lay beside me. "Meg?" I asked before I saw dust lying undisturbed on her open eyes. Blood flowed sluggishly from her nose and mouth, but the arrow shaft over her heart seemed strangely bloodless. I whispered, "Mara's alive, Mara's all right." More blood pooled on the dry ground, as though the soil had rejected it.

Hidden in the grass, my dog whistles lay along the line of her outstretched arm, as though she had been reaching for them. I hid them in my sash, stood and walked shakily away.

My dogs were scattered dead through the area, even some of the ones I had whistled away on tasks. Some looked asleep. One, the second lead male, had died biting at the arrow that pinned him by the flank to the ground.

Several were missing altogether. Blood trails dribbled through the long grasses where dogs had been strong enough to escape or to find a private place to die. I thought of the whistle, but there would be no point to calling an injured one in to death.

One of the missing dogs was the clan dog, a great long-legged golden male. His main duty was to run if anything happened to my family, to run and find the Moot as we had trained him to, my father and I. He would be seen there. The clan flag on his collar would be recognized and they would know my family was dead. Whoever was at the Moot would mourn us, and our scrolls would be closed and the name Winden remembered only in chants.

Several dogs were not dead but I had no knife, no pain-killers to ease their suffering. I knelt in the bloodstained grass holding my gasping brindle bitch until my captor ran up and caught my arm. "You do not leave us," he said. Her head hit the ground as I was jerked upright.

"Kill her," I said.

He started to pull me toward the camp. I ripped myself free and pointed at the dying bitch. "Kill them all. Finish it."

"They are dogs." He spat on the ground. "Unclean."

"Kill them." I met his eyes until he said something guttural and gestured one of the others toward us, a youth barely into adulthood, more boy than man. They spoke back and forth for a moment, and the boy walked toward the dogs, pulling a long knife free. My uncle Bran's knife. I recognized the notch at the tip.

The leader bound my wrists with black cords and lifted me onto a horse, where he tied my feet to the stirrups. The strangers had taken nothing but my parfleches, the clan's sextant, and a packet of gold and metal from ancient Earth that the family kept for bartering. Had kept. These were loaded on the backs of two mares. Mara seemed unconscious, held in front of her captor. The leader saw me staring at her. "To keep you honest," he said.

Riding and shouting, the other barbarians circled the loose mare-herd until they gathered into a ragged bunch, the queen watching the strangers warily. Through the smoke, I listened to their talk, for they seemed to speak Trade among themselves. I learned there were seven of them instead of the five I saw; two were scouts. The barbarians were going to move fifty mares and thirty-five foals with five riders and no dogs.

The leader looked around and called, "Shen!"

The boy dropped Bran's knife in the grass and ran back to us, mounted a horse. He caught my eye. "Finished," he said, not unkindly. "It was not painful."

My captor caught my reins and shouted to the others. We began to move toward Morning. Soon the camp was gone, the dark puddles of its collapsed tents no more than shadows. My family and my dogs would lie there until their bones baked in Noon and were lost forever. They would never return to n'dau.

My family usually traveled only as much as we needed to keep the sun at n'dau or to find a trade fair or the Moot. I had never traveled like this: endless whiles of arrowing north and dawnward, riding until dirty foam flecked the horses' coats and their riders fell asleep against their necks. I was bound too securely to escape, even were I free of the smoke, the not-caring. After a time, the woman, Suhui, handed my niece to the boy, Shen, as they rode. Mara's face was dirty and she slept in the crook of his arm as though waking were too painful.

I felt this way. I was awake, but the smoke was thick between me and the world. Nothing mattered, not even when I saw the gelding herd wandering far dawnward, Dana and Willem's flattened shelter a shadow on the ground. The raiders had stopped there first, but they couldn't bring the geldings into the mare herd, not with new foals.

The barbarians ate as they rode. I took strips of jerky in my bound hands when Huer gave them to me, but eventually my hands forgot their presence and they fell uneaten to the ground. I did not worry: the dogs would find them, and then remembered the dogs were gone. I swallowed when he held a waterskin to my lips. It was too much work to reject it.

We left the ribbon of Earth grasses and crossed a ragged plateau scoured nearly bare of soil, leaving only stones of every size. Dry as it was, velvet Ping-moss filled each rock's short shadow with dark green. Dawnward, when the sun had been lower in the sky, the moss had filled in longer shadows; dying as the shadows shortened, the moss became soil for pockets of Earth grass. Ping-moss was poisonous to horses but grass was edible, and the horses snatched mouthfuls, until they walked in an ankle-deep cloud of pollen.

We came to a brackish stream, a thread following the broad bed of its Dawn self. The lead mare stopped, and the herd with her. Huer called a command and the riders moved upstream. Mara was awake. Shen swung her down to Suhui, who held her by the hand while pulling packs from horseback.

"You will not run." Huer stood beside my mare, hands busy on the cords that held my feet in the stirrups.

The smoke in my head made it hard to think. I would not leave Mara. And where would I go, alone and unarmed, horseless and dogless, with a small child? They would catch me before I had gone a thousand paces. "I won't run," I said.

He nodded and pulled me from the horse's back. "Mei," he said to the junior of the two women. "Take her."

Shrugging, Mei caught the trailing rope that led to my wrists. "Come." On my leash like a dog in training, I moved into the long reeds away from the others to relieve myself, and then to rinse my face and throat with water that smelled of sulfur. Led back to the camp, I leaned against the mossy Dawn side of a rock. The shadow barely covered my knees when it should have spread over me like a blanket. So far from n'dau.

Mei started a fire that bled thin smoke. From a fitted felt case, she pulled a large silver metal bowl beaten thin as a leaf. She filled the bowl with water and hung it over the flames.

Once they had their saddle pads and bridles removed, the raiders' mares mingled with my clan's horses. There was some fighting, but less than I would have expected. The strange horses stood head and shoulders higher as they all waded into the stream. One of the riders, Ko, patrolled the opposite bank on horseback. As he cantered opposite us, he rubbed his dusty face wearily. My dogs would have guarded better.

Mara sat on the cracked-mud bank beside Shen. He was making something with reeds he had pulled.

"Mara." My voice sounded blurred in my ears.

She turned slightly, perhaps afraid to look directly at me. "Aunt Katia?"

"Yes." Meaning to reach for her, I lifted my hands until the cord stopped me.

"'Tia!" She bolted into my lap and clung to my neck.

"Are you all right?" I asked her.

She nodded, and her dusty, sweaty hair scratched my throat. She looked healthy, if tired and drawn. As well as I could, I felt her for injuries. She had a bruise on one shin, but I thought I remembered that from before the barbarians.

I had never been comfortable with the family's children. I tended them when it was my turn but never asked to hold them or taught them the small-child things. After my father died, I showed Mara the things he had taught me when I was her size: how to clean the horses' hooves, how to make a tablet from herbs or powders. I dealt with her best if I remembered my father teaching me, but now I had to deal with her. There was no one left.

"Where are Mama and Papa?" she asked.

Dust on Megan's long-lashed eye; the ragged red gash left by an arrow removed from Daved's side. "You don't remember?" I finally said.

"Shen says they had to go away but that he'll take care of me." She frowned. "You're dirty, 'Tia. You should wash."

Dried blood flecked her cheek. "You should wash, too, Mara."

"That's what Shen says but I don't want to. Shen says that where he's from is so cold that water is like sand on the ground."

"Snow," I said. "At Dawn. I saw it once when I was smaller than you."

"Shen says I'll see it." She blinked sleepily. "Why are you tied up like that? Were you bad like a dog?"

"No. You don't remember the camp?"

She shook her head.

Shen came closer and squatted on his heels. He looked as tired as the rest of them, but he smiled at Mara and held out for her a small shape woven of reeds. "I have a sister her age," he said to me. "Wulin. She is full of questions, too."

"Shen says I may have the straw pony," Mara said. "He made it."

I watched through the smoke. Mara had already forgotten.

I slept until I was drugged with it. I woke once and staggered to the water's edge to drink the silty water. My hands were bound in such a way that I could not cup water, so I dipped my face like a dog or a horse. When I was done, I knelt back, and picked at the knot with my teeth as I looked around me.

Shen and Ko slept nearby. Mara was cuddled against the youth. Mei guarded the horses and the camp; I saw her astride the one-eared mare from my family's herd. She slowed when she saw me but did not stop. I could go nowhere and I was no threat; Shen and Ko lay with their knives and bows within arm's reach.

I heard the murmur of voices, Huer and Suhui talking. They stood away from the herd with a single horse, the gray mare Suhui had first ridden. The gray held her head rigid as though afraid to move it, and barked a single shallow cough. Her halter was hung with prayer flags no longer than my finger.

Suhui soothed the horse. "Hush, daughter, easy." The raiders all called one another family words—daughter, sister, father.

"The lesions and now the coughing," Huer said.

"Yes," Suhui said.

"Then the mare is already dead," he said slowly. "I am sorry."

"I understand." Even at that distance I saw how pale she was, her gold-skinned face leached a muddy white. "But the others, the strange horses—they do not have the lesions, do they? They might not have it?"

"You saw them yourself. You looked in their mouths. No sores."

"Every other horse on Ping seems to have them." Suhui's voice sounded bitter. "How are these free of them?"

"The handler," Huer said. "Or she has something in her packs. Daughter, she might know how to cure your mare."

Suhui's voice was hopeless. "The pneumonia, maybe. The plague? Not even Earth medicine could cure her of that. It must be luck that her herd has not caught it. It was a mistake to take her, father."

"Perhaps," Huer said. "But it may not be luck. She may know things. Could I leave her behind?"

She said slowly, "She is too unwrinkled to be a great healer. I think there is more to it than this."

"There is nothing," he said harshly.

"She might poison her horses rather than see them become ours. Have you thought of that?"

"We have the child, what is it—Mara. She will not endanger her."

"She might not care."

The gray mare coughed again, once, shallowly, seemingly afraid of the pain. Huer touched her neck. "We cannot let her give this cough to the others, if she has not already. The handler may something to make this easier for her."

"No. I will do it myself, as it has always been done." The horse shifted at the grief in Suhui's voice. "Would you trust the stranger if it were your horse dying?"

"We may all have to learn to, daughter," Huer said wearily. "Her horses are well and ours are dying."

Suhui removed the halter and walked away, singing softly to the mare. The gray's ears pricked forward, and she followed slowly. They moved out of sight around a curve of the stream bed, Suhui plucking the prayer flags from the halter as they walked.

"And will you poison them?" Huer's voice so close to my ear startled me. He stood a bare arm's length from me, watching me watch Suhui.

I said nothing. I had thought of it but they were my family's horses, all that was left of the Winden clan beyond Mara and me and the clan dog—if he lived. And to kill them would take me out of the smoke, to somewhere I did not want to be. "What sickness?" I asked finally.

"You don't know." I started to pick at the knots with my teeth again. "There is a plague. Everywhere on Ping, the horses are dying. The horses get sores in their mouths and then any illness kills them whether it is serious or not. It takes a long while for them to die. A dying mare can foal before she dies. But the foal is dying before it is born.

"Many leagues south of where I am from, back in Dawn, there were a people with a million horses. We used to raid them, but their horses are all dead now. Dead or dying. The Emperor sent us out, a thousand of us, while our horses were still well enough to carry us. To find information or anything that might help."

"And so you killed my family and let me live."

"You are an idea I had. That you might be able to heal the horses. Bringing you and the child to the capital may anger the Emperor. He may kill us."

"Unless I keep the horses well?"

"Even then. I broke my orders."

"Then why bring me back at all?"

"Because my death isn't as important as saving the horses, if you can do that." He shrugged. "We are horse people. The Emperor rules by the speed of our horses. When the horses die, we also die. I will only die a little faster than my people."

Suhui was quiet, swollen-eyed and hard-jawed when she came back. She selected one of the bays from the Winden mares and looked her over carefully; the horse was young, so she danced as the woman did this, tossing her head high. Suhui seemed to like this and haltered her with the gray's halter, tying a single prayer flag to her cheek strap.

We left the stream and traveled again.

There were fifty horses in the Winden herd, as well as the ones we rode. The queen mare decided she did not like being pushed so hard and kept moving the herd in other directions, away from north and dawnward. The riders exhausted their mounts trying to stop this. The barbarians' gray horse that I rode trailed the herd, directed by Huer's shouted commands. More often than not, Mara rode before Shen. When she did ride with me, she chattered about the strange world of the riders.

"Shen says we're going to a city," she said. "That's where his family is from and he will introduce me to his sister."

"City," I murmured after her. An unfamiliar word, even in Trade.

"That is like a bunch of houses, only huge. Shen says that many more than a thousand people live just in that place. The emperor—that's their group leader, 'Tia, like the Moot-leader—has a herd of a many more than a thousand horses, and they feed them with grain from farmers from all around, instead of eating it themselves. Shen says—"

"Who are your parents, Mara?" I interrupted.

"My mother is Meg Weaver of the Winden clan of the Moot people. My father is Daved Handler of the Leydet clan, crossed into the Windens," she recited. "When are Mama and Papa coming back?"

"You won't forget that, will you?" I asked. "Your clan? Your parents? No matter what happens?"

She twisted in my arms to look at me. "That's silly, 'Tia. I have to say that every time we come to Moot."

"But if you never go to a Moot again, Mara. Promise."

"But—" Her face twisted. "Where's Mama?"

"Gone," I said. I still saw through the smoke; I had no resources on which to draw to explain things gently, or at all, to a child. Meg, Daved: dead, leagues noonward.

"When will they come back?" I recognized the signs of coming tears in the tension in her body and the tightening of her voice. "You have to tell me."

"I don't know," I said.

She screamed and hit me. "You do know! You won't let me talk to them. You're here and they're not. I hate you, I hate you!"

At her first screams, Shen and Huer left their places by the herd and galloped toward us.

"Hush, daughter, hush." Shen pulled her from my arms and into his own. "Wulin is your size and she never cries anymore. Do you want her to think you are a baby when you meet her?" He met my eyes momentarily over her heaving shoulders; I saw anger that I had made her cry. "Let me show you a marker cairn, how we show a way for the horses to go home." Still murmuring in her ear, he kicked his horse into a canter toward the front of the herd.

Huer barked a word; my mare, who had started after Shen's, stopped in her tracks. "You are all right?" he asked.

"Yes," I said.

"Your face——" He gestured toward his own cheeks. I raised my hands, but they stopped halfway, stopped by the short lead around my waist.

"Wait," he said, and pulled free his knife and leaned across. The cords fell from my wrists and waist to the ground beside my horse, a tangle of black. "Now."

My arms were stiff when I lifted them. My face was wet. "She is mine," I said finally. "She is my clan, the only——" My throat closed.

"No one steals her," he said softly.

I knew that; she gave herself away, to Shen and his family I had never seen.

For the Moot people, finding places is not so hard; we have the sextant to tell us how far north or south we are; and the angle of the sun shows us that we are where we belong, at the center of things. Rivers and hills and lakes and plains all move under us, but we and the sun stay still: n'dau.

The raiders did not use a sextant, although they had my clan's as well as their own. Instead, we passed cairns no higher than my ankle, made of gold-pink stones—laid by the advance horsemen finding a route for so many horses. I did not know how anyone saw the cairns on a plain littered with gold-pink stones.

We ate on horseback. There was more water now, easy to find at the center of the soil ribbons we crossed. We stopped to sleep only when the lead mare refused to travel. Even through the smoke, I remembered to examine the horses of the herd, looking in their mouths for sores, but the Winden mares were healthy, if tired. Amazingly, the foals were all keeping up. The barbarians' horses were not so well. None had caught pneumonia from Suhui's mare before it had died, but they were more exhausted than they should be, even for the work they were doing.

Back with my family, I had always slept in a tent, but I got used to resting as the barbarians did, with a dark cloth thrown over my face to cut the sun's bite. In the brief time between lying down and exhausted sleep,

I looked up and saw the ball of the sun filtered through fabric and the smoke in my head to a hard hot ball. Still too high.

After a while, we crossed another ribbon of vegetation, this time mixed thorn bushes as high as my chest. Some were from Earth, but here they bloomed and seeded at the same time so that the tangle was filled with tiny yellow-green flowers and brighter wax-yellow berries. A small stream ran along the ribbon's center. The herd drank there, but Huer said there was more water and better grazing ahead of us, and we did not stop for long.

They had not tied my hands again but the blazed gray mare I rode still had no reins. Perhaps she was the best trained for voice commands, because I never rode another, even when she was tired and fell to the back of the group. I had memorized one of the words Huer used on her, the command for *stop*. Her ears flicked back when I tried the word, but she plodded on. At last, impatient, I slid from her saddle and ran to her head, caught the cheek straps of her halter and forcibly halted her.

Her head hung as she labored for breath. She was sweating too hard for the work she was doing, as I am small and she was a big horse. Her coat was stained dark. When I laid my ear against her side I heard her heartbeat, too fast. Looking for a sign of the fever I already knew she had, I peeled her lip back. Her gums were pale.

But the inside of her lip and her gums were also covered with weeping sores, some the size of my thumb. The flesh around them was hot red, inflamed. She flinched when I touched her mouth, even with cool hands, even a finger's length from the sores.

I heard a shout from the herd: Ko's voice, calling for Huer. Perhaps he had seen me off my horse. But where would I go afoot? To the ribbon behind us, to squat among thorns? No: Ko galloped past me, back toward the ribbon.

Huer rode up. "The mare," he said harshly. "The pregnant sorrel. She's left the herd."

I stared at him. "Bring her back, then."

"Have you been watching? She's shedding, drinking a lot. It is her time. Mount."

I looked at my heaving horse. "I don't think mine can carry me."

"Behind me, then," he said impatiently, and leaned over, his hand outstretched. I laid mine in it; he heaved me up in front of him. He pivoted his mare and we followed Ko, back the way we came.

Ko had found her almost immediately, and we followed his shouts to a place in the thorns just south of where we had crossed the water. We stopped where Ko's horse stood. Ko paced beside a gap in the thorns. Huer pulled me down, caught my wrist, and dragged me down a short path.

The sorrel stood in a small clearing, pawing at the blossom-dusted ground. When she noticed us, she charged a step. Huer and I stepped back into the path's mouth and silently knelt to watch. Perhaps this was distance enough, for she ignored us there.

Something was wrong. She acted as any mare delivering would: shimmied her huge bulk as though uncomfortable, then laid down with her legs tucked under her like a crouching dog. And then up again and then down, twisting restlessly.

"No," I said, realizing.

"What?" Huer said behind me, his breath warm on my ear.

"She's not eating," I murmured. "She should be eating everything she can reach."

He left me and moved back. I heard him say in a low voice, "Get her medicines." Ko mounted and left at a gallop.

When Huer returned, I said without looking back, "Wasted effort."

"What?"

The sorrel was rolling on her back, heaving her huge torso from side to side. "It's colic. I can do nothing."

"Is this the plague?"

I turned to look at him. "No. The mare is damaged internally somehow: the foal kicked her intestinal wall or has been lying across a vein in her belly. Or she's eaten something strange."

"Did the plague make her susceptible?"

"No," I said impatiently. "There have always been difficult deliveries, colics."

Her neck was stretched straight out, her throat muscles working. Her legs thrashed as she tried to shift her bulk. The coppery coat was streaked dark and light with sweat and foam. The eye I could see was rimmed with panic-white. Huer said, "You must do something."

The spasms stopped and she lay on her side, heaving. The hard drying mud of the clearing was spangled with tiny fallen green-yellow blossoms. I moved to her and stroked the long bone of her face.

"There's nothing I can do," I said without looking up.

He crossed the clearing in two strides and pulled my face to his, until his gold eyes were a flat angry glow a hand's width from mine. "You can try, Katia. You can fight for her life."

"Why?" I said wearily. He had never called me by my name before. None of them had. "So that she can bear foals for you?"

"Better that she bear foals for someone," he said grimly. "Yours is the first pregnant horse I have seen in six of Suhui's menstrual cycles. If they cannot be infected, your horses, their foals, will save us all. You will not let her die of colic."

"Important? Nothing is so important that you had to kill Ricard and Jena. Meg. Daved. The boys. The dogs." My words came as croaks. My eyes felt pressured by poisonous, unshed tears.

"Do you think I do not have a family, Katia of the Winden Clan? That I do not have brothers, a sister married to a book-saver in the city? A son, too young to leave his mother and join me? I have family and I fear for them. Without horses we will die. There will be no way to communicate, no way to gather tribute. We will starve. Save this foal."

"Or what? You will kill me? Mara?"

A horse galloped up. Its rider dismounted and pushed through the gap in the thorns with the first of my parfleches.

For a moment Huer's eyes glittered. He looked away before I did. "No," he said. "The child learns our tongue from Shen. She is already loved as a sister by one of us. We will not kill her. Or you."

My clan was gone: my dogs, my family. Even Mara, forgetting it all. But I still had the parfleches and my knowledge. And somehow his admitting he would not kill me freed me to do what I was meant to.

"Bring me the parfleche with the red beads."

"You will save her?" he asked.

She began heaving beside me. "I told you. No one can. But I can kill the pain, and help her deliver even though she dies."

She was thrashing again, and I had retreated to the path before he got the parfleche to me. I laid it out quickly. I knew what Huer saw, leaning over my shoulder: a horsehide packet filled with small cloth- or leather-wrapped bundles, each tied with dyed cord hung with beads. But I saw the contents instead: boxes of powdered leaves and roots and molds and earths, stoppered jars of honeys and tinctures, knives and threads and needles, splints and bowls; a waxed sack filled with clay dust, for casts.

"When she relaxes again, cut her in the neck, a slice this long." I showed him the first joint of my thumb. "And then hold her."

I mixed water and tincture, sucked them into a bamboo straw cut to a point at the bottom, and stoppered the top with my tongue, which instantly went numb.

When she stopped thrashing for a moment, he dug the point of his knife in, just above the shoulder. She flinched and prepared to fight, but she was tired and in pain, and I was faster: I jammed the straw's sharp end into the hole he had made and blew hard, then jumped back before she could knock my teeth out with her tossing head. Blood sprayed from the cut.

"That will work?" Huer said, panting.

I nodded. "I was in muscle. She will calm."

Which she did. Tired and drugged, she writhed less and less, until she died.

We cut the live foal from her belly. While Huer and Ko wiped him clean, I milked the dead mare out. Ko took the waterskin filled with milk and cut a tiny hole in a leg, which he thrust into the tiny colt's questing mouth. He drank greedily.

"Look how healthy," Ko said. Tears fell down his face. "He will father many foals." Huer sent him back to the herd, colt and milk laid over his mare's neck, to find a milk-mother as soon as possible.

I still knelt with my hand on the mare's sagging, empty belly. I began heaving. It was a while before I realized this sickness was sobs. I cried for a while. When I was done, Huer gave me water and rode with me back to the herd, now far ahead. I heard a feral dog howling at a great distance. It was a lonely noise and I was grateful for the first time for the company of the barbarian.

We rode. My numbness was over, replaced by a raw ache. The sun scarcely moved in the sky. I watched my short shadow and cried steadily.

Shen's dark bay got sick: a runny nose and fever, then influenza. By the time we noticed it was more than her usual exhaustion from the early stages of the plague, all the other horses had it, as well: the raiders' horses and the new colt worst, my herd no worse than they ordinarily would be in influenza, coughing and staggering their way through the disease's course.

We were passing a drying lake that stretched dawnward to the horizon. Far to the south, a group of small buildings stood where the lake's shore had once been, not much more than dark blots on the horizon. People had lived there when this place was closer to Dawn, then abandoned their village as the lake withdrew and the mud bed cracked.

"We will stop here," Huer said. He slid from his mare's back and laid his hand on her neck. Her coat was flecked with foam, though the air was cooler than it had been. Mucus hung in a thick rope from her panting mouth. "She has suffered enough. They all have, our horses. No. We will let them die in peace here. When they are gone, we will put saddles on mares from the Winden herd."

And so we stayed for a while.

For the first time, the raiders set up a true camp. There was a single tent, which Huer used for his own purposes, and a regular fire, fueled with dried Ping-moss and the branches of the soft-wooded trees that grew and seeded and died in a single dog's lifetime. Mei gave me a jacket, a short version of her quilted riding coat, to keep away the chill of the steady wind that blew across the lake from Dawn. The felted wool smelled like my father's sleep tent had. Its warmth was comforting after the steady despair of working with the dying horses.

The outriders came in once, a grim-faced man and a tiny woman with eyes that might once have been merry if they had not been so weary. They slept through a full sleep-and-wake cycle, and into the next sleep cycle; when they woke they left their dying horses with me, and took six

Winden horses before heading off northward along the shore of the dried lake.

Even after I sent Huer's mare to death, there were still seven of the raider's horses alive: Mei's, Shen's, and Ko's riding mares; one horse with a misshapen hoof that they had used for carrying supplies; and the three left by the outriders, two mounts and one baggage mare. There were still forty-three Winden horses, and eleven of the foals had survived, the losses all being normal to a large herd traveling hard. The Winden horses showed no signs of the disease that killed the others, though several were tired from the journey and a couple of them still struggled through the last of the influenza. Perhaps my mares truly were resistant to whatever killed the tall horses of the barbarians. But the other horses died, one after the other, and I gave them what medications I could to ease their passing.

Huer watched me often as I moved among the horses. He seemed to be brooding, but when he spoke to me, it was only to ask about my treatments.

His sick mare lingered. We had separated her from the others, more for her comfort than from any hope of preventing anything, and Huer spent much of his time with her, weaving paper flags into her halter, talking in the universal wordless language between men and horses. After a time she stopped responding, and instead hung her head and hacked out streamers of mucus that trailed from her cracked lips onto the dust. I watched him watch her, remembering the pain of my first horse's death, remembering my father's death, remembering Meg and Ricard and the rest of my clan, dead.

"Please," I said finally. "Let me help her."

"No." Huer's face was expressionless. "It is not yet time."

"I'm not going to kill her. I just want her to suffer less."

"No," he said. "We do not do things this way."

"Your people have allowed me to help their horses. You thought I might do some good for the horses! Are you too proud of your ways to prevent her pain?" The anger I felt was welcome: it made a change.

"No," he said. "Proud is not the word."

———

Shen's mare fell at last, still heaving but no longer able to stand. "Shen! Oh, Shen!" Mara cried, and then something in the raiders' tongue. She threw herself sobbing into his arms. Shen cradled her in one arm, tears glittering on his face.

"May I help?" I asked.

"Your medicines have made it easier for her," Shen said, "but now it is my turn." He pulled his knife free.

"Mara?" I asked. "Come with me. This isn't going to be nice."

Mara looked at Shen, who watched her in silence. "No," she said finally. "Wulin would stay." She did not flinch when the knife bit into the mare's throat.

I turned on my heel.

"Stop." Huer strode across to me. "What are you doing?"

I pointed southward, to the distant turf houses. "There may be flitterlass nests there. I need their honey."

"Take Suhui." I glanced at her where she leaned against a dead Ping-tree rebraiding a leather rein. The woman shrugged.

"If Mara does not come, alone."

"No," he said. "It is not safe."

"What does that matter?" I snarled. "If anything happens to me, you will still have Mara and the horses."

He looked at me for a time. "Take this then." He handed me his knife.

"Wait!" Suhui straightened. "You cannot—"

He held up his hand to silence her. "Protect yourself. There are wild dogs around."

They had not let me use knives before. Even eating, Huer or one of the others had cut anything that needed to be cut. I took it in silence and left on one of my horses before he could say more.

I stopped my horse just beyond the ragged ring of turf houses. She was exhausted already, her coat smeared with pale gold froth, her nostrils pulling hard at the air. Too hard. I knew what I would find but I looked anyway. Inside her mouth was a single sore, the size of my fingertip.

The turf houses were dried and empty as husks, hardly more than humps of dead grass and dirt. Plumes of dust like dark veils tore from their corners and stung my eyes. I looked in one doorway and saw light where the turf roof had crumbled into the single room. Low benches ringed the space; a stone-lined fire pit squatted in its center. There was a gleam in one corner. When I crouched to look at it, I found a tiny medal such as a child might wear made of gold-colored metal, forgotten in the room's gloom when its inhabitants had abandoned their homes and turned back to Dawn to build anew.

So much work, all abandoned to dry into dust. When I was a child, my family had seen a few of these places, where people settled only to move half a lifetime later, as the planet dragged their sturdy little houses toward Noon. Even then it had seemed nonsense when one could move so easily with tents and horses and dogs. The only stable things on Ping were the sun at n'dau and us: my family at the still center of things. Except that my family was dead and the sun had been a long time from n'dau.

There were no flitterlass nests. I had not expected them, after all: flitterlasses lived among the ruehoney bushes that only grew farther dawnward, but I knew the raiders would not know that.

I stepped into the next house. I was thirsty and tired of walking. I sat on the bench that ringed the wall and drank from my waterskin, warm and flat as the liquid was. The roof was intact and the doorway small. Inside was darker than anywhere I had ever been. It seemed darker than a sleep-tent's interior, darker than the insides of my eyelids, darker than all the legends of Night.

I could kill myself. I touched the thought with my mind, like feeling a strange fabric at the Moot. Everyone else was dead. I tried to remember them as they had been alive, but all I saw was Stivan with the arrow in his breastbone, Daved curled like a child around the arrow in his gut.

I looked at the knife Huer had given me, a dim gleam in the darkness. It would be easy enough. Huer thought I was past this cold place or he would not have given me the knife. Well, he would be wrong. He would still have my horses and my medicines, useless though they were against this plague. I was irrelevant.

I do not know how long the breathing went on before I noticed. It had been so silent but now I heard it, steady if rasping, in the doorway. It was not a human's breathing.

I knew suddenly that I wanted to live despite everything. I did not want my bones to follow my family's, baked in Noon and lost at last under the ice sheets of Evening. Anything was better than that. Even slavery. Even sorrow. I stood, prepared to fight.

A single whine, familiar to me as Mara's sleep-noises. "Dog?" I asked in wonder, and softly whistled: *everyone*, and *come in from wherever you are.*

A lone dog moved shakily into the doorway, a black outline. One of my males, the rangy red one with the white ear. Here. Alive. I scrambled toward him.

His coat was caked with dark mud. It took a moment to realize the mud was made of blood and dirt. I felt him with frightened fingers and found a great jagged tear along one flank where he must have ripped free of an arrow, but the wound was cool to the touch and crusted over. A scab: he was healing. His footpads were hot and rough and cracked. He had tracked me all these weary leagues.

A small dark circle appeared on the dust of his back, then another. It was a while before I realized they were my tears.

I cried for a time and fell asleep just inside the doorway to darkness with my face pressed against his flank.

"Katia?" Huer's voice awakened me. He was moving through the circle of huts. He had not seen me; I lay close to the ground, dirt-colored in my stained clothes, hidden in the constant Night of the hut.

I fingered the knife. I had a waterskin, a knife, a horse—at least until she died—and now, incredibly, a dog. I could travel to the Moot, reopen the Winden scrolls, train new dogs, start a new horse herd if it was possible to stop the plague. Huer was all that stood between me and this. He knew about the knife but not about the dog, nor about my awakening from the smoke and the sorrow. It would be a small thing, a simple thing, to kill him. There would be a long while before they realized what had happened and came after me—if they did; they might assume he and

I were lost, killed by dogs perhaps. They might continue on north and dawnward, back to their Emperor with my horses and Mara, who was barely Winden any more.

"Where are you?" he said. His voice sounded weary. "Please."

I do not know why I did not kill him and leave. The leagues between me and Moot; the fact that no reclaimed clan would be *my* family; the gentleness in his voice then and there—I do not know. I only know that I walked from the doorway, the dog beside me.

He saw the dog as soon as he saw me. He had not replaced the knife he had given me. He said nothing, did nothing, stood empty-handed. I had nothing to say. The balance between us shifted like Dawnlands in earthquake, the river uncertain which way to go: the old channel where the way was already cut, or the new channel which might lead nowhere.

"How did you get here?" I asked.

His face was a mask. "I rode."

"But your mare—" I began.

He cut me off. "She is suffering too much. I asked this one last thing of her, that she would bring me here. Perhaps you will be merciful and send her to rest."

"You are planning to walk back?" It was too far, unless the other raiders meant to ride down and meet him here.

"No," he said. "I have no plans for returning. Suhui knows what I do. She takes the herd and your medicines on to the emperor's city. I will stay with you."

I shook my head violently. "I can't save the horses. I think they will all die. I don't know how the disease transmits, but now mine have it too, and they're going to die too. I can heal a rash, soothe a fever, splint some leg breaks. I can help a mare deliver. But I can't cure this plague. I don't think anyone can."

"So there will be no more horses."

"No more," I said.

Silence fell again. I could hear my dog's breathing; the soft wheezing of the horses; the hushing nose of the Dawn winds.

"Your family," he said finally. "I am sorry. I was wrong. I should have asked aid first."

I said nothing.

"You were a tool to me. A new knife, a magical medicine. But you have not been able to help, and still I—find I value you. Esteem you. I was wrong to kill. Even to save my people it was wrong."

There was anger in me, and pain. But surprisingly I had no wish to speak of these things. "Your people will survive," I said. "They will find another way. They will heal the horses or they will learn another way, a way without horses."

"No," Huer said. "There is no way without horses for us. We are an empire spread across a thousand leagues."

"Then you will become a smaller empire. But you will survive." I knew this. I had survived.

"How?" he said bitterly.

"For them, I do not know. But watch." I whistled and my red dog shook and launched upright. I whistled *dance* and he performed an odd little step, crossing paws as he moved sideways, first one way, then the other. I whistled *hold*, and he stopped, one foot still lifted in the step, his eyes shining with happiness.

"What—?"

"He hunts. And used to herd for us. Takes messages. Watches when we sleep. And he has been trained to defend. To guard. I had a dozen dogs like him before your people killed them. I can breed and train others."

"Dogs can do so much."

I ruffled the fur on my dog's head. "Yes. And haul and run. I cannot ride a dog but they allow us to stay in touch, my people."

"Ah," Huer nodded once. "Perhaps such a thing is possible."

"Where is your horse?" I asked.

When it was done, Huer pulled free one of the prayer flags from his mare's halter. I turned it over: it was of vellum, stained dark gold with wear, still warm from his dead mare's skin.

"Tie it to the dog's collar," he said. "All animals need prayers."

"I am leaving," I said.

"I will come with you," he said. "I owe you a life. A dozen lives, but I can only repay one."

The river dropped into its new course. He never asked for the knife back.

We turned to the south. If we walked far enough, we would be able to pass the lake and then head north again, toward where the Moot should be.

I had not noticed the sun, my shadow. But it was closer to n'dau and soon it would be entirely there. Huer had made a mistake, had slipped from the right center of things. It was a terrible thing, and my family died for it. The horses die for another reason, but they die. But life continues, and I and Mara and Huer and my dog are the proof of that. The sun hangs where it should in the sky, and I walk beneath it in my right place, n'dau, which never stops moving, which is eventually everywhere.

Dia Chjerman's Tale

We tell these tales, we who lived on the Ship. We do this so that our home planets and our time on the Ship will not be forgotten—so that *we* will not be forgotten. To the men of the Ship, our planets were disobedient fiefs, then nonrenewable resources. Our grandmothers and mothers were objects to fight over, breeding stock. We have always been more than this.

It has been more than six hundred years since this story was first told by my twenty-seven-times grandmother, Dia Chjermen. The way it is told, she cried silently for a month after Delmoni was destroyed and she was taken aboard Empire Ship Delta. And then she stopped crying and wiped her eyes, and told this tale to the other women of the Ship. And now I tell you, so that Dia and Delmoni will not be forgotten.

My planet was Delmoni Prime. We were a beautiful world, fourth from the amber-colored star, also called Delmoni. We turned on the very edge of the galactic disk and depending on the season, our night sky was just a thin scattering of stars, like a pinch of salt thrown on a black skirt, or it was a shell over us, striped with bands of light. Our trees had leaves so dark they looked black, but our lichens—and we had many of them—were bright, green and gold and pink, glowing as though lit from within. Most of our insects and animals were brightly colored as well, with many legs.

We knew we belonged to the Empire, almost an accidental addendum to some declaration covering our entire sector. But why should they care about us one way or another? We had no resources not readily available closer to the Empire's core. Faster-than-light travel would have made us more accessible to them, but this was still an unattainable dream: men and women were not meant to travel through warping time. *Space* could be warped, but only the Empire Ships were large enough to carry the black hole necessary to do so. Even supralight communications took many years to get to us, forwarded along the pipeline from the Empire's heart, so no time was wasted on politics or power. Communications were all of technology and trade. The Empire offered us information that would improve our food production and our trade potential. Everyone was always grateful for the Empire's help. That is how they had grown so great and powerful.

Because of this, and because we were just one of ten thousand planets in their domain, we foolishly thought the Empire did not care about us. So we minded our business and sent occasional unmanned ships off toward the core of Empire, filled with whatever tax they demanded. Mostly we forgot about them.

And then we found a drone in our solar system, sent—not from Empire or the galaxy's cluttered heart—but from outside, apparently from a star beyond what we thought of as the Edge. It was an alien drone and based on our interpretation of certain symbols carved along its carapace, it appeared to ask for a benign exchange of information. We deliberated for half a century and agreed, sending a drone in reply. We hoped they would be able to read our instructions for radio and supralight technologies.

We did not bother to tell the Empire of this. We didn't want to pass on news until we had something back from the aliens, something worth the expense of a pipeline communication. Though the likeliest star was only a few light years away, still, they might have died off hundreds of years ago, or they might be from another galaxy altogether. And to be honest, we might not want to share what we found. We had elected a new ruler in the last decade of this time, and she began building a small spacefaring force suitable for impressing the aliens, if they did indeed still exist.

Perhaps it was this small handful of ships that attracted the Empire's attention somehow, because that's when the message came. My twenty-seven-times grandmother Dia Chjermen did not hear it, but her great-grandmother did. "Empire Ship Delta here. Delmoni, we are on our way."

That was it. There's never any more to the messages—no accusation, no judgment, no verdict, no threat. This message came in the Year of the Empire 3658.

Everyone knew of the Ships and called them Blood Ships. They existed only to terrify and to punish. They traveled to a recalcitrant planet, they destroyed that place, and they moved on. Depending on where it was when it started its trek toward a planet, a Ship might take years to arrive, decades or centuries, but it would inevitably arrive. It was said that each Ship carried a hundred thousand fighting men, a hundred million, a billion. There was one Ship, a dozen Ships, a hundred. What did we know except horror stories?

Worldwide riots began immediately, as though we were unwilling to wait for the Ship to arrive, and chose instead to destroy ourselves. Even before the message was verified, the people revolted and the leader who had built the space force was quartered in the streets of the capital. Dia's great-grandmother killed five men with a cooking knife as she escaped from the silver-walled city of Telete with her two daughters.

For years, we sent countless messages down the pipeline to the galaxy's heart, pleading with the Empire to forgive us. We heard nothing. Others among us sent panicked requests for aid to any world in range. The nearest human planet responded twelve years after the Ship announced itself to us. They were very sorry and wished us luck. But, they said, please don't try to seek refuge here. We heard the threat beneath the polite words and turned to other options.

We scrambled to establish communications with the aliens who, it turned out, were alive and located around the close star we had identified as likeliest. Our linguists rushed to establish a workable, mutual language. Supralight messages whirled back and forth. Their technology was considerably advanced compared to ours, but centered entirely around agricultural technology and weather modification. They had nothing to help us fight the Ship.

Eight years after the message, the aliens offered to take refugees. Perhaps they did not understand the full power of the Ships or what the Ship might do to their own planet; or perhaps they didn't believe the Ship would care about them. Or perhaps they did not have the nightmares we did, raised as we were for millennia with tales of the Blood Ships ringing in our infants' ears.

This lasted until the aliens realized that it was not a thousand nor a hundred thousand people who craved sanctuary, but a billion. They closed communications with Delmoni. We did send our embryonic space force there to beg or force them to accept us. Ten years later, we received a supralight transmission—human screams and another message from the aliens: so sorry, we disgrace ourselves doing this, but our people must be first in our concerns. That was the last we heard from the aliens.

We agonized about what we might have done to bring a Blood Ship to us. Was it the radio message to the aliens? The tiny space fleet? Electing an ambitious leader? Was it because the aliens had contacted us, instead of the Empire? We never found out and this made it somehow worse.

After twenty years, the Ship had not yet come. The world government collapsed. The global riots had formalized themselves into gangs that alternated between ritualized but bloody combat among themselves, and killing sprees. Thirty-four years after the message, Dia's great-grandmother was raped and killed by a handful of young boys from one of these gangs. Dia's grandmother was barely twenty but she killed three of them before she was herself killed, leaving a sister who would start screaming when she heard certain noises—a door being opened, a light flicking on—and a baby girl abruptly weaned by circumstance. Dia's mother.

The people of Delmoni Prime settled into a desperate clawing depression. Like animals in a trap, they alternated between flailing furiously against the jaws of the planet that held them, and biting at themselves. Those who could afford to do so built personal spaceships and bolted for anywhere in the galaxy but Delmoni's lavender skies. Some of those ships were shoddily built and exploded during liftoff.

Decades passed and the Ship did not come. Children were born and grew up in its shadow and died. Dia sometimes told her daughters—and they their daughters, down to me—the stories she read as a girl, when Delmoni still lived. There were two sorts: airy bright fantasies filled with miraculous rescues, and the other ones, the realistic ones, grim lightless tales about how it feels to be living dead. Sex became a desperate escape or else a subdued instinctual thing, joyless. Rape became common.

After a time, a small but vocal group began their talk. Perhaps, they said, the Ship would not come after all. Decades had passed and there had been no sign of it. Perhaps the crew had mutinied, or the vessel had been destroyed or ordered elsewhere. Perhaps the very notice of its coming and the outside verification had been a clever trick. No one would come; it was time for us to put our fear behind us, to come together again as a planet and build a glorious new future. Churches sprang up, and new benevolent societies, and then trickled into silence to be replaced by new groups. In our hearts we knew they all lied, but we cheered and pretended to forget this. Hope, even a hope built on impossibilities, was the only luxury we could afford. The Ship would come. The Ship always came.

Eighty-four years after the message, Dia Chjermen was eight. That was the year the first wave began. Every tale we Shipwomen tell has this part in it. Millions of microscopic drone fighters churned out of a wormhole into the Delmoni system. They immediately ate the home-guard ships we had been able to throw together, then settled not on our planet but on our asteroids and moons and the other planets, shredding the crusts to supply materials to build more microrobots. When there were enough, they gathered in the skies over Delmoni, hovering, a haze like the gauze of darkmatter. And then they fell in shimmering curtains, like distant rain away or a dark veil trailing onto the ground.

The microrobots didn't kill anyone, not yet, only ate our electronics and refined metals, turning them into still more robots. Some of the robots targeted concretes and even fired bricks—anything we had touched, altered for our convenience—but nothing harmed the people's flesh. Half-naked and unsheltered, we starved and we fought. There were no means of gathering crops, no roads and nothing to travel on them. We thought the riots would be the worst: after all, we had seen men and women tortured and killed, buildings smashed into shards of metal and earth. But nothing prepared us for this. There was no one visible doing this. Our world dissolved into dust and mist.

Dia had a little receiver she used to listen to speeches. She told of watching its surface seethe like a body covered with vermin. Its shape softened and shifted and began suddenly to smoke away like fog rising from water. She watched closely—she was a small girl—and saw tiny, tiny bits zip into the air. After a time, there was no receiver left. That's when she realized her synthetic parka had also been eaten away.

I don't know how many people died during the twenty years before the microbots at last died and settled ankle-deep across the surface of

Delmoni. More than in the eighty before, I suppose. Dia lost her aunt, her cousins—everyone in her town. She was claimed by a strong man who defended them both until he died trying to trap something to eat; Dia never told what it was but we have told these tales enough to guess. By then she was old enough and strong enough to tend to herself. After that, she was alone in what had once been her village, the only person alive for a day's walk in any direction. She knew this because she walked a day out once and circled back in a giant spiral closing on the place where her village had stood. She saw no sign of anyone as she waded through the dead microrobots, pulling and eating the struggling plants as she walked.

Dia was twenty-eight when the Ship itself came through the wormhole and settled into orbit. A terrible wind started and she ran for the cave she had been living in. She watched lights on the horizon and clouds that moved too quickly toward her. What looked like sheets of black rain fell from them, darker than the first fall of microrobots had been years before. The wind that blew in her face stank of heat, and she realized at last that it was the start of the Bombing. She ran as deep into the cave as she could, hiding in a hollow beside an underground stream.

She stayed there for forty days and nights, a magic number the Ships chose for the length of their bombings. The earth shook overhead. Flame-scented winds snaked through the narrow passages to find her. The only food she had was an animal she had captured just before the bombing had begun, and a creature which she found after a few days, hiding close by. The water she drank from the river was good at first, but after a time chemicals from above leached into it and made her sick. She had wood and torches enough for a week, then they were gone and she lay in absolute darkness, wrapped in her furs and screaming. The bombing overhead seemed to come in regular waves; after a time she slept through them, not because she was accustomed to them but because she could not stay awake and sane. She slept curled tight in a fetal position, waking every eternity to drink more of the water that made her sick. One of these times, she noticed dully there wasn't any bombing overhead, and she crawled from the darkness.

The light blinded her at first. Hungry as she was, she couldn't go out into the world until night fell. At first she thought everything was absolutely gone. All she saw was ashes and broken charred trees. Eventually she saw that there was still some life, animals that looked as stunned and shock-struck as she, stumbling across the wasteland. She caught one and ate it alive, blood sweet as rain on her tongue.

Then nothing happened for a time in Dia's world. She didn't know that a hundred million Empire Shipmen had landed. They established what they called a One-Generation Punitive Governorship, killed most of the remaining men, and enslaved the rest. During this time they buried their stored dead in elaborate stone tombs carved from living rock by the slaves, took on fresh water and food plants, and mined nuclear materials for their onboard power supply. They recruited from the few surviving men to renew their numbers. The men were grateful: at least they would live this way. Shipmen were always looking for men to replenish their losses. They were not kind, even to themselves.

And they took the women of Delmoni, the strong women who had survived the twenty years of destruction and the Bombing, for breeding stock to strengthen the Shipmen of the future. A group of Shipmen happened upon Dia hiding with a stone knife. She gutted one and slashed another across the face before, laughing, they disarmed her and told her she would be taken to the Ship. She was raped fifteen times in the first two days, though that word was meaningless aboard Ship. She memorized the faces of the men who raped her, swearing to kill each of them, but she did not. Few do.

Dia was one of the last Delmoni women to be pulled onto the Ship. Shortly after the arrival of her group, the Punitive Governorship was recalled and the Ship crammed itself and its horde of surviving bots back through the wormhole.

Dia's story ends here. Many of our tales end that way, with the sight of our planet dwindling in the aft screens. After that we were Shipwomen. We learned to survive in the Ships, raised children. A few of us grew to love the fierce Ship's men and the sharp edge of Ship life; some of us rebelled in secret ways. Most of us hunkered down, numb when we needed to be, and passed to our daughters these tales.

I do not know what happened to Delmoni. There were people still alive there, and perhaps they interbred with the Shipmen left behind as permanent occupation forces and became ardent supporters of the Empire. This is what the men of Blood Ship Delta told us. Perhaps only a handful still live. Perhaps more. Perhaps none.

But I am the twenty-seven-times granddaughter of Dia Chjerman, and I know many other tales about Dia and Delmoni, and of others: of Jennhl and her home, the satellite half lost in Parucek Tertia's rings, and her poems, written by pressing thorns into her skin to save their words; of Constanzia Allameda, who dared the Ship's captain to single combat under the red skies of Li Po; of Meg Backus of Archimedes 6, who had twelve children when the drones began and kept them all alive; of Trian HBjorhus of Uth 67-b, who cursed Empire Ship Iota, and it died ninety-nine days later. There are a thousand tales: a million.

And all our stories end thus: when the Empire Ship at last died, we the women of Delmoni and all the other conquered places walked free from the ruins and felt sunlight on our faces again. They still exist, Parucek and Li Po and all the others. And Delmoni exists still, in Dia Chjermen's tale and now in your memories.

—for Chris McKitterick

My Wife Reincarnated as a Solitaire—Exposition on the Flaws in My Wife's Character—The Nature of the Bird—The Possible Causes— Her Final Disposition.

My wife seems returned to me as a solitaire: a great ugly mean-spirited bird, feathered and stubby of physique; with a great bulging beak, a surly mien, and an omnipresent squawk. To deny so unnatural a fact would be a comfort; but a sensible man faces difficult truths.

Having accepted so extra-ordinary a change, her new form is unsurprising. She was ever a squat, awkward woman; resentful in nature; recalcitrant as to a wife's right duties of acknowledging her husband's sovereignty and holding household to his general betterment; and importunate in her demands regarding that amative act that leads to the wife's other great labour, the bearing of progeny.

While her new physical form is unappealing, even by those standards which one must apply to fat wingless fowl, they are at least collected into a form that scarce reaches my thigh:—and in three things at least she is considerably improved by the change: firstly, that such sounds as fall from her, one can no longer say *lips* but must now say *beak*, may the more readily be ignored without unfavorable judgement, when even the most assiduous listener—such as our vicar Mr. White, who has, perhaps to a fault, exhibited a most accommodating charity with regard to my wife; proof that a man of the cloth indeed suffers much in his duties—can find no meaning to them; secondly, that she no longer makes unreasonable demands upon my pocket for house-keeping, clothing, or other extravagant purposes; and thirdly, that her transmutation into a bird has brought completely to an end those impositions of an intimate nature which she hitherto had made with such frequency as might nearly constitute harassment—though in truth, they had abated somewhat in her last months and final illness.

It was Mr. White who recognized her species, when first we returned to my wife's room after she had breathed, for so we imagined it, her last; and found there, instead of the relict—the cast-off shell—, this large gray bird, its inutile wings a-flail as it sought to hop from the bed. At this sight he grew most excited, and even, as one might say, exalted.

—She is become *Pezohaps solitaria*! said he.

—Indeed! said I;—How do you know what bird she is become? 'Tis most specific, sir.

—'Tis a lucky guess, says he, and picks her up with somewhat of a grunt (for even as a bird she remained plump) and feeling over her limbs with curiosity,—there are plates in the *Transactions*—'tis the Rodrigues solitaire, as you might call it; 'tis related closely to the dodo; and 'tis said to be extinct, these twenty years and more.

—If 'tis my wife, in some fashion changed, said I:—then, extinct indeed, and yet not extinct enough. Perhaps for the salvation of her soul, we would be wiser to dispatch it immediately.

—'Tis your wife, sir! said Mr. White:—You can say this?

—'Tis a bird now, sir, said I;—a great homely one, too.

—Well, if you feel thus, said Mr. White,—perhaps you shall not think so ill of remanding her: it, I should say: to my care, so that I might demonstrate it to the members of the Royal Society upon my next visit to town.

Mr. White is, as apparently are all vicars, a natural philosopher and member of the Royal Society;—which honour I might myself have claimed, for, while I do not like to boast, my intelligence is such that I have been flattered many times by the deference shown my opinions when I have found occasion to bring them forth at the Crossroads, at the Shoes & Keys, or even at Eeles's coffee-house in Town; which respect all auditors have each time demonstrated by falling silent as I spoke; and by a certain fixity of expression about the eyes, as they struggled to keep pace with the rapidity of my processes.

Since his arrival at the parish, some months ago, after Lord C_____ gave him the preferment, Mr. White has been often at my house. 'Tis my wife's doing, for, while Mr. White is not of such acuity as might make him an ideal companion for a rational man—yet he was peer enough for my wife; who, I am sorry to say, reading and but imperfectly absorbing such books as fall to her hand, sets herself up as a wit, the unhappy result of a father's overindulgence in his senescence; and she often suggested that the vicar join us to dine or for tea.

—Poor man, said she;—He has few enough good meals, eating whatever that slattern thinks to give him; he'll never have had tarts like ours: for my wife disliked Mr. White's cook, calling her slovenly, lazy, and ill-mannered; which slur, which might with equal accuracy be directed in a more immediate direction, caused me more than once to bite my lips.

—Wife, I had several occasions to remark:—'Tis an act of charity to feed Mr. White at our board, but to do so thus often becomes an affront, implying as it does that he has not the good sense to keep his own house, but instead must rely upon the generosity and kindness of others.

Said she, most contentious:—'Tis not about him but about your own cheeseparing nature; 'twill not kill you to feed your betters once and a while.

Said I,—'Tis not *once and a while* that bothers me: 'tis his almost constant attendance; but she paid little attention to my reasonable and—despite her unkind and inaccurate words—selfless concerns. He thus dined often with us; and he managed to put away his bottle a night.

Mr. White was quite a favourite of my wife's. In his courtesy, he allowed her to draw him away from our own more rational discourses, and they thus spent hours in close converse: I asked her of what they spoke and she said, matters of doctrine and faith; and indeed, though I was often barred from their conversations by Mr. White's over-developed sense of the sanctity of confession: a belief so extreme in his case that it seemed quite Roman—their conversations did have a beneficent effect in one matter at least; for, though their colloquy sometimes distracted her from her household labours to the extent that I came home more than once from the Shoes & Keys to find dinner burnt, the kitchen maid flirting at the back gate with the carrier, and even my wife's attire in some disarray, as though she neglected even that spousal duty to keep herself presentable and pleasant-appearing to her husband:—still their discussions brought decrease in her *attentions vitale*, as Mr. White led her with his counsel to understand the *proportionateness* to be sought in this, as in all other, behaviours.

Her illness came upon her some weeks after Mr. White's arrival; and it proved most difficult, indeed impossible, to diagnose: our Dr. Thrale confessed himself at a loss and proposed that he send for a physician from Town; but, for once in her life my wife refused to spend money upon herself, even saying that, should the London doctor be summoned, she would go so far as to lock her door and deny him entrance: even the suggestion by Dr. Thrale so offending her that she barred her door even to him, preferring, as she said, to die attending most carefully to Mr. White's good counsel regarding her immortal soul, even excluding me from her chamber as he answered her questions and brought her to, as I hoped, a gentle acceptance and remorse for her many failings.

Then came the day, when Mr. White walked into my library uninvited—his constant attendance in my house made him sometimes unrespecting of the little proprieties that make our Civilisation so shining an example to the World at large—and said: Sir, it is nearly done: she shall pass on this very evening.

—Then I shall speak with her, said I.

—I do not think that will be wise, sir, said he:—she should instead devote her final energies to contemplation of the Divine.

—I am not an unreasonable man, said I:—if she apologize for her contumacity, for subverting all my plans and desires, and for her importunate demands on my pocketbook, time, and person, I shall most willingly forgive her, and she may pass from this world with her conscience cleared of these sins.

—Well, sir, said he after some coughing:—in that case I only request that you be brief.

When I came to see her upon her death-bed, she indeed did seem at peace, calm, and even content: surprisingly pink (as Mr. White assured me she would seem, giving as cause the fever that scorched her very body; though I felt little enough of it when I took her hand): yet much exhausted.

—Well, she said: or rather croaked, for she was quite hoarse from crying out in recent nights, her pain spurring her to such great volume that at last I had taken to sleeping in the library, in an elbow-chair; waking up each morning with a great pain in my neck that left me quite weak;—You'll be rid of me soon enough.

—Wife, said I:—What is this! I want only your happiness and well-being; and a few tears dript from my face and nose.—A moment later, I realized it would have been a delicate sentiment to have said,—and your health; but the time was past.

—B********, said she: employing a word I did not know she knew and which made me despair of her future bliss:—Well, it hardly matters now: You are rid of me; and I escape to a better place.

—I hope, said I,—that this is true, though I must confess as your loving husband—, at which point she made a noise that has no orthographic equivalent,—that I have some slight doubts about your welcome in Paradise; for, forgive me, but you have shown but little understanding of your duties as a Christian, a woman, and a wife.

This was an unfortunate statement and, had I not been in considerable pain from my sleepless night, I would not have demonstrated so great a failure of judgement, which opened me to her subsequent calumny; for my benignant counsel brought forth from her an unreasonable fervid tirade about my flaws as Christian, man, and husband, decaying into such libelous peroration that there is no point to recording it.

—'Twas my own fault, said she when her spleen was spent:—Father wanted me to wait to wed, but I was too eager:—as indeed she was, demonstrating in our early months of matrimony so high a level of ardour that my health suffered as under unsavoury siege: though after a time I had often been able to divert her attentions into argument.

I shook my head in sorrow: I ventured a few gentle words meant to direct her thoughts to more proper channels for a woman who walked in the very shadow of Death; but she raised herself from her bed to hurl an empty jug at me, which only narrowly missed and shattered against the door-jamb: a valuable white-ware jug from my great-uncle's estate; and then falling back, she coughed feebly and said:—I fail. Send Mr. White to me.

I hastened to my library where Mr. White sat alone reading a book my wife had some weeks before taken from my library; instantly seeing its inappropriate and irreligious nature and showing a judgement otherwise occasionally lacking in his bookishness, Mr. White had confiscated it; and was reading it, attempting, as he said, to learn in what fashion its contents might have damaged her hopes for Paradise; and informed him of her request.

This book is perhaps of interest at this point in my recital; for in it, as I have come to believe since her demise, is the profane cause of her change into a solitaire. As a youth, my father expended considerable resources (though to be sure no more than he could or should have, in the education of his sole son and heir) in sending me upon the Grand Tour; and in my travels in distant Turkey, I met a man in an opium den, which I visited for the sake of my education, seeking to learn what I might of even man's lowest estate. He was an Englishman and spoke in an educated tone, though it was only that of Cambridge; but he wore mere rags, and was thin and ill, the result as he averred of years spent in the Himalayan mountains with Bhuddist priests; but which I attributed to pernicious opium.

From that Englishman I purchased the notebook of his researches there, in part the translation, as he assured me, of a work sacred to the heathens. 'Twas illustrated with his own drawings in coloured inks, of the pagan temples, peoples, and mountains he had observed; and it seemed a most useful document to me, of such nature that I might impress my father with the breadth of my learning, were I to offer it as my own accomplishment—for the Tour had been far more expensive than my father's frugality had budgeted for, and our correspondence was of not such volume or frequency that I thought he would detect the difference in hand-writing.

The Englishman wished to sell it for five pounds, but with my superior skills in bargaining, I was able to acquire it for the local equivalent of eighteen and sixpence—and I should have been able to get it for much less, had he not rallied from his coughing-fit and stood fast at that sum. The work proved to be of great utility: my Latin language was a trifle unpolished, for it had been some time since I had attended to it, preferring instead to devote my thoughts to more important topics; but the pictures were of great use in generating stories: my father knew nothing of Thibet and thus accepted any statement I made; the men at Eeles's and the Shoes & Keys listened to every word I chose to utter with flattering attention; and the locale was sufficiently removed from the normal circuits that no-one asked questions, which might be difficult or awkward to address.

I knew even from the title on the cover that it was an impious work; 'twas styled *De mysteriis orientalibus thibetensibusque cum philosophiis magiae mortis vitaeque futurae liturgiis ex originalibus conversis*; the words for *Magic*, *Life*, and *Death* clear enough that even my wife must have understood them; though I had had no idea her father's ill-considered opinions about the education of women—to my mind of no great value, making them sullen, contentious and froward: my wife as exemplar of this—had extended to the language of scholarship.

My book remaining yet in Mr. White's hands, he went upstairs to attend her death-bed. His calling demands that he walk into humble places and show concern about the souls of even low men: still, my wife's character must have made attendance nearly as onerous for him as would have been time spent with thieves and poachers—though, to be sure, he did not in general meet with any but the neighbourhood's best company; but instead sent his curate.

A scarce hour later, he came back into the library.—Alas, your wife has passed from this life! said he.—But she is happy at last, in the bosom of her Lord. He seemed tranquil, as befits a man of the cloth in the face of that most natural of processes, that of life into death; though he was clearly tired, with great circles of fatigue under his eyes and some disorder in his dress that hinted at her final throes.

I leapt up, the journal I had been reading slipping from my hand. I said some words of loss, and wept for quite a minute; before accompanying him to her bedside to view the empty husk that was all that remained of her.

However, as I have described earlier, there was instead that bird, its head tipped sideways to stare at me with one small unintelligent black eye. Having gathered it up, Mr. White brought the solitaire down most carefully into the library and stood it upon my desk, where it looked again at me and then left a gleaming grey-white turd in the exact centre, upon the funeral notice I had been attempting to draft.

—'Twas that ****** book, said I, in my indignation incautious with my language; though he did not seem over-bothered, perhaps understanding my extremity:—She has done this solely to haunt me for-ever.

—Perhaps, said Mr. White,—her existence *mortuus* is not fixed upon you, but her conversion to this form has been for some other reason; and when I further questioned him, he offered three possible Causes: first, that she had died and been reincarnated, which was my own suspicion; second, that she was being punished in this fashion for some sin—perhaps, as I suppose, for her amative tendencies, for, except for that season in which it mates, the solitaire remains much alone, hence its name; and third, that she was truly and forever dead, and that this bird had spontaneously and instantly generated from her corpus, as maggots from meat, but consuming it utterly.

Mr. White, to my surprize, seemed less interested in these possibilities, than in the question of why she had appeared as *P. solitaria*.—There was nothing to indicate this result, he said: I must research further. I rolled my eyes, for philosophers, even natural historians, are ever impractical; and the proper inquiry was not, what she was—the solitaire's close relation to the dodo was, to my mind, reason enough—but what was to do with her, in this inextinct form?—which concern I voiced.

—Perhaps, said he,—you will allow me to take her to the vicarage tonight: it, I *should* say—and the bird nipped his hand where he ruffled its feathers; and he emended himself:—Very well, said he:—*her*, to better consider what next to do.

—I do not know about that, said I:—dead or not, she is my wife; it would hardly be proper for her to share a roof with a single man, even as a bird.

For the first time, the burdens of long attendance on my wife, offering what was clearly unheeded counsel, and his fatigue at ministering to her final hour: caused a certain nevertheless unwarranted shortness in his reply:—For G**'s sake, said he:—Do you want her or don't you?

To be honest I have no use for a bird that is thought to be extinct, even a relict of my wife; and so I sent him off, the solitaire under one arm and the Thibetan book, its presence undoubtedly forgotten, under the other.

Surprisingly, despite his passion for acquiring the bird,—in the two weeks since that date he has not yet taken it up to London, to the Royal Society for their inspection, at all. In plain fact, I have not seen the bird; which contents me considerably, for I have no interest in seeing my wife in whatever form. He claims to keep the bird inside, to guard it from the harmful rays of the sun and to better explore its natural functions. He claims as well, that the bird is as gentle as a lamb with him; though character will out, I am sure: and the bird shall eventually prove as great a burden to him as ever my wife was to me.

Yet he still speaks of taking it up to London, and even of staying some months there, leaving the parish in the curate's care. This may be a blessing for us all, for I have in recent nights, before the curtains are drawn, seen him sitting with a woman in his library: presumably his housewife, for what other woman shares his household? And I am sorry to report that I did upon one occasion—though I was in no way attempting to observe his actions; I merely walked in the lane relishing my widowed state; his actions were visible even to the most uninterested eye—observe him embrace that woman most ardently. These manners may do for London, but have nothing to do with Plainfield.

Schrödinger's Cathouse

Bob is driving down Coney Island Avenue in the rain. His dust-blue Corolla veers a little as he struggles with a small box wrapped in brown paper with no return address. He was going to take it home from the post office and open it there but he got curious at a stoplight and now, even though the light's changed and he's splashing toward Brighton Beach in medium traffic, he's still picking at the tape that holds the top shut. A bus pulls in front of him just as the tape peels free and the box opens.

Bob looks around. The room in which he has suddenly found himself is large. The walls are covered with vividly flocked paper, fuschia and crimson in huge swirls that look a little like fractals. He blinks: no, the pattern is dark blue with silver streaks like the lines of electrons made in a cloud chamber. The bar in front of him is polished walnut, ornately carved with what might be figures and might only be abstract designs. No, it's chrome, cold and smooth under his fingers. Wait a second, he thinks, and he remembers driving his Corolla down Coney Island Avenue in the rain. The box. Bob blinks again: the walls are red and fuschia again.

There are people in the room. He sees them reflected in the mirror behind the bar. They drape over wing chairs that are covered in a violent red velvet, or they walk across the layered Oriental rugs in poses of languor. They all wear suggestive clothes or things that might pass for clothes: A lilac corset with lemon-yellow stockings and combat boots. A motorcycle jacket over a cropped polo shirt with a popped collar. A red chain harness over a crisp lace-edged white camisole and pantaloons that appear not to have a crotch. A man's red union suit with black Mary

Janes. There is something unsettling about them all but Bob isn't sure what it is.

"Well?" The dark bartender slaps a glass onto the walnut bar in front of Bob.

"What?" he says, startled. The bar used to be—something else, he thinks. The man snorts impatiently.

The people reflected in the mirror—what sex are they? Bob turns to look. It's very hard to tell. The men—the ones dressed somewhat like men, anyway—are rather small and fine-boned, and the women—or the ones dressed in corsets and such—seem fairly large. They lounge on what are now aqua leather couches, move across what is now pale gray carpet.

"What can I get you?" The bartender doesn't sound the least curious.

Bob licks his lips, which are suddenly dry, and turns around. The man now has a blond moustache that curls up at the tips. His skin is very pale.

"Didn't you used to be darker?" Bob asks.

The man snorts. "What're you drinking?"

"Gin and—I don't even know *where* I'm drinking."

Now clean-shaven and dark-skinned, the bartender walks away. "But my drink—" Bob starts.

The bartender picks up another glass.

Bob looks down and there is a glass of oily clear fluid on the bar, which is now chrome dully reflecting the blue-and-silver wallpaper. Bob squeezes his eyes shut.

"I know, it's strange." The voice in Bob's ear is calm and slightly amused. A cool hand touches his wrist. "The first visit is very unsettling. You have to figure out what you know and then you'll feel better."

"I don't know what you mean," Bob says, eyes still closed.

"There's always a bar." The voice sounds as though it's cataloguing. "There is always a mirror. The seating is always in the same places. It changes, though, which can be upsetting if you're sitting on it. The beds upstairs—they stay. Well, of course they would. We are a whorehouse. Members of the staff change a bit, but after a few visits you'll be able to recognize most of us most of the time. It's not so bad. Open your eyes."

"Where am I?" Bob asks.

"La Boîte." The voice sounds amused. "C'mon."

Bob slits one eye at his drink. The bar is walnut again but his drink is still clear. He picks it up, lifts it to his mouth. The gin is sharp and spicy, ice-cold. He gasps a little and opens his other eye. A mirror: yes. The people are still reflected in it. Or Bob thinks so; they could be different people. The aqua couches with the blue walls; when he blinks, yes, red armchairs again with the flocked wallpaper. Next to the cash register on the bar is a card with the Visa and Mastercard icons on it and in handwriting beneath them: CASH OR CHARGE ONLY—NO CHECKS! The cash register doesn't change, he notes.

"Feel better?"

Bob does feel better. He takes another drink—still gin, still ice cold, still a little like open-heart massage—and eyes his reflection. Still Bob. He turns to the person who's been speaking to him.

She—if it is a she—is a redhead, with a smooth flat haircut that stops at her strong jaw line. She's wearing a fur coat, apparently with nothing else. Bob gets glimpses of peach-colored skin and downy blond hairs where the coat falls away from her thigh. In her left ear she wears a single earring, a crystal like a chandelier's drop. Her? *Hot*, he thinks, *if it's a woman.*

"I'm Jacky," she says and holds out her hand. It seems big for a woman's hand but maybe a little small for a man.

"Bob," Bob says. "Um, where exactly am I? You said but I didn't quite...."

"La Boîte." She picks up a stemmed glass filled with something pink. "'The Box.' Ha ha, right? One of the Boss's little jokes."

"The Boss?"

"Mr. Schrödinger." Jacky tilts her head to one side so that her earring hangs away from her face. It's in her right ear now.

Bob clenches his eyes shut again. "Jesus Christ."

Jacky's voice continues. "It's your first time, poor thing. No one's explained any of this, have they?"

"Just go away. You're all some sort of dream."

There is a sound that might be a fingernail pushing an ice cube around a lowball glass. "Well, you know about the cat, don't you? Everyone does. She's around but we can't let her into the bar because of health regulations. So," she says, and she sounds like she's spelling something out to a slow child. "This. Is. The. Box."

Bob maneuvers the glass he still holds to his lips and drains it. Still gin. He glances sidelong at Jacky. Earring in the left ear. Was that where it was last time? The gin is making itself felt. "This is like limbo?"

Jacky shrugs and the fur slips fetchingly, briefly exposing a smooth shoulder, broad but still well within range for a woman. "It's a lot more like a whorehouse. I'm thirsty."

Bob leans across the bar and taps the bartender on the shoulder.

Jacky sips something pink from her full glass.

"Jesus, how do you guys *do* that?" Bob asks. "It was empty a second ago."

Jacky smirks. "It both was and was not empty. It partook of both states at once." She holds up her hand as Bob opens his mouth. "I don't understand it either, so don't ask me. Look at your glass. Empty or full?"

Bob looks down. "Empt—No, it's—" he stops.

"Don't think too much. Take a sip."

Bob sips. Gin. He gulps. When his eyes have stopped watering, he says, "This is all pretty confusing."

"That's okay. Are you interested in going upstairs?"

His cock hardens when he thinks of it. But the broad shoulders, the big hands—"Uh, no thanks."

She pouts. "Are you sure? If you would prefer someone else, perhaps we can—"

"No," Bob says and swallows hard. "No, I like you fine, I like you best of everyone here, you're very, uh, attractive. But I think my type is more, well, feminine." The earring has changed places once more, he's positive of it this time. That long neck . . . He's getting hard again and hopes she won't notice.

But she slides her hand down his belly, cupping his cock through his jeans in her broad fingers. The pressure makes his heart skip a beat. "I thought you preferred me?"

It's getting difficult to think. "Well, what are you?"

Jacky laughs something that would be a giggle if Bob were a little more sure of her gender, and drops her fur from her shoulders. Her skin is smooth and she is moderately muscled, with small nipples half-erect in the air. Jacky has soft ash-blonde pubic hair, with a small trail of fur leading down from her navel. What Jacky *doesn't* have is sexual characteristics: no penis, no breasts, no labia. She's—Bob's not certain of that she again—too muscled to look comfortably feminine, too smooth to be really male. "I might be either. It changes."

Bob can feel himself shriveling, looking at her. "How can you do this?"

"I can be whatever I want here," Jacky says. "How often can you say you have that choice? Back out there, would you fuck a man?"

"No," he admits. "*Would* I be fucking a man?"

"Maybe. What's inside the box? Me. And I could be a pussy, or I could be a pistol." She leans forward until her face is inches from Bob's. Her breath is warm against his lips, "Either way, I'll be the best fuck you've ever had."

"All—" Bob stops and clears his throat. "Can we go upstairs now?"

Jacky leads him up a broad flight of stairs lavishly ornamented with statuary depicting fauns and satyrs being ravished by nymphs—or is it the other way around? Bob's looking at Jacky, cannot wait to pull aside that coat and do whatever it is they're about to do. Jacky keeps moving up the stairs, pulling him along by the fur that he is trying to pull off Jacky.

He pulls Jacky close at the door to a room, kissing hard, Jacky's body pressed against him, the flatness of chest and silky skin stretched over hard muscle, a hand sliding under his belt flat-palmed against his belly, moving down until his rigid cock throbs. Bob fumbles the door open and they cascade into a room that might be red or might be honey-colored. They pull apart for a second. Jacky drops the fur coat. At the sight of the body Bob hesitates again.

"What's wrong?" Jacky says, moving to stand chest to chest with him. Jacky is just his height.

"I just wish I knew what you are, that's all."

Jacky laughs once, a low bark. "Except you never do know. You only think you do."

———

The bus accelerates until Bob can see around it. The box from the post office lies in his lap, its flaps folded closed. Rain's smearing the windshield. Bob adjusts the timer and turns on the headlights before he remembers the whorehouse. The bar that kept changing, Jacky and that strange conversation, and the room—So which was she—he?

Bob's most of the way to Brighton Beach before he figures it out. The Box is closed, after all.

Chenting, in the Land of the Dead

In the end, the only job that presented itself was the governorship of a remote province in the land of the dead. Chenting was the name of the place, and the scholar and his concubine Ah Lien talked of it often as they lay entangled in their sweaty robes after lovemaking.

It would be a place of fields, he said. The peasants will farm rice and raise oxen. The air will smell a bit like the smoke from the false money that is burned to give one influence among the dead; but it will also be rich with perfumes, the scents that only dogs and pigs can smell in this world.

No, she said. It shall be like distant Tieling, where the fields lead up to the mountains, except that the mountains will never stop but will go up and up; and gray snow shall blow like dust across the fields, and the sky will be the purple-black of a thundercloud's heart or a marten's wing. And it will be lonely, she said, and held him tighter, pressing her face against his neck.

He was dying; they both knew that. The man with the eyes of smoke, the man who had come to tell him of the post at Chenting, had said so.

"But I am waiting to hear how I performed at the examinations!" the scholar had said to him. "I was hoping for a position somewhere."

The man bowed as he had at the start of the conversation: as before, the bow seemed both perfunctory and punctilious. "And well you might hope. Hope is the refuge of the desperate. But please allow me to be candid here. You are poor, and cannot afford the bribes or fees for anything better than, let us say, a goatherdship. And this governorship in Chenting, in the land of the dead, is available immediately."

The scholar stroked his chin. "But I am not dead."

"You shall be soon enough," the man said. "It is as certain as, well, taxes."

The scholar frowned. "Are there no other candidates for this position, that you seek a living man to fill it?"

"As I have said, you shall not live many months longer, making this point moot."

"Well then, are there other dead candidates?—Or soon to be dead," the scholar added.

"Well, yes, there are always candidates. But I feel sure that your qualifications shall prevail." The man with eyes of smoke made a gesture like two coins clinking together.

"But—" the scholar began and stopped. "I must consult."

The man bowed yet again and left.

"Well?" the scholar said to the empty room. There was a soft brushing of fabric and Ah Lien glided from behind the patched screen with the painted camellias. She was better than he deserved, the lovely Ah Lien, with eyes as narrow and long and green as willow leaves, better than he could afford, except that her birth was common and the eyes were considered a questionable asset for a woman in her position.

"You heard," he said. A statement, not a question. Of course she had heard. She was one ear, he was the other.

"Chenting," she whispered. "In the land of the dead. When must you leave, my lord?"

And that was that. There was no choice about his dying, only about his position in the scheme of things after his death, and both knew it was better to be a dead governor than a dead scholar.

But he lingered for a time with her, and they talked often of Chenting.

The governor's palace, he said, will be built of white stone and then plastered over, so that even where the plaster has cracked the walls will glow like bleached silk. And the roof will be covered with ceramic tiles the color of daylilies. The gardens will have countless enclosed roofless areas, each filled with hanging baskets containing small pines whose needles chime when one passes.

No, she said, the gardens are cold and abandoned. Winds blow through the empty rooms, and sometimes one sits by an unglazed window, watching the patterns made by dead leaves blown in the air.

It cannot be like that, he said. It must be as I see it.

If it is, she murmured, summon me to your side and I will come.

They had already decided she could not accompany him. The man with eyes like smoke had said nothing of her, and Ah Lien was understandably reluctant to die. She loved the scholar dearly but she had aging parents to consider and an ancestral shrine to tend. Still: she was willing.

His death when it came was a comparatively simple one. He coughed a bit as the winter began to take hold. Ah Lien held him close and warmed him when chills shook him. Then they talked of Chenting.

The bedrooms of the governor's palace, he said, and paused to catch his breath. The bedrooms have braziers of porcelain shaped like horses, and each horse bears a silver saddle on its back, and each saddle holds a fire of charcoal. The smoke that curls up smells of sandalwood and jasmine. And the bed is soft, covered with silk, with pillows carved of black wood. And the pillow book there has positions we have never imagined.

No, she said, the beds at Chenting are cold and narrow and hard, made of wheat husks in hemp bags. The smoke smells of funeral biers, but the fires are cold and colored the blue of foxfire in the marshes at night. "Do not leave me, my love," she said.

"I will send for you," he promised, and died.

When he awakened in Chenting he was amazed at first at how well he felt. There was no pain, no trouble breathing, no aches from holding a brush too tightly or walking in new shoes. And Chenting was everything he had imagined and more. The fields were lusher than he had expected and seemed to be near harvest. The air smelled as rich as he had dreamed. And he had much money to spend, for Ah Lien had sold her hair ornaments to buy paper money, and burnt it so that it would follow him.

He missed her and wanted her beside him, and since Chenting was warm and beautiful and not like the cold visions she had feared, he sent a message to her. "Come," it read. "I have seen Chenting and it is as fair as I envisioned. The birds are the colors of flames, and their songs are sharp as the crackling of fire. Come sit beside me." He sent a messenger off, with an entourage to show her the honor she deserved.

The messenger returned. "She is coming," he said.

Many days later, the entourage at last arrived, brilliant with tassels, loud with flutes. The governor of Chenting straightened his cap and calmed his heart, and descended the red stairs leading to the courtyard where his entourage milled about the sedan chair he had sent for her. He brushed aside the chair's gold-thread curtain. "Ah Lien—" he began.

For an instant he heard Ah Lien sobbing, and then that was gone. The sedan chair was empty and silent.

The governor of Chenting stormed and raged and ordered great punishments for the entourage that had failed to keep her safe. But even as he wept and cursed, he knew what had happened.

He had found Chenting just as he had expected, a place where an old man's pains were eased. But she had imagined another Chenting, a place where youth is irrelevant and even beauty is lonely. He did not know the Chenting she had gone to, but he knew it was not his.

The Empress Jingu Fishes

The empress Jingu fishes. The little mountain stream before her is fast but smooth, and clear enough that she can see a trout near the bottom, though it is nearly hidden by tree shadows above and the busy pattern of the river bed below: gold and russet and gray rocks, waving tangled weeds. The trout does not see her, or does not care whether she sees it, only hovers there, as unconcerned and self-absorbed as the gods.

She is not hungry for she has just eaten. Beside a small slender stone as long as her thumb is a tipped cedarwood box. Cooked rice spills from it, the remains of her meal. She picks up the stone and tucks it into her sash. She will need it later, and it will be just the right size and shape. Jingu knows this as clearly as she knows the death-name of the unborn son in her belly or the date of her own death, forty years from now. Past and future are equally immediate to the gods, and thus to her, their shaman, to whom and through whom they speak.

Half a year from now, she will be in the kingdom of Silla on the Korean peninsula, completing a task the gods have set her. It will be bitterly cold, a pale-skied day with snow in the air. Though it will be six months before she sees it, she knows that Silla's capital is built on the Chinese plan, its walls twenty feet high and roofed with tile to protect the city against flaming arrows, roads from the gates scattering across a treeless plain—the perfect place for her to draw up her troops. Though she is pregnant with her son, who will be due—and overdue—by then, Jingu is on horseback at their head, dressed in armor, her long hair tied close in a man's style. Her bow lies across her horse's neck and she runs a crow-feathered arrow between her fingers. She longs for the Sillans to attack, longs for their king to open the gates of the capital and ride out to meet her. She has wanted this since her husband Chuai died. The gods demanded he take Silla; when he refused they killed him. She cannot avenge herself on the gods, but aches to kill someone, anyone.

That is half a year from now. Now, this instant, she looks at the trout suspended in water as clear and cold and pitiless as the future.

Eight years ago. Jingu is to be married. She kneels on a litter hung so heavily with silk and paper and tree branches that she can see nothing, but she sees anyway. She is carried through the emperor's temporary palace; though it is only a month before they move to their next home, the many wood-and-plaster buildings are solidly constructed, with graceful tall roofs. Her husband the emperor will be called Chuai when he is dead. This is his name to her even now, before she has seen his face—though she must remember to address him as "husband" or "your highness." The future is uncomfortable enough to a woman who is born to it, and she knows already that he will be afraid of the gods that speak through her, that he will ignore them and die.

Her robes are heavy with appliqué and silver. Her crown's dangling ornaments tickle her face when she tips back her head. The soles of her shoes are hung with silver charms shaped like fish. Her bracelets of jade are narrow but so deep that they form broad flat disks around her wrists. She cannot walk, cannot pick up anything. Her wedding-dress is nearly as heavy as the armor she will wear eight years from now, after the gods speak and her husband dies.

Her husband has other, older wives and even two grown sons. This will be a problem when her child is born, for a time anyway. She sees her stepsons' deaths, unavoidable as soon as they raise arms against the boy. Her son will prevail and become emperor. Many generations from now he will be a god, the god of peace and then the god of war, Hachiman. She smiles and touches her virgin belly. It is appropriate that his mother will conquer a land across the sea for him.

Five months from now. Jingu crouches alone in a shrine, a building sunk half into the earth, its roof far over her head. The roof's supports make strange angled shadows against the morning light that sifts from the steep triangles of the eave openings. The air is thick with the scents of horses and hot metal, latrines and cooking fish, all the smells of an army. Outside the shrine she hears her war leader Takeuchi talking with her guard. It is Takeuchi who will stop the rebellious stepsons for her, but that is years in the future. Jingu has a war to fight and a son to bear before then.

She does not pray for her troops' safety in crossing the sea or a victory in Silla, for she has seen these things already. No: she is nine months' pregnant and her child frets to be born. The contractions drive her to her knees, panting. Her urine runs into the hard-packed earth; snot and saliva and sweat drip from her face. She prefers not to embarrass herself in front of her troops. The privacy of the shrine is welcome.

Jingu has been careful to show none of the weakness that can come of pregnancy, though hers has not been an easy one. Her chest hurts, and her bowels, pelvis, legs, back—everything. She finds herself panting at even slight exertion. Her breasts have begun to weep and the cotton with which she binds them chafes. Inside her, Ojin grows large and kicks, searching for a comfortable position.

Things have grown a little easier since her son dropped in her belly. It's easier to breathe, easier to move. The clear fluid seeping from her loins to stain her saddle is only a minor inconvenience.

She wears the torso of her armor, though its metal plates are very heavy and, since she is still in Japan, their value is based only in her troops' morale. There are ordinarily four panels but she has removed a side plate, claiming that her belly is too great to secure the fourth piece. In truth, she simply chooses to lighten the armor by removing some of it, and it is easy enough to see that the panel turned away from the enemy is useless. The weight: she already carries sorrow heavy as stone bracelets, and her child like iron in her womb.

When the contraction ends at last, she collapses on her left side— the unarmored side. Her tears leak to the ground. "Not now," she says aloud to the gods and her son. "Wait. When I've returned from Silla. Then."

She has brought with her the slender smooth stone she found beside the trout's stream. She slides it into her vagina, a cold weight. The stone frets. Gods are not all great gods and this stone longs for its icy riverbed, for the company of its fellows. It has no choice but to stay, for she wraps hemp cloth tightly around her loins to hold stone and child in place, and ties a knot.

The stone, the army, the horse before the walls of Silla's capital—they are in the future. In the meantime, Jingu stands on the riverbank and eyes the trout. It remains supremely unconcerned with her shadow over it, her loss and anger, her war and the forty years of her life that stretch beyond, each day without Chuai. The fish does not care. "You horror," she says aloud and sets out to catch it, though she is not hungry.

Like every woman, whether peasant or empress, she has a needle, though hers is of silver, a treasure from beyond the same sea she will cross in six months. She draws it from her sash and bends it easily between her fingers into a hook. It looks fragile but will be sturdy enough for the trout, which is small.

The gods have taken even luck from Jingu; there is no serendipity to the fact she snagged her robe on a *sakaki* shoot when she walked to the stream's edge. She crouches and rocks back on her heels, and worries at the frayed thread, tugging until it starts to slide past its fellows. Its absence leaves a tiny flaw in the fabric, a puckered line that is more sensed than seen. When she has pulled half a dozen strands of the dark silk, she twists them together, and when this is done, she tugs on the thread, hard as a fish fighting to live. She will not lose this trout because she underestimates the power of denial and despair. It holds. She threads the bent needle and ties a knot.

Problems with the natives. It is a year ago. Jingu and Chuai are well content with one another, though Jingu already mourns him in her heart. The blurring of present and future has consequences both large and small: unexpected minor advantages have been Jingu's ability to sexually please her husband from the beginning and the passion they share even after seven years of marriage, fueled on her part by the knowledge that she will lose him so soon. And not so minor: the two older wives are nearly forgotten, and it is Jingu who travels with Chuai now.

Chuai (though she remembers to call him "beloved") has for several years fought with the Kumaso, ill-mannered and independent-minded locals from a southern island, who refuse to pay their taxes. The battles with the Kumaso have been inconclusive at best—it is never easy to force recalcitrants to battle on their own terrain—but Chuai remains confident. He has called a council of his generals in Na, a strange little barbarian town on the island. Jingu walks the hills outside of Na, weeping, waiting for the dream that she knows is coming.

Still, when the dream takes her it is like a rape, and she awakens screaming. Her husband holds her until her muscles unclench and the tears begin. She speaks then, the gods' voice scraping from between her clenched teeth. *"Ignore the Kumaso,"* it says. *"There is a rich land across the water to the north and west. Silla. Take it."*

Chuai has seen her weakness in the hands of the terrible gods before this. He knows that they tell the truth through her. But he is emperor and understands (better than the gods, perhaps) the intricate exchanges of power and influence that are necessary to rule a land. "Why?" he says to Jingu. "It has taken years to bring this together. We can't leave this campaign to start another somewhere none of us have ever seen." The gods do not permit her to say what crowds in her mind: *Because they will kill you.*

In the morning, Chuai leads Jingu to the tallest hill they can see from Na, and together they climb it. There are no fish on the soles of her shoes this time, and it is a simple walk, if long. The autumn sky is very blue, the oak and maple trees in their first startling change from green to gold and red. For an instant she pretends that she and Chuai are not emperor and consort but ordinary people gathering sticks or hunting, free to live as they wish, to say without constraint, "Do that," or, "Don't do this." The illusion is gone as quickly as it comes.

They come to the hill's top and look around them. The island they stand on stretches away to the south and west. To the north and east is the main island. To the north and west, where Silla is supposed to be, is nothing but water and sky and a few fishing boats, small as fallen leaves on a lake. He says, "There is nothing there, nothing to conquer, nothing to point to and strive for. Whereas here"—his sweeping arm encompasses the hill, little Na at its feet, the island they stand on—"are the Kumaso. Enemies we can see and destroy. Which do you think my commanders will see as the wiser course?"

"The gods—" she whispers past her strangled throat.

Chuai rubs his face with his hand. "The gods are unreasonable and they are not all allies. The gods can be treacherous."

She knows this better than he ever will. The words come out in a rush: "They will kill you if you do not."

He touches the tears growing cold on her cheeks. "You've already seen your life without me, haven't you?" She cannot meet his weary eyes. "Then I am already dead."

Some months later, the gods do kill him, with a Kumaso arrow in the chest, an infected wound, and a quick uncomfortable death. There are times in the last days when he asks about the future, but she has nothing to tell him for none of it has to do with him, none but the barely begun son in her belly: Prince Homuda, who will be Ojin after he has died, and then the god Hachiman.

Knowing her husband will die is not the same as losing him. She is numb as she stumbles through the purification retreat and rituals. Past and future are meaningless to the gods and thus to Jingu. The pain never lessens. Each moment of each day contains the first shock and the endless ache of his death. Forty years before she dies.

A fish is not seduced by bait. When it grows hungry, it eats whichever mosquito egg or dragonfly happens to be closest. If one is fortunate or destined, it is one's bait that is closest at that moment. But it is chance that fish and bait are in the right places at the right time. There may be no fish there or a different fish, or the wrong bait, or the fish may not be hungry. The woman who hopes to catch a fish knows she offers nothing to the fish that it cannot find for itself—and better, for her bait comes with a hook and a thread, and death.

The spilled rice on the ground is cold. Grains stick to her hand when she picks up one and presses it onto the needle. It looks like the tiny things that live at the water's surface and become mosquitoes.

She stands slowly and looks down into the stream, down at the shimmering motionless uncaring trout. "You horror," she says again. "Prove to me that I should go to Silla."

Jingu knows what the gods want. They toss their demands at her, knowing she will meet them: a dozen shrines to this god or that, rice fields and offerings, priestesses in Nagata and Hirota. And Silla.

Chuai died because he sought to conquer the Kumaso rather than Silla, but the gods allow Jingu to defeat the Kumaso in mere months. Past and future blur in the gods' minds. They knew, and know, that this is how things will happen. Chuai's death was arbitrary and meaningless, proof that the gods are either ironical or cruel or simply do not care. The gods may define her actions but they do not care what she feels, the sorrow and anger and love and grief that are always with her, always as intense as the first moments she feels them.

For a time after his death she performs divination after divination, all asking, *Shall I conquer Silla?* Catching trout with a needle is part of this. She will also watch a rock crumble and allow water to irrigate a rice field she has planted. She will bathe in a river and feel the water in her hair, drawing conclusions from the currents that pull it this way and that. She knows what the answer will be—it is as familiar to her as a song she will sing to her infant son when he is born—but her only power over the gods is this, that they must tell her what they want for her to give it to them. And so she asks them to repeat themselves and takes a chill comfort in hearing their voices and pretending they care.

There are places in Japan where the gods do not permit men to fish during spawning, for they cannot understand and will not properly respect the fish's feelings. Jingu often fishes as a child before she becomes consort and then empress, and old skills come back easily when the past is eternally now. It is still some months before Ojin disrupts her balance, so she stands precariously on the little river's bank, the thread coiled in one hand, the baited needle in the other.

The sun has moved barely a hand's breadth in the sky since she first saw the trout; still, this is a long time for a fish to stay in one place. Perhaps the trout must be here as surely as she is. She frowns as she calculates and tosses the hook through the air. It settles just before the trout, light as an insect.

Six months from now, Jingu sits astride her horse before the walls of Silla's capital, longing to kill. She strokes the feathers of the arrow in her hand and dreams a little dream: the king will open the gates and emerge at the head of his armies, all dressed in armor from beyond China, riding tigers and breathing fire. With Chuai alive beside her, she will ride to meet the Sillans, and her own people with them. She will empty her quiver and then draw her sword, and she will cut and cut and cut. Men's blood will soak her hair and there will be no gods, nothing but the random terror and delight of a life without certainties. Chuai might die or he might not. And she might die here, today, instead of forty long years from now, years already laid out before her as clear and cold and pitiless as a mountain stream.

It is only a dream, of course. She knows the shape of this victory in all its details. She has seen it since the first of her trances, when the gods broke down the walls between the past and the future. The king of Silla also has diviners, perhaps his own instructions to follow. In any case he has problems of his own: violent Paekche to the east, to the west China's looming shadow. He opens the gates and sends out not armies but emissaries.

Silla falls to Japan without an arrow fired. The king surrenders and swears fealty, annual shipments of horses and gold. The only weapon hurled in anger is the spear that Jingu drives into the ground before the king's palace, the symbol of the conquest. Her rage is intact when she returns to Japan and bears her son, the emperor who will become the god of war, Hachiman.

———

The bent needle and its bait lie on the stream's surface just above the trout's head. Jingu can only wait, for she knows she will catch it, bring it to shore, and watch it die gasping in the unbreathable air. This will prove yet again that she is to go to Silla, to conquer a land she does not care about for gods she hates, who have killed her husband and will steal her son and make him one of them.

All moments are this moment. Past and future jumbled together: Jingu cannot say which is which. And because everything—sorrow and anger and love and grief—is equally immediate, she finds herself strangely distanced from her own life. It is as though she listens to a storyteller recite a tale she has heard too many times, the tale of the empress Jingu.

She lives this tale divorced from past and future, separated even from what is and what is not. The fragments of her life are stolen from later empresses: this woman will take Silla without a fight; that woman will manage the land for weary years after her husband's death. Jingu is no more than the tale of the empress Jingu, forced through the patterns of the storytelling, again and again and again. But she nevertheless feels, and she aches to kill something, anything.

The trout strikes and the hook sets. She hauls it in.

At the Mouth of the River of Bees

It starts with a bee sting. Linna exclaims at the sudden sharp pain; at her voice, her dog Sam lifts his head where he has settled his aging body on the sidewalk in front of the flower stand.

Sucking at the burning place, Linna looks down at the bouquet in her hand, a messy arrangement of anemones and something loose-jointed with tiny white flowers, dill maybe. The flowers are days from anywhere that might have bees. But she sees one, dead or dying on the yellow petal of one of the flowers.

She tips the bouquet to the side. The bee slides from the petal to the ground. Sam leans his dark head over and eats it.

Back in her apartment, she plucks the stinger from her hand with tweezers. It's clear that she's not going to die of the sting or even swell up much, though there's a white spot that weeps clear fluid and still hurts, still burns. She looks out the windows of her apartment: a gray sky, gray pavement and sidewalks and buildings, trees so dark they might as well be black. The only colors are those on signs and cars.

"Let's go, Sam," she says to the German shepherd. "Let's take a road trip. We need a change, don't we?"

Linna really only intended to cross the Cascades—go to Leavenworth, maybe as far as Ellensburg and then home—but now it's Montana. She drives as fast as the Subaru will go, the purple highway drawing her east. Late sun floods the car. The honey-colored light flattens the brush and rock of the badlands into abrupt gold and violet shapes as unreal as a hallucination. It's late May and the air is hot and dry during the day, the nights cold with the memory of winter. She hates the air conditioner so she doesn't use it, and the air thrumming in the open window smells like hot dust and metal and, distant as a dream, ozone and rain. Her hand still burns. She absently sucks on the sting as she drives.

There are thunderheads ahead, perhaps as far away as North Dakota. Lightning flashes through the gold-and-indigo clouds, a sudden silent flicker of white so bright that it is lilac. Linna eyes the clouds. She wants to drive through the night, wonders whether she will drive through rain, or scurry untouched beneath their pregnant weight.

The distance between Seattle and her present location is measured in time, not miles. It has been two days since she left Seattle, hours since she left Billings. Glendive is still half an hour ahead. Linna thinks she might stop there, get something to eat, let Sam stretch his legs. She's not sure where she's going or why. Her mind whispers *east, toward sunrise,* and then *my folks live in Wisconsin; that's where I'm going,* but she knows neither are the real answer. Still, the road feels good. Sam sleeping in the back seat is good.

A report would say traffic is light, but that is an overstatement. In the past twenty minutes, she has seen exactly two vehicles going her way on the interstate. Ten minutes ago she passed a semi with the word COVENANT on the side. And just a moment ago, a rangy Montana State Patrol SUV swept past with its lights flashing at a hundred miles an hour to her eighty-five. As the siren Dopplered past, Sam heaved upright and barked once. Linna glances into her mirror: he's asleep again, loose-boned across the back seat.

Linna comes over a small hill to see emergency lights far ahead: red, blue, a lilac-white bright as lightning. The patrol SUV blocks the freeway. There are six cars stopped in the lanes behind it, patient as cows lined up at the door of the barn. The sun is too low behind her to light the dip in the highway ahead of the cars. The air collected there seems dark.

Sam wakes up and whines when the car slows. Linna stops next to a night-blue Ford, an Explorer. The other drivers and the state trooper are out of their cars, so she turns off the Subaru's engine. It has run, with occasional stops for gas and food and dog walks and a half-night of sleep snatched at a Day's Inn outside of Missoula, for two days. The silence is deafening. The wind that parched Linna's skin and hair is gone. The air is still and warm as dust, and spicy with asphalt and sage.

Linna lifts Sam from the back seat, places him on the scrub grass of the median. He would have been too heavy to carry last year, but his muscles atrophy as his spine fuses, and he's lost weight. Sam stretches painfully, a little urine dribbling. He can't help this; the nerves are being pinched. Linna has covered the back seat of the Subaru with a waterproof tarp and a washable blanket. She's careful when she takes corners, not wanting him to slide.

Whatever else he is (in pain; old; dying), Sam is still a dog. He hobbles to a shrub with tiny flowers pale as ghosts against the leaves, and sniffs it carefully before marking. He can no longer lift his leg so he squats.

The only sunlight that Linna can still see fades on the storm clouds to the east, honey to rust. The rest of the world is already dim with twilight: ragged outlines of naked rock, grass, and brush stained imperfect grays. A pickup pulls up behind her car and, a moment later, the Covenant truck beside it. Another patrol vehicle blocks the westbound lanes, but its light bar seems much too faint, perhaps a reflection of the sky's dying light. If time is the measure for distance, then dusk can be a strange place.

Linna clips Sam onto his leash and loops it over her wrist. She rubs at her sore hand as she walks to the patrol SUV. The people standing there stare at the road to the east, but there's nothing to see.

Linna knows suddenly that this is not twilight or shadows. The air over the road truly *is* flowing darkness, like ink dropped in moving water. "What *is* that?" she asks the patrolman, who is tall with very white skin and black hair. Sam pulls to the end of his leash, ears and nose aimed at the darkness.

"The Bee River is currently flooding east- and westbound lanes of Ninety-four, ma'am," the patrolman says. Linna nods. All the rivers here seem to have strange names: Tongue River, Automatic Creek. "We'll keep the road closed until it's safe to pass again, which—"

".The *freeway's* closed?" A man holds a cell phone. "You can't do that! They *never* close."

"They do for floods and blizzards and ice storms," the patrolman says. "And the Bee River."

"But I have to get to Bismarck tonight!" The man's voice shakes; he's younger than he looks.

"That's not going to be possible," the trooper says. "Your options would be Twelve and Twenty, and they're blocked, too. Ninety's okay, but you'll have to backtrack. It's going to be a day or two before anyone can head east here. Town of Terry's just a couple of miles back and you might be able to find lodging there. Otherwise, Miles City is about half an hour back."

Linna watches the seething darkness, finally hears what her engine-numbed ears had not noticed before: the hum, reminding her of summers growing up in Iowa, hives hot in the sun. "Wait," she says: "It's all bees. That is a river of *bees.*"

A woman in a green farm coat laughs. "Of course it is. Where you from?"

"Seattle," Linna says. "How can there be a river of bees?" Someone new arrives and the patrolman turns to him, so the woman in the green coat answers.

"Same way there's a river of anything else, I suppose. It happens sometimes in June, July. Late May sometimes, like now. The river wells up, floods some roads, runs through some ranch yards."

"But it's *not* water," Linna says. Sam pushes against her knees. His aching spine stiffens up quickly; he wants to move around.

"Nope. Nice dog." The woman waggles her fingers at Sam, who pushes his head beneath them. "What's wrong with him? Spinal fusion?"

"Yeah," Linna says. "Arthritis, other stuff."

"That's not good. Not much they can do, is there? We used to raise shepherds. Lot of medical problems."

"He's old." Linna stoops to wrap an arm around his ribcage, to feel his warmth and the steady thumping of his heart.

The woman pats him again. "Well, he's a sweetie. Me and Jeff are going to turn back to Miles City, try and get a room and call Shelly—that's our daughter—from there. You?"

"I'm not sure."

"Don't wait too long to decide, hon. The rooms fill fast."

Linna thanks her and watches her return to their pickup. Headlights plunge as it feels its cautious way across the median to the other lanes. Other cars are doing the same, and a straggling row of tail lights heads west.

Some vehicles stay. "Might as well," says the man with the Covenant truck. He is homely, heavyset; but his eyes are nice as he smiles at Linna and Sam. "Can't turn the rig around anyhow, and I want to see what a river of bees looks like with the light on it. Something to tell the wife." Linna smiles back. "Nice pup," he adds, and scratches Sam's head. Leaning heavily against Linna's leg, Sam stands patiently through it, like a tired but polite child.

She walks Sam back to the Subaru and feeds him on the grass, pouring fresh water into a plastic bowl and offering food and a Rimadyl for the pain. He drinks the water thirstily while she plays with his ears. When he's done, she lifts him carefully onto the back seat, lays her face against his head. He's dozing when she rolls his window down and returns to the river of bees.

A patrol car has rolled up the outside shoulder to park beside the SUV, and a second officer has joined the first. Lit by their headlights, the young man with the cell phone still pleads. "I don't have a *choice*, officers."

"I'm sorry, sir." The patrolman shakes his head.

The man turns to the other officer, a small woman with dark hair in an unruly braid stretching halfway down her back. "I have a Ford Explorer. This—river—is only twenty, thirty feet wide, right? *Please.*"

The patrolwoman shrugs, says, "Your call, Luke."

The patrolman sighs. "Fine. Sir, if you insist on trying this—"

"Thank you," the man says.

"—I have a winch on the patrol vehicle. We'll attach it to your rear axle, so I can pull you out of trouble if you stall partway. Otherwise unhook it on the other side and I'll drag it back. Keep all vents and windows closed, parking lights only. Tap your brakes if you need a pull. As slow as the truck will go. And I am serious, sir: the river is dangerous."

"Yes, of course," the man says. "I'm really grateful, Officer Tabor."

"All right then," the patrolman, Tabor, says, and sighs again. He talks into the radio on his shoulder. "Tim, I've got someone who's going to try and crawl through. I've warned him of the dangers, but his wife's in the hospital in Bismarck, he really wants to try. If he gets through, can you make sure he's okay?" Indecipherable squawks. "Right, then."

Linna and the Covenant driver (his name is John, he tells her as they wait, John Backus, from Iowa City originally, now near Nashville, trucking for twelve years, his wife Jo usually comes along but she's neck-deep in preparations for the oldest's wedding, on and on) watch the huge Ford roll forward, trailing cable like a dog on an inertia-reel leash. Barely lit by its parking lights, the truck inches onto, into, the dark patch of highway. Blackness curls like smoke, drifts over the truck. It revs its engine for a moment and then dies. Brake lights tap on, and Tabor sighs a third time, sets the winch in motion, and pulls the truck back.

The air is cold, the sky moonless but bright with stars. To warm herself, Linna walks along the line of cars and trucks. People sleep across their front seats, or read or talk or play cards under dome lights. Engines purr, running heaters. The air is sweet with exhaust, an oddly comforting smell. An older couple sit in lawn chairs by their parked RV; the woman offers Linna a Styrofoam cup of coffee and the chance to use their bathroom. Linna accepts both gratefully, but refuses their offer to sleep on the couch.

She does not think she'll be able to sleep. Stars pace across the sky, their dim light somehow deeper than blackness and yet too bright to sleep through. A coyote or perhaps a dog barks once, a long way away. Back at the car, Linna watches Sam chase something in his sleep, paws twitching in the rhythm of running. *Live forever*, she thinks, and wills his twisted spine and legs straight and well.

It is very cold and the sky through the windshield is the color of freshwater pearls when Linna wakes, blinks, and remembers. There is half a cup of coffee on the floor of the passenger seat. It's cold and acidic, but the familiar bitterness anchors her. Sam is still sleeping. He never liked morning, and they moved to Mountain Time as they drove yesterday, so whatever local time it is (4:53, the dashboard clock tells her when she looks), it is actually an hour earlier for them. Once out of the car, she stretches. Her eyes are sticky and her back aches, but the time before dawn is a strange land to her, and she finds herself surprisingly happy.

She walks to the patrol SUV. Tabor sits with the door open, drinking directly from a thermos. "Coffee," he says. "Still hot. Want some? I lost the cup, though."

She takes the steel cylinder. The smaller patrol car and its driver are gone, as are the big Ford and the distraught young man. "What happened to the guy who had to get to his wife?"

"We scraped all the bees off the air intakes and got the truck running again. He drove back to Ninety. It's adding three, four hundred miles, but he's going to try and go around."

Linna nods and drinks. The coffee *is* hot, and it warms her to her toes. "Oh," she says with delight: "That's good." She returns the thermos.

"You get stung last night?" Tabor has seen the white spot on her hand.

She rubs it and laughs a little, oddly embarrassed. "No, right before I left Seattle. And now here's a river of them. Small world," she says and looks toward the fog collected in the dip.

"Hmm." Tabor drinks off some of the coffee. Then: "Listen for it," he says.

Linna listens. The SUV's idling engine throbs. A car door clicks open, far back in the line. There's no wind, no whispering grass or rubbing leaves—but there is a humming, barely audible. "That's *them*." She whispers, as though her voice might disturb them.

"Yeah. The fog is clearing. Look."

She walks a little toward where the river should be, will be. "No closer," Tabor behind her warns and she stops. A tiny breeze brushes her cheek. Mist recoils, and patches of darkness show through: asphalt black with sleeping bees. The sky lightens, turns from pearl to lavender to blue. The clouds are gone and the eastern horizon glows. The fog retreats. There is the river.

The river is a dark changeable mist like the shifting of a flock of flying starlings, like a pillar of gnats over a highway in hot August dusk, like a million herring turning. South to north, the river runs like cooling lava, like warm molasses. It might be six feet deep, though in places it is much less, in others much more. It alters as she watches.

The river of bees streams as far as she can see. It flows from the south, down a butte beside the freeway and across the road and into the river bed of the Yellowstone, then pours up over the side of a gully to the northwest. As she watches, more sleeping bees wake and lift to join the deepening river. The buzz grows louder.

Tabor stands beside her now but she cannot look away. "Where does it begin?" she says at last. "Where does it end?"

He is slow answering and she knows he is as trapped in its weird beauty as she. "No one knows," he says: "Or no one says. My dad used to tell me tales, but I don't know that he knew, either. Maybe there's a spring of bees somewhere, and it sinks underground somewhere else. Maybe the bees gather, do this thing, and then go home. There's no ocean of bees, anyway."

Others join them, talking in loud and then hushed voices; there are snapshots, videos—"not that the pictures ever come out," a voice grumbles. This is peripheral. Linna watches the bees. The sun rises, a cherry ovoid blur that shrinks and resolves as it pulls away from the horizon. Pink-gold light fills the hollow. The river quickens and grows. People watch for a time and then walk back to their cars. Their voices grow louder as they move away, conversations full of longing for coffee and breakfast and hot showers and flush toilets. They reassure themselves with the ordinary.

Linna does not move until she hears Sam bark once, the want-to-go-out-*now* bark. Even then, she walks backward.

"This is going to sound strange," Linna says to Tabor.

She walked Sam until his joints loosened and he no longer dragged his hind legs. She exchanged pleasantries with the man from the Covenant truck, though now she remembers nothing but his expression, oddly distant and sad as he watched her rub her hand. She drank orange spice tea and ate a fried-egg sandwich when the woman at the RV offered them, and used the little stainless steel bathroom again. The woman's husband was cooking. He flipped an egg to the ground between Sam's feet. Sam ate it tidily and then smiled up at the cook. Linna spoke at random, listening for the bees' hum. "Excuse me," she remembers saying to the couple, interrupting something. "I have to go now." She has led Sam back to the patrol SUV, and says:

"This is going to sound strange."

"Not as strange as you probably think," Tabor says. He's typing something into the computer in his vehicle. "Let me guess. You're going to follow the river."

"Can I?" she says, her heart leaping. She knows he shouldn't know this, shouldn't have guessed; knows she won't be allowed, but she asks anyway.

"Can't stop you. There's the River, and then I saw the sting and I knew. My dad—he was a trooper, back twenty and more years ago. He told me it happens like this sometimes. There's always a bee sting, he said. Let me see your car."

She leads Tabor back to the Subaru, lifts Sam into the back seat. The trooper makes her open the back hatch, sees the four gallon jugs of water there. "Good, but could be better. What about food?" She shows him what she has, forty pounds of dog food (she bought it two weeks ago, as though it were a charm to make Sam live long enough to eat it all) and two boxes of granola bars. "Gas?" She has half a tank: just under two hundred miles' worth maybe. "Get some, next time you're near a road," Tabor says. "Subaru, that's good," he adds, "but you don't have much clearance in a Forester. Be careful when you're off-road."

"I won't go off-road," Linna says. "There's just too much that can go wrong."

"Yes, you will," Tabor says. "You'll follow the river to its mouth, whatever and wherever that is. I can't stop you, but at least I can make sure you don't get into trouble on the way."

Tabor brings her a heavy canvas bag from his SUV. "This is sort of an emergency kit," he says. "My dad put it together before he retired. We've been keeping it at the base ever since. Got the report and hauled it down with me, figuring someone might show up needing it. Heavy gloves, snakebite kit, wire, some other stuff."

"Do people get back?" Linna says.

Tabor unzips the bag a few inches, drops a business card in. "Don't know. But when you get wherever it is, you're going to send all this gear back to me. Or leave it. Or—" he pauses, looks again at the river.

She laughs, suddenly ashamed. "How can you be so calm about this? I know this is all insane and I'm *still* doing it, but you—"

"This is Montana, ma'am," Tabor says. "Good luck."

The aqua clock says 6:08 and the sun is two hands above the horizon when Linna puts the Subaru into gear and eases across the median.

Linna is lucky at first. The exit to Terry and its bridge across the Yellowstone are only a couple of miles back, and she learns her first lesson about following the river: she doesn't have to *see* the river of bees because she can taste its current in the air. Terry is a couple of gas stations and fast-food places, a handful of trailers and farmhouses, everything shaded by cottonwoods, their leaves a harsh silver-green when the wind moves through them.

Her second lesson: the river tells her where to go. There is only one road out of Terry, but there is no chance she might make a mistake and take another. She stops long enough to buy gas and road food and breakfast, and eats in the car on her way out of town. Sam is interested, of course, so she feeds him a hash-brown cake by holding it over her shoulder. Soft lips lift the cake from her hand. The vet would not be pleased, but she's not here and Linna and Sam are.

The road is two empty lanes of worn pavement following a dry streambed through soft-edged badlands. She knows the bees are a mile or two to the east. Gravel roads branch off to the north from time to time. She longs to take one, to see the bees again, but she knows the roads will taper off, end in a farmyard, or turn abruptly in the wrong direction. It will be many miles before she reaches the river's mouth. These roads will not take her there.

The road changes from worn to worse, and then decays to gravel. Linna slows and slows again. The sun that pours in the passenger windows loses its rosy glow as it climbs, turns flat and hot. The only traffic she sees is a single ancient tractor that might once have been orange, heading into town. The old man driving it wears a red hat. He salutes her with a thermos. She salutes with her own cup of fast-food coffee. The dust he's raised pours into the car until she rolls the windows closed.

Once, when she crosses the mouth of a little valley, Linna can see the bees at a distance. She stops there to walk and water Sam and to drink stale water from one of the jugs. The cooling engine ticks a few times, then leaves her in the tiny hissing of the wind in the grasses. The river of bees cannot be heard from here, but she feels the humming in her bones, like true love or cancer.

She opens the bag that Tabor gave her. There are all the things he mentioned, and others besides: wire-cutters and instructions for mending barbed wire; a Boy Scout manual from the '50s; flares; a spade; a roll of toilet paper that smells of powder; tweezers and a magnifying glass and rubbing alcohol; stained, folded geological survey maps of eastern Montana; a spare pair of socks; bars of chocolate and water purification tablets; a plastic star map of the northern hemisphere in summer—and a note. *Do not damage anything permanently. Close any gates you open—mend any fences you cut—Cattle, tractors and local vehicles receive right of way—Residents mostly know about the river. They'll allow you to pass through their property so long as you don't break the fences.* It was signed: *Richard Tabor.* Officer Luke Tabor's father, then.

In another small town—the sign says Brockway—the road tees into another dusty two-lane, this one going east-west. She finds a gravel road heading northwest, but it turns unexpectedly and eventually leaves her in a ranch yard in an eddy of barking dogs, Sam yelling back. The next road she tries turns east, then north, then east again. The gravel that once covered it is long gone. The Subaru humps its way through gullies and potholes. She drives over a rise, and the river streams in front of her, blocking off the road.

She's close enough to see individual bees but only for an instant before they drop back into the texture of the river. Brownian motion: she can see the bee but she cannot see the river; or she sees the current but not the bees.

What am I doing? she asks herself. She is fifty miles off the freeway, following hypothetical roads through an empty land in pursuit of something beautiful but impossible and so very dangerous. This is when she learns the third lesson: she cannot help doing this. She backtracks to find a better road, but she keeps slewing around to look behind her as though she has left something behind, and she cries as she drives.

So she threads her way across eastern Montana, gravel to dirt to cracked tar to dirt, always north, always west. Sometimes she's in sight of the river. More often it's only a nagging in her mind: *this way.* She drives past ranches and ruined lonely barns, past a church of silver wood with daylight shining through its walls. She drives across an earthen dam, a narrow paved ridge between afternoon sunlight on water and a small town straggling under cottonwoods, far below what would be water level if it weren't for the dam. She crosses streams and dry runs with strange names: Powder Creek, Milk River. When she slows on the narrow bridges to look down, she does not see powder or milk, just water or nothing. Only the river of bees is what it claims to be.

When she crosses U.S. Highway 2, Linna stops for a while in Nashua. Sam is asleep, adrift in Rimadyl. She parks in the shade and leaves her windows open, and sits under the glare of fluorescent lights in a McDonald's, stirring crushed ice in a waxed cup. Conversations wash over her. The words are as strange as a foreign language after the hours alone: the river of bees (which blocks Highway 2 less than a mile east of town), but also feline asthma, rubber flip-flops for the twins, and Jake's summer job canning salmon in Alaska.

The bees pour north. The roads Linna follows grow sketchier. The Subaru is all-wheel drive and set fairly high, but it lurches through potholes and washouts, and scrapes its undercarriage. Sam pants in her ear until Linna slows to a crawl. He relaxes a little, lies back down. The sun crawls northwest, scalding Linna's arm and neck and cheek. She thinks sometimes of using the air conditioner but finds she cannot. The dust, the heat, the sun: they are all part of driving to the river's mouth. Sam seems not to mind the heat, though he drinks almost a gallon of water.

Linna is able to stay close enough to the river that individual bees sometimes stray into an open window. Black against sun-gold and dust-white, they inscribe intricate calligraphy in the air. Linna cannot read their messages.

———

Linna stops when the violet twilight starts to hide things from her. She parks on a ridge beside a single ragged tree that makes the air sharp with juniper. Thinking of snakes, she walks Sam carefully, but it is growing dark and cold and only the hot-blooded creatures remain awake. A bat or perhaps a swift or a small owl veers overhead with the almost inaudible whirring of wings. A coyote barks. Sam pricks his ears but does not respond, except to urinate on a shrub he has been smelling.

She does not sleep well that night. At one point, great snorting animals surround the Subaru for what seem hours, occasionally bumping into it as they pass. Sam is as awake as she. At first she thinks they're bears, that she has stumbled somehow upon a river of bears, but starlight shows they are steers. For some reason they are not asleep but travel under the spinning sky, toward water or away from something or out of simple restlessness. Still, she cannot sleep until they are long gone, no more than a memory of shuffling and grunts.

It is past dawn when Linna brings herself to admit she won't be sleeping anymore. After the steers passed she couldn't stop shivering, so she crawled awkwardly over the front seats to curl up with Sam, and pulled his soft blanket over them both. Now his spine presses against her thigh. Each bone is sharp as a juniper knurl. He smells of stale urine and sickness, but behind that is the sweetness that has always been his. She presses her face to his shoulder and inhales deeply. His muskiness works its way into her lungs, her blood and bones.

People have smells like this, smells that she has collected to herself and stored in the memory of her body; but Sam has been part of her life for longer than anyone but parents and siblings. For the first time, she thinks that perhaps she should have stayed on the road, closer to where veterinarians and their bright clean buildings live; but she has enough Rimadyl to kill Sam if he needs it, and she thinks that death is the only gift she or anyone can give him now.

At last she climbs from the car, stretches in the surprising simultaneous sensations of cold air and sun's warmth. "Come on, pup," she says aloud. Her voice startles her. It's the first she's heard since Nashua—yesterday, was it? It seems longer. Sam staggers upright and she lifts him to the ground. He creeps a few steps and then urinates, creeps a few more and pauses to smell a tuft of something yellow-green. She doesn't bother with the leash.

Perhaps a hundred yards away, the river hums along, broader and slower now. Linna can see individual straying bees as she squats to urinate, grateful again for the toilet paper in the kit the officer, Tabor, gave her. Something wild and sweet-smelling grows all around her. It might be lavender, though she thinks of lavender as something polite and domesticated, all about freshly ironed sheets and bath salts and tussie-mussies. Bath salts: she sniffs her armpits as she squats and then recoils. Well, dogs like stink.

The wandering bees explore the flowers around her, spiraling and arrowing like electrons in a cloud chamber. One lands on her stung hand as it rests on her knee. The slight touch of its legs might be no more than an imagined tickle if she did not also see its stocky, velvety bulk. It's the Classic bee: yellow-and-black striped, small-bodied, dark transparent wings folded tidily. It strokes the air with tiny feelers, then leans its head over and touches its mouth to the white spot on her hand, as though tasting her. For a dizzying moment she wonders if it's going to snap her up the way Sam snapped up the bee that gave her the sting back in Seattle.

Behind her, Sam gives a yelp, all surprise and pain. Linna whirls around and feels a drop of her urine splash against her knee as she stands. There is a hot sharp shock to her hand. A bee sting.

"Sam?" she shouts and stumbles forward, dragging her pants up, feverish with panic or the sting. She knows he's going to die, *but not yet,* her mind tells her. *Too soon.*

Sam limps to her, a comical look of distress on his face. She's reassured, as she's seen this expression before and it doesn't mesh with her fears. She folds to her knees beside him (lightheaded or concerned) and looks at the paw he's lifting. A tiny barb against a pale patch of skin on his pad. She finds herself laughing hysterically as she removes the stingers, first from his paw and then from her hand. Officer Tabor's father knew what he was doing.

———

Linna has not driven more than five miles an hour since awakening, though these terms—mile, hour—seem irrelevant. It might be better or more accurate to say she has driven down forty little canyons and up thirty-nine of them, and crossed twelve ridges and two surprising meadows, softly sloped as any Iowa corn field and spangled with flowers that are small and very blue: time measured as distance. She thinks perhaps she's crossed into Canada but there's been nothing to indicate this. She's running low on water and is tired of granola bars, but she hasn't seen anything that looked like a town since Nashua.

The trail she follows is a winding cow or deer path. She keeps one set of tires on the track and hopes for the best, which works well so long as she goes slowly enough. She keeps inspecting where the bee stung her earlier. There is an angry swelling across her hand, centered on a weeping white spot, half an inch from the first. What is half an inch, if measured in time? Linna doesn't know but she worries over the question, as though there might be an answer.

Since the sting the light has seemed very bright, and she is by turns hot and cold. She wonders whether she should turn around and try to find a hospital (where? how can she know when she measures distance by event?). But the calligraphy of the bees hovers; she is just on the edge of making sense of it; she is reluctant to give this up.

The Subaru grinds to a stop in a gully that is too deep to cross. Linna feels the river: *close*, it says, *so close*; so she lifts Sam out and they walk on. He is very slow. There are bees everywhere, like spray thrown from a mountain stream. They rest on her hands and tickle her face with their feather-tip feet, but she is not stung again. Sam watches them, puffs air at one that clings to the silver-furred leaves of a plant. They cross a little ridge and then a second one. There is the mouth of the river of bees.

The bees pool in a grassy basin. As she watches, the river empties a thousand—a million—more into the basin, but the level never changes and she never sees bees leave. It is as though they sink into the ground, into some secret ocean.

She knows she is hallucinating, because at the bank of the lake of bees is an unwalled tent hung with tassels and fringe. Six posts hold a white silk roof. The sunlight through it is intimate, friendly. And because this is a hallucination Linna approaches without fear, Sam beside her, his ears pricked forward.

Linna cannot later say whether the creature under the tent was a woman or a bee, though she is sure this is the queen of the bees, as sure as she is of death and sunlight. She knows that—if the creature was a woman—she had honey-colored eyes and black hair, with silver streaks glinting in both. And if the creature was a bee, her faceted eyes were deep as Victorian jet, and her voice held a thousand tones at once.

But it's easier to think of the queen of the bees as a woman. The woman's gold skin glows against her white gown. Her hands are very long and slender, with almond-shaped nails. They pour tea and arrange cakes on plates ornamented with pink roses. For a disconcerting moment, Linna sees slim black legs arrange the cakes and blinks the image back to hands. Yes, better to think of her as a woman. "Please," the queen of the bees says. "Join me."

In the shade of the awning are folding teakwood chairs draped with white fringed shawls. Linna sinks into one, takes a cup that is as thin as eggshell, and sips. Its contents are warm and clearly tea, but they are also cooling and sweet and fill her with a sudden happiness. She watches the queen of the bees place a saucer filled with tea on the ground beside Sam (a thousand dark facets reflect his face. No. Simple gold eyes, caught in a mesh of laugh-lines fine as thread that smile down at him). He drinks it thirstily, grins up at the woman.

"What is his name?" she says. "And yours?"

"Sam," says Linna. "I'm Linna."

The woman gives no name for herself but gestures to her skirts as they swirl around her ankles. A small cat with long gray-and-white fur and startling blue eyes sits against one foot. "This is Belle."

"You have a cat," Linna says. Of all the things she has seen today, this seems the strangest somehow.

The woman reaches down a hand. Belle walks over to sniff her fingers. Her fur is thick but it doesn't conceal how thin she is. Linna can see the bumps of her spine in sharp outline. "She's very old now."

"I understand," Linna says softly. She meets the woman's eyes, sees herself reflected in their gold, their black depths.

Silence between them stretches, defined by the eternal unchanging humming of the river of bees, the scent of sage and grass in the sun. Linna drinks her tea and eats a cake. Across from her the bee's body glows brilliantly in the silk-muted sun.

Linna holds out the injured hand. "Did you do this?"

The woman touches Linna's hand where the two stings burn. The pain is there, under fingers that flicker soft as antennae, and then it is not. Linna inspects her hand. The white spots are gone. Linna's mind is as clear as the dry air, so she knows this is an illusion. She must still be having some sort of reaction, or everything—the tent, the woman, the lake of bees—would be gone. "Can you heal your cat like this?"

"No." The woman bends to pick up Belle, who curls up in her thin black insect's legs. Belle's blue eyes blink up at the face of the queen of the bees. "I cannot stop death, only postpone it for a time."

Linna's mouth is dry. "Can you do that for Sam? Make him run again?" She leans over to touch Sam's ruff. The blood rushing to her head turns everything red for a moment.

"I cannot say. I hope that you and I will talk a while. It's been many years since I had someone to talk to, since the man who brought me Belle. She couldn't eat. Her jaw—" the cat purrs against the bee's thorax "—it was ruined, a cancer. He walked the last day after his car gave up, carrying her. We talked for a time, and then he gave her to me and left. So long ago now."

"What was his name?" Linna thinks of a canvas bag back in the Subaru, filled with all the right things.

"Tabor," she says. "Richard Tabor."

And so they talk, eating cakes and drinking tea under the silk awning of the queen of the bees. Linna recalls certain things, but cannot later say whether they are hallucinations; or stories she was told or told herself; or things she did not speak of but knew. She remembers the taste of sage pollen, bright and smoky on what might be her tongue or might be her imagination. They talk of (or visit, or dream of) countless infants, creamy smooth and packed safe in their close cribs; small towns in the middle of nowhere; great cities; towers and highways seething with urgent activity. They talk of (or visit, or dream of) great tragedies—disaster, whole races destroyed by disease or cruelty or misfortune—and small ones, drizzly days and mislaid directions and dirt and vermin. Later, Linna cannot recall which stories or visions or dreams were about people and which were about bees.

The sun eases into the west. Its light crawls onto the table. It touches the black forefoot of the queen of the bees. She stands and stretches, then gathers Belle into her arms. "I must go."

Linna stands as well and notices for the first time that the river is gone, leaving only the lake of bees, and even this is smaller than it was. "Can you heal Sam?" she says suddenly.

"He cannot stay with you and stay alive." The woman pauses, as though choosing her words. "If you and Sam chose, he could stay with me."

"Sam?" Linna puts down her cup carefully, trying to conceal her shaking hands. "I can't give him to anyone. He's old, he's too sick. He needs pills." She slips from her seat to the dry grass beside Sam. He struggles to his feet and presses his face against her chest, as he has since he was a puppy.

The queen of the bees looks down at them both, stroking Belle absently. The cat purrs and presses against her black-velvet thorax. Faceted eyes reflect a thousand images back to Linna, her arms around a thousand Sams.

"He's mine. I love him, and he's *mine*." Linna's chest hurts.

"He's Death's now," the woman says. "Unless he stays with me."

Linna bends her face to his ruff, smells the warm living scent of him. "Let me stay with him then. With you." She looks up at the queen of the bees. "You miss company. You said so."

The black heart-shaped head tips back. "No. To be with me is to have no one."

"There'd be Sam. And the bees."

"Would they be enough for you? A million million subjects? Ten thousand lovers, all as interchangeable and mindless as gloves? No friends, no family, no one to pull the sting from your hand?"

Linna's eyes drop. She cannot bear to look into that fierce face, proud and searingly alone.

"I will love Sam with all my heart," the queen of the bees continues in a voice soft as a hum. "Because I will have no one else."

Sam has rolled to his side, waiting patiently for Linna to remember to scratch him. *Live forever*, she thinks, and wills his twisted spine and legs straight and well.

"All right then," she whispers.

The queen of the bees exhales sweet air. Belle makes a tired cranky noise, a sort of question. "Yes, Belle," she says, and touches her with what might be a long white hand. Belle sighs once and is still.

"Will you——?" the queen of the bees asks.

"Yes." Linna stands, takes the cat from her black arms. The body is light as wind. "I will bury her."

"Thank you." The queen of the bees kneels and places her long hands on either side of the dog's muzzle. "Sam? Would you like to be with me for a while?"

He says nothing, of course, but he licks the soft black face. The woman touches him and he stretches lavishly, like a puppy awakening after a long afternoon's sleep. When he is done, his legs are straight and his eyes are very bright. Sam dances to Linna, bounces onto his hind legs to lick the tears from her face. She buries her face in his fur a last time. The smell of sickness is gone, leaving only Sam. *Live*, she thinks. When she releases him, he races once around the little field before he returns to sit beside the queen of the bees, smiling up at her.

Linna's heart twists inside her but it's the price of knowing he will live. She pays it, but cannot stop herself from asking, "Will he forget me?"

"I will remind him every day." The queen rests her hand on his head. "And there will be many days. He will live a long time, and he will run and chase what might as well be rabbits, in my world."

The queen of the bees salutes Linna, kissing her wet cheeks, and then she turns and walks toward the rising darkness that is the last of the lake of bees and also the dusk. Linna watches hungrily. Sam looks back once, confused, and she nearly calls out to him, but what would she be calling him back to? She smiles as best she can and he returns the smile, as dogs do. And then he and the queen of the bees are gone.

Linna buries Belle using the spade in the canvas bag. It is almost dark before she is done, and she sleeps in her car again, too tired to hear or see or feel anything. In the morning she finds a road and turns west. When she gets to Seattle (no longer gray, but green and blue and white with summer), she sends the canvas bag back to Officer Tabor—Luke, she remembers—along with a letter explaining everything she has learned of the river of bees.

She is never stung again. Her dreams are visited by bees, but they bring her no messages; the calligraphy of their flights remain mysterious. Once she dreams of Sam, who smiles at her and dances on young straight legs, just out of reach.

—*for Sid and Helen*

Story Kit

Six story types, from Damon Knight:
1. The story of resolution. The protagonist has a problem and solves it, or doesn't.
2. The story of explanation.
3. The trick ending.
4. A decision is made. Whether it is acted upon is irrelevant.
5. The protagonist solves a puzzle.
6. The story of revelation. Something hidden is revealed to the protagonist, or to the reader.

It has to start somewhere, and it might as well be here.

Medea. Hypsipyle. Ariadne. *Tess of the d'Urbervilles. Madame Butterfly. Anna Karenina.* Emma Bovary. Ophelia.

Dido. *The Aeneid.* Letter 7 of Ovid's *Heroides.* Lines 143–382 of *The House of Fame.* Lines 924–1367 of *The Legend of Good Women.* A play by Marlowe. An opera by Purcell.

Wikipedia: *Dido. Aeneas.*

The pain of losing something so precious that you did not think you could live without it. Oxygen. The ice breaks beneath your feet: your coat and boots fill with water and pull you down. An airlock blows: vacuum pulls you apart by the eyes, the pores, the lungs. You awaken in a fire: the door and window are outlined in flames. You fall against a railing: the rusted iron slices through your femoral artery. You are dead already.

I can write about it if I am careful, if I keep it far enough away.

The writer is over it. It was years ago.

Dido's a smart woman and she should have predicted his betrayal, as Aeneas has always been driven before the gusting winds that are the gods. His city Troy falls to their squabbling, the golden stones dark with blood dried to sticky dust and clustered with flies: collateral damage, like a dog accidentally kicked to death in a brawl. Aeneas huddles his few followers onto ships and flees, but Juno harries him and sends at last a storm to rip apart his fleet. He crash-lands in a bay near Carthage. His mother— Venus; another fucking god—guides him to shelter.

Dido is Reynard; she is Coyote. No gods have driven *her*, or if they have, she has beaten them at their own game. She also was forced from her land but she avenged her father first, then stole her brother's ships and left with much wealth and a loyal, hard-eyed army. Rather than fight for a foothold on the Libyan shore, she uses trickery to win land from the neighboring kings. They cannot reclaim it except through marriage, so she plays the Faithful Widow card, and now they cannot force her into marriage, either. If she continues to play her cards well, the city she founds here will come to rule the seas, the world. The neighboring kings understandably resent how this is working out.

She begins to build. When Aeneas arrives on her shores, Carthage is a vast construction site threaded with paths, its half-finished walls fringed with cranes and scaffolds, and hemmed with great white stones waiting to be lifted into place. *[A textile metaphor—Ariadne's thread leading Jason through the labyrinth—she also was betrayed and died.]*

Aeneas comes to her court a suppliant, impoverished and momentarily timid. He is a good-looking man. If anything, his scars emphasize that. The aura of his divine failure wraps around him like a cloak. Dido feels the tender contempt of the strong for the unlucky, but this is mixed with something else, a hunger that worms through her bones and leaves them hollow, to be filled with fire.

There is a storm. They take shelter in a cave where they kiss, where for the first time she feels his weight on her. Words are exchanged.

And afterward, when they lie tangled together and their sweat dries to cold salt on her skin, he tells Dido that Jupiter has promised him a new land to replace his lost Troy. Italy. He is somewhat evasive but in any case she does not listen carefully, content to press her ear to his breast and hear the rumble of his voice stripped of meaning.

There is every reason to believe he will be no stronger against the gods this time, but Dido loves him.

Some losses are too personal to write about, too searing to face. Easier to distance them in some fashion: zombies or a ghost story. Even Dido may be too direct.

She kneels on the dark tiles of the kitchen floor and begs: anything, anything at all. She will die, she tells him. She will not survive this loss. Her face is slick with snot. *There's blood on your face*, he says. Her tears are stained red from where she has broken a vein in her eye. Her heart is skipping beats, trying to catch up to this new rhythm that does not include him. She runs to the bathroom, which a year ago they painted the turquoise of the sea. He kneels beside her as she vomits but does not touch her, as though he wishes he could help but does not know how.

She cannot figure out what has happened. It seems he cannot either, but the wind fills his sails. He is already gone.

1,118,390 words before these. The writer's craft is no longer a skill she has learned but a ship she sails. It remains hard to control in strong winds.

Aeneas will be tall and broad-shouldered because heroes and villains usually are. Probably in his thirties. Scarred from the Trojan wars and a bad sleeper. He thinks he has lost everything, but he still has his health, his wits, some followers.

Aeneas is from the eastern Mediterranean. He will not be half-French. He will not have blue eyes, nor wear horn-rimmed glasses. He will not have a tattoo that says CAVEAT EMPTOR on his left shoulder, nor a misshapen nail from when he caught his finger in the car door when he was ten; nor sleep on his right side and occasionally sleepwalk.

Perhaps he will have survivor guilt.

- the sound of the words
- what the words mean
- how they string together into phrases, like the linked bubbles of sea wrack
- the structure
- the plot
- memories and lies
- the theme
- the feeling she wants to inspire in readers

Lost her wallet. Lost her virginity. Lost her way. Lost the big game. Lost his phone number. Lost the horses. Lost the rest of the party. Lost the shotgun. Lost the antidote. Lost the matches. Lost her brother. Lost her mother. Lost

Wikipedia: *Carthage.*

Though the real Carthage is on the Libyan shore, for purposes of this story it will look like a Greek island. There will be a cliff breached by a narrow road that hairpins up from a harbor to the city's great gates of new oak bound with iron. Carthage will someday be a great seafaring nation so the writer adds wharves and warehouses by the harbor, but they are unpeopled in her mind, wallpaper.

It was March when she stayed on Ios—not the season for tourists, so she saw no one beyond two scuba divers and a couple of shivering Australians pausing in their wanderings. Ios was mostly stone-walled fields with goats and windmills and weeds, but Virgil's Carthage did not have fields and neither will hers.

She hiked a lot, and climbed down to the water. The sea was clear as air. She saw anemones and a fish she did not recognize. The rock looked gray until she came close and its uniformity broke into rose and white and smoke-colored quartz crystals, furry with black and gold lichens.

It was cold on Ios. In the mornings, her breath puffed from her like smoke. When she climbed the cliffs, mist rose from her sweating skin and caught the sun. Her feet were always cold. *[Perhaps I am mixing up Ios with some other place I have been: Oregon or Switzerland. But these rocks, these anemones— they are real.]*

There needs to be a bay just up the coast, because Aeneas will land there. It is a horseshoe tucked between stone arms, a lot like the little cove where the scuba divers would spend their days. His ship will ride at anchor, the torn sails laid out on the dark sand; the sail-makers will shake their heads but mend them anyway because these are the only ones they have.

Aeneas will climb the cliffs. The air will smell of wet earth and the bright salt sea, so far below. The writer can use Aeneas's responses to the forest—which will be of short, slim-needled pines, maybe some oaks too, why not?—and the boulders to develop his character. Or Dido's, to develop hers.

There will need to be a cave, as well.

Does Carthage even have forests? Did Virgil know for sure or was it just convenient for his story? Virgil was a professional liar. This would not be the only place where he pruned the truth until it was as artificial as an espaliered pear tree against a wall, forced to an expedient shape and bearing the demanded fruit.

The moan that ice makes underfoot. The taste of salt. The smells of ash and copper. A dog barking at a great distance. A bone cracking in your leg. The gray scouring pain of sleet. She stumbles and falls against a rusted railing. The taste of pears.

Dido is playing her cards poorly, making her discards at random.

Her need for Aeneas burns through her hollowed bones. He said something about leaving someday, but she did not believe him. Men say that kind of shit all the time and then change their minds. What does she really know of him, anyway? Stories carved on the walls of temples.

Dido gives him the keys to her apartment. He can share her kingdom to replace the one he lost: a king for the Queen of Carthage. In her distraction, construction on the city's white walls slows and then ceases. They remain half-built, cranes akimbo and unused. Her neglected armies grow sullen and fall into disarray.

The hot-eyed Gaetulian king who is her neighbor wants his land back and, not incidentally, hungers to prove his right to it upon her body. Her faithful widowhood was more effective than a naked sword in guarding her honor and Carthage's boundaries, but now she has taken Aeneas into her bed, felt his weight on her body, bowed her head to him. She has laid aside that sword.

But it will all still be fine, so long as he stays.

Poor Dido. She is dead already. The writer knows it. You know it. I know it.

The sentence, "She was hollow, as though something had chewed a hole in her body and the hole had grown infected," unless it's been used before by someone else in a story she cannot recall.

And there is the rage sometimes, the rage of a smart woman betrayed by her own longing. It runs under her skin, too hot to be visible. Her breath is smoke; her skin steams. Her tears freeze to slush. Her cheeks bleed.

The writer stalks the winter streets at dusk and imagines him dead. She imagines their house a smoking, freezing ruin. The fire trucks are gone; all that remains is black wreckage outlined by tape that says DO NOT CROSS. She imagines her town a glassy plain, every dog in the world dead, the Earth's atmosphere ripped off by a colliding asteroid, the universe condensed to an icy point.

[*A flute made of a woman's bones*]

She walks the streets. Her pain cannot permit her to exist in a world where he also exists, and yet she does. Her feet are always cold.

She can use this.

Virgil walked the streets of Rome as he composed. It could take all day to polish a couplet.

Dido knows what happens if Aeneas leaves. Her hot-eyed neighbor, the Gaetulian king, will denounce her inconstancy and send his armies. Her own army's resistance will be half-hearted. They want a ruler who is strong, and perhaps a king will be better after all, more trustworthy than a woman however clever and just.

The Gaetulian king will attack, break her gates, and claim her white- walled city. He will find Dido and her personal guard in the great courtyard, on the steps that lead to her palace. She retains this much pride at least, that she will not be hunted through her own rooms. No, that is wrong. It is not pride that holds her here, chin lifted and a naked sword in her hand. Despair and fury burn like lye through her veins.

The Gaetulian king will slay her guard to the last man.

He will mount the steps to her. He will strike the sword from her hand. In the presence of his own hard-eyed guard, he will force her to her knees, his hand knotted in her hair. When she refuses to open her mouth to him, he will throw her to the ground and rape her as she lies in the cooling blood of her dead men. This will be almost enough pain to make her forget Aeneas's betrayal. This will be almost enough pain to make the writer forget.

The Gaetulian king will hang Dido with chains and march her through the streets, scratch marks on her face, blood running down her leg. He will raze her city. He will disband her armies. Carthage, which was to rule the world, will dwindle to a footnote in someone else's tale.

Plus, Aeneas will be gone. Dido has courage for the rest of it, but not for that.

————

Some stories are not swallowed but sipped, medicines too vile to be taken all at once.

"What am I supposed to say here? I'm sorry?"
  "Please. Please just still love me."
  [pause] "Well. It's just. You know."

Considering the pain it gave the writer when her husband said those words, she imagines it will break Dido's heart as well. But really, it is pretty banal, written down.

Demia looked forward, squinting. The dimming ~~sunset~~ [no, it's dusk] sky outlined the crags ahead ~~of them~~. The hermitage was there somewhere, safe haven if they could just reach it before ~~dusk~~ dark.

A howl interrupted her thoughts. Her mare jumped as though she had been struck but did not bolt, Demia's long hands strong on her reins. [POV?]

"Lady," Corlyn said, his voice suddenly ~~tense~~ urgent. "The athanwulfen / athanhunds. They are hunting." His own horse twisted ~~against its reins~~ under him.

"Too soon," Demia murmured, but no: dusk [twilight? nearly dark?] already. "I wish——"

Her brothers could have defended them all, but they were dead. She and Corlyn had found them ~~on the Richt Desert~~ at the ~~dead~~ oasis, miles to the east—or what was left of them—their bones picked clean and drilled through ~~in many places~~, hollowed by the narrow barbed tongues of the athanwulfen / athanhunds. Stivvan, Ricard, Jenner, Daved / David / Davell? She clenched her teeth against the loss. There was no time.

Corlyn lit a torch and was outlined by ~~the flame~~ the leaping flame——

No Corlyn, no horses, no torch. But athanhunds, yes. Demia must lose *everything*, her own bones hollowed. Otherwise it will not hurt enough.

No "suddenly"s. Nothing is sudden. When the tornado hits, the house comes apart in a few seconds, but before that there was a barbed curve on the NOAA map, a front coming in from the southwest, clouds and cold and a growing wind.

In fact, no adverbs in general. Verbs happen, unmediated. Leave, abandon, lose. The next day the videos show you amid the ruins, clutching a cat carrier and a framed photo from someone else's wedding.

[ANGER SHAME DERANGEMENT]
   [ALL BETRAYALS ARE THE SAME STORY]
   [at least dido had warning]

Aeneas does not stay. He says that of course he loves her. He feels terrible about all this. It's not his fault; it's the gods that whip him from her side. His words mound up like slush under her feet, slippery and treacherous. He is unworthy—every word proves it—but it's too late for that to make a difference. He is sorry, so sorry, but he did warn her, after all. It's not his fault that she didn't believe him. Etc.

Dido abases herself, kneels before Aeneas. She has broken a vein in her eye and she sees through a red haze. Her heart skips beats. She fights not to vomit. Her fingertips are bloody from clawing herself.

He promises to stay, presumably because he wants her to lighten up, but he slips from her arms as she sleeps. There is no time, she will wake soon; so he runs to his ships, cuts his anchor cables, and sails out on the tide. When she sees them at dawn, he is far out to sea. He has lain with her, lied to her, for the last time.

Diera Vallan's tears fell unheeded as the V-5f life pod crashed through the meteor field, all that remained of her shattered planet. So many millions, she thought, and the tears fell faster. Her own husband, the Windhover King, was dead, flayed alive by—"

Not that, either.

———

The writer still has her health, her wits, the cat. Many people have lost more. There are plagues, earthquakes, fires and starvation. Children run down in the street. A man's legs crushed between two cars as he tries to jump-start a Ford on a winter's night. A woman losing her ability to form words as the tumor webs across her brain. A couple waiting for the stillborn birth of their already-dead son. Farming accidents. Alzheimer's.

And other divorces. She is not unique. She is not even unusual. Perhaps this has more in common with a wedding ring lost by the pool at a vacation hotel, or blood poisoning from a cat bite.

- 237 "the"s. They are words that dry to invisibility, Elmer's Glue-all to anchor nouns.
- 104 "and"s; 30 "but"s. Apparent correlation.
- Too many semicolons.
- Clean out the passive constructions. Dido was there. She did things and some of them were wrong.

She has a dream in which he's still there. He has not yet betrayed her and she is still sane. They huddle together in a mountain cave where they have found shelter from the night's storm. The world outside roars with rain, broken timber, falling stones. The air here is chill but they are safe.

All things are new, all things are possible. In the darkness, she sees him only with her fingertips: his eyelids, his curling lashes, the complex shapes of his ears. His lips smile against her palm. He opens his mouth. She feels his breath. They lie in a nest they make of their clothing, the things they have cast aside.

They are not cold. She runs her hand down the long smooth planes of his body. She feels a scar. He says it still hurts when it is touched. She understands this; she has her own.

In the darkness he strokes her and she feels outlined in light. Her skin is afire. She sobs under his hand, his mouth, the weight of his long, scarred body.

I want to leave them dreaming there, Dido and the writer both, for lines and lines. It is a lie I am telling them.

Are grammar and syntax correct? Is there enough setting? Were the senses engaged? Is this the best start to the story? Does it end too soon/ too late/too abruptly? Are the characters realistic? Is the story from the right point of view? What is the theme? What is the subtext?

The story betrays us all.

I spend the entire night rewriting, changing things around, hoping for a better result. The story doesn't do what I wish. Dido always dies. The writer always finds herself alone, a flute made of a woman's bones.

She does not want to face the raw, whole thing, so she takes it in pieces. She transfers, distances, sublimates. She cannot sit at her keyboard for long. She is haunted. The apartment is cold and smells of chicken. The cat turns over the bones she forgot to put in the trash.

Rewriting ends when the deadline comes. Even then, she will attach the file to an email and send it, and wish there had been more time.

The onshore wind blows through Carthage. His ships are far off, flecks smaller than snowflakes on the dark sea. He is still in sight but he cannot return: the winds forbid it. In any case, he was gone already, before ever he cut his cables and sailed at dawn—before the cave and the first time he held her in his arms, even.

In the great courtyard before the palace, Dido, Queen of Carthage, orders a pyre built. She will burn all the things he left here: the clothes and jewels she gave him, the shield and sword he left beside her bed. She holds the naked sword in her hand.

She is dead already. She has been dead since he was first brought to her, sea-stained and despairing, and the flame of her hunger gnawed into her bones.

She curses him. She curses him. She curses him.
But it is herself she kills.

Delete.
Undo.

It is not just that the writer needs the safe distance of a zombie story, a ghost story. It is that no story can carry so much sorrow and anger without being crushed beneath its weight, without bursting into flames, without drowning.

What really happened—the careful stacking of pebbles in the path of the landslide that was the last year of their marriage, the woman from the gym, the months of listening to his voice make promises for the bitter false comfort of it—those words cannot contain her feelings.

Even her imagined Dido cannot contain them, as she bleeds upon the oil-soaked pyre in those seconds before her heart stops struggling to fill the hole left by the sword. A torch stabs into the stacked wood. Flames run along each tier.

Her skin breathes a mist. She is for a moment outlined in light. Then the fire bursts upward and she becomes a burning pillar, a tower, a beacon, and she is dead; and he looks back and does not see the thing that he has destroyed, only the flames upon the half-built walls of Carthage, and he wonders what message they send and to whom.

Not Medea's frenzy, not Ariadne's broken thread. Anna under the train's wheels. Butterfly holding the blade to her breast. None of the betrayed women, that commonest story of all.

Not even Troy itself and all its deaths: the bitter siege and ten years from home, Penelope's tears and the Trojan women's torn breasts and Iphigenia's sacrifice, the ruined towers, the blood dried to dust on the golden stones; the anguish of Paris; Aeneas's own pain—even these cannot contain her rage, her loss.

Words fail.

She found herself in a room with ivory-painted wainscoting and a floor tiled with black and white marble. There were no furnishings, only a single glass table at the hall's center. There were no doors. The narrow windows were too high to reach, though she tired herself through the long afternoon, jumping for them.

When it grew dark at last, she huddled against the wall on the cold marble and slept, and tried to remember the flowers that had been in the garden.

Dido dies on the sword. She hits CTRL-S. I type "End." We will do this again.

Wolf Trapping

He was saving the laptop's battery and the generator was down, so Richard was transcribing his field notes into a notebook by lamplight when the wolf's scream of pain cut through the walls of the cabin. He dropped his pen on the open page. He'd known a poacher would be coming after the wolves, when he saw the rabbit snare a few weeks back. He picked up his emergency pack and the Winchester thirty-thirty, and slung them over the parka he already wore against the cabin's cold. He stuffed the handcuffs into one pocket.

The early winter evening caught instantly at his lungs when he ran out the door; it had been a cold day, the coldest yet. The wolf was still howling: south he thought, though it was hard to tell much in this dead air. He couldn't tell whose voice it was. He dragged on his gloves and outer mittens, kicked his bear-paw snowshoes into the snow, and stamped his boots onto their frames.

The howling raised in pitch—not far away at all—and now there were growls. Richard ran south along the nameless creek that led from Horsehead Mountain, ahead.

The wolf's sounds cut off abruptly. He was crossing a small clearing among the trees, where salmonberry bushes made a bramble; he stopped to get his bearings but heard nothing over his own panting and the light wind hissing through the bare alder branches.

Running sounds, and a wolf broke from a deer trail in the trees ahead, a mass of fur and teeth and eyes. Richard tripped, crossed his shoes, and fell floundering helplessly backward. The wolf stumbled to a halt ten feet from him.

It was the gray female, Genna, one of the lower-ranked wolves of the Horsehead pack, gamma or delta depending on the day. She held her left forepaw slightly raised. Blood spattered the pale fur of her breast and dripped slowly onto the snow, where it melted a red uneven hole. He looked at her eyes, for the white ring of panic around them or visible distress, but she only watched him warily, unafraid in spite of the injury. Even in the dimming daylight, her eyes were golden, with a pale and wild gaze.

From the ground, she was bigger than he had imagined. He rolled to his side, eased himself into a crouch. The snowshoes made a sound like sticks rubbing but she did not move. He realized he was speaking to her as though she might be soothed by a man's voice: "Let me look at the foot," he murmured. "Pretty girl, pretty girl." Her eyes tracked him as he leaned toward her.

She bolted, and the suddenness of it rocked him back so that he fell again. He rolled upright in time to watch her vanish into the trees, limping but moving fast, the padding of her feet swallowed immediately by the air. He stared after her a minute. He'd never been so close to a free wolf.

Close ahead, Richard heard the heavy whack of a trap's metal jaws snapping shut. He ran again, crashing through the salmonberry bushes and then the brush under the alders, jamming his fingers into the lever action of the rifle as he backtracked Genna along the deer trail: easy to follow when drops of blood marked the way. The cold of the rifle bit through his glove.

He found the trapper crouching in the trail, in a dirty red parka and camouflage pants, at the center of a circle of snow torn up by frantic bloody claw marks. It was dark under the trees but Richard recognized the trap in the other's hands, a Newhouse Number 114, an ugly toothed half-circle of steel longer than his hand. If it had caught Genna's foot wrong, it would have crushed her bones, crippled or killed her. He lifted the rifle over his head and fired, and snow cascaded down from the branches onto them both.

The trapper stood unsteadily, sinking shin-deep into the snow. Richard chambered another round. Dark eyes looked past the dirty fur that fringed the parka hood, and with a shock Richard realized that the trapper was a woman, and under-equipped, too: no snowshoes, no rifle, no pack.

"She went your way," the woman said in a hoarse voice. "Is she okay?"

"She's fine," he said harshly. "Considering."

She appeared not to hear his anger. "She looked all right to me. Broken skin but no bone damage. She's never, none of them have ever let me get so close before." She paused, seemed to look at Richard for the first time. "You're the one who watches the pack. The naturalist."

"Do you know what kind of trouble you're in? Trapping," he added when she stared blankly at him, and pointed the rifle's muzzle at the Newhouse.

"Wait. You think—"

"I saw the wolf, and here you are."

"I *freed* her," the woman said. "I heard her howl and came running. I pulled the trap open for her—she let me get that close. The trap has been here for months. *Look* at it." She held it out.

"Throw it here."

It landed in the snow between them, and when he picked it up he saw she was right. New scratches of bright metal shone through a fog of rust, tracing the arc of the trap's motion. Flakes of dislodged rust still clung to its jaws.

She said, "It must have been set and then lost. It happens, you *know* it does."

Richard eyed her for a moment. She was clearly exhausted. Her knees were wet from kneeling in the snow: her pants were not waterproof. He slid his Winchester into the scabbard lashed to his backpack and rolled his shoulders, releasing the tension. "What are you doing out here? Tourists all left a month ago."

"I'm staying for the winter." The woman hunched her shoulders and coughed, and her breath clouded between them.

Richard looked up. The trees were nearly black now, the scraps of visible sky fading red. He hefted the Newhouse. "Where's your place?"

"Here. Wherever the wolves are."

"I mean your real place. Your cabin."

She gestured. "No cabin. No tent, no hotel room with a hot tub. Just what's on me."

The wind was picking up and one of the cords that tightened his parka hood snapped in his face. "Fuck. My cabin's about a mile from here. Come back with me and we'll figure this out."

———

She led the way, retracing his trail without trouble through the ribbon forests of fir and spruce and the clearings between them. The snow was knee-high in places, all new and still soft, but there had been hard frost for enough nights that any water hidden beneath it was frozen solid. It was full dark, Richard leading the way now with his headlamp, when they walked across the last narrow meadow toward the boulders and ice on the southern shore of Lake Juhl.

The cabin hunched against a large rock outcropping fifty feet from shore, a small box made of insulation, plywood sheets, and caulking that showed as white strips against the wood. Cords of wood formed a windbreak to the north and west. The single small window glowed dimly.

The cabin door was shielded by an alcove. Richard gestured her through, removed his snowshoes, and followed her.

"Did you put this together?" she asked as he entered. The cabin was small, barely enough floor space for them both to stand, and imperfectly lit by his lamp and the stove. Most everything was packed already in plastic crates in the alcove, but the shelves that lined the walls were still piled with food packets, tin pans and eating utensils, the pieces of a shortwave transmitter, replacement tools and equipment, his laptop and its spare batteries, and books, hundreds of books. A narrow iron bed heaped with his sleeping bags pressed against one wall.

Richard said, "It was here when I came last year, mostly like this. But abandoned. It was all mice and squirrels." A small table was built into one corner, cluttered with a handful of black notebooks and pens, a few books and printouts from other researchers. He pushed everything aside and dropped the Newhouse on the table. The tea in his cup had already grown a hard shell of ice. He stoked the stove.

"It's not very warm." The woman sat on the bed, the only possibility other than the table's single chair.

Richard shrugged. "There's a generator but I didn't want to refill the tank this close to the end of the season. I fly out in a couple of days, anyway."

She had removed her leather mittens and gloves and pushed back her hood. She would have been a thin woman in any case—she had the strong lean bones he associated with people of Finnish blood—but now she was half-starved and her emaciated wrists were like birds' legs. Her fingertips were discolored. There were frozen frostbite sores on her dirty cheeks, white patches that sloughed off when she wearily rubbed her face.

"Jesus Christ, what happened?" Richard said, appalled. "You should have said something." He put an ice-skinned pan of water onto the stove and slid the aluminum first-aid box from under the table.

"I'm fine."

He pulled out gauze pads and antibiotic cream, and crouched beside her. "I'll clean what I can, but the frost burns on your cheeks are going to hurt when you start to warm up. And your fingertips—"

"I'm *fine*," she said, and struck the gauze from his hand. Her eyes when they met his were cold and full of anger, but instantly she tipped her face away and they were hidden by a straight fall of greasy hair.

Richard laid the gauze and cream on the bed beside her and stood. "You can do it, then. What's your name?" He thought he sounded unnaturally calm.

"Adela Bjorhus. Addie."

He looked down at her for a moment. "Coming close to an injured wolf. She might have hurt you."

"She wouldn't have."

"She's a wolf. She's dangerous." Richard suddenly remembered Genna a short leap from him, himself crawling toward her—"pretty girl, pretty girl"—as though she had been harmless, a frightened child. He turned back to the stove. The ice in the pan was melting, leaving little floes that grew smaller as he watched.

Something in his pocket shifted. He pulled free the handcuffs, key swinging, and dropped them onto the desk beside the trap and the books. She looked at them.

"Handcuffs," he said. "Stating the obvious. Six weeks ago I saw a snare, so I had Jeff bring them when he delivered supplies last time. I thought there might be a poacher. If he came after the wolves, I was going to stop him."

"That was my snare, for rabbits." The anger seemed to be gone.

"You've been here for six weeks? Why haven't I seen you?"

"You weren't looking." She reached across to the table and picked up one of his notebooks. "Who are you, anyway?"

"Richard. Richard Montaigne."

She raised her face. Exhaustion had circled her eyes with dark rings that spread onto her cheekbones. "I've read your books about the North Range pack. What are you doing this far south?"

"Research. Second-tier pack hierarchy, specifically. You've read my stuff? It's heavy going for a nonspecialist."

"I've read everything about wolves." She leaned back stiffly, propping her feet on the bed's frame. There was a crack in the leather between the upper and the sole of one shoe. "It's solid research, but it's not like being with them."

"Nothing is like that." He shook milk powder and sugar and the freeze-dried contents of a couple of pouches into the pan. He watched it for a time before he asked, "Why are you out here?"

"I'm doing it the way the wolves do, except that I need a hatchet and snares. I don't have teeth like theirs."

"You can't survive here without the right equipment. Plus, it's almost winter." Richard poured the soup into a bowl and handed it to her. She huddled over it greedily, gulping almost without breathing. "When was the last time you ate?"

She frowned. "Yesterday, I think," she said when her mouth was clear. "A hare."

"Raw?"

"I didn't bring matches." She pulled her lips back from her teeth in something that was not a smile. "I'll get used to it."

"No one gets used to that," Richard said grimly. "You can't really be planning on staying."

Addie was silent.

"You'll die."

She lifted one shoulder, and Richard's throat tightened. "Don't you care? What's so bad that coming out here to freeze to death is easier?"

She looked up and he saw again the flash of absolute wildness in her eyes, lamplight reflected flat and gold as she stared at the trap on the table.

"Nothing," she said finally. "Nothing at all." She lay down and wrapped herself in one of the sleeping bags, face to the cold wall.

He watched her, but she didn't move and she didn't relax into sleep. She said nothing more, even when he powered up the transmitter to call Jeff and make a time for him to fly them out the day after the next.

Richard woke to a gust of cold air. He pushed his sleeping bag away and looked around. The cabin had gotten cold in the night, and his breath was visible, thick as smoke. Predawn gray seeped through the small window. A puff of unmelted snow lay just inside the door. Addie was gone.

Outside, the sky over the cabin was just brightening with the cold blue of dawn. The wind had died in the night, and the air was sharp, perfectly still. To the far north Richard saw the first streamers that presaged storm clouds.

The snow on the ground gleamed softly, and Addie's footprints were nearly invisible. Cold air needling his lungs with each breath, he followed the prints due south across the meadow, toward the ridge where Genna had been hurt. He found the stains on the snow where the trap had been, but Addie's footprints slogged past. The sky was gold and delicate pink by the time he found her. He crested a hill by a half-grown fir, where Addie's footprints ran to the right along the bowl of a small valley. He saw her halfway down the slope, a flash of dirty red nylon behind three small trees.

The pack was on the opposite side of the valley, apparently undisturbed by the arrival of Addie and Richard. Genna was there, absently licking her paw. She didn't appear to be in pain. The young, darker wolf, Murie, lay curled beside her with his head pillowed on her ribcage. Primadonna, the alpha female, stood in place, pressed close by half-grown cubs licking her face and tugging at her ears and tail. When the alpha male, Black, trotted down through the firs at the valley's head, the pack rose and converged on him. He lowered his head and regurgitated meat for the three cubs, which they attacked with growls that were audible even across the valley.

Black started the howl. 'Donna joined in, then one by one the other wolves until even the cubs sang. Richard leaned against a tree, weak-

149

kneed as he always was at the sound, the knots of pitch and overtone. The voices seemed many more than seven. Richard closed his eyes: so much of what he did was intellectual, rational; but there was always this, the woods and the smell of cold air and the loose twining braid of the howl.

The last voice to join came from his side of the valley. He opened his eyes. The wolves were all visible, but Black stared toward the brush below Richard. He could just see Addie behind the young firs: crouched on all fours in the snow, her chest pressed against one knee, her head tilted back and her eyes closed. Her voice was different, higher and rougher, lacking the fluid drop of the wolves' song. He could not stop watching her, even after the howl died and the pack moved off. She half-ran, half-slid down the hill and stumbled a few steps after them. The trailing wolf, Murie, turned to look at her and continued on.

Only when the wolves were gone could Richard move. He walked down to stand beside her.

"They never let me run with them," she said softly. "Sometimes I trap for them and they'll eat what I leave, but they never let me run with them."

"You howled," he said, half angry, half in wonder.

"Why didn't you?" She squinted at the interlaced trails of the wolves. "I'm going to follow."

"You'll never catch up with them," he said with a certain satisfaction and then felt ashamed.

"But you'll try, too, won't you?" Addie burst into a run, snow kicking up under her feet. Richard followed.

She traveled quickly despite the lack of snowshoes or other equipment. The trail went northwest for several miles, heading back toward Lake Juhl, to the western arm a couple of miles from the cabin. She moved at a quick constant trot, plowing without pause through the calf-deep snow. *How can she do it?* he wondered as he stumped after her, laboring in places, until he dropped behind and had to hurry to overtake her before the next hill's crest.

She rose suddenly in front of him, her finger to her lips. Richard stopped. She approached until they stood within a few feet of one another. "Moose over the hill on Lake Juhl, and the wolves have vanished. They're stalking."

"You don't—" he began in annoyance, but she was already gone, back up the slope to settle on her belly in the snow at the crest. He crept up to lie beside her.

Moose had paired off for the rut season, so there were two animals here. The bull looked large, over eight feet tall at the shoulders and very healthy, though still young, judging by the size of his antlers: it made no sense for the pack to waste its effort on so healthy an animal. The small female looked weaker and kept shaking her head as though to dislodge something, screw worm probably. The bull held his head high, wary. Richard suspected that the smell of the wolves—or perhaps the humans—was making him nervous.

Richard leaned over until his mouth was a few inches from Addie's ear. His breath touched her in a fog. "They can't win this one. The bull can fight them off."

Addie gestured impatiently.

The bull nosed at the air, trying to pull scents from it. He shifted restlessly from foot to foot, dropped his head and thrust his antlers into the snow.

Murie and Black and one of the cubs broke from cover just above the pair, vocalizing in sharp yelps. The cow backed across the ice as the bull bellowed, a huge sound that seemed to fill the valley, and charged the three wolves. They evaded him easily and began running south along the shore, just out of reach of his huge hooves, turning to jump at his hocks and pendulous nose whenever he slowed.

The rest of the wolves—Richard saw Genna with them, favoring her leg—broke cover a short distance south of the first ambush, neatly cutting the cow's route to the bull. The cow sank back on her haunches, for a moment meeting the eyes of the gray female, 'Donna. The cow wheeled and ran north, calling as she fled, but the bull was still hampered by Black, who jumped at him whenever he tried to turn and follow.

'Donna got in front of the running cow and jumped at her nose, sinking jaw-deep into the fleshy tip. The cow wailed and threw her head upward, 'Donna flopping into the air like a half-filled bag, still clinging. The cow shook again and 'Donna flew twenty feet to slam into a boulder.

Addie leapt up and ran down the hillside.

"Addie!" Richard grabbed for her ankle as she passed. His hands came down empty in the snow. He sank to his elbows, struggling to get free.

The bull moose roared and kicked at the circling wolves. Murie shied away and the bull galloped through the gap that left. He charged toward the wolves harassing the cow—toward 'Donna, inert.

Addie screamed as she ran toward 'Donna and the cow, and the running bull and wolves. She had her hatchet in her hand.

"Addie!" Richard shouted again.

The bull moose had seen Addie and veered to charge her, his head low. Richard pulled the rifle free and squeezed off two shots. He missed, so he emptied the Winchester. The bull kept running, but each bullet slowed him until he was staggering, and he collapsed to his knees, blood pumping onto the snow around him, twenty yards from Addie. 'Donna lifted her head at the sound of the shots, stood and shook herself. All the wolves appeared to make an instantaneous and unanimous decision. They streamed past Addie toward the bull.

The bull staggered upright. Before the pack could close the circle, he feinted again at Murie, and again ran out the gap. The bull fled north across the lake, and even at this distance Richard could see the bloody trail like red ribbons unfurled against the snow. The wolves ran after him, and the cow followed, as though uncertain where else to go.

When they were past, Richard ran to where Addie stood in the bloody snow. She dragged heavy breaths into her lungs, her arms wrapped tight around herself.

"What were you *doing?*" he shouted.

"He would have killed her."

"You're *fucking* with them when you do this!" Richard stopped shouting, out of breath in the cold air.

Without speaking, Addie thrust her axe in her pocket and walked quickly off the lake ice, back toward the cabin. She maintained the day's pace, but by the time they got there, she was staggering with exhaustion. Only after the cabin warmed a bit and Richard placed porridge and beef jerky and hot sugared tea in front of her, did they speak again.

"Addie, what the hell was that about?"

She was eating ravenously but automatically, but now she looked up. "I'm not supposed to help them? I can't let them die."

"Wolves dying is a part of things. Like moose, like rabbits." He pointed at her snare and the axe on the table, where she had cleared her pockets. For a moment he had a visceral memory of the moose he'd shot, the way it had staggered and then fallen to its knees at the bullets' impact, the ribbons of blood.

As though reading his mind, she said, "So why did you shoot the bull, then? Why didn't *you* let him kill her?"

"I would have," he said. "But I was saving you."

She rocked forward and grabbed the side of the bed frame. Her bare hands were clenched white on the metal. "You would let one die. They're, we're, not all just pieces in a puzzle, fit them in and they're just part of the picture. They're individuals. Do you have any idea who these wolves are? How they feel when they play or howl? What it's like for them to babysit the cubs?"

Richard rubbed his eyes. "No one can know that."

"I will." Addie pushed the tin bowl onto the floor and pulled the blankets around her.

Richard jerked awake, already losing the dream that had awakened him. He was slumped fully dressed over the table, so that his face rested in an open notebook a few inches from the jumble of metal that was the wolf trap, the rabbit snare, the handcuffs, and Addie's hand axe. The stove had burned down and the cabin was frigid. He was alone again.

He walked outside. It was after midnight and nearly pitch dark. There was a full moon somewhere overhead, but heavy clouds concealed most of the sky. The wind was stronger, pushing loose snow along the ground in needling waves. There would be no way to follow her tonight. She would have to find her own way home.

"Addie," he yelled. "Addie, goddammit, where are you?" The wind swallowed the noise. Richard yelled again; the shout lengthened, rose in pitch; and then he was howling, hoarse and not wolf-like at all, but his voice carrying in the way a shout could not.

He was surprised at the power of his lungs, at the volume he could produce when unhampered by the need to make words and sense. He did not stop until his anger had drained from him and his throat hurt from the icy air. Only then did he hear, far to the northwest, the pack howling in response, their interwoven voices muddied by the wind. He could not tell if Addie's was among them.

Morning light gleamed through the cabin's window when Richard heard the sound of her feet outside. The door flew open in the wind, flakes whirling to settle everywhere. Addie was silhouetted in the doorway. "I thought you'd be gone by now."

"Jeff will land right out here." Richard had spent most of the morning hauling the crates he was taking out with him down to the ice; he slammed a notebook into a last half-filled pack. "You shouldn't have gone, Addie. We can't make him wait, not with the weather like this."

"I was with the wolves." She stepped forward into the room. Light from the lamp and the window fell on her face. It was masked in gouts of blood and sinew.

"You're covered in blood," he said with horror.

She rubbed at the gelled stains that darkened her parka. "I'm fine. It's from the moose. They accepted me. They got the male they were chasing, the one you shot. The alpha saw me, he let me feed off the kill. I came back for my axe."

"The wolves let you approach?"

"They let me *in*." She reached across him for the hatchet and the snare and dropped them into her pocket. "I followed them. The kill smelled good and I've been hungry, so I crawled down to it. The alpha watched and let me feed. He was three feet from me. I could smell his fur. It was just dawn. He accepted me." Through the blood, she smiled at him, radiant, beautiful in that moment with her mad golden eyes.

"The pack accepted you?" he repeated.

"I ate so much and then we slept together," she continued, not hearing. She was stuffing packs of food into her pockets. "I could reach out and touch one of the cubs, the pale red one, I was that close. I have to go back now. As soon as the moose is done, we're going to the south end of the range, by the foot of Horsehead Mountain."

One of the sores on her cheek was beginning to ooze. She rubbed it absently, smearing moose blood into the pus there, apparently without pain. "There are caribou by the mountain. We'll—"

"Addie," Richard said. "You're imagining it all."

She looked at him for a moment. "You'll never dance with us. You'll never feel the cubs' noses against your face."

"There *is* no 'us.' It's not real, Addie. Jeff will take us—*us*, you and me, the humans—to Yellowknife, and we'll get help there."

She turned away. "They're waiting."

"They're not. You're sick. You need help." Richard reached for her hand, but she brought the heel of her palm up to his chin hard, and punched him twice under the ribs.

Richard lunged for Addie. She jumped back and cracked the back of her knees against the bed frame. Before she could regain her balance, he caught both her wrists. For a moment they stood toe to toe. She glared into his eyes, her teeth bared and the cords of muscle in her jaw sharp beneath her blistered skin.

The cuffs still lay on the table behind him. Richard grabbed the hoops, snapped one around her thin wrist. She pulled back and fell onto the bed. She kicked him in the thigh and he dropped to his knees. Grabbing the open hoop as it swung, he snapped it shut on the bed frame. He ripped the key from its lock and dropped it into a pocket.

Addie fell heavily against him. Thinking she'd fainted, he caught her shoulders and tried to rebalance her before he noticed she was scrabbling at his pocket, the one with the key. He knocked it from her hand. It hit the door and fell beside the stove. Addie howled and lunged after it. Caught short by the cuff, she slammed onto her side on the floor, whimpering in pain, her arm wrenched high over her head.

Richard slid the key into the wrist of the gloves he was wearing, where it settled cold in his palm. He looked down at Addie. Her face lay against the floor, dust and snow catching in the blood and blisters.

Tears seeped from her closed eyes. She shook, but he couldn't tell if it was from sickness or grief. She made a horrible whining noise, like an injured animal.

"Addie," he said, afraid of the sound, "I had to." He crouched beside her. "You know I have to do this, don't you? I can't let you kill yourself like this."

The whining continued.

"We'll get you out of here. You'll be fine. You'll be warm, it will be okay." He reached for her hand, curled close to her face. She snatched it away. Her other hand, still stretched over her head, pulled at the handcuffs.

"You don't know," she said in anguish. "They accepted me. They let me share a kill. They let me sleep with them. They're *waiting* for me."

"Maybe you're prey, Addie."

"You can't know what it's like, to want to be with them—" Her voice broke.

"Don't I?" he said softly. "I used to watch the pack in Como Zoo. They paced a dirt path twelve inches from the wire fence, all around. I could see the road on the other side of the enclosure, sometimes cars, sometimes other people watching. The wolves ignored us all, just kept walking. Except once, the alpha, a long-bodied gray, he looked at me, not afraid, just curious. That's all we get."

She raised her face to look at him. The tears had cleared tracks through the mask of blood and dirt and pus. "Let me go."

Richard turned his head away from the terrible wild eyes that glowed within the mask. "I can't."

She said no more. He packed the rest of his things, then sat staring at the meaningless marks of his writing on the cover of a notebook, trying not to hear her hopeless crying.

When Richard heard the first sounds of an engine, he ran outside and to the lake shore. The wind snapped heavy flakes in his face. He couldn't see the plane but the drone grew louder. It was a full minute before the Beaver appeared in the southeast, facing into the wind for a landing. It hit the ice on one ski and bounced sideways before it settled onto both skis and ran smoothly away from him. For a moment, the plane sounded as though it masked a wolf's howl, but it was only the overtones of the slowing engines. It slowed to a crawl, turned and began taxiing back. Richard waved his arms at the small figure behind the windscreen and ran back toward the cabin.

"Addie," he yelled as he approached. "He's here, we're getting out." He scrambled around the rock that hid the cabin.

There was blood everywhere by the entrance, splashed red against the white snow and the pale walls. Indistinct footprints and a broad trail of bloody marks wove southwest across the meadow into the ribbon forest, toward Horsehead Mountain.

Richard ran into the cabin. Sheathed in blood, the cuffs still hung from the bed frame, one hoop swinging closed and empty. The chain between the rings had been smashed by something sharp but was unbroken. Blood soaked the bed's blankets and heavy drops trailed down the walls. In a pool of gelling blood by the bed lay a severed hand, bones extending just past the ragged cut.

Richard staggered out the door, away from the thick cold smell, to fall vomiting by the cabin, holding a corner until he could stand alone and look again at the path that led into the fir and spruce.

She couldn't be far away, losing blood as she was. He'd easily overtake her. He looked at her path, the mountain beyond it, and the clouds dark behind that. New snow was falling, drifting over the stains. After a long moment, Richard turned his back and walked north, to Lake Juhl and the waiting plane.

Ponies

The invitation card has a Western theme. Along its margins, cartoon girls in cowboy hats chase a herd of wild Ponies. The Ponies are no taller than the girls, fat and bright as butterflies, with short, round-tipped unicorn horns and small fluffy wings. At the bottom of the card, newly caught Ponies mill about in a corral. The girls have lassoed a pink-and-white Pony. Its eyes and mouth are surprised round Os. There is an exclamation mark over its head.

The little girls are cutting off its horn with curved knives. Its wings are already removed, part of a pile beside the corral.

> You and your Pony ___[and Sunny's name is handwritten here in puffy girl-letters]___ are invited to a cutting-out party with TheOtherGirls! If we like you, and if your Pony does okay, we'll let you hang out with us.

"Yay!" Sunny says. "I can't wait to have friends!" She reads over Barbara's shoulder, her rose-scented breath woofling through Barbara's hair. They are in the big backyard next to Sunny's pink stable.

Barbara says, "Do you know what you want to keep?"

Sunny's tiny wings are a blur as she hops into the air, loops and then hovers, legs curled under her. "Oh, being able to talk, absolutely! Flying is great but talking is way better!" She drops to the grass. "I don't know why any Pony would keep her horn! It's not like it does anything!"

This is the way it's always been, as long as there have been Ponies. All ponies have wings. All Ponies have horns. All Ponies can talk. Then all Ponies go to a cutting-out party with AllTheGirls and they give up two of the three, because that's what has to happen if a Girl is going to fit in with TheOtherGirls. The Ponies must all keep their voices because Barbara's never seen one that still had her horn or wings after her cutting-out party.

Barbara sees TheOtherGirls' Ponies all the time, peeking in the classroom windows just before recess or clustered at the bus stop after school. They're baby pink and lavender and daffodil-yellow, with flossy manes in ringlets and tails that curl to the ground. When not at school and cello lessons and ballet class and soccer practice and play group and the orthodontist's, TheOtherGirls spend their days with their Ponies.

The party is at TopGirl's house, which has a mother who's a pediatrician and a father who's a cardiologist and a small barn and giant trees shading the grass where the Ponies are playing games. Sunny walks out to them nervously. They touch her horn and wings with their velvet noses and then the Ponies all walk out to the lilac barn at the bottom of the pasture where a bale of hay is broken open for them.

TopGirl meets Barbara at the fence. "That's your Pony?" she says without greeting. "She's not as nice as mine."

Barbara is defensive. "She's beautiful!" She knows this is a misstep and adds, "Yours is so pretty!" And TopGirl's Pony Starblossom *is* pretty. Her tail is every shade of purple and glitters with stars; but Sunny's tail is creamy white and shines with honey-colored light, and Barbara knows that Sunny's the most beautiful Pony ever.

TopGirl walks away, saying over her shoulder, "There's Rock Band in the family room and a bunch of TheOtherGirls are hanging out on the deck and Mom bought some cookies and there's Coke Zero and Diet Red Bull and diet lemonade."

"Where are you?" Barbara asks.

"*I'm* outside," TopGirl says so Barbara gets a Crystal Light and three frosted raisin-oatmeal cookies and follows her. TheOtherGirls outside are listening to an iPod plugged into speakers and playing Wii tennis and watching the Ponies play HideAndSeek and Who'sPrettiest and ThisIsTheBestGame. They are all there, SecondGirl and SuckUpGirl and EveryoneLikesHerGirl and the rest. Barbara only says anything when she thinks she'll get it right. It seems as though it's going okay.

And then it's time. TheOtherGirls and their silent Ponies collect in a ring around Barbara and Sunny. Barbara feels sick.

TopGirl says to Barbara, "What did she pick?"

Sunny looks scared but answers her directly. "I would rather talk than fly or stab things with my horn."

TopGirl says to Barbara, "That's what Ponies always say." She gives Barbara a curved knife with a blade as long as a woman's hand.

"Me?" Barbara says. "I thought someone else did it, a grownup."

TopGirl says, "Everyone does it for their own Pony. I did it for Starblossom."

In silence Sunny stretches out a wing.

It's not the way it would be, cutting a real pony. The wing comes off easily, smooth as plastic, and the blood smells like cotton candy at the fair. There's a shiny trembling oval where the wing was as though Barbara cut rose-flavored Turkish Delight in half and saw the pink under the powdered sugar. Barbara thinks, *It's sort of pretty,* and throws up.

Sunny shivers, her eyes shut tight. Barbara cuts off the second wing and lays it beside the first.

The horn is harder, like paring a real pony's hooves. Barbara's hand slips and she cuts Sunny and there's more cotton-candy blood. And then the horn lies in the grass beside the wings.

Sunny drops to her knees. Barbara throws the knife down and falls beside her, sobbing and hiccuping. She scrubs her face with the back of her hand and looks up at the circle. "Now what?"

Starblossom touches the knife with her nose, pushes it toward Barbara with one lilac hoof. "You're not done yet," TopGirl says. "Now the voice. You have to take away her voice."

"But I already cut off her wings and her horn!" Barbara throws her arms around Sunny's neck. "Two of the three, you said!"

"That's the cutting-out, yeah," TopGirl says. "That's what *you* do to be OneOfUs. But the Ponies pick their own friends and that costs, too." Starblossom tosses her violet mane. For the first time Barbara sees that there is a scar shaped like a smile on her throat. All the Ponies have one.

"I can't!" Barbara tells TheOtherGirls, TopGirl, Starblossom, Sunny. But even as she cries until her face is caked with snot and tears, she knows she's going to. When she's done she picks up the knife and pulls herself upright.

Sunny stands up beside her on trembling legs. She looks very small without her horn, her wings. Barbara's hands are slippery. She tightens her grip.

"No," Sunny says suddenly. "Not even for friends. Not even for you."

And Sunny spins and runs, runs for the fence in a gallop as fast and beautiful as a real pony's. But there are more of the others and they are bigger, and Sunny doesn't have her wings to fly or her horn to fight. They pull her down before she can jump the fence into the woods beyond. Sunny cries out and then there is nothing, only the sound of pounding hooves from the tight circle of Ponies.

TheOtherGirls stand, frozen, their blind faces turned toward the Ponies.

The Ponies break their circle, trot away. There is no sign of Sunny beyond a spray of cotton-candy blood and a coil of her mane torn free and fading as it falls to the grass.

Into the silence TopGirl says, "Cookies?" Her voice sounds fragile and false. TheOtherGirls crowd into the house, chattering in equally artificial voices. They start up a game, drink more Diet Coke. Soon they sound almost normal.

Barbara stumbles after them into the family room. "What are you playing?" she says uncertainly.

"Why are *you* here?" FirstGirl says, as though noticing her for the first time. "You're not OneOfUs."

TheOtherGirls nod. "You don't have a pony."

The Cat Who Walked a Thousand Miles

Chapter I
The Garden

At a time now past, a cat was born. This was not so long after the first cats came to Japan, so they were rare and mostly lived near the capital city.

This cat was the smallest of her litter of four. Her fur had been dark when she was born but as she grew it changed to black with speckles of gold and cinnamon and ivory. She had a little gold-colored chin, and her eyes were gold, like a fox's.

She lived in the gardens of a great house in the capital. They filled a city block and the house had been very fine once but that was many years ago. The owners moved to a new home in a more important part of the city, and left the house to suffer fires and droughts and earthquakes and neglect. Now there was very little left that a person might think of as home. The main house still stood but the roofs leaked and even had fallen in places. Furry green moss covered the walls. Many of the storehouses and other buildings were barely more than piles of wood. Ivy filled the garden and water weeds choked the three little lakes and the stream.

But it was a perfect home for cats. The stone wall around the garden kept people and dogs away. Inside, cats could find ten thousand things to do. There were trees and walls to climb, bushes to hide under, corners to sleep in.

Food was everywhere. Delicious mice skittered across the ground and crunchy crickets hopped in the grass. The stream was full of slow, fat frogs. Birds lived in the trees and occasionally a careless one came within reach.

The little cat shared the grounds with a handful of other female cats. Each adult claimed part of the gardens, where she hunted and bore her kittens alone; but the private places all met at the center like petals on a flower, in a courtyard beside the main house. The cats liked to gather here and sleep on sunny days, or to groom or watch the kittens playing. No males lived in the garden except for boy-kittens who had not gotten old enough to start their prowling, but tomcats visited and a while later there were new kittens.

The cats shared another thing: their *fudoki*. The fudoki was the collection of stories about all the cats that had lived in a place. It described what made it a home and what made the cats a family. Mothers taught their kittens the fudoki. If the mother died too soon, the other cats, the aunts and cousins, would teach the kittens. A cat with no fudoki was a cat with no family, no home and no roots. The small cat's fudoki was many cats long and she knew them all—The Cat From The North, The Cat Born The Year The Star Fell, The Dog-Chasing Cat.

Her favorite was The Cat From The North. She had been her mother's mother's mother's aunt, and her life seemed very exciting. As a kitten she lived beside a great hill to the north. She got lost when a dog chased her and tried to find her way home. She escaped many adventures. Giant oxen nearly stepped on her. Cart wheels almost crushed her. A pack of wild dogs chased her into a tree and waited an entire day for her to come down. She was insulted by a goat that lived in a park. She stole food from people. She met a boy but she ran away when he tried to pull her tail. At last she came to the garden. The cats there called her The Cat From The North and as such she became part of the little cat's fudoki.

The ancestors and the aunts were all clever and strong and resourceful. More than anything, the little cat wanted to earn the right for her story and name to be remembered alongside theirs. And when she had kittens, she would be part of the fudoki that they would pass on to their own kittens.

The other cats had started calling her Small Cat. It wasn't an actual name but it was a beginning. She knew she would have a story worth telling someday.

———

Chapter 2
The Earthquake

One day, it was beautiful and very hot. It was August, though overnight the first leaf in the garden had turned bright yellow. A duck bobbed on the lake just out of reach but the cats were too lazy to care as they dozed in the courtyard or under the shadow of the trees. A mother cat held down her kitten with one paw as she licked her ears clean, teaching her the fudoki as she did so. Small Cat wrestled, not very hard, with an orange-striped boy-kitten almost old enough to leave the garden.

A wind started. The duck on the lake burst upward with a flurry of wings, quacking with panic. Puzzled, Small Cat watched it race across the sky. There was nothing to scare the duck, so why was it so frightened?

Suddenly the ground heaved underfoot. An earthquake. Small Cat crouched to keep her balance while the ground shuddered, as though it were a giant animal stretching itself after waking up and she a flea clinging to its hide. Tree branches clashed against one another. Leaves rustled and rained down. Just beyond the garden walls, people shouted, dogs barked, horses whinnied. There was a crashing noise like a pile of pottery falling from a cart—which is exactly what it was. A temple bell rang as it tossed in its frame. And the strangest sound of all: the ground itself groaned.

The older cats had been through earthquakes before, so they crouched wherever they were and waited for it to end. Small Cat knew of earthquakes through the stories but she'd never felt one. She hissed and looked for somewhere safe to run, but everything around her rose and fell. It was wrong for the earth to move!

The old house cracked and boomed. Blue pottery tiles slid from the roof to shatter in the dirt. A wood beam in the main house broke in half with a cloud of flying splinters. The roof collapsed in on itself, and crashed into the building with a wave of white dust. The crash was too much for even the most experienced cats, and they ran in every direction.

Small Cat staggered and fell. Cones and needles rained down from a huge cedar tree. It was shaking, but trees shook all the time in the wind so maybe it would be safer up there. She bolted up the trunk. She ran through an abandoned birds' nest tucked on a branch, the babies grown and flown away and the adults nowhere to be found. A squirrel chattered as she passed it, more upset by Small Cat than the earthquake.

Small Cat paused and looked down. The ground had stopped moving. As the dust settled, she saw most of the house and garden. The courtyard was piled with beams and branches, but there was still an open space to gather and tell stories, and new places to hunt or play hide-and-seek. It was still home.

Aunts and cousins emerged from their hiding places. Slinking or creeping or just trotting out, they were too dusty to tell who was who, except for The Cat With No Tail, who sniffed and pawed at a fallen door. Other cats hunched in the remains of the courtyard, or paced about the garden, or groomed themselves as much for comfort as to remove the dirt. She didn't see everyone.

She fell asleep the way kittens do, suddenly and all at once and wherever they happen to be. She had been so afraid during the earthquake that she fell asleep lying flat on a broad branch with her claws sunk into the bark.

When she woke up with her whiskers twitching, the sun was lower in the sky. What had awakened her? The air had a new smell, bitter and unpleasant. She wrinkled her nose and sneezed.

She crept along a branch until she saw out past the tree's needles and over the garden's stone wall.

The city was on fire.

Chapter 3
The Fire

Fires in the capital were even more common than earthquakes. Buildings were made of wood with paper screens and straw mats. In August the gardens were dry, the weeds so parched that they broke like twigs. Across the city, a lamp tipped over in the earthquake. No one noticed until the fire leapt to a bamboo blind and then to a wall and from there into a garden, and by that time it couldn't be stopped.

Smoke streamed across the city: thin white smoke where grass sizzled, thick gray plumes where some great house burned. The smoke concealed most of the fire, even though in places the flames were as tall as trees. People fled through the streets wailing or shouting, and their animals added to the din. But beneath those noises, even at this distance, the fire roared.

Should she go down? Other cats in the fudoki had survived fires—The Fire-Tailed Cat, The Cat Who Found The Jewel—but the stories didn't say *what* she should do. Maybe one of her aunts or cousins could tell her but where were they?

Smoke drifted into the garden.

She climbed down and meowed loudly. No one answered, but a movement caught her eye. One of her aunts, The Painted Cat, trotted toward a hole in the wall, her ears pinned back and tail low. Small Cat scrambled after her. A gust of smoky wind blew into her face until she squeezed her eyes tight, coughing and gasping. When she could see again her aunt had gone.

She retreated up the tree and watched houses catch fire. At first, smoke poured from their roofs, and then flames roared up and turned each building into a pillar of fire. Each house was closer than the last. The smoke grew so thick that she could only breathe by pressing her nose into her fur and panting.

Her house caught fire just as the sky grew dark. Cinders rained on her garden. The grass beside her lake hissed as it burned like angry kittens. The fires crawled up the walls and slipped inside the doors. Smoke gushed through the broken roof. Something collapsed inside the house with a huge crash and the flames shot up, higher even than the top of Small Cat's tree.

The air was too hot to breathe. She moved to the opposite side of the tree, and dug her claws into the bark as deep as they would go, and huddled down as small as she could get.

Fire doesn't always burn everything in its path. It can leave an area untouched that is surrounded by nothing but smoking ruins. The house burned until it was just blackened beams and ashes. Beside it, Small Cat's tree got charred but the highest branches stayed safe.

Small Cat stayed there all night long and by dawn the tall flames in the garden were gone and the smoke didn't seem so thick. At first she couldn't get her claws to let go or her muscles to carry her, but at last she managed to climb down.

Much of the house remained but it was roofless now, hollowed out and charred. Other buildings were no more than piles of smoking black wood. With their leaves burned away the trees looked like skeletons. The pretty bushes were gone. Even the ground smoked in places, too hot to touch.

There was no sound of any sort: no morning songbirds, no people going about their business on the street. No cats. All she could hear was a small fire still burning in an outbuilding. She rubbed her sticky eyes against her shoulder.

She was very thirsty. She trotted to the stream, hopping from paw to paw on the hot ground. Chalky-white with ashes, the water tasted bitter but she drank until her stomach was full. She was hungry so she ate a dead bird she found beside the stream, burnt feathers and all.

From the corner of her eye, she caught something stirring inside a storehouse. Maybe it was an aunt who had hidden during the fire or maybe The Painted Cat had come back to help her! She ran across the hot ground and into the storehouse but there was no cat. What had she seen? There, in a window, she saw the motion again. It was just an old bamboo curtain.

She searched everywhere. The only living creature she saw was a soaked rat climbing from the stream. It shook itself and ran beneath a fallen beam, leaving nothing but tiny wet paw prints.

She found no cats or any signs of what had happened to them.

Chapter 4
The Burnt Paws

Cats groom themselves when they're upset, so Small Cat sat down to clean her fur, making a face at the taste of the ashes. For comfort she recited the stories from the fudoki: The Cat Who Ate Roots, The Three-Legged Cat, The Cat Who Hid Things, every cat all the way down to

The Cat Who Swam, her youngest aunt, who had just taken her place in the fudoki.

The fudoki was more than just stories. The cats of the past had claimed the garden and made it home for those who lived there now. If the cats were gone, was this still home? Was it still her garden if nothing looked the same and it all smelled like smoke? Logs and broken roof tiles filled the courtyard. The house was a ruin. There were no frogs, no insects, no fat ducks, no mice. No cats.

Small Cat cleaned her ear with a paw, thinking hard. No, she wasn't alone. She didn't know where the other cats had gone, but she had seen The Painted Cat run through a hole in the wall just before the fire, so if Small Cat could find her there would be two cats. That would be better than one. The Painted Cat would know what to do.

A big fallen branch leaned against the wall just where the hole was. She inched carefully across the ground, still hot in places, twisting her face away from the fumes wherever something smoked. There was no way to follow The Painted Cat by pushing through the hole. Small Cat didn't mind that: she had always liked sitting on top of the wall watching the outside world. She crawled up the branch.

There were people on the street carrying bundles or boxes or crying babies. Many looked lost or frightened. A wagon pulled by a single ox passed, and a cart pushed by a man and two boys that had been heaped high with possessions. A stray flock of geese were eating the fallen rice from a tipped cart. Even the dogs looked weary.

There was no sign of The Painted Cat. Small Cat climbed higher.

The branch she stood on cracked in half. She crashed to the ground and landed on her side on a hot rock. She twisted upright and jumped away from the terrible pain, but when she landed, it was with all four paws on a smoldering beam. She howled and started running. Every time she put a foot down, the agony made her run faster. She ran across the broad street and through the next garden, and the next.

Small Cat stopped running only when her exhaustion became stronger than her pain. She scarcely made it off the road before she slumped to the ground, and she was asleep immediately. People and carts and even dogs tramped past but no one bothered her, a small filthy cat lying in the open and looking dead.

When Small Cat woke up, she was surrounded by noise and tumult. Wheels rolled past her head. She jumped up, her claws out. The searing pain in her paws made her almost forget herself again but she managed to limp into a clump of weeds.

Where was she? Nothing looked or smelled familiar. She didn't recognize the street or the buildings. She did not know that she had run nearly a mile in her panic, but she knew she would never find her way back.

She had collapsed beside an open market. Even so soon after the earthquake and fire, merchants set up new booths to sell things, rice and squashes and tea and pots. Even after a great disaster people are hungry, and broken pots always need to be replaced.

If there was food for people, there would be food for cats. Small Cat limped through the market, staying away from the big feet of the people. She stole a little silver fish from a stall and crept inside a broken basket to eat it. When she was done she licked her burnt paws clean.

She had lost The Painted Cat and now she had lost the garden. The stories were all she had left. But the stories were not enough without the garden and the other cats; they were just a list. If everyone and everything was gone, did she even have a home? She could not help the cry of sadness that escaped her.

It was her fudoki now, hers alone. She had to find a way to make it continue.

Chapter 5
The Strange Cats

Small Cat was very careful to keep her paws clean as they healed. For the first few days she only left her basket when she was hungry or thirsty. It was hard to hunt mice yet, so she ate things she found on the ground: fish, rice, once even an entire goose wing. Sad as she was, she found interesting things to do as she got stronger. Fishtails were fun to bat at and she liked to crawl under tables of linen and hemp fabric, and tug the threads that hung over the edges.

As she got better, she began to search for her garden. Since she didn't know where she was going, she wandered, hoping that something would look familiar. Her nose didn't help because for days she couldn't smell anything but smoke. She was slow on her healing paws. She stayed close to trees and walls. She couldn't run fast and she had to be careful about dogs.

There was a day when Small Cat limped along an alley so narrow that the roofs on either side met overhead. She had seen a mouse run down the alley and vanish into a gap between two walls. She wasn't going to catch it by chasing it, but she could always wait in the gap beside its hole until it emerged. Her mouth watered.

Someone hissed. Another cat squeezed from the gap, a striped gray female with a mouse in her mouth. Her mouse! Small Cat couldn't help but growl and flatten her ears. The stranger hissed, arched her back, and ran away.

Small Cat trailed after the stranger with her heart beating so hard she could barely hear the street noises. She had not seen a single cat since the fire. One cat might mean many cats. Losing the mouse would be a small price to pay for that.

The stranger spun around. "Stop following me!" she said through a mouthful of mouse. Small Cat sat down instantly and looked off into the distance, as though she just happened to be traveling the same direction. The stranger glared and stalked off. Small Cat jumped up and followed. Every few steps the stranger whirled and Small Cat pretended not to be there, but after a while, the stranger gave up and trotted to a tall bamboo fence, her tail bristling with annoyance. With a final hiss she squeezed under the fence. Small Cat waited a moment before following.

She was behind a tavern, in a small yard filled with barrels. And cats! There were six of them that she could see and she knew others would be in their private ranges, prowling or sleeping. She meowed with excitement. She could teach them her fudoki and they would become her family. She would have a home again.

Cats don't like new things very much. The strangers all stared at her, every ear flattened, every tail bushy. "I don't know why she followed me," the striped cat said sullenly. "Go away!"

The others hissed agreement: "No one wants *you*."

Small Cat backed out under the bamboo fence but she didn't leave. Every day she came to the tavern yard. At first the strange cats drove her off with scratches and hisses, but she always returned to try again and each time she got closer before they attacked her. After a while they ignored her and she came closer still.

One day the strange cats gathered beneath a little roof attached to the back of the tavern. It was raining, so when Small Cat jumped onto a stack of barrels under the roof, no one seemed to think it was worthwhile to chase her away.

The oldest cat, a female with black fur growing thin, was teaching the kittens their fudoki. The stories were told in the correct way: The Cat Inside The Lute, The Cat Born With One Eye, The Cat Who Bargained With A Flea. But these strangers didn't know the right cats: The Cat From The North or The Cat Who Chased Foxes or any of the others. Small Cat jumped down, wanting to share.

The oldest cat looked sidelong at her. "Are you ready to learn our stories?"

Small Cat felt as though she'd been kicked. Her fudoki would never belong here. These strangers had their own stories, for different aunts and ancestors and for a different place. If she stayed she would no longer be a garden cat, but a cat in the tavern yard's fudoki, The Cat After The Fire or The Burnt-Paw Cat. If she had kittens they would learn about the aunts and ancestors of the tavern-yard cats. There would be no room for her own.

She arched and backed away, tail shivering, teeth bared; and when she was far enough from the terrible stories she turned and ran.

Chapter 6
The Rajo Gate

Small Cat came to the Rajo Gate at sunset. Rain fell on her back, so light that it didn't soak through but instead slid off her fur in drops. She inspected the weeds beside the street as she walked. She had eaten three mice for dinner but a fourth would make a nice snack.

She looked up and saw a vast dark building looming ahead, a hundred feet wide and taller than the tallest tree she had ever climbed, made of wood that had turned black with age. There were actually three gates in the Rajo Gate. The smallest one was fifteen feet high and wide enough for ox carts, and it was the only one still open.

A guard by the door held a corner of a cape over his head against the rain. "Gate closes at sunset," he shouted. "No one wants to be wet all night. Hurry it up!" People crowded through. A man carrying geese tied together by their feet narrowly missed a fat woman carrying a bundle of blue fabric and dragging a goat on a rope.

The guard bent down. "What about you, miss?" Small Cat pulled back. Usually no one noticed her but he was talking to her, smiling and wiggling his fingers. Should she bite him? Run? Smell his hand? She leaned forward, trembling but curious.

Through the gate behind him she saw a wide busy road half-hidden by the rain. The guard pointed. "That's the Tokaido," he said, as though she had asked a question. "The Great North Road. It starts right here and it goes all the way to the end of Japan." He shrugged. "Maybe farther. Who knows?"

North! She had never thought about it before this, but The Cat From The North must have come from somewhere before she became part of Small Cat's fudoki. And if she came *from* somewhere, Small Cat could *go* there. There would be cats and they would have to accept her—and they would have to accept a fudoki that included one of their own.

Unfortunately, The Cat From The North's story didn't say where North was. Small Cat kneaded the ground, uncertain.

The guard straightened and shouted, "Last warning!" Looking down he added in a softer voice, "That means you, too, young lady. Stay or go?"

Suddenly deciding, she dashed through the gate, right into the path of an ox cart. A wheel rolled by her head, close enough to bend her whiskers back. She scrambled out of the way, and tumbled in front of a man on horseback. The horse shied as Small Cat leapt aside. Small Cat streaked into the nearest yard and crouched beneath a wagon.

The Rajo Gate shut with a great crash. She was outside.

The rain got harder as the sky dimmed. She needed a place to rest and think, out from underfoot until morning. She explored warily, avoiding a team of steaming oxen that entered the yard. She was in an inn yard full of wagons and carts. Light shone from the inn's paper windows and the sound of laughter and voices poured out. Too busy! The back of the building was quiet and unlit, with a single window cracked open to let in the night air. Perfect. She jumped onto the sill.

A voice screeched inside the room and a heavy object hurtled past her head. Small Cat fell from the sill and bolted back to the wagon. Maybe not so perfect.

But where else could she go? She couldn't stay here, because someone would step on her. Everything she might climb onto was wet. And she didn't want to hide in the forest behind the inn. It smelled strange and deep and frightening, and night is not the best time for adventures.

But there was a promising shape in a corner of the yard. When she approached, it turned out to be a small shed with a shingled roof, knee-high to a person and open in front. It was a shrine to a *kami*. Kami are the spirits and gods that exist everywhere in Japan, and their shrines can be as large as palaces or as small as doll houses. She pushed her head into the shed. Inside was an even smaller building, barely bigger than she was. This was the shrine itself. Its doors were shut tight. In front of the shed, two stone foxes stood on either side of a ledge with little bowls and pots. She smelled cooked rice.

"Are you worshipping the kami?" a voice said behind her. She whirled, bumped into the shed, and knocked over the rice.

A Buddhist monk stood in the yard. He was very tall and thin and wore a straw cape over his red-and-yellow robes, and a pointed straw hat on his head. Except for his smiling face, he looked like a pile of wet hay,

"Are you catching mice, or just praying to catch some?"

The monk worshipped Buddha, who had been a very wise man who taught people how to live properly. But the monk also respected Shinto, which is the religion of the kami. Shinto and Buddhism did not war between themselves and many Buddhist temples had Shinto shrines on their grounds. And so the monk was happy to see a cat do something so wise.

Small Cat had no idea of any of this. She watched suspiciously as he put down his basket to place his hands together and murmur for a moment. "There," he said, "I have told the Buddha about you. I am sure he will help you find what you seek." And he bowed and took his basket and left her alone, her whiskers twitching in puzzlement.

She fell asleep curled against the shrine inside the little shed, still thinking about the monk. And in the morning she headed north along the Tokaido.

Chapter 7
The Tokaido

At first the Tokaido looked a lot like the streets of the city. It was packed earth just as the streets had been, fringed with buildings and overshadowed by trees so close that they dropped needles onto the road. She recognized most of the sorts of buildings but some she had never seen before, houses like barns where people and animals lived under a single high thatched roof.

At first she stayed in the brush beside the road and hid whenever anything approached—and there was always something! People crowded the Tokaido: peasants and carpenters and charcoal-sellers, monks and nurses. There were carts and wagons, honking geese and quacking ducks. She saw a man on horseback and a very small boy leading a giant black ox by a ring through its nose. Everyone except the ox seemed in a hurry to go somewhere and then to get back from there just as fast as they could.

She stayed out of their way until she realized that no one had paid any attention to her, not since the guard and the monk back at Rajo Gate. Even if they did notice her, everyone was too busy to bother with her. Well, everyone except dogs anyway, and she knew what to do about dogs: make herself look large and then get out of reach.

The Tokaido followed a broad valley divided into fields and dotted with trees and farmhouses. The mountains beyond that were dark with pine and cedar trees, bright with larches and birch trees. As she traveled, the road left the valley and crossed hills and other valleys. There were fewer buildings and more fields and forests and lakes. The Tokaido grew narrower. Other roads and lanes left it, but she always knew where to go. North.

She did leave the road a few times when curiosity drove her.

In one place, where the road clung to the side of a wooded valley, a rough stone staircase climbed up into the forest. She glimpsed the flicker of a red flag. It was a hot day, maybe the last hot day before autumn and then winter settled in. She might not have investigated except that the stair looked cool and shady.

She padded into a graveled yard surrounded by red flags. There was a large Shinto shrine and many smaller shrines and buildings. She walked through the grounds, sniffing statues and checking offering bowls to see if they were empty. Acolytes washed the floor of the biggest shrine. She made a face—too much water!—and returned to the road.

Another time, she heard a crowd of people approaching and she hid in a bush to watch them pass. It was a row of sedan chairs, which looked exactly like people-sized boxes carried on poles by two strong men each. Other servants tramped along. The chairs smelled of sandalwood perfume.

The chairs and servants turned onto a narrow lane. Small Cat followed them to a Buddhist monastery with many gardens. The sedan chairs stopped in front of a building. And then nothing happened.

Small Cat prowled around inside but no one did much in there either, mostly just knelt and chanted. There were many monks but none of them was the monk who had spoken to her beside the tiny shrine. She was coming to realize that there were many monks in the world.

When it was time to sleep, she hid in storehouses, boxes, barns, the attics where people kept silkworms in the spring, any place that would keep the rain off and some of her warmth in. But sometimes it was hard to find safe places: one afternoon she was almost caught by a fox, who had found her half-buried inside a loose pile of straw.

And there was one gray windy day when she napped in a barn, in a coil of rope beside the oxen. She awoke when a huge black cat leapt on her and scratched her face.

"Leave or I will kill you," the black cat snarled. "I am The Cat Who Killed A Hawk!"

Small Cat ran. She knew The Cat From The North could not have been kin to so savage a cat. After The Cat Who Killed A Hawk, she saw no more cats.

She got used to her wandering life. At first she did not travel far in any day, but she soon learned that a resourceful cat could hop into the back of a cart just setting off and get many miles along her way without lifting a paw.

There was food everywhere, fat squirrels and absent-minded birds, mice and voles. She loved the tasty crunch of crickets and beetles which got easier to catch as the weather got colder. She stole food from storehouses and trash heaps and even learned to eat vegetables. There were many things to play with, as well. She didn't have other cats to wrestle, but mice were a constant amusement, as was teasing dogs.

North was turning out to be a long way away. Day followed day and still the Tokaido went on. She did not notice how long she had been traveling. There was always another town or village or farmhouse, always something else to eat or look at or play with. The leaves on the trees turned red and orange and yellow, and fell to crackle under Small Cat's feet. Evenings grew colder. Her fur got thicker.

She recited the stories of her fudoki as she walked. Someday, she would get to wherever The Cat From The North came from, and she wanted to have them right.

Chapter 8
The Approach

One morning a month into her journey, Small Cat awoke in the attic of an old farmhouse. When she had stopped the night before, it was foggy and cold, as more and more nights were lately. She wanted to sleep near the big charcoal brazier at the house's center but there was an old dog dozing there and Small Cat worried that he might wake up. It had seemed smarter to slip upstairs and sleep where the floor was warm above the fire.

Small Cat stretched and scrubbed her whiskers with a paw. What sort of day was it? She saw a triangular opening in the thatched roof overhead, a gap where smoke could leave. It was easy enough to climb up and peek out.

It would be a beautiful day. The fog was thinning and the sky glowed pale pink with dawn. The farmhouse was on a plain near a broad river, with fields of buckwheat ready to be harvested. Beyond everything the dim outlines of mountains were just beginning to appear as the light grew. The Tokaido meandered across the plain, narrow because there was not very much traffic here.

The sun rose and daylight poured across the valley. And there, far in the distance, was a mountain bigger than anything Small Cat had ever seen, so big it dwarfed every other mountain. This was Fujisan, the great mountain of Japan. It was still more than a hundred miles away, though she didn't know that.

Small Cat had seen many mountains by now but Fujisan was different: a perfect snow-covered cone with a thin line of smoke that rose straight into the sky. It was a volcano, though it had been many years since it had erupted. The ice on its peak never melted. Snow came halfway down its slopes.

Could that be where The Cat From The North had come from? The fudoki said that she had begin her wanderings beside a big hill. This was so much more than a hill but the Tokaido seemed to lead toward Fujisan. Even if it weren't The Cat From The North's home, surely Small Cat would be able to see her hill from a mountain that high.

That day Small Cat didn't linger over her morning grooming and she ate a squirrel for breakfast without playing with it. In no time at all, she trotted down the road. And even when the sky grew heavy the next day and she could no longer see Fujisan, she kept going.

It was fall now, so there was more rain and whole days of fog. In the mornings puddles had a skin of ice, but her thick fur kept her warm. She was too impatient to do all the traveling on her own paws, so she stole rides on wagons, and the miles added up, eight or even ten in a day.

The farmers finished gathering their buckwheat and rice and the root vegetables that would feed them for the winter, and then they set their pigs loose in the fields to eat the stubble. Small Cat caught the sparrows that joined them. After the first time, she never forgot to pull off the feathers before eating!

But she was careful. The people here had never even heard of cats. She frightened a small boy so much that he fell from a fence and ran off screaming, "Demon! A demon!" Small Cat fled before his parents arrived. Another night, a frightened grandfather threw hot coals at her. A spark caught in her fur, and Small Cat ran into the darkness in panic, remembering the fire that destroyed her home. She slept cold and wet that night under a pile of logs. After that Small Cat made sure not to be seen again.

Fujisan was always hidden by *something*. Even when there was a break in the forests and the mountains, the low never-ending clouds concealed it. Then there was a long period when she never saw farther than the next turn of the road, everything gray in the pouring rain. She trudged on, cold and miserable. Water dribbled from her whiskers and drooping tail. She couldn't decide which was worse, walking down the middle of the road so that the trees overhead dropped cold water on her back, or brushing through the weeds beside the road and soaking her belly. She groomed herself whenever she could, but even so she was always muddy.

The longer this went, the more she turned to stories. But these were no longer the fudoki of her aunts and ancestors, the stories that taught Small Cat what home was like. She made up her own stories about The Cat From The North's home, and how well Small Cat would fit in there, how thrilled everyone would be to meet her.

After many days of this, she was filthy and frustrated. She couldn't see anything but trees and the fallen leaves underfoot were an awful-feeling, slippery, sticky brown mass. The Tokaido seemed to go on forever.

Had she lost the mountain?

Finally one day, the sky cleared as she came up a long hill. She quickened her pace. Once she got to the top she might see a village nearby. She was tired of mice and sparrows; cooked fish would taste good.

She came to the top of the hill and sat down, hard. She hadn't lost the mountain. There was no way she could possibly lose the mountain. Fujisan seemed to fill the entire sky now, so high that she tipped her head to see the top. It was whiter that it had been, for the clouds that rained on the Tokaido had snowed on Fujisan. Small Cat would be able to see the entire world from a mountain that tall.

Chapter 9
Fujisan

Fujisan loomed to the north, closer and bigger each time Small Cat saw it. The Tokaido threaded through the forested hills and came to a river valley that ended on a large plain. That was where she had to leave the Tokaido, for the road skirted the mountain, going east instead of north.

The plain was famous for its horses which were praised even in the capital for their beauty and courage. Small Cat tried to stay far from the galloping hooves of the herds, but the horses were fast and she was not. She woke up one day to find herself less than a foot from a pair of nostrils bigger than her entire body. It was a red mare snuffling the weeds where she hid. Small Cat leapt in the air, the mare jumped back, and they pelted in opposite directions, tails streaming behind them. Horses and cats are both curious but there is such a thing as too much adventure.

She traveled as quickly as a small cat can when she is eager to get somewhere. The mountain towered over her, its white slopes leading into the sky. The bigger it got, the more certain she was that if she climbed to the top of Fujisan, she would see The Cat From The North's home, and then everything would be perfect. She wanted this to be true so much that she ignored all the doubts that came to her. What if she *couldn't* find them? What if she was already too far north, or not north enough? What if they didn't want her?

And because she was ignoring so many important things, she started ignoring other important things as well. She stopped being careful where she walked and she scraped her paws raw on the rough rock. She got careless about her grooming and her fur grew dirty and matted. She stopped repeating the stories of her fudoki and instead just told the fantasy-stories of how she wanted everything to be.

The climb went on and on. She trudged through the forests. The narrow road she followed turned to a lane and then a path and started zigzagging through the rock outcroppings that were everywhere. The mountain was always visible because she was on it.

There were only a few people, just hunters and once a small tired woman in a blue robe lined with feathers, with a bundle on her back. But she saw strange animals everywhere. There were deer almost small enough to catch and white goats with long beards that stared down their noses at her, and once a troop of pink-faced monkeys that surprised her when they tore through the trees overhead.

At last even the path ended, but Small Cat kept climbing through the trees until she saw daylight ahead. Maybe *this* was the top of Fujisan! She hurried forward. The trees ended abruptly. She staggered sideways, hit by a icy wind so strong that it threw her off her feet. There was nothing up here to stop the wind, because trees did not grow higher than this. She staggered to the sheltered side of a rock.

This wasn't the top. It was nowhere near the top. She was in a rounded basin cut into the mountain and she could see all the way to the peak itself. The slope above her grew still steeper and craggier. Above that it became a smooth glacier, and wind pulled snow from the peak in white streamers.

She looked the way she had come. The whole world seemed made of mountains. Except for the plain she had come across, mountains and hills stretched as far as she could see. The villages she had passed were too far away to see, though in places wood smoke rose from the trees. She looked for the capital but it was hundreds of miles away, so far away that there was nothing to see, not even the Rajo Gate.

She had never imagined that all those days and all those miles had added up to something so immense. She could never go back so far and she could never find anything as small as a single hill, a single family of cats.

A flash of color caught her eye, a man huddled behind another rock just a few feet away. She had been so caught up in the mountain that she hadn't even noticed him. Under a padded brown coat, he wore the red-and-yellow robes of a Buddhist monk, with thick straw sandals tied tightly to his feet. His face was red with cold.

How had he gotten up here and why? He was staring up the mountain as though trying to see a path, but why was he doing that? He saw her and his mouth made a circle of surprise. He crawled toward her and ducked into the shelter of her rock. They looked up at the mountain. "I didn't know it would be so far," he said, as though they were in the middle of a conversation.

She looked at him.

"We can try," he added. "I think we'll die but sometimes pilgrimages are worth it."

They sat there for a while longer, as the sun grew lower and the wind grew colder. "But we don't have to," he said. "We can go back down and see what happens next."

They started off the mountain together.

Chapter 10
The Monk

Small Cat and the monk stayed together for a long time. In many ways they were alike, both journeying without a goal, free to travel as fast or as slow as they liked. Small Cat continued north because she had started on the Tokaido, and she might as well see what lay at the end of it. The monk went north because he could beg for rice and talk about the Buddha anywhere, and he liked adventures.

It was winter now, and a cold, snowy one. It seemed as though the sun barely rose before it set behind the mountains. The rivers they crossed were sluggish, and the lakes were covered with ice as smooth as the floorboards in a house. It seemed to snow every few days, sometimes in clumps heavy enough to splat when they landed, sometimes with tiny flakes so light they tickled her whiskers. Small Cat didn't like snow. It looked like feathers, but it just turned into water when it fell on her.

Small Cat liked traveling with the monk. When she had trouble wading through the snow, he let her hop onto the big straw basket he carried on his back. When he begged for rice, he shared whatever he got with her. She learned to eat bits of food from his fingers and would stick her head into his bowl if he set it down. One day she brought him a bird she had caught as a gift. He didn't eat the bird, just looked sad and prayed for its fate, so after that she killed and ate her meals out of his sight.

The monk told stories as they walked. She lay comfortably on the basket and watched the road unroll slowly under his feet as she listened to stories about the Buddha's life and his search for wisdom and enlightenment. She didn't understand what enlightenment was exactly, but it seemed very important, for the monk said he also was looking for it. Sometimes on nights where they didn't find anywhere to stay and had to shelter under the heavy branches of a pine tree, he told stories about himself as well, from when he was a child.

And then the Tokaido ended.

It was a day that Small Cat could tell was about to finish in a storm. The first flakes of snow whirled down from low dark clouds that promised more to come. Small Cat huddled atop the basket on the monk's back, her face pressed into the space between her front paws. She didn't look up until the monk said, "There! We can sleep warm tonight."

There was a village at the bottom of the hill they were descending. The Tokaido led through a double handful of buildings scattered along the shore of a storm-tossed lake, but it ended at the water's edge. The opposite shore—if there was one!—was hidden by snow and the gathering dusk. Now what? She mewed.

"Worried, little one?" the monk said over his shoulder. "You'll get there! Just be patient."

One big house rented rooms as though it were an inn. When the monk called outside its door, a small woman with short black hair emerged and bowed many times. "Come in, come in! Get out of the weather." The monk took off his straw sandals and put down his basket with a sigh of relief. Small Cat leapt down and stretched.

The innkeeper screeched and snatched up a hoe to jab at Small Cat, who leapt behind the basket.

"Wait!" The monk put his hands out. "She's traveling with me."

The innkeeper lowered the hoe a bit. "Well, she's small at least. What is she then?"

The monk looked at Small Cat. "I'm not sure. She was on a pilgrimage when I found her on Fujisan."

"Hmm," the woman said, but she put down the hoe. "Well, if she's with you..."

The wind drove through every crack and gap in the house, so that everyone gathered around a big brazier set into the floor of the centermost room, surrounded by screens and shutters to keep out the cold. Besides the monk and Small Cat and the members of the household, there were two farmers—a young husband and wife—on their way north.

"Well, you're here for a while," the innkeeper said as she poured hot broth for everyone. "The ferry won't run for a day or two, until the storm's over."

Small Cat stretched out so close to the hot coals that her whiskers sizzled, but she was the only one who was warm enough. Everyone else huddled inside the screens. They drank tea, wrapping their hands around their cups to warm their fingers; and they ate rice and barley and dried fish cooked in pots that hung over the brazier

She hunted for her own meals. The mice had gnawed a secret hole into a barrel of rice flour, so there were a lot of them. Whenever she killed one she brought it back to the brazier's warmth where she could listen to the people.

There was not much for them to do but talk and sing, so they talked and sang a lot. They shared fairy tales and ghost stories. They told funny stories about themselves or the people they knew. People had their own fudoki, Small Cat realized, though there seemed to be no order to the stories and she didn't see yet how they made a place home. They sang love songs and songs about foolish adventurers. Songs were stories, as well.

At first the servants in the house kicked at Small Cat whenever she was close, but the monk stopped them.

"But she's a demon!" the young wife said.

"If she is," the monk said, "she means no harm. She has her own destiny. She deserves to be left in peace to fulfill it."

"What destiny is that?" the innkeeper asked.

"Do you know *your* destiny?" the monk asked. She shook her head and slowly all the others shook theirs as well. The monk said, "Well, then. Why should she know hers?"

The young husband watched her eat her third mouse in as many hours. "Maybe catching mice is her destiny. Does she always do that? Catch mice?"

"Anything small," the monk said, "but mice are her favorite."

"That would be a useful animal for a farmer," the husband said. "Would you sell her?"

The monk frowned. "No one owns her. It's her choice where she goes."

The wife scratched at the floor, trying to coax Small Cat into playing. "Maybe she would come with us! She's so pretty." Small Cat batted at her fingers for a while before she curled up beside the brazier again. But the husband looked at Small Cat thoughtfully.

Chapter 11
The Abduction

It was two days before the snowstorm stopped, and another day before the weather cleared enough for them to leave. Small Cat hopped onto the monk's straw basket and they left the inn, blinking in the daylight after so many days lit only by dim lamps and the brazier.

Sparkling new snow hid everything and made it strange and beautiful. Waves rippled the lake, though the frothing whitecaps whipped up by the storm were gone. The Tokaido, now no more than a broad flat place in the snow, ended at a dock on the lake. A big man wearing a brown padded jacket and leggings made of fur took boxes from a boat tied up there. Two other men carried them into a covered shelter close by.

The Tokaido only went south from here, back the way she had come. A smaller road, still buried under the snow, followed the shoreline to the east and west but she couldn't see where the lake ended. The road might go on forever and *never* turn north! Small Cat mewed anxiously.

The monk turned his head a little. "Still eager to travel?" He pointed to the opposite shore. "They tell me the road starts again on the other side. The boat's how we can get there."

Small Cat growled.

The farmers tramped down to the boat with their packs and four shaggy goats that were tugging and bleating and cursing as goats do. The boatman accepted their fare, counted out in old-fashioned coins. He offered to take the monk for free. He frowned at Small Cat and said, "That thing too, whatever it is."

The boat was the most horrible thing that had ever happened to Small Cat, worse than the earthquake, worse than the fire. It heaved and rocked, tipping this way and that. She crouched on top of a bundle with her claws sunk deep, drooling with nausea and meowing with panic. Equally unhappy, the goats jostled against one another.

She would run if she could, but there was nowhere to go. They were surrounded by water in every direction and too far from the shore to swim. The monk offered to hold her but she hissed and tried to scratch him. She kept her eyes fixed on the hills to the north.

The moment the boat bumped against the dock, she streaked ashore and crawled as far into a little roadside shrine as she could get.

"Sir!" A boy stood by the dock, hopping from foot to foot. He bobbed a bow at the monk. "My mother isn't well. I saw you coming and was so happy! Could you please come see her and pray for her?" The monk bowed in return and the boy ran down the lane.

The monk knelt beside Small Cat's hiding place. "Do you want to come with me?" he asked. She stayed where she was, trembling. He looked a little sad. "All right, then."

"Oh sir, please hurry!" the boy shouted from down the lane.

The monk stood. "Be clever and brave, little one. And careful!" And he trotted after the boy.

From her hiding place, Small Cat watched the husband and the boatman wrestle the goats to shore. The wife walked to the roadside shrine and squatted in front of it, peering in.

"I saw you hide," she said. "Were you frightened on the boat? I was. I have rice balls with meat. Would you like one?" She bowed to the kami of the shrine and pulled a packet from her bundle. She laid a bit of food in front of the shrine and bowed again. "There. Now some for you."

Small Cat inched forward. She felt better now and it did smell nice.

"What did you find?" The farmer crouched behind his wife.

"The little demon," she said. "See?"

"Lost the monk, did you? Hmm." The farmer looked up and down the lane before he pulled an empty sack from his bundle. He bowed to the kami, reached in, and grabbed Small Cat by the scruff of her neck.

Nothing like this had ever happened to her! She yowled and scratched but the farmer kept his grip and managed to stuff her into the sack. He lifted it to his shoulder and started walking.

She swung and bumped for a long time.

———

Chapter 12
The Farmhouse

Small Cat gave up fighting after a while, for she was squeezed too tightly in the sack to do anything beyond make herself even more uncomfortable. It was cold in the sack. Light filtered in through the coarse weave, but she could see nothing. She could smell nothing but onions and goats. She meowed until she was hoarse.

Night fell before the jostling ended and she was carried indoors. Someone laid the sack on a flat surface and opened it. It was the farmer. Small Cat clawed him hard, as she emerged. She was in a small room with a brazier. With a quick glance she saw a hiding place and she stuffed herself into a corner where the roof and wall met.

The young husband and wife and two alarmed farmhands stood looking up at her, all wide eyes and opened mouths.

The husband sucked at the scratch marks on his hand. "She's not dangerous," he said, a little doubtfully. "I think she is a demon for mice, not for us. Well, except for this."

Small Cat stayed in her high place for two days. The wife put scraps of chicken skin and water on top of a huge trunk, but the people mostly ignored her. Though they didn't know it, this was the perfect way to treat a frightened cat in an unfamiliar place. Small Cat watched the activity of the farmhouse at first with suspicion and then with growing curiosity. At night, after everyone slept, she saw the mice sneak from their holes and her mouth watered.

By the third night her thirst overcame her nervousness. She slipped down to drink. She heard mice in another room and quickly caught two. She had just caught her third when she heard the husband rise.

"Demon?" he said softly. He came into the room. She backed into a corner with her mouse in her mouth. "There you are. I'm glad you caught your dinner." He chuckled. "We have plenty more just like that. I hope you stay."

Small Cat did stay though it was not home. She had never expected to travel with the monk forever but she missed him anyway: sharing the food in his bowl, sleeping on his basket as they hiked along. She missed his warm hand when he stroked her.

Still, this was a good place to be, with many mice to eat and only a small yellow dog to fight her for them. No one threw things or cursed her. The people still thought she was a demon but she was *their* demon now, as important a member of the household as the farmhands or the dog. And the farmhouse was large enough that she could get away from everyone when she wished.

In any case she didn't know how to get back to the road. The path had vanished with the snowfall, so she had nowhere to go but the wintry fields and the forest.

Though she wouldn't let the farmer touch her, she liked to follow him and watch as he tended the ox and goats or went to kill a goose for dinner. The husband talked to her just as the monk had, as though she understood him. Instead of the Buddha's life, he told her what he was doing when he repaired harness or set tines in a new rake, or he talked about his brothers who lived not so very far away.

Small Cat liked the wife better than the husband. *She* wasn't the one who had thrown Small Cat into a bag. She gave Small Cat bits of whatever she cooked. Sometimes, when she had a moment, she tossed a goose feather or a small knotted rag for her, but it was a working household and there were not many moments like that.

Busy as the wife's hands might be, her mind and her voice were free. She talked about the baby she was hoping to have and her plans for the gardens as soon as the soil softened with springtime. When she didn't talk, she sang in a voice as soft and pretty as a dove's. One of her favorite songs was about Fujisan. This puzzled Small Cat. Why would anyone tell stories of a place so far away? With a shock, she realized her stories were about a place even more distant.

Small Cat started reciting her fudoki again, putting the stories back in their proper order: The Cat Who Ate Dirt, The Earless Cat, The Cat Under The Pavement. Even if there were no other cats to share it with, *she* was still here. For the first time, she realized that The Cat From The North might not have come from very far north at all. There hadn't been any monks or boats or giant mountains in The Cat From The North's story, just goats and dogs. The more she thought about it, the more it seemed likely that she'd spent all this time looking for something she left behind before she even left the capital.

The monk had told her that courage and persistence would bring her what she wanted, but was this it? The farm was a good place to be: safe, full of food. But North went on so much farther than The Cat From The North had imagined. If Small Cat could not return to the capital, she might as well find out where North really ended.

A few days later, a man hiked up the snow-covered path. It was one of the husband's brothers come with news about their mother. Small Cat waited until everyone was inside and then trotted briskly down the way he had come.

Chapter 13
The Wolves

It was much less pleasant to travel alone in the coldest part of winter. The monk would have carried her or kicked the snow away so that she could walk more easily; they would have shared food; he would have found warm places to stay and talked the people they met into not hurting her. He would have spoken to her and tickled her ears when she wished.

Without him, the snow came to her shoulders. She had to stay on the road itself, which was slippery with packed ice and had deep slushy ruts that froze into slick flat ponds. Small Cat learned how to hop without being noticed onto the huge bundles of hay that oxen sometimes carried on their backs.

She found somewhere to sleep each night by following the smell of smoke. She had to be careful, but even the simplest huts had corners and cubbyholes where a small dark cat could sleep in peace—provided no dogs smelled her and sounded the alarm. But there were fewer leftover scraps of food to find. There was no time or energy to play.

The mice had their own paths under the snow. On still days she could hear them creeping through their tunnels, too deep for her to catch, and she had to wait until she came to shallower places under the trees. At least she could find and eat the dormice that hibernated in tight little balls just under the surface of the snow, and the frozen sparrows that dropped from the bushes on the coldest nights.

One night it was very cold. She was looking for somewhere to stay but she hadn't smelled smoke or heard anything promising.

There was a sudden rush from the snow-heaped bushes beside the road. She tore across the snow and scrambled high into a tree before turning to see what had chased her. It was bigger than the biggest dog she had ever seen, with a thick ruff and flat gold eyes. A wolf! It was a hard winter for wolves, and they were coming down from the mountains and eating whatever they could find.

This wolf glared and then sat on its haunches and tipped its head to one side, looking confused. It gave a puzzled yip. Soon a second wolf appeared from the darkening forest. It was much larger and she knew that the first one was young.

They looked thin and hungry. The two wolves touched noses for a moment and the older one called up, "Come down, little one. We wish to find out what sort of animal you are."

She shivered. It was bitterly cold this high in the tree but she couldn't trust them. She looked around for a way to escape. The tree was isolated. There was nowhere to jump to.

"We can wait," the older wolf said, and settled onto its haunches.

She huddled against the tree's trunk. The wind shook ice crystals from the branches overhead. If the wolves waited long enough she would freeze to death, or her paws would go numb and she would fall. The sun dipped below the mountains and it grew much colder.

The icy air hurt her throat so she pressed her face against her leg to breathe through her fur. It reminded her of the fire so long ago back in the capital, the fire that had destroyed her garden and her family. Had she come so far just to freeze to death and be eaten by wolves?

The stars were bright in the clear night. The younger wolf was curled up tight in a furry ball, but the old wolf sat looking up, its eyes shining in the darkness. It said, "Come down and be eaten."

Her fur rose on her neck. She dug her claws deep into the branch. She couldn't feel her paws anymore.

The wolf growled softly, "I have a pack, a family. This one is my son and he is hungry. Let me feed him. You have no one."

The wolf was right. She had no one.

It sensed her grief and said, "I understand. Come down. We will make it quick."

Small Cat shook her head. She would not give up, even if she did die like this. If they were going to eat her, at least there was no reason to make it easy for them. She clung as hard as she could.

Chapter 14
The Bear Hunter

In the distance, a dog barked and a second dog joined the first, their sharp voices carrying through the still air. Small Cat was shivering so hard that her teeth chattered and she couldn't tell how far they were, down the valley or even miles away.

The wolves pricked their ears. The barking stopped for a moment and then began again, each bark closer. Two dogs hurtled into sight at the bottom of the valley. The wolves vanished into the forest without a sound.

The dogs were still barking as they raced up to the tree. They were a big male and a smaller female, with thick golden fur that covered them from their toes to the tips of their round ears and their high, curling tails. The female ran a few steps after the wolves and returned to sniff the tree. "What's that smell?"

They peered up at her. She tried to climb higher and loose bark fell into their surprised faces.

"I better get the man," the female said and ran off, again barking.

The male sat just where the big wolf had sat. "What are you, up there?"

Small Cat ignored him. She didn't feel so cold now, just very drowsy. She didn't even notice when she fell from the tree.

Small Cat woke up slowly. She was warm, curled up on something dark and furry, and for a moment she imagined she was home, dozing with her aunts and cousins in the garden, light filtering through the trees to heat her whiskers.

She heard a heavy sigh, a dog's sigh. This wasn't the garden! She was somewhere indoors and everything smelled of fur. She leapt to her feet.

She stood on a thick pile of bear hides in a small hut, dark except for the tiny flames in a brazier set into the floor. The two dogs from the forest slept in a pile beside it.

"You're awake then," a man said. She hadn't seen him, for he had wrapped himself in a bear skin. Well, he hadn't tried to harm her. Wary but reassured, she drank from a bowl on the floor, and cleaned her paws and face. He still watched her.

"What are you? Not a dog or a fox. A *tanuki*?" Tanuki were little red and white striped animals that could climb trees and ate almost anything. The hunter lived a long way from where cats lived, so how would he know better? She mewed. "Out there is no place for a whatever-you-are, at least until spring," he added. "You're welcome to stay until then, if the dogs let you."

The dogs didn't seem to mind though she kept out of reach at first. She found plenty to do. An entire village of mice lived in the hut, helping themselves to the hunter's rice and having babies as fast as they could. Small Cat caught so many at first that she didn't bother eating them all and just left them on the floor for the dogs to crunch up when they came in from outdoors. Within a very few days the man and the dogs accepted her as part of the household, even though the dogs still pestered her to find out what she was.

The man and the dogs were gone a lot. They hunted bears in the forest, dragging them from their caves while they were sluggish from hibernation. The man skinned them and planned to sell their hides when summer came. If they were gone for a day or two the hut got cold for there was no one to keep the charcoal fire burning, but Small Cat didn't mind. She grew fat on all the mice and her fur got thick and glossy.

The hut stood in a meadow with trees and mountains on either side. A narrow stream cut through the meadow. It moved too fast to freeze, and the only crossing was a single fallen log that shook from the strength of the water rushing beneath it. The forest crowded close to the stream on the other side.

There was plenty to do, trees to climb and birds to catch. Small Cat watched for wolves but daylight wasn't their time and she was careful to be inside before dusk. She never saw another human.

Each day the sun got brighter and stayed up longer. It wasn't spring yet but Small Cat could smell it. The snow got heavy and wet, and she heard it slide from the trees in the forest with thumps and crashes. The stream swelled with snowmelt.

The two dogs ran off for a few days. When they came back the female was pregnant. At first she acted restless and cranky and Small Cat kept away, but once her belly started to get round with puppies she calmed down. The hunter started leaving her behind. He would tie her with a rope to the hut; she barked and paced but she didn't try to pull free, and after a while she didn't bother to do even that.

Small Cat was used to the way people told stories. The bear hunter had his stories as well, about hunts with the dogs and legends he had learned from the old man who had taught him to hunt so long ago. Everyone had a fudoki. Everyone had their own stories and the stories of their families and ancestors. There were adventures and love stories, or tricks and jokes and funny things that had happened, or disasters.

Everyone wanted to tell their stories and to know where they fit in their own fudoki. She was not that different.

Chapter 15
The Bear

The last bear hunt of the season began on a morning that felt like the first day of spring, with a little breeze full of the smell of growing things. The snow had a dirty crust and it had melted away in places to leave mud and the first tiny green shoots pushing through the dead grass of the year before.

Fat with her puppies, the female lay on a straw mat the bear hunter had laid over the mud for her. The male paced eagerly, his ears pricked and tail high. The man sat on the hut's stone stoop. He was sharpening the head of a long spear. Small Cat watched him from the doorway.

The man said, "Well, you've been lucky for us this year. Just one more good hunt, all right?" He looked along the spear's sharp edge. "The bears are waking up and we don't want any angry mothers worried about their cubs, we don't. We have enough of our own to think about!" He patted the female dog, who woke up and heaved herself to her feet.

He stood. "Ready, boy?" The male barked happily. The bear hunter shouldered a small pack and picked up his throwing and stabbing spears. "Stay out of trouble, girls," he said.

He and the male filed across the log. The female pulled at her rope but once they vanished into the forest she slumped to the ground again with a heavy sigh. They would not be back until evening or even the next day.

Small Cat had already eaten a mouse and a vole for her breakfast. She prowled the edges of the meadow more for amusement than because she was hungry. She ended up at a large black rock right next to the log across the stream. It was warmed and dried by the sun. She could look down from there into the creamy, racing water. It was a perfect place to spend the middle of the day. She settled down comfortably. The sun on her back was almost hot.

A sudden sense of danger made her muscles tense up. She lifted her head but she saw nothing. The female sensed it too, for she also was sitting up, intently staring toward the forest beyond the stream.

The bear hunter burst from the woods, running as fast as he could. He had lost his spear. The male dog wasn't with him. Right behind him a giant black shape crashed from the forest—a black bear, bigger than he was! Small Cat could hear them splashing across the mud, and the female behind her barking hysterically.

It happened too fast to be afraid. The hunter bolted across the shaking log just as the bear ran onto the far end. The man slipped as he passed Small Cat and he fell to one side. Small Cat had been too surprised to move, but when he slipped she leapt out of his way sideways—onto the log!

The bear was a heavy black shape hurtling toward her. She could see the little white triangle of fur on its chest. A paw slammed into the log so close that she felt fur touch her whickers. With nowhere else to go, she jumped straight up and for an instant, she stared right into the bear's red-rimmed eyes.

The bear reared up at Small Cat's leap. It lost its balance, fell into the swollen stream and was carried away, roaring and thrashing. The bear had been swept nearly out of sight before it managed to pull itself from the water on the opposite bank. Droplets scattered as it shook itself. It swung its head from side to side looking for them, and finally shambled back into the trees far downstream. A moment later, the male dog limped from the trees and across the fallen log to them.

The male whined but sat quiet as the bear hunter cleaned out his foot. He had stepped on a stick and torn the pad. When the hunter was done, he leaned against the wall, the dogs and Small Cat tucked close.

They had found a bear sooner than expected, he told them: a female with her cub just a short walk into the forest. She saw them and attacked immediately. He used his throwing spears but they didn't stick, and she broke his stabbing spear with a single blow of her big paw. The male dog slammed into her from the side, giving him time to run for the hut, where there was a rack of spears on the wall beside the door.

"I knew I wouldn't make it," the hunter said. His hand still shook a little when he finally took off his pack. "But at least I wasn't going to die without trying."

Small Cat meowed.

"Exactly," the hunter said. "You don't give up, ever."

Chapter 16
The North

Small Cat left not so many days after the bear attacked. She pushed under the door flap while the hunter and the dogs dozed beside the fire. She stretched all the way from her toes to the tip of her tail, and she stood tall on the step, looking around.

It was just at sunset, the bright sky dimming to the west. To the east she saw the first bit of the full moon crawling from the trees. Even at dusk the forest looked different now, the bare branches softened with buds. The air smelled fresh with spring growth.

She paced the clearing looking for a sign of the way to the road. She hadn't been conscious when the bear hunter had brought her. In any case it was a long time ago.

Someone snuffled behind her. The female stood blinking outside the hut. "Where are you?" she asked. "Are you gone already?"

Small Cat walked to her.

"I knew you would leave," the dog said. "This is my home but you're like the puppies will be when they're born. We're good hunters so the man will be able to trade the puppies for fabric or even spear heads." She sounded proud. "They will go other places and have their own lives. You're like that too. But you were very interesting to know, whatever you are."

Small Cat came close enough to touch noses with her.

"If you're looking for the road," the female said, "it's on the other side, over the stream." She went back inside and the door flap dropped behind her.

Small Cat sharpened her claws and trotted across the log, back toward the road.

At first, traveling got harder as spring grew warmer. Helped along by the bright sun and the spring rains, the snow in the mountains melted quickly. The rivers were high and icy cold with snowmelt. No cat, however tough she was, could hope to wade or swim them, and sometimes there was no bridge. Whenever she couldn't cross, Small Cat waited a day or two until the water went down or someone passed.

People seemed to like seeing her. This surprised her. Maybe it was different here. They couldn't know about cats but maybe demons did not frighten them so far north, especially small ones. She wasn't afraid of the people either, so she sniffed their fingers and ate their offerings, and rode in their wagons whenever she had the chance.

The road wandered down through the mountains and hills, into little towns and past farmhouses. Everything seemed full of new life. The trees were loud with baby birds and squirrels. The wind rustled through the new leaves. Yellow and pink flowers spangled the meadows and smelled so sweet and strong that she sometimes stepped right over a mouse and didn't notice until it jumped away. The fields were full of new plants, and the pastures and farmyards were full of babies: goats and sheep, horses, oxen and geese and chickens. Goslings, it turned out, tasted delicious.

Journeying was a pleasure now but she knew she was almost ready to stop. She could have made a home anywhere, she realized—strange cats or no cats, farmer or hunter, beside a shrine or behind an inn. It wasn't about the stories or the garden. It was about her.

But she wasn't quite ready. She had wanted to find The Cat From The North's home, and when that didn't happen she had gone on, curious to find how far the road went. And she didn't know yet.

Then there was a day when it was beautiful and bright, the first really warm day. She came around a curve in the road and looked down into a broad valley with a river flowing to a distant bay that glittered in the sun. It was the ocean, and Small Cat knew she had come to the end of her travels. This was North.

Chapter 17
Home

There was a village where the river and the ocean met. The path that led there passed through fields green with new shoots and full of people planting things or digging with hoes. The path became a lane and others joined it.

Small Cat trotted between the double row of houses and shops. Every window and door and screen was open to let the winter out and the spring in. Bedding and robes fluttered as they aired. Young grass and white flowers glowed in the sun, and the three trees in the center of the village were bright with new leaves.

Everyone seemed to be outside doing something. A group of women sang a love song as they pounded rice in a wood mortar to make flour. A man with no hair wove sturdy sandals of straw to wear in the fields; he told a story about catching a wolf cub by falling on it when he had been a child. The girl sitting on the ground beside him listened as she finished a straw cape for her wooden doll and then ran off calling for her mother. The geese who had been squabbling over a weed scrambled out of her way.

A man on a ladder tied new clumps of thatch onto a roof where the winter had worn through. Below him, a woman laid a bearskin across a rack. She tied her sleeves back to bare her arms, and hit the skin with a stick. Clouds of dirt puffed out with each blow. In between blows, she shouted instructions up to the man on the roof, and Small Cat recognized that this was a story, too: the story of what the man should do next.

A small Buddhist temple peeked from a grove of trees, with stone dogs guarding a gate into the grounds. A boy swept the ground in front of a Shinto shrine there. Small Cat smelled dried fish and mushrooms that had been left as offerings. It might be worth her while later to find out more.

Two young dogs wrestled in the dirt by a pen until they noticed her. They jumped to their feet and raced about, barking, "Cat! Cat!" She wasn't afraid of dogs anymore, not happy dogs like these, with their heads high and their ears pricked; but still, she hopped onto a railing where they couldn't accidentally bowl her over. They milled about wagging their tails.

A woman stretching fabric on a frame started to say something to the dogs. When she saw Small Cat, her mouth made an O of surprise. "A cat!" She whirled and ran toward the temple. "A cat! Look, come see!"

The woman knew what a cat was, and so had the dogs! Ignoring the dogs, ignoring all the people who were suddenly looking at her, Small Cat pelted after the woman.

The woman burst through a circle of children gathered around a seated man. He was dressed in red and yellow, his shaved head shiny in the sun: a monk but not her monk, she knew right away; this one was rounder though his face was still open and kind. He stood up as the woman pointed at Small Cat. "Look, look! Another cat!"

The monk and the children all started talking at once. And in the middle of all the noise, Small Cat heard a meow.

Another cat?

A ginger-and-white striped tomcat stood on a stack of boxes nearby, looking down at her. His golden eyes were bright and huge with excitement, and his whiskers vibrated. He jumped down and ran to her.

"Who are you?" he said. His tail waved. "Where did you come from?"

When she had decided to make this her home, she hadn't thought she might be sharing it. He wasn't much bigger than she was or any older, and right now he was more like a kitten than anything, hopping from paw to paw. She took a step toward him.

"I am so glad to see another cat!" he said. He purred so hard that his breath wheezed in his throat. "The monk brought me here last year to

197

catch mice, all the way from the capital in a basket! It was very exciting. There are so many things to do here! I have a really nice secret place to sleep but I'll show it to you." He touched her nose with his own.

"There's no fudoki," he said, a little defensively. "There's just me."

"And me now," said The Cat Who Walked A Thousand Miles, and she rubbed her cheek against his. "And I have such a tale to tell!"

Spar

In the tiny lifeboat, she and the alien fuck endlessly, relentlessly.

They each have Ins and Outs. Her Ins are the usual, eyes ears nostrils mouth cunt ass. Her Outs are also the common ones: fingers and hands and feet and tongue. Arms. Legs. Things that can be thrust into other things.

The alien is not humanoid. It is not bipedal. It has cilia. It has no bones, or perhaps it does and she cannot feel them. Its muscles, or what might be muscles, are rings and not strands. Its skin is the color of dusk and covered with a clear thin slime that tastes of snot. It makes no sounds. She thinks it smells like wet leaves in winter, but after a time she cannot remember that smell, or leaves, or winter.

Its Ins and Outs change. There are dark slashes and permanent knobs that sometimes distend, but it is always growing new Outs, hollowing new Ins. It cleaves easily in both senses.

It penetrates her a thousand ways. She penetrates it, as well.

The lifeboat is not for humans. The air is too warm, the light too dim. It is too small. There are no screens, no books, no warning labels, no voices, no bed or chair or table or control board or toilet or telltale lights or clocks. The ship's hum is steady. Nothing changes.

There is no room. They cannot help but touch. They breathe each other's breath—if it breathes; she cannot tell. There is always an Out in an In, something wrapped around another thing, flesh coiling and uncoiling inside, outside. Making spaces. Making space.

She is always wet. She cannot tell whether this is the slime from its skin, the oil and sweat from hers, her exhaled breath, the lifeboat's air. Or come.

Her body seeps. When she can, she pulls her mind away. But there is nothing else, and when her mind is disengaged she thinks too much. Which is: at all. Fucking the alien is less horrible.

She does not remember the first time. It is safest to think it forced her.

The wreck was random: a mid-space collision between their ship and the alien's, simultaneously a statistical impossibility and a fact. She and Gary just had time to start the emergency beacon and claw into their suits before their ship was cut in half. Their lifeboat spun out of reach. Her magnetic boots clung to part of the wreck. His did not. The two of them fell apart.

A piece of debris slashed through the leg of Gary's suit to the bone, through the bone. She screamed. He did not. Blood and fat and muscle swelled from his suit into vacuum. Out.

The alien's vessel also broke into pieces, its lifeboat kicking free and the waldos reaching out, pulling her through the airlock. In.

Why did it save her? The mariner's code? She does not think it knows she is alive. If it did it would try to establish communication. It is quite possible that she is not a rescued castaway. She is salvage, or flotsam.

She sucks her nourishment from one of the two hard intrusions into the featureless lifeboat, a rigid tube. She uses the other, a second tube, for whatever comes from her, her shit and piss and vomit. Not her come, which slicks her thighs to her knees.

She gags a lot. It has no sense of the depth of her throat. Ins and Outs.

There is a time when she screams so hard that her throat bleeds.

———

She tries to teach it words. "Breast," she says. "Finger. Cunt." Her vocabulary options are limited here.

"Listen to me," she says. "Listen. To. Me." Does it even have ears?

The fucking never gets better or worse. It learns no lessons about pleasing her. She does not learn anything about pleasing it either: would not if she could. And why? How do you please grass and why should you? She suddenly remembers grass, the bright smell of it and its perfect green, its cool clean soft feel beneath her bare hands.

She finds herself aroused by the thought of grass against her hands, because it is the only thing that she has thought of for a long time that is not the alien or Gary or the Ins and Outs. But perhaps its soft blades against her fingers would feel like the alien's cilia. Her ability to compare anything with anything else is slipping from her, because there is nothing to compare.

She feels it inside everywhere, tendrils moving in her nostrils, thrusting against her eardrums, coiled beside the corners of her eyes. And she sheathes herself in it.

When an Out crawls inside her and touches her in certain places, she tips her head back and moans and pretends it is more than accident. It is Gary, he loves me, it loves me, it is a He. It is not.

Communication is key, she thinks.

She cannot communicate, but she tries to make sense of its actions.

What is she to it? Is she a sex toy, a houseplant? A shipwrecked Norwegian sharing a spar with a monolingual Portuguese? A companion? A habit, like nail biting or compulsive masturbation? Perhaps the sex is communication and she just doesn't understand the language yet.

Or perhaps there is no It. It is not that they cannot communicate, that she is incapable; it is that the alien has no consciousness to communicate with. It is a sex toy, a houseplant, a habit.

———

On the starship with the name she cannot recall, Gary would read aloud to her. Science fiction, Melville, poetry. Her mind cannot access the plots, the words. All she can remember is a few lines from a sonnet, "Let me not to the marriage of true minds admit impediments"—something something something—"an ever-fixèd mark that looks on tempests and is never shaken; it is the star to every wand'ring bark...."

She recites the words, an anodyne that numbs her for a time until they lose their meaning. She has worn them treadless, and they no longer gain any traction in her mind. Eventually she cannot even remember the sounds of them.

If she ever remembers another line, she promises herself she will not wear it out. She will hoard it. She may have promised this before, and forgotten.

She cannot remember Gary's voice. Fuck Gary, anyway. He is dead and she is here with an alien pressed against her cervix.

It is covered with slime. She thinks that, as with toads, the slime may be a mild psychotropic drug. How would she know if she were hallucinating? In this world, what would that look like? Like sunflowers on a desk, like Gary leaning across a picnic basket to place fresh bread in her mouth. The bread is the first thing she has tasted that feels clean in her mouth, and it's not even real.

Gary feeding her bread and laughing. After a time, the taste of bread becomes "the taste of bread" and then the words become mere sounds and stop meaning anything.

On the off-chance that this will change things, she drives her tongue though its cilia, pulls them into her mouth and sucks them clean. She has no idea whether it makes a difference. She has lived forever in the endless reeking fucking now.

Was there someone else on the alien's ship? Was there a Gary, lost now to space? Is it grieving? Does it fuck her to forget, or because it has forgotten? Or to punish itself for surviving? Or the other, for not?

Or is this her?

———

When she does not have enough Ins for its Outs, it makes new ones. She bleeds for a time and then heals. She pretends that this is a rape. Rape at least she could understand. Rape is an interaction. It requires intention. It would imply that it hates or fears or wants. Rape would mean she is more than a wine glass it fills.

This goes both ways. She forces it. Her hands are blades that tear new Ins. Her anger pounds at it until she feels its depths grow soft under her fist, as though bones or muscle or cartilage have disassembled and turned to something else.

And when she forces her hands into the alien? If intent counts, then what she does, at least, is a rape—or would be if the alien felt anything, responded in any fashion. Mostly it's like punching a wall.

She puts her fingers in herself, because she at least knows what her intentions are.

Sometimes she watches it fuck her, the strange coiling of its Outs like a shockwave thrusting into her body, and this excites her and horrifies her; but at least it is not Gary. Gary, who left her here with this, who left her here, who left.

One time she feels something break loose inside the alien, but it is immediately drawn out of reach. When she reaches farther in to grasp the broken piece, a sphincter snaps shut on her wrist. Her arm is forced out. There is a bruise like a bracelet around her wrist for what might be a week or two.

She cannot stop touching the bruise. The alien has had the ability to stop her fist inside it, at any time. Which means it has made a choice not to stop her, even when she batters things inside it until they grow soft.

This is the only time she has ever gotten a reaction she understands. Stimulus: response. She tries many times to get another. She rams her hands into it, kicks it, tries to tear its cilia free with her teeth, claws its skin with her ragged, filthy fingernails. But there is never again the broken thing inside, and never the bracelet.

For a while, she measures time by bruises she gives herself. She slams her shin against the feeding tube, and when the bruise is gone she does it again. She estimates it takes twelve days for a bruise to heal. She stops after a time because she cannot remember how many bruises there have been.

She dreams of rescue, but doesn't know what that looks like. Gary, miraculously alive pulling her free, eyes bright with tears, I love you he says, his lips on her eyelids and his kiss his tongue in her mouth inside her hands inside him. But that's the alien. Gary is dead. He got Out.

Sometimes she thinks that rescue looks like her opening the lifeboat to the deep vacuum, but she cannot figure out the airlock.

Her anger is endless, relentless.

Gary brought her here, and then he went away and left her with this thing that will not speak, or cannot, or does not care enough to, or does not see her as something to talk to.

On their third date, she and Gary went to an empty park: wine, cheese, fresh bread in a basket. Bright sun and cool air, grass and a cloth to lie on. He brought Shakespeare. "You'll love this," he said, and read to her.

She stopped him with a kiss. "Let's talk," she said, "about anything."

"But we are talking," he said.

"No, you're reading," she said. "I'm sorry, I don't really like poetry."

"That's because you've never had it read to you," he said.

She stopped him at last by taking the book from his hands and pushing him back, her palms in the grass; and he entered her. Later, he read to her anyway.

If it had just been that.

They were not even his words and now they mean nothing, are not even sounds in her mind. And now there is this thing that cannot hear her or does not choose to listen, until she gives up trying to reach it and only reaches into it, and bludgeons it and herself, seeking a reaction, any reaction.

"I fucking hate you," she says. "I hate fucking you."

The lifeboat decelerates. Metal clashes on metal. Gaskets seal.

The airlock opens overhead. There is light. Her eyes water helplessly and everything becomes glare and indistinct dark shapes. The air is dry and cold. She recoils.

The alien does not react to the light, the hard air. It remains inside her and around her. They are wrapped. They penetrate one another a thousand ways. She is warm here, or at any rate not cold: half-lost in its flesh, wet from her Ins, its Outs. In here it is not too bright.

A dark something stands outlined in the portal. It is bipedal. It makes sounds that are words. Is it human? Is she? Does she still have bones, a voice? She has not used them for so long.

The alien is hers; she is its. Nothing changes.

But. She pulls herself free of its tendrils and climbs. Out.

The Man Who Bridged the Mist

Kit came to Nearside with two trunks and an oiled-cloth folio full of plans for the bridge across the mist. His trunks lay tumbled like stones at his feet where the mailcoach guard had dropped them. The folio he held close, away from the drying mud of yesterday's storm.

Nearside was small, especially to a man of the capital where buildings towered seven and eight stories tall, a city so large that even a vigorous walker could not cross in a day. Here hard-packed dirt roads threaded through irregular spaces scattered with structures and fences. Even the inn was plain, two stories of golden limestone and blue slate tiles with (he could smell) some sort of animals living behind it. On the sign overhead, a flat, pale blue fish very like a ray curvetted against a black background.

A brightly dressed woman stood by the inn's door. Her skin and eyes were pale, almost colorless. "Excuse me," Kit said. "Where can I find the ferry to take me across the mist?" He could feel himself being weighed, but amiably: a stranger, small and very dark, in gray—a man from the east.

The woman smiled. "Well, the ferries are both on this side, at the upper dock. But I expect what you really want is someone to oar the ferry, yes? Rasali Ferry came over from Farside last night. She's the one you'll want to talk to. She spends a lot of time at The Deer's Hart. But you wouldn't like The Hart, sir," she added. "It's not nearly as nice as The Fish here. Are you looking for a room?"

"I hope I'll be staying in Farside tonight," Kit said apologetically. He didn't want to seem arrogant. The invisible web of connections he would need for his work started here with this first impression, with all the first impressions of the next few days.

"That's what *you* think," the woman said. "I'm guessing it'll be a day or two—or more—before Rasali goes back. Valo Ferry might, but he doesn't cross so often."

"I could buy out the trip's fares, if that's why she's waiting."

"It's not that," the woman said. "She won't cross the mist 'til she's ready. Until she feels it's right, if you follow me. But you can ask, I suppose."

Kit didn't follow but he nodded anyway. "Where's The Deer's Hart?"

She pointed. "Left, then right, then down by the little boat yard."

"Thank you," Kit said. "May I leave my trunks here until I work things out with her?"

"We always stow for travelers." The woman grinned. "And cater to them too, when they find out there's no way across the mist today."

The Deer's Hart was smaller than The Fish, and livelier. At midday the oak-shaded tables in the beer garden beside the inn were clustered with light-skinned people in brilliant clothes, drinking and tossing comments over the low fence into the boat yard next door where, half lost in steam, a youth and two women bent planks to form the hull of a small flat-bellied boat. When Kit spoke to a man carrying two mugs of something that looked like mud and smelled of yeast, the man gestured at the yard with his chin. "Ferrys are over there. Rasali's the one in red," he said as he walked away.

"The one in red" was tall, her skin as pale as that of the rest of the locals, with a black braid so long that she had looped it around her neck to keep it out of the way. Her shoulders flexed in the sunlight as she and the youth forced a curved plank to take the skeletal hull's shape and clamped it in place. The other woman, slightly shorter, with the ash-blond hair so common here, forced an augur through the plank and into a rib, then hammered a peg into the hole she'd made. After three pegs the boatwrights straightened. The plank held. *Strong,* Kit thought. *I wonder if I can get them for the bridge?*

"Rasali!" a voice bellowed, almost in Kit's ear. "Man here's looking for you." Kit turned in time to see the man with the mugs gesturing, again with his chin. He sighed and walked to the waist-high fence. The boatwrights stopped to drink from blueware bowls before the one in red and the youth came over.

"I'm Rasali Ferry of Farside," the woman said. Her voice was softer and higher than he had expected of a woman as strong as she, with the fluid vowels of the local accent. She nodded to the boy beside her: "Valo Ferry of Farside, my brother's eldest." Valo was more a young man than a boy, lighter-haired than Rasali and slightly taller. They had the same heavy eyebrows and direct amber eyes.

"Kit Meinem of Atyar," Kit said.

Valo asked, "What sort of name is Meinem? It doesn't mean anything."

"In the capital, we take our names differently than you."

"Oh, like Jenner Ellar." Valo nodded. "I guessed you were from the capital—your clothes and your skin."

Rasali said, "What can we do for you, Kit Meinem of Atyar?"

"I need to get to Farside today," Kit said.

Rasali shook her head. "I can't take you. I just got here and it's too soon. Perhaps Valo?"

The youth tipped his head to one side, his expression suddenly abstract. He shook his head. "No, not today, I don't think."

"I can buy out the fares if that helps. It's Jenner Ellar I am here to see."

Valo looked interested but said, "No," to Rasali, and she added, "What's so important that it can't wait a few days?"

Better now than later, Kit thought. "I am replacing Teniant Planner as the lead engineer and architect for construction of the bridge over the mist. We start work again as soon as I've reviewed everything. And had a chance to talk to Jenner." He watched their faces.

Rasali said, "It's been a year since Teniant died. I was starting to think Empire had forgotten all about us and that your deliveries would be here 'til the iron rusted away."

Valo frowned. "Jenner Ellar's not taking over?"

"The new Department of Roads cartel is in my name," Kit said, "but I hope Jenner will remain as my second. You can see why I would like to meet him as soon as is possible, of course. He will—"

Valo burst out, "You're going to take over from Jenner after he's worked so hard on this? And what about us? What about *our* work?" His cheeks were flushed an angry red. *How do they conceal anything with skin like that?* Kit thought.

"Valo," Rasali said, a warning tone in her voice. Flushing darker still, the youth turned and strode away. Rasali snorted but said only: "Boys. He likes Jenner and he has problems with the bridge, anyway."

That was worth addressing. *Later.* "So what will it take to get you to carry me across the mist, Rasali Ferry of Farside? The project will pay anything reasonable."

"I cannot," she said. "Not today, not tomorrow. You'll have to wait."

"Why?" Kit asked, reasonably enough, he thought; but she eyed him for a long moment as though deciding whether to be annoyed.

"Have you gone across mist before?" she said at last.

"Of course," he said.

"But not the river," she said.

"Not the river," he agreed. "It's a quarter-mile across here, yes?"

"Yes." She smiled suddenly, white even teeth and warmth like sunlight in her eyes. "Let's go down and perhaps I can explain things better there." She jumped the fence with a single powerful motion, landing beside him to a chorus of cheers and shouts from the garden's patrons. She slapped hands with one, then gestured to Kit to follow her. She was well liked, clearly. Her opinion would matter.

The boat yard was heavily shaded by low-hanging oaks and chestnuts, and bounded on the east by an open-walled shelter filled with barrels and stacks of lumber. Rasali waved at the third boat maker, who was still putting her tools away. "Tilisk Boatwright of Nearside. My brother's wife," she said to Kit. "She makes skiffs with us but she won't ferry. She's not born to it as Valo and I are."

"Where's your brother?" Kit asked.

"Dead," Rasali said and lengthened her stride.

They walked a few streets over and then climbed a long even ridge perhaps eighty feet high, too regular to be natural. *A levee,* Kit thought, and distracted himself from the steep path by estimating the volume of earth and the labor that had been required to build it. Decades, perhaps, but how long ago? How many miles did it stretch? Which department had overseen it, or had it been the locals? The levee was treeless. The only feature was a slender wood tower hung with flags on the ridge, probably for signaling across the mist to Farside since it appeared too fragile for anything else. They had storms out here, Kit knew; there'd been one the night before. How often was the tower struck by lightning?

Rasali stopped. "There."

Kit had been watching his feet. He looked up and nearly cried out as light lanced his suddenly tearing eyes. He fell back a step and shielded his face. What had blinded him was an immense band of mist reflecting the morning sun.

Kit had never seen the mist river itself, though he bridged mist before this, two simple post-and-beam structures over narrow gorges closer to the capital. From his work in Atyar, he knew what was to be known. It was not water nor anything like. It formed somehow in the deep gorge of the great riverbed before him. It found its way some hundreds of miles north, upstream through a hundred narrowing mist creeks and streams before failing at last in shreds of drying foam that left bare patches of earth where they collected.

The mist stretched to the south as well, a deepening, thickening band that poured out at last from the river's mouth a thousand miles south, to form the mist ocean, which lay on the face of the salt-water ocean. Water had to follow the river's bed to run somewhere beneath or through the mist, but there was no way to prove this.

There was mist nowhere but this river and its streams and sea, but the mist split Empire in half.

After a moment, the pain in Kit's eyes grew less and he opened them again. The river was a quarter-mile across where they stood, a great gash of light between the levees. It seemed nearly featureless, blazing under the sun like a river of cream or of bleached silk, but as his eyes accustomed themselves, he saw the surface was not smooth but heaped and hollowed, and that it shifted slowly, almost indiscernibly, as he watched.

Rasali stepped forward and Kit started. "I'm sorry," he said with a laugh. "How long have I been staring? It's just—I had no idea."

"No one does," Rasali said. Her eyes when he met them were amused.

The east and west levees were nearly identical, each treeless and scrub-covered, with a signal tower. The levee on their side ran down to a narrow bare bank half a dozen yards wide. There was a wooden dock and a boat ramp, a rough switchback leading down to them. Two large boats had been pulled onto the bank. Another, smaller dock was visible a hundred yards downstream, attended by a clutter of boats, sheds and indeterminate piles covered in tarps.

"Let's go down." Rasali led the way, her words coming back to him over her shoulder. "The little ferry is Valo's. *Pearlfinder. The Tranquil Crossing's* mine." Her voice warmed when she said the name. "Eighteen feet long, eight wide. Mostly pine, but a purpleheart keel and pearwood headpiece. You can't see it from here, but the hull's sheathed in blue-dyed fishskin. I can carry three horses or a ton and a half of cartage or fifteen passengers. Or various combinations. I once carried twenty-four hunting dogs and two handlers. Never again."

Channeled by the levees, a steady light breeze eased down from the north. The air had a smell, not unpleasant but a little sour, wild. "How can you manage a boat like this alone? Are you that strong?"

"It's as big as I can handle," she said. "but Valo helps sometimes for really unwieldy loads. You don't paddle through mist. I mostly just coax the *Crossing* to where I want it to go. Anyway, the bigger the boat, the more likely that the Big Ones will notice it—though if you *do* run into a fish, the smaller the boat, the easier it is to swamp. Here we are."

They stood on the bank. The mist streams he had bridged had not prepared him for anything like this. Those were tidy little flows, more like fog collecting in hollows than this. From this angle, the river no longer seemed a smooth flow of creamy whiteness, nor even gently heaped clouds. The mist forced itself into hillocks and hollows, tight slopes perhaps twenty feet high that folded into one another. It had a surface but it was irregular, cracked in places and translucent in others. The boundary didn't seem as clearly defined as that between water and air.

"How can you move on this?" Kit said, fascinated. "Or even float?" The hillock immediately before them was flattening as he watched. Beyond it something like a vale stretched out for a few dozen yards before turning and becoming lost to his eyes.

"Well, I can't, not today," Rasali said. She sat on the gunwale of her boat, one leg swinging, watching him. "I can't push the *Crossing* up those slopes or find a safe path unless I feel it. If I went today, I know—I *know*—" she tapped her belly—"that I would find myself stranded on a pinnacle or lost in a hole. *That's* why I can't take you today, Kit Meinem of Atyar."

When Kit was a child, he had not been good with other people. He was small and easy to tease or ignore, and then he was sick for much of his seventh year and had to leave his crèche before the usual time, to convalesce in his mother's house. None of the children of the crèche came to visit him but he didn't mind that. He had books and puzzles, and whole quires of blank paper that his mother didn't mind him defacing.

The clock in the room in which he slept didn't work, so one day he used his penknife to take it apart. He arranged the wheels and cogs and springs in neat rows on the quilt in his room, by type and then by size; by materials; by weight; by shape. He liked holding the tiny pieces, thinking of how they might have been formed and how they worked together. The patterns they made were interesting but he knew the best pattern would be the working one, when they were all put back into their right places and the clock performed its task again. He had to think that the clock would be happier that way, too.

He tried to rebuild the clock before his mother came upstairs from her counting house at the end of the day, but when he had reassembled things, there remained a pile of unused parts and it still didn't work; so he shut the clock up and hoped she wouldn't notice that it wasn't ticking. Four days more of trying things during the day and concealing his failures at night, and on the fifth day the clock started again. One piece hadn't fit anywhere, a small brass cog. Kit still carried that cog in his pen case.

Late that afternoon, Kit returned to the river's edge. It was hotter and the mud had dried to cracked dust. The air smelled like old rags left too long in a pail. He saw no one at the ferry dock, but at the fisher's dock upstream people were gathering, a score or more of men and women with children running about.

The clutter looked even more disorganized as he approached. The fishing boats were fat coracles fashioned of leather stretched on frames, all tipped bottom up to the sun and looking like giant warts. The mist had dropped so that he could see a band of exposed rock below the bank. He could see the dock's pilings clearly. They were not vertical but had been set at an angle to make a cantilevered deck braced into the stone underlying the bank. The wooden pilings had been sheathed in metal.

He approached a silver-haired woman doing something with a treble hook as long as her hand. "What are you catching with that?" he said.

Her forehead was wrinkled when she looked up, but she smiled when she saw him. "Oh, you're a stranger. From Atyar, dressed like that. Am I right? We catch fish—" Still holding the hook, she extended her arms as far as they would stretch. "Bigger than that, some of them. Looks like more storms, so they're going to be biting tonight. I'm Meg Threehooks. Of Nearside, obviously."

"Kit Meinem of Atyar. I take it you can't find a bottom?" He pointed to the pilings.

Jen Threehooks followed his glance. "It's there somewhere, but it's a long way down and we can't sink pilings because the mist dissolves the wood. Oh, and fish eat it. Same thing with our ropes, the boats, us— anything but metal and rock, really." She knotted a line around the hook's eye. The cord was dark and didn't look heavy enough for anything Kit could imagine catching on hooks that size.

"What are these made of, then?" He squatted to look at the framing under one of the coracles.

"Careful, that one's mine," Meg said. "The hides—well, and all the ropes—are fishskin. Mist fish, not water-fish. Tanning takes off some of the slime so they don't last forever either, not if they're afloat." She made a face. "We have a saying: foul as fish-slime. That's pretty nasty, you'll see."

"I need to get to Farside," Kit said. "Could I hire you to carry me across?"

"In my boat?" She snorted. "No, fishers stay close to shore. Go see Rasali Ferry. Or Valo."

"I saw her," he said ruefully.

"Thought so. You must be the new architect—city folk are always so impatient. You're so eager to be dinner for a Big One? If Rasali doesn't want to go then don't go, stands to reason."

Kit was footsore and frustrated by the time he returned to The Fish. His trunks were already upstairs, in a small cheerful room overwhelmed by a table that nearly filled it, with a stiflingly hot cupboard bed. When Kit spoke to the woman he'd talked to earlier, Brana Keep, the owner of The Fish (its real name turned out to be The Big One's Delight) laughed. "Rasali's as hard to shift as bedrock," she said. "And truly, you would not be comfortable at The Hart."

By the next morning, when Kit came downstairs to break his fast on flatbread and pepper-rubbed water-fish, everyone appeared to know everything about him, especially his task. He had wondered whether there would be resistance to the project, but if there had been any it was gone now. There were a few complaints, mostly about slow payments—a universal issue for public works—but none at all about the labor or organization. Most in the taproom seemed not to mind the bridge, and the feeling everywhere he went in town was optimistic. He'd run into more resistance elsewhere, building smaller bridges.

"Well, why should we be concerned?" Brana Keep said to Kit. "You're bringing in people to work, yes? So we'll be selling room and board and clothes and beer to them. And you'll be hiring some of us and everyone will do well while you're building this bridge of yours. I plan to be wading ankle-deep through gold by the time this is done."

"And after," Kit said, "when the bridge is complete—think of it, the first real link between the east and west sides of Empire. The only place for three thousand miles where people and trade can cross the mist easily, safely, whenever they wish. You'll be the heart of Empire in ten years. Five." He laughed a little, embarrassed by the passion that shook his voice.

"Yes, well," Brana Keep said in the easy way of a woman who makes her living by not antagonizing customers, "we'll make that harness when the colt is born."

For the next six days, Kit explored the town and surrounding countryside.

He met the masons, a brother and sister that Teniant had selected before her death to oversee the pillar and anchorage construction on Nearside. They were quiet but competent and Kit was comfortable not replacing them.

Kit also spoke with the Nearside ropemakers, and performed tests on their fishskin ropes and cables, which turned out even stronger than he had hoped, with excellent resistance to rot and to catastrophic and slow failure. The makers told him that the rope stretched for its first two years in use, which made it ineligible to replace the immense chains that would bear the bridge's weight; but it could replace the thousands of vertical suspender chains that that would support the roadbed with a great saving in weight.

He spent much of his time watching the mist. It changed character unpredictably: a smooth rippled flow, hours later a badland of shredding foam, still later a field of steep dunes that joined and shifted as he watched. The river generally dropped in its bed each day under the sun and rose after dark, though it wasn't consistent.

The winds were more predictable. Hedged between the levees, they streamed southward each morning and northward each evening, growing stronger toward midday and dusk, and falling away entirely in the afternoons and at night. They did not seem to affect the mist much except for tearing off shreds that landed on the banks as dried foam.

The winds meant that there would be more dynamic load on the bridge than Teniant Planner had predicted. Kit would never criticize her work publicly and he gladly acknowledged her brilliant interpersonal skills, which had brought the town into cheerful collaboration, but he was grateful that her bridge had not been built as designed.

He examined the mist more closely, as well, by lifting a piece from the river's surface on the end of an oar. The mist was stiffer than it looked, and in bright light he thought he could see tiny shapes, perhaps creatures or plants or something altogether different. There were microscopes in Atyar, and people who studied these things; but he had never bothered to learn more, interested only in the structure that would bridge it. In any case, living things interested him less than structures.

Nights, Kit worked on the table in his room. Teniant's plans had to be revised. He opened the folios and cases she had left behind and read everything he found there. He wrote letters, wrote lists, wrote schedules, wrote duplicates of everything, sent to the capital for someone to do all the subsequent copying. His new plans for the bridge began to take shape. He started to glimpse the invisible architecture that was the management of the vast project.

He did not see Rasali Ferry except to ask each morning whether they might travel that day. The answer was always no.

One afternoon, when the clouds were heaping into anvils filled with rain, he walked up to the building site half a mile north of Nearside. For two years, off and on, carts had tracked south on the Hoic Mine road and the West River Road, leaving limestone blocks and iron bars here in untidy heaps. Huge dismantled shear-legs lay beside a caretaker's wattle-and-daub hut. There were thousands of large rectangular blocks.

Kit examined some of the blocks. Limestone was often too chossy for large-scale construction but this rock was sound, with no apparent flaws or fractures. There were not enough, of course, but undoubtedly more had been quarried. He had written to order resumption of deliveries and they would start arriving soon.

Delivered years too early, the iron trusses that would eventually support the roadbed were stacked neatly, painted black to protect them from moisture, covered in oiled tarps, and raised from the ground on planks. Sheep grazed the knee-high grass that grew everywhere. When one eyed him incuriously, Kit found himself bowing. "Forgive the intrusion," he said and laughed: too old to be talking to sheep.

The test pit was still open, with a ladder on the ground nearby. Weeds clung when he moved the ladder as though reluctant to release it. He descended.

The pasture had not been noisy but he was startled when he dropped below ground level and the insects and whispering grasses were suddenly silenced. The soil around him was striated shades of dun and dull yellow. Halfway down, he sliced a wedge free with his knife: lots of clay, good foundation soil as he had been informed. Some twenty feet down, the pit's bottom looked like the walls, but when he crouched to dig at the dirt between his feet with his knife, he hit rock almost immediately. It seemed to be shale. He wondered how far down the water table was. Did the Nearsiders find it difficult to dig wells? Did the mist ever backwash into one? There were people at University in Atyar who were trying to understand mist, but there was still so much that could not be examined or quantified.

He collected a rock to examine in better light and climbed from the pit in time to see a teamster approaching, leading four mules, her wagon groaning under the weight of the first new blocks. A handful of Nearsider men and women followed, rolling their shoulders and popping their joints. They called out greetings and he walked across to them.

When he got back to The Fish hours later, exhausted from helping unload the cart and soaked from the storm that had started while he did so, there was a message from Rasali. *Dusk* was all it said.

Kit was stiff and irritable when he left for *The Tranquil Crossing*. He had hired a carrier from The Fish to haul one of his trunks down to the dock but the others remained in his room, which he would probably keep until the bridge was done. He carried his folio of plans and paperwork himself. He was leaving duplicates of everything on Nearside, but after so much work it was hard to trust any of it to the hands of others.

The storm was over and the clouds were moving past, leaving the sky every shade between lavender and a rich purple-blue. The largest moon was a crescent in the west, the smaller a half circle immediately overhead. In the fading light, the mist was a dark, smoky streak. The air smelled fresh. Kit's mood lightened and he half-trotted down the final slope.

His fellow passengers were there before him: a prosperous-looking man with a litter of piglets in a woven wicker cage (Tengon whites, the man confided, the best bloodline in all Empire); a woman in the dark clothes fashionable in the capital, with brass-bound document cases and a folio very like Kit's; two traders with many cartons of powdered pigment;

a mail courier with locked leather satchels and two guards. Nervous about their first crossing, Uni and Tom Mason greeted Kit when he arrived.

In the gathering darkness the mist formed tight-folded hills and coulees. Swifts darted just above the surface, using the wind flowing up the valley, searching for insects, he supposed. Once a sudden black shape, too quick to see clearly, appeared from below. Then it, and one of the birds, was gone.

The voices of the fishers at their dock carried to him. They launched their boats and he watched one and then another and then a gaggle of the little coracles push themselves up a slope of the mist. There were no lamps.

"Ready, everyone?" Kit had not heard Rasali approach. She swung down into the ferry. "Hand me your gear."

Stowing and embarkation were quick, though the piglets complained. Kit strained his eyes but the coracles could no longer be seen. When he noticed Rasali waiting for him, he apologized. "I guess the fish are biting."

Rasali glanced at the river as she stowed his trunk. "Small ones. A couple of feet long only. The fishers like them bigger, five or six feet, though they don't want them too big, either. But they're not fish, not what you think fish are. Hand me that."

He hesitated a moment, then gave her the folio before stepping into the ferry. *The Tranquil Crossing* sidled at his weight but sluggishly: a carthorse instead of a riding mare. His stomach lurched. "Oh!" he said.

"What?" one of the traders asked nervously. Rasali untied the rope holding them, pulled it into the boat.

Kit swallowed. "I had forgotten. The motion of the boat. It's not like water at all."

He did not mention his fear but there was no need. The others murmured assent. The courier, her dark face sharp-edged as a hawk, growled, "Every time I do this, it surprises me. I dislike it."

Rasali unshipped a scull and slid the great triangular blade into the mist, which parted reluctantly. "I've been on mist more than water but I remember the way water felt. Quick and jittery. This is better."

"Only to you, Rasali Ferry," Uni Mason said.

"Water's safer, anyway," the man with the piglets said.

Rasali leaned into the oar and the boat slid away from the dock. "Anything is safe until it kills you."

The mist absorbed the quiet sounds of shore almost immediately. One of Kit's first projects had been a stone single-arch bridge over water, far to the north in Eskje province. He had visited before construction started, and he was there for five days more than he had expected, caught by a snowstorm that left nearly two feet on the ground. This reminded him of those snowy moonless nights, the air as thick and silencing as a pillow on the ears.

Rasali did not scull so much as steer. It was hard to see far in any direction except up, but perhaps it was true that the mist spoke to her for she seemed to know where best to position the boat for the mist to carry it forward. She followed a small valley until it started to flatten and then mound up. The *Crossing* tipped slightly as it slid a few feet to port. The mail carrier made a noise and immediately stifled it.

Mist was a misnomer. It was denser than it seemed. Sometimes the boat seemed not to move through it so much as across its surface. Tonight it seemed like the dirty foam that strong winds could whip from Churash Lake's waves, near the western coast of Empire. Kit reached a hand over the boat's side. The mist piled against his hand, almost dry to the touch, sliding up his forearm with a sensation he could not immediately identify. When he realized it was prickling, he snatched his arm back in and rubbed it on a fold of his coat. The skin burned. Caustic, of course.

The man with the pigs whispered, "Will they come if we talk or make noise?"

"Not to talking or pigs' squealing," Rasali said. "They seem to like low noises. They'll rise to thunder sometimes."

One of the traders said, "What are they if they're not really fish? What do they look like?" Her voice shook. The mist was weighing on them all, all but Rasali.

"If you want to know you'll have to see one for yourself," Rasali said. "Or try to get a fisher to tell you. They gut and fillet them over the sides of their boats. No one else sees much but meat wrapped in paper or rolls of black skin for the ropemakers and tanners."

"*You've* seen them," Kit said.

"They're broad and flat. But ugly."

"And Big Ones?" Kit asked.

Her voice was harsh. "*Them* we don't talk about here."

No one spoke for a time. Mist—foam—heaped up at the boat's prow and parted, eased to the sides with an almost inaudible hissing. Once the mist off the port side heaved and something dark broke the surface for a moment, followed by other dark somethings, but they were not close enough to see well. One of the merchants cried without a sound or movement.

The Farside levee showed at last, a black mass that didn't get any closer for what felt like hours. Fighting his fear, Kit leaned over the side, keeping his face away from the surface. "It can't really be bottomless," he said half to himself. "What's under it?"

"You wouldn't hit the bottom, anyway," Rasali said.

The Tranquil Crossing eased up a long swell of mist and into a hollow. Rasali pointed the ferry along a crease. And then they were suddenly a stone's throw from the Farside dock and the light of its torches.

People on the dock moved as they approached. Just loudly enough to carry, a soft baritone voice called, "Rasali?"

She called back, "Ten this time, Pen."

"Anyone need carriers?" A different voice. Several passengers responded.

Rasali shipped the scull while the ferry was still some feet away from the dock, and allowed it to ease forward under its own momentum. She stepped to the prow and picked up a coiled rope there, tossing one end across the narrowing distance. Someone on the dock caught it and pulled the boat in, and in a very few moments the ferry was snug against the dock.

Disembarking and payment was quicker than embarkation had been. Kit was the last off and after a brief discussion he hired a carrier to haul his trunk to an inn in town. He turned to say farewell to Rasali. She and the man—Pen, Kit remembered—were untying the boat. "You're not going back already," he said.

"Oh, no." Her voice sounded loose, content, relaxed. Kit hadn't known how tense she was. "We're just going to tow the boat down to where the

Twins will pull it out." She waved with one hand to the boat launch. A pair of white oxen gleamed in the night, at their heads a woman hardly darker.

"Wait," Kit said to Uni Mason and handed her his folio. "Please tell the innkeeper I'll be there soon." He turned back to Rasali. "May I help?"

In the darkness he felt more than saw her smile. "Always."

The Red Lurcher, more commonly called The Bitch, was a small but noisy inn five minutes' walk from the mist, ten (he was told) from the building site. His room was larger than at The Fish, with an uncomfortable bed and a window seat crammed with quires of ancient hand-written music. Jenner stayed here, Kit knew, but when he asked the owner (Widson Innkeep, a heavyset man with red hair turning silver), he had not seen him. "You'll be the new one, the architect," Widson said.

"Yes," Kit said. "When he gets in, please tell Jenner I am here."

Widson wrinkled his forehead. "I don't know, he's been out late most days recently, since—" He cut himself off, looking guilty.

"—since the signals informed him that I was here," Kit said. "I understand the impulse."

The innkeeper seemed to consider something for a moment, then said slowly, "We like Jenner here."

"Then we'll try to keep him," Kit said.

When the child Kit had recovered from his illness, he did not return to the crèche—which he would have been leaving in a year in any case—but went straight to his father. Davell Meinem was a slow-talking humorous man who nevertheless had a sharp tongue on the sites of his many projects. He brought Kit with him to his work places: best for the boy to get some experience in the trade.

Kit loved everything about his father's projects: the precisely drawn plans, the orderly progression of construction, the lines and curves of brick and iron and stone rising under the endlessly random sky.

For the first year or two, Kit imitated his father and the workers, building structures of tiny beams and bricks made by the woman set to mind him, a tiler who had lost a hand some years back. Davell collected the boy at the end of the day. "I'm here to inspect the construction," he said, and Kit demonstrated his bridge or tower, or the materials he had laid out in neat lines and stacks. Davell would discuss Kit's work with great seriousness until it grew too dark to see and they went back to the inn or rented rooms that passed for home near the sites.

Davell spent nights buried in the endless paperwork of his projects, and Kit found this interesting as well. The pattern that went into building something big was not just the architectural plans or the construction itself; it was also labor schedules and documentation and materials deliveries. He started to draw his own plans but he also made up endless correspondences with imaginary providers.

After a while, Kit noticed that a large part of the pattern that made a bridge or a tower was built of people.

The knock on Kit's door came very late that night, a preemptory rap. Kit put down the quill he was mending and rolled his shoulders to loosen them. "Yes," he said aloud as he stood.

The man who stormed through the door was as dark as Kit, though perhaps a few years younger. He wore mud-splashed riding clothes.

"I am Kit Meinem of Atyar," Kit said.

"Jenner Ellar of Atyar. Show it to me." Silently Kit handed the cartel to Jenner, who glared at it before tossing it onto the table. "It took long enough for them to pick a replacement."

Might as well deal with this right now, Kit thought. "You hoped it would be you."

Jenner eyed Kit for a moment. "Yes. I did."

"You think you're the most qualified to complete the project because you've been here for the last—what is it? year?"

"I know the sites," Jenner said. "I worked with Teniant to make those plans. And then Empire sends—" He turned to face the empty hearth.

"—Empire sends someone new," Kit said to Jenner's back. "Someone with connections in the capital, influential friends but no experience with this site, this bridge. It should have been you, yes?"

Jenner was still.

"But it isn't," Kit said, and let the words hang for a moment. "I've built eight bridges in the past fifteen years. Four suspension bridges, two major spans. Two bridges over mist. You've done three, and the biggest span you've directed was three hundred and fifty feet, six stone arches over shallow water and shifting gravel on Mati River."

"I know," Jenner snapped.

"It's a good bridge." Kit poured two glasses of whiskey from a stoneware pitcher by the window. "I coached down to see it before I came here. It's well made and you were on budget and nearly on schedule in spite of the drought. Better, the locals still like you. Asked how you're doing these days. Here."

Jenner took the glass Kit offered. *Good.* Kit continued, "Meinems have built bridges—and roads and aqueducts and stadia, a hundred sorts of public structures—for Empire for a thousand years." Jenner turned to speak but Kit held up his hand. "This doesn't mean we're any better at it than Ellars. But Empire knows us—and we know Empire, how to do what we need to. If they'd given you this bridge, you'd be replaced within a year. But I can get this bridge built and I will." Kit sat and leaned forward, elbows on knees. "With you. You're talented. You know the site. You know the people. Help me make this bridge."

"It's real to you," Jenner said finally. Kit knew what he meant: *You care about this work. It's not just another tick on a list.*

"Yes," Kit said. "You'll be my second for this one. I'll show you how to deal with Atyar and I'll help you with contacts. And your next project will belong entirely to you. This is the first bridge but it isn't going to be the only one across the mist."

Together they drank. The whiskey bit at Kit's throat and made his eyes water. "Oh," he said, "that's *awful.*"

Jenner laughed suddenly and met his eyes for the first time: a little wary still but willing to be convinced. "Farside whiskey is terrible. You drink much of this, you'll be running for Atyar in a month."

"Maybe we'll have something better ferried across," Kit said.

———

Preparations were not so far along on this side. The heaps of blocks at the construction site were not so massive and it was harder to find local workers. In discussions between Kit, Jenner and the Near- and Farside masons who would oversee construction of the pillars, final plans materialized. This would be unique, the largest structure of its kind ever attempted: a single-span chain suspension bridge a quarter of a mile long. The basic plan remained unchanged: the bridge would be supported by eyebar-and-bolt chains, four on each side, allowed to play independently to compensate for the slight shifts that would be caused by traffic on the roadbed. The huge eyebars and their bolts were being fashioned five hundred miles away and far to the north, where iron was common and the smelting and ironworking were the best in Empire. Kit had just written to the foundries to start the work again.

The pillar and anchorage on Nearside would be built of gold limestone anchored with pilings into the bedrock; on Farside they would be pink-gray granite with a funnel-shaped foundation. The towers' heights would be nearly four hundred feet. There were taller towers back in Atyar, but none had to stand against the compression of a bridge.

The initial tests with the fishskin rope had showed it to be nearly as strong as iron without the weight. When Kit asked the Farside tanners and ropemakers about its durability, he was taken a day's travel east to Feknai, to a waterwheel that used knotted belts of the material for its drive. The belts, he was told, were seventy-five years old and still sound. Fishskin wore like maplewood so long as it wasn't left in mist, but it required regular maintenance.

He watched Feknai's little river for a time. There had been rain recently in the foothills and the water was quick and abrupt as light. *Water bridges are easy*, he thought a little wistfully, and then: *Anyone can bridge water.*

Kit revised the plans again to use the lighter material where they could. Jenner crossed the mist to Nearside to work with Daell and Stivvan Cabler on the expansion of their workshops and ropewalk.

Without Jenner (who was practically a local, as Kit was told again and again), Kit felt the difference in attitudes on the river's two banks more clearly. Most Farsiders shared the Nearsiders' attitudes—money is money and always welcome—and there was a sense of the excitement that comes of any great project, but there was more resistance here. Empire was effectively split by the river, and the lands to the east—starting with Nearside—had never seen their destinies as closely linked to Atyar in the west. They were overseen by the eastern capital, Triple, and their taxes went to building necessities on their own side of the mist. Empire's grasp on the eastern lands was loose and had never needed to be tighter.

The bridge would change things. Travel between Atyar and Triple would grow more common and perhaps Empire would no longer hold the eastern lands so gently. Triple's lack of enthusiasm for the project showed itself in delayed deliveries of stone and iron. Kit traveled five days along the Triple Road to the district seat to present his credentials to the governor, and wrote sharp letters to the Department of Roads in Triple. Things became a little easier.

It was midwinter before the design was finished. Kit avoided crossing the mist. Rasali Ferry crossed seventeen times. He managed to see her nearly every time, at least for as long as it took to drink a beer.

The second time Kit crossed, it was midmorning of an early spring day. The mist mirrored the overcast sky above: pale and flat, like a layer of fog in a dell. Rasali was loading the ferry at the upper dock when Kit arrived and to his surprise she smiled at him, her face suddenly beautiful. Kit nodded to the stranger watching Valo toss immense cloth-wrapped bales to Rasali, then greeted the Ferrys. Valo paused for a moment but did not return Kit's greeting, only bent again to his work. Valo had been avoiding him since the beginning of his time there. With a mental shrug, Kit turned from Valo to Rasali. She was catching and stacking the enormous bales easily.

"What's in those? You throw them as though they were—"

"—paper," she finished. "The very best Ibraric mulberry paper. Light as lambswool. You probably have a bunch of this stuff in that folio of yours."

Kit thought of the vellum he used for his plans, and the paper he used for everything else: made of cotton from the south, its surface buffed until it felt hard and smooth as enamelwork. Ibraric paper was only useful for certain kinds of printing. He said, "All the time."

Rasali piled on bales and more bales until the ferry was stacked three high. He added, "Is there going to be room for me in there?"

"Pilar Runner and Valo aren't coming with us," she said. "You'll have to sit on top of the bales, but there's room as long as you sit still and don't wobble."

As Rasali pushed away from the dock Kit asked, "Why isn't the trader coming with her paper?"

"Why would she? Pilar has a broker on the other side." Her hands busy, she tipped her head to one side in a gesture that somehow conveyed a shrug. "Mist is dangerous." Somewhere along the River a ferry was lost every few months: horses, people, cartage, all lost. Fishers stayed closer to shore and died less often. It was harder to calculate the impact to trade and communications of this barrier splitting Empire in half.

This journey—in daylight, alone with Rasali—was very different from Kit's earlier crossing: less frightening but somehow wilder, stranger. The cold wind down the river was cutting and brought bits of dried foam to rest on his skin, but they blew off quickly without pain and left no mark. The wind fell to a breeze and then to nothing as they navigated into the mist.

They moved through what looked like a layered maze of cirrus clouds. He watched the mist along the *Crossing*'s side until they passed over a small hole like a pockmark, straight down and no more than a foot across. For an instant he glimpsed open space below them. They were floating on a layer of mist above an air pocket deep enough to swallow the boat. He rolled onto his back to stare up at the sky until he stopped shaking; when he looked again, they were out of the maze, it seemed. The boat eased along a gently curving channel. He relaxed a little and moved to watch Rasali.

"How fares your bridge?" Rasali said at last, her voice muted in the muffled air. This had to be a courtesy—everyone in town seemed to know everything about the bridge's progress—but Kit was used to answering questions to which people already knew the answers. He had found patience to be a highly effective tool.

"Farside foundations are doing well. We have maybe six more months before the anchorage is done, but pilings for the pillar's foundation are in place and we can start building. Six weeks early," Kit said a little smugly, though this was a victory no one else would appreciate and in any case the weather was as much to be credited as any action on his part. "On Nearside, we've run into basalt that's too hard to drill easily so we sent for a specialist. The signal flags say she's arrived, and that's why I'm crossing."

She said nothing, seemingly intent on moving the great scull. He watched her for a time, content to see her shoulders flex, hear her breath forcing itself out in smooth waves. Over the faint yeast scent of the mist, he smelled her sweat, or thought he did. She frowned slightly but he could not tell whether it was due to her labor or something in the mist, or something else. Who was she, really? "May I ask a question, Rasali Ferry of Farside?"

Rasali nodded, eyes on the mist in front of the boat.

Actually, he had several things he wished to know: about her, about the river, about the people here. He picked one almost at random. "What is bothering Valo?"

"He's transparent, isn't he? He thinks you take something away from him," Rasali said. "He is too young to know what you take is unimportant."

Kit thought about it. "His work?"

"His work is unimportant?" She laughed, a sudden puff of an exhale as she pulled. "We have a lot of money, Ferrys. We own land and rent it out—The Deer's Hart belongs to my family; did you know that? But he's young and he wants what we all want at his age, a chance to test himself against the world and see if he measures up. And because he's a Ferry he wants be tested against adventures. Danger. The mist. Valo thinks you take that away from him."

"But he's not immortal," Kit said, "whatever he thinks. The river can kill him. It will, sooner or later. It—"

—*will kill you.* Kit caught himself, rolled onto his back again to look up at the sky.

In The Bitch's taproom one night, a local man had told him about Rasali's family: a history of deaths, of boats lost in a silent hissing of mist, or the rending of wood, or screams that might be human and might be a horse. "So everyone wears ash-color for a month or two, and then the next Ferry takes up the business. Rasali's still new, two years maybe. When she goes, it'll be Valo, then Valo's sister. Unless Rasali or Valo have kids by then.

"They're always beautiful," the man had added after some more porter, "the Ferrys. I suppose that's to make up for having such short lives."

Kit looked down from the paper bales at Rasali. "But you're different. You don't feel you're losing anything."

"You don't know what I feel, Kit Meinem of Atyar." Cool light moved along the muscles of her arms. Her voice came again, softer. "I am not young; I don't need to prove myself. But I will lose this. The mist, the silence."

Then tell me, he did not say. *Show me.*

She was silent for the rest of the trip. Kit thought perhaps she was angry, but when he invited her, she accompanied him to the building site.

The quiet pasture was gone. All that remained of the tall grass was struggling tufts and dirty straw. The air smelled of sweat and meat and the bitter scent of hot metal. There were more blocks here now, a lot more. The pits for the anchorage and the pillar were excavated to bedrock, overshadowed by mountains of dirt. One sheep remained, skinned and spitted, and greasy smoke rose as a boy turned it over a fire beside the temporary forge. Kit had considered the pasture a nuisance, but looking at the skewered sheep he felt a twinge of guilt.

The rest of the flock had been replaced by sturdy-looking women and men who were using rollers to shift stones down a dugout ramp into the hole for the anchorage foundation. Dust dulled their skin and muted the bright colors of their short kilts and breastbands. In spite of the cold, sweat had cleared tracks along their muscles.

One of the workers waved to Rasali and she waved back. Kit recalled his name: Mik Rounder, very strong but he needed direction. Had they been lovers? Relationships out here were tangled in ways Kit didn't understand. In the capital such things were more formal and often involved contracts.

Jenner and a small woman knelt conferring on the exposed stone floor of the larger pit. When Kit slid down the ladder to join them, the small woman bowed slightly. Her eyes and short hair and skin all seemed to be turning the same iron gray. "I am Liu Breaker of Hoic. Your specialist."

"Kit Meinem of Atyar. How shall we address this?"

"Your Jenner says you need some of this basalt cleared away, yes?"

Kit nodded.

Liu knelt to run her hand along the pit's floor. "See where the color and texture change along this line? Your Jenner was right: this upthrust of basalt is a problem. Here where the shale is, you can carve out most of the foundation the usual way with drills, picks. But the basalt is too hard to drill." She straightened and brushed dust from her knees. "Have you ever seen explosives used?"

Kit shook his head. "We haven't needed them for any of my projects. I've never been to the mines, either."

"Not much good anywhere else," Liu said, "but very useful for breaking up large amounts of rock. A lot of the blocks you have here were loosed using explosives." She grinned. "You'll like the noise."

"We can't afford to break the bedrock's integrity."

"I brought enough powder for a number of small charges. Comparatively small."

"How—"

Liu held up a weathered hand. "I don't need to understand bridges to walk across one. Yes?"

Kit laughed outright. "Yes."

Liu Breaker was right; Kit liked the noise very much. Liu would not allow anyone close to the pit but even from what she considered a safe distance, behind a huge pile of dirt, the explosion was an immense shattering thing, a crack of thunder that shook the earth. There was a second of echoing silence. After a collective gasp and some scattered screams, the workers cheered and stamped their feet. A small cloud of mingled smoke and rock dust eased over the pit's edge, sharp with the smell of saltpeter.

The birds were not happy; with the explosion, they had burst from their trees and wheeled nervously.

Grinning, Liu climbed from her bunker near the pit, her face dust-caked everywhere but around her eyes, which had been protected by the wooden slit-goggles now hanging around her neck. "So far so good," she shouted over the ringing in Kit's ears. Seeing his face she laughed. "These are nothing—gnat sneezes. You should hear when we quarry granite up at Hoic."

Kit was going to speak more with her when he noticed Rasali striding away, toward the river. He had forgotten she was there. He followed her, half shouting to hear himself. "Some noise, yes?"

Rasali whirled. "What are you *thinking?*" She was shaking and her lips were white.

Taken aback, Kit answered, "We are blowing the foundations." *Rage? Fear?* He wished he could think a little more clearly but the sound seemed to have stunned his wits.

"And making the earth shake! The Big Ones come to thunder, Kit!"

"It wasn't thunder," he said.

"Tell me it wasn't worse!" Tears glittered in her eyes. Her voice was dulled by the drumming in his ears. "They will come, I *know* it."

He reached a hand out to her. "It's a tall levee, Rasali. Even if they do, they're not going to come over that." His heart in his chest thrummed. His head was hurting. It was so hard to hear her.

"*No one* knows what they'll do! They used to destroy whole towns, drifting inland on foggy nights. Why do you think they built the levees a thousand years ago? The Big Ones—"

She stopped shouting, listening. She mouthed something but Kit could not hear her over the beating in his ears, his heart, his head. He realized suddenly that these were not the after-effects of the explosion; the air itself was beating. He was aware at the edges of his vision of the other workers, every face turned toward the mist. There was nothing to see but the overcast sky. No one moved.

But the sky was moving.

Behind the levee the river mist was rising, a great boiling upheaval of dirty gray-gold against the steel-gray of the clouds, at least a hundred feet high, to be seen over the levee. The mist was seething, breaking open in great swirls and rifts, everything moving, changing. Kit had seen a great fire once when a warehouse of linen had burned in Atyar, where the smoke had poured upward and looked a little like this before bring torn apart by the wind.

Gaps opened in the mountain of mist and closed, and others opened, darker the deeper they were. And through those gaps, in the brown-black shadows at the heart of the mist, was movement.

The gaps closed. After an eternity the mist slowly smoothed and then settled back behind the levee and could no longer be seen. He wasn't really sure when the thrumming of the air blended back into the ringing of his ears.

"Gone," Rasali said with a sound like a sob.

A worker made one of the vivid jokes that come after fear; the others laughed, too loud. A woman ran up the levee and shouted down, "Farside levees are fine; ours are fine." More laughter: people jogged off to Nearside to check on their families.

The back of Kit's hand was burning. A flake of foam had settled and left an irregular mark. "I only saw mist," Kit said. "Was there a Big One?"

Rasali shook herself, stern now but no longer angry or afraid. Kit had learned this about the Ferrys, that their emotions coursed through them and then dissolved. "It was in there. I've seen the mist boil like that before but never so big. Nothing else could heave it up like that."

"On purpose?"

"Oh, who knows? They're a mystery, the Big Ones." She met his eyes. "I hope your bridge is very high, Kit Meinem of Atyar."

Kit looked to where the mist had been, but there was only sky. "The deck will be two hundred feet above the mist. High enough. I hope."

Liu Breaker walked up to them, rubbing her hands on her leather leggings. "So, *that's* not something that happens at Hoic. *Very* exciting. What do you call that? How do we prevent it next time?"

Rasali looked at the smaller woman for a moment. "I don't think you can. Big Ones come when they come."

Liu said, "They do not always come?"

Rasali shook her head.

"Well, cold comfort is better than no comfort, as my Da says."

Kit rubbed his temples. The headache remained. "We'll continue."

"Then you'll have to be careful," Rasali said, "or you will kill us all."

"The bridge will save many lives," Kit said. *Yours, eventually.*

Rasali turned on her heel.

Kit did not follow her, not that day. Whether it was because subsequent explosions were smaller ("As small as they can be and earn my fees," Liu Breaker said) or because they were doing other things, the Big Ones did not return, though fish were plentiful for the three months it took to plan and plant the charges, and break the bedrock.

There was also a Meinem tradition of metal working, and Meinem reeves, and many Meinems went into fields altogether different, but Kit had known from nearly the beginning that he would be one of the building Meinems. He loved the invisible architecture of construction, looking for a compromise between the vision in his head and the sites, the materials, and the people that would make them real. The challenge was to compromise as little as possible.

Architecture was studied at University. His tutor was a materials specialist, a woman who had directed construction on an incredible twenty-three bridges. Skossa Timt was so old that her skin and hair had faded together to the white of Gani marble, and she walked with a cane she had designed herself for efficiency. She taught him much. Materials had rules, patterns of behavior: they bent or crumbled or cracked or broke under quantifiable stresses. They augmented or destroyed one another. Even the best materials in the most stable combinations did not last forever—she tapped her own forehead with one gnarled finger and laughed—but if he did his work right, they could last a thousand years or more. "But not forever," Skossa said. "Do your best but don't forget this."

The anchorages and pillars grew. Workers came from towns up and down each bank, and locals were hired on the spot. The new people were generally welcome. They paid for rooms and food and goods of all sorts. The taverns settled into making double and then triple batches of everything, threw out new wings and stables. Nearside accepted the new people easily, the only fights late at night when people had been drinking and flirting more than they should. Farside had fist fights more frequently, though they decreased steadily as skeptics gave in to the money that flowed into Farside, or to the bridge itself, its pillars too solid to be denied.

Farmers and husbanders sold their fields and new buildings sprawled out from the towns' hearts. Some were made of wattle and daub, slapped together over stamped-earth floors that still smelled of sheep dung. Others, small but permanent, went up more slowly, as the bridge builders laid fieldstones and timber in their evenings and on rest days.

The new people and locals mixed together until it was hard to tell the one from the other, though the older townfolk kept scrupulous track of who truly belonged. For those who sought lovers and friends, the new people were an opportunity to meet someone other than the men and women they had known since childhood. Many took casual lovers, and several term-partnered with new people. There was even a Nearside wedding, between Kes Tiler and a black-eyed builder from far to the south called Jolite Deveren, whatever that meant.

Kit did not have lovers. Working every night until he fell asleep over his paperwork, he didn't miss it much, except late on certain nights when thunderstorms left him restless and unnaturally alert, as though lightning ran under his skin. Some nights he thought of Rasali, wondered whether she was sleeping with someone that night or alone, and wondered if the storm had awakened her, left her restless as well.

Kit saw a fair amount of Rasali when they were both on the same side of the mist. She was clever and calm and the only person who did not want to talk about the bridge all the time.

He did not forget what Rasali said about Valo. Kit had been a young man himself not so many years before, and he remembered the hunger that young men and women felt to prove themselves against the world. Kit didn't need Valo to accept the bridge—he was scarcely into adulthood and his only influence over the townspeople was based on his work—but Kit liked the youth, who had Rasali's eyes and her effortless way of moving.

Kij Johnson

Valo started asking questions, first of the other workers and then of Kit. His boat-building experience meant the questions were good ones. Kit passed on the first things he had learned as a child on his father's sites and showed him the manipulation of the immense blocks and the tricky balance of material and plan, the strength of will that allows a man to direct a thousand people toward a single vision. Valo was too honest not to recognize Kit's mastery and too competitive not to try and meet Kit on his own ground. He came more often to visit the construction sites.

After a season, Kit took him aside. "You could be a builder if you wished."

Valo flushed. "Build things? You mean bridges?"

"Or houses or granges or retaining walls. Or bridges. You could make peoples' lives better."

"Change peoples' lives?" He frowned suddenly. "No."

"Our lives change all the time whether we want them to or not," Kit said. "Valo Ferry of Farside, you are intelligent. You are good with people. You learn quickly. If you were interested, I could start teaching you myself or send you to Atyar to study there."

"Valo Builder..." he said, trying it out, then: "No." But after that, whenever he had time free from ferrying or building boats, he was always to be found on the site. Kit knew that the answer would be different the next time he asked. There was for everything a possibility, an invisible pattern that could be made manifest given work and the right materials. Kit wrote to an old friend or two, finding contacts that would help Valo when the time came. He would not be ashamed of this new protegé.

The pillars and anchorages grew. Winter came and summer, and a second winter. There were falls, a broken arm, two sets of cracked ribs. Someone on Farside had her toes crushed when one of the stones slipped from its rollers and she lost the foot. The bridge was on schedule even after the delay caused by the slow rock-breaking. There were no problems with payroll or the Department of Roads or Empire, and only minor, manageable issues with the occasionally disruptive representatives from Triple or the local governors.

Kit knew he was lucky.

———

The first death came during one of Valo's visits.

It was early in the second winter of the bridge, and Kit had been in Farside for three months. He had already learned that winter meant gray skies and rain and sometimes snow. Soon they would have to stop the heavy work for the season. Still, it had been a good day and the workers had lifted and placed most of a course of stones.

Valo had returned after three weeks at Nearside building a boat for Jenna Bluefish. Kit found him staring up at the slim tower through a rain so faint it felt like fog. Halfway up the pillar, the black opening of the roadway arch looked out of place.

Valo said, "You're a lot farther along since I was here last. How tall now?"

Kit got this question a lot. "A hundred and five feet, more or less. A little over a quarter finished."

Valo smiled, shook his head. "Hard to believe it'll stay up."

"There's a tower in Atyar, black basalt and iron, five hundred feet. Five times this tall."

"It just looks so delicate," Valo said. "I know what you said, that most of the stress on the pillar is compression, but it still looks as though it'll snap in half."

"After a while you'll have more experience with suspension bridges and it will seem less ... unsettling. Would you like to see the progress?"

Valo's eyes brightened. "May I? I don't want to get in the way."

"I haven't been up yet today and they'll be finishing up soon. Scaffold or stairwell?"

Valo looked at the scaffolding against one face of the pillar, the ladders tied into place within it, and shivered. "I can't believe people go up that. Stairs."

Kit followed Valo. The steep internal stair was three feet wide and endlessly turning, five steps up and then a platform, turn to the left and then five more steps and turn. Eventually the stairs would be lit by lanterns set into alcoves at every third turning, but today Kit and Valo felt their way up, fingers trailing along the cold damp stone, a small lantern in Valo's hand. The stairwell smelled of water and earth and the thin smell of the burning lamp oil. Some of the workers hated the stairs and preferred the ladders outside, but Kit liked it here. For these few moments he was part of his bridge, a strong bone buried deep in flesh he had created.

They came out at the top and paused a moment to look around the unfinished course, and at the black silhouette of the crane against the dulling sky. The last few workers were breaking down a shear-leg that had been used to move blocks. A lantern hung from a pole jammed into one of the holes the laborers would fill with rods and molten iron. Kit nodded to them as Valo went to an edge to look down.

"It is wonderful," Valo said, smiling. "Being high like this—you can look right down into people's kitchen yards. Look, Teli Carpenter has a pig smoking."

"You don't need to see it to know that," Kit said dryly. "I've been smelling it for two days."

Valo snorted. "Can you see as far as White Peak yet?"

"On a clear day, yes," Kit said. "I was up here two—"

A heavy sliding sound and a scream. Kit whirled to see one of the workers on her back, one of the shear-leg's timbers across her chest. Loreh Tanner, a local. Kit ran the few steps to Loreh and dropped beside her. One man, the man who had been working with her, said, "It slipped—oh, Loreh, please hang on," but Kit could see already that it was futile. She was pinned against the pillar, chest flattened, one shoulder visibly dislocated, unconscious, breathing labored. Foam bloomed from her lips, black in the lantern's bad light.

Kit took her cold hand. "It's all right, Loreh. It's all right." It was a lie and in any case she could not hear him, but the others would. "Get Hall," one of the workers said and Kit nodded: Hall was a surgeon. And then, "And get Obal, someone. Get her husband." Footsteps ran down the stairs and were lost into the hiss of rain just beginning and someone's crying and Loreh's wet breathing.

Kit glanced up. His chest heaving, Valo stood staring. Kit said to him, "Help find Hall," and when the boy did not move he repeated it, his voice sharper. Valo said nothing, did not stop looking at Loreh until he spun and ran down the stairs. Kit heard shouting far below as the first messenger ran toward the town.

Loreh took a last shuddering breath and died.

Kit looked at the others around Loreh's body. The man holding Loreh's other hand pressed his face against it crying helplessly. The two other workers left here knelt at her feet, a man and a woman, huddled close though they were not a couple. "Tell me," he said.

"I tried to stop it from hitting her," the woman said. She cradled one arm: obviously broken though she did not seem to have noticed. "But it just kept falling."

"She was tired. She must have gotten careless," the man said, and the broken-armed woman said, "I don't want to think about that sound."

Words fell from them like blood from a cut. This was what they needed right now, to speak and to be heard. So he listened, and when the others came, Loreh's husband Obal, white-lipped and angry-eyed, the surgeon Hall, and six other workers, Kit listened to them as well, and gradually moved them down through the pillar and back toward the warm lights and comfort of Farside.

Kit had lost people before and it was always like this. There would be tears tonight, and anger at him and at his bridge, anger at fate for permitting this. There would be sadness and nightmares. And there would be lovemaking and the holding close of children and friends and dogs—affirmations of life in the cold wet night.

His tutor at University had said, during one of her frequent digressions from materials and the principles of architecture, "Things will go wrong."

It was winter, but in spite of the falling snow they walked slowly to the coffee house, as Skossa looked for purchase for her cane. She continued, "On long projects, you'll forget that you're not one of them. But if there's an accident? You're slapped in the face with it. Whatever you're feeling? Doesn't matter. Guilty, grieving, alone, worried about the schedule. None of it. What matters is *their* feelings. So listen to them. Respect what they're going through."

She paused then, tapped her cane against the ground thoughtfully. "No, I lie. It does matter but you will have to find your own strength, your own resources elsewhere."

"Friends?" Kit said doubtfully. He knew already that he wanted a career like his father's. He would not be in the same place for more than a few years at a time.

"Yes, friends." Snow collected on Skossa's hair but she didn't seem to notice. "Kit, I worry about you. You're good with people, I've seen it. You like them. But there's a limit for you." He opened his mouth to protest but she held up her hand to silence him. "I know. You do care. But inside the framework of a project. Right now it's your studies. Later it'll be roads and bridges. But people around you—their lives go on outside the framework. They're not just tools to your hand, even likable tools. Your life should go on, too. You should have more than roads to live for. Because if something does go wrong, you'll need what *you're* feeling to matter, to someone somewhere, anyway."

Kit walked through Farside toward The Bitch. Most people were home or in one of the taverns by now, a village turned inward; but he heard footsteps running behind him. He turned quickly. It was not unknown for people reeling from a loss to strike at whatever they blamed, and sometimes it was a person.

It was Valo. Though his fists were balled, Kit could tell immediately that he was angry but that he was not looking for a fight. For a moment Kit wished he didn't need to listen, that he could just go back to his rooms and sleep for a thousand hours, but there was a stricken look in Valo's eyes: Valo, who looked so much like Rasali. He hoped that Rasali and Loreh hadn't been close.

Kit said gently, "Why aren't you inside? It's cold." As he said it, he realized suddenly that it *was* cold. The rain had settled into a steady cold flood.

"I will. I was, I mean, but I came out because I thought maybe I could find you, because—" The boy was shivering.

"Where are your friends? Let's get you inside. It'll be better there."

"No," he said. "I have to know first. It's like this always? If I do this, build things, it'll happen for me? Someone will die?"

"It might. It probably will, eventually."

Valo said an unexpected thing: "I see. It's just that she had just gotten married."

The blood on Loreh's lips, the wet sound of her crushed chest as she took her last breaths—"Yes," Kit said. "She had."

"I just...I had to know if I need to ready for this. I guess I'll find out."

"I hope you don't have to." The rain was getting heavier. "You should be inside, Valo."

Valo nodded. "Rasali—I wish she were here. She could help maybe. You should go in too. You're shivering."

Kit watched him go. Valo had not invited him to accompany him back into the light and the warmth. He knew better than to expect that, but for a moment he had permitted himself to hope otherwise.

Kit slipped through the stables and through the back door at The Bitch. Wisdon Innkeep, hands full of mugs for the taproom, saw him and nodded, face unsmiling but not hostile. That was good, Kit thought, as good as it would get tonight.

He entered his room and shut the door, leaned his back to it as if to hold the world out. Someone had already been in his room. A lamp had been lit against the darkness, a fire laid, and bread and cheese and a tankard of ale set by the window to stay cool. He began to cry.

The news went across the river by signal flags. No one worked on the bridge the next day or the day after that. Kit did all the right things, letting his grief and guilt overwhelm him only when he was alone, huddled in front of the fire in his room.

The third day, Rasali arrived from Nearside with a boat filled with crates of northland herbs on their way east. Kit was sitting in The Bitch's taproom, listening. People were coping, starting to look forward again. They should be able to get back to it soon, the next clear day. He would offer them something that would be an immediate, visible accomplishment, something different, perhaps guidelining the ramp.

He didn't see Rasali come into the taproom, only felt her hand on his shoulder and heard her voice in his ear. "Come with me," she murmured.

He looked up puzzled, as though she were a stranger. "Rasali Ferry, why are you here?"

She said only, "Come for a walk, Kit."

It was raining but he accompanied her anyway, pulling a scarf over his head when the first cold drops hit his face.

She said nothing as they splashed through Farside. She was leading him someplace but he didn't care where, grateful not to have to be the decisive one, the strong one. After a time she opened a door and led him through it into a small room filled with light and warmth.

"My house," she said. "And Valo's. He's still at the boatyard. Sit."

She pointed and Kit dropped onto the settle beside the fire. Rasali swiveled a pot hanging from a bracket out of the fire and ladled something into a mug. She handed it to him and sat. "So. Drink."

It was spiced porter and the warmth eased the tightness in his chest. "Thank you."

"Talk."

"This is such a loss for you all, I know," he said. "Did you know Loreh well?"

She shook her head. "This is not for me, this is for you. Tell me."

"I'm fine," he said, and when she didn't say anything, he repeated with a flicker of anger: "I'm *fine*, Rasali. I can handle this."

"Probably you can," Rasali said. "But you're not fine. She died and it was your bridge she died for. You don't feel responsible? I don't believe it."

"Of course I feel responsible," he snapped.

The fire cast gold light across her broad cheekbones when she turned her face to him, but she said nothing, only looked at him and waited.

"She's not the first," Kit said, surprising himself. "The first project I had sole charge of, a toll gate. Such a little project, such a silly little project to lose someone on. The wood frame for the passageway collapsed before we got the keystone in. The whole arch came down. Someone got killed." It had been a very young man, slim and tall with a limp. He was raising his little sister. She hadn't been more than ten. Running loose in the fields around the site, she had missed the collapse, the boy's death. Dafuen? Naus? He couldn't remember his name. And the girl—what had her name been? *I should remember. I owe that much to them.*

"Every time I lose someone," he said at last, "I remember the others. There've been twelve in seventeen years. Not so many, considering. Building's dangerous. My record's better than most."

"But it doesn't matter, does it?" she said. "You still feel you killed each one of them, as surely as if you'd thrown them off a bridge yourself."

"It's my responsibility. The first one, Duar—" *that* had been his name; there it was. The name loosened something in Kit. His face warmed: tears, hot tears running down his face.

"It's all right," she said. She held him until he stopped crying.

"How did you know?" he said finally.

"I am the eldest surviving member of the Ferry family," she said. "My father died. My mother. My aunt died seven years ago. And then I watched my brother leave to cross the mist, three years ago now. It was a perfect day, calm and sunny, but he never made it. He went instead of me because the river felt wrong to me that day. It could have been me. It should have, maybe. So I understand."

She stretched a little. "Not that most people don't. If Petro Housewright sends his daughter to select timber in the mountains and she doesn't come back—eaten by wolves, struck by lightning, I don't know—is Petro to blame? It's probably the wolves or the lightning. Maybe it's the daughter, if she did something stupid. And it *is* Petro, a little; she wouldn't have been there at all if he hadn't sent her. And it's her mother for being fearless and teaching that to her daughter, and Thom Green for wanting a new room to his house. Everyone except maybe the wolves feels responsible. This path leads nowhere. Loreh would have died sooner or later." Rasali added softly, "We all do."

"Can you accept death so readily?" he asked. "Yours even?"

She leaned back, her face suddenly weary. "What else can I do, Kit? Someone must ferry and I am better suited than most—and by more than my blood. I love the mist, its currents and the smell of it and the power in my body as I push us all through. Petro's daughter Cilar— she did not want to die when the wolves came, I'm sure, but she loved selecting timber."

"If it comes for you?" he said. "Would you be so sanguine then?"

241

She laughed and the pensiveness was gone. "No indeed. I will curse the stars and go down fighting. But it will still have been a wonderful thing, to cross the mist."

At University, Kit's relationships had all been casual. There were lectures that everyone attended, and he lived near streets and pubs crowded with students; but the physical students had a tradition of keeping to themselves that was rooted in the personal preferences of their predecessors and in their own. The only people who worked harder than the engineers were the ale-makers, the University joke went. Kit and the other physical students talked and drank and roomed and slept together.

In his third year, he met Domhu Canna at the arcade where he bought vellums and paper: a small woman with a heart-shaped face and hair in black clouds that she kept somewhat confined by gray ribbons. She was a philosophical student from a city two thousand miles to the east, on the coast.

He was fascinated. Her mind was abrupt and fish-quick and made connections he didn't understand. To her, everything was a metaphor, a symbol for something else. People, she said, could be better understood by comparing their lives to animals, to the seasons, to the structure of certain lyrical poems, to a gambling game.

This was another form of pattern-making, he saw. Perhaps people were like teamed oxen to be led, or like metals to be smelted and shaped to one's purpose, or like the stones for a dry-laid wall, which had to be carefully selected for shape and strength, sorted, and placed. This last suited him best. What held them together was not external mortar but their own weight and the planning and patience of the drystone builder. But it was an inadequate metaphor. People were this, but they were all the other things as well.

He never understood what Domhu found attractive in him. They never talked about regularizing their relationship. When her studies were done halfway through his final year, she returned to her city to help found a new university, and in any case her people did not enter into term marriages. They separated amicably and with a sense of loss on his part at least, but it did not occur to him until years later that things might have been different.

The winter was rainy but there were days they could work and they did. By spring, there had been other deaths unrelated to the bridge on both banks: a woman who died in childbirth, a child who had never breathed properly in his short life, two fishers lost when they capsized, several who died for the various reasons that old or sick people died.

Over the spring and summer they finished the anchorages, featureless masses of blocks and mortar anchored to the bedrock. They were buried so that only a few courses of stone showed above the ground. The anchoring bolts were each tall as a man, hidden behind the portals through which the chains would pass.

The Farside pillar was finished by midwinter of the third year, well before the Nearside tower. Jenner and Teniant Planner had perfected a signal system that allowed detailed technical information to pass between the banks, and Kit took full advantage of it. Documents traveled each time a ferry crossed. Rasali made thirty-eight trips. Though he spent much of his time with Kit, Valo made nineteen. Kit did not cross the mist at all unless the flags told him he must.

It was early spring and Kit was in Farside when the signals went up: *Message. Imperial seal.* He went to Rasali at once.

"I can't go," she said. "I just got here yesterday. The Big Ones—"

"I have to get across and Valo's at Nearside. There's news from the capital."

"News has always waited before."

"No it hasn't. News waited restlessly, pacing along the levee until we could pick it up."

"Use the flags," she said impatiently.

"The seals can't be broken by anyone but me or Jenner. He's over here. I'm sorry," he said, thinking of her brother, dead four years before.

"If you die no one can read it," she said, but they left just after dusk anyway. "If we must go, better then than earlier or later."

He met her at the upper dock at dusk. The sky was streaked with bright bands of green and gold, clouds catching the last of the sun so that they glowed but radiated no light. The current down the river was steady. The mist between the levees was already in shadow, smooth dunes twenty feet high.

Rasali waited silently, coiling and uncoiling a rope in her hands. Beside her stood two women, a man, and a dog: dealers in spices returning from the plantations of Gloth, the dog whining and restless. Kit was burdened with document cases filled with vellum and paper rolled tightly and wrapped in oilcloth. Rasali seated the merchants and their dog in the ferry's bow, their forty crates of cinnamon and nutmeg amidships, Kit in the back near her. In silence she untied and pushed away from the dock.

She stood at the stern, braced against the scull. For a moment he could pretend that this was water they moved on and he half expected to hear sloshing, but the big paddle made no noise. It was so quiet that he could hear her breath, the dog's nervous panting in front, and his own pulse, too fast. Then the *Crossing* slid up the long smooth slope of a dune and there was no possibility that this could be anything but mist.

He heard a soft sighing, like air entering a once-sealed room. It was hard to see so far, but the lingering light showed him mist heaving on the face of a neighboring dune, like a bubble coming to the surface of mud. The dome grew and then burst. There was a gasp from one of the women. A shape rolled away, too dark for Kit to see more than its length.

"What—" he said in wonder.

"Fish," Rasali breathed to Kit. "Not small ones. They are biting tonight. We should not have come."

It was night now. The first tiny moon appeared, followed by stars. Rasali oared gently through the dunes, face turned to the sky. At first he thought she was praying but she was navigating. There were more fish now: each time the sighing sound, the dark shape half seen. He heard someone singing, the voice carrying somehow, from far behind.

"The fishers," Rasali said. "They will stay close to the levees tonight. I wish...."

But she left the wish unspoken. They were over the deep mist now. He could not say how he knew this. He had a sudden vision of the bridge overhead, a black span bisecting the star-spun sky, the parabolic arch of the chains perhaps visible, perhaps not. People would stride across the river an arrow's flight overhead, unaware of this place beneath. Perhaps they would stop and look over the bridge's railings but they would be too high to see the fish as any but small shadows—supposing they saw them at all, supposing they stopped at all. The Big Ones would be novelties, weird creatures that caused a safe shiver, like hearing a frightening story late at night.

Perhaps Rasali saw the same thing for she said suddenly, "Your bridge. It will change all this."

"It must. I am sorry," he said again. "We are not meant to be here on mist."

"We are not meant to cross this without passing through it. Kit—" Rasali said as though starting a sentence and then fell silent. After a moment she began to speak again, her voice low, as though she were speaking to herself. "The soul often hangs in a balance of some sort. Tonight do I lie down in the high fields with Dirna Tanner or not? At the fair, do I buy ribbons or wine? For the new ferry's headboard, do I use camphor or pearwood? Small things. A kiss, a ribbon, a grain that coaxes the knife this way or that. They are not, Kit Meinem of Atyar. Our souls wait for our answer because any answer changes us. This is why I wait to decide what I feel about your bridge. I'm waiting until I know how I will be changed."

"You never know how things will change you," Kit said.

"If you do not, you have not waited to find out." There was a popping noise barely a stone's throw to starboard. "Quiet."

On they moved. In daylight, Kit knew, the trip took less than an hour but now it seemed much longer. Perhaps it was. He looked up at the stars and thought they had moved but perhaps not.

His teeth were clenched, as were all his muscles. When he tried to relax them, he realized it was not fear that cramped him but something else, something outside him. Rasali's stroke faltered.

He recognized it now, the sound that was not a sound, like the deepest pipes on an organ, a drone too low to hear but which turned his bones to liquid and his muscles to flaked and rusting iron. His breath labored from his chest in grunts. His vision narrowed. Moving as though through honey, he strained his hands to his head, cradling it. He could not see Rasali except as a gloom against the slightly less gloom of the mist but he heard her pant, tiny pain-filled breaths like an injured dog.

The thrumming in his body pounded at his bones now, dissolving them. He wanted to cry out but there was no air left in his lungs. He realized suddenly that the mist beneath them was raising itself. It piled up along the boat's sides. *I never got to finish the bridge,* he thought. *And I never kissed her.* Did Rasali have any regrets?

The mound roiled and became a hill, which became a mountain obscuring part of the sky. The crest melted into curls and there was a shape inside, large and dark as night itself, that slid and followed the collapsing mist. It seemed not to move, but he knew that was only because of the size of the thing, that it took ages for its full length to pass. That was all he saw before his eyes slipped shut.

How long he lay there in the bottom of the boat, he didn't know. At some point he realized he was there. Some time later he found he could move again, his bones and muscles back to what they should be. The dog was barking. "Rasali?" he said shakily. "Are we sinking?"

"Kit." Her voice was a thread. "You're still alive. I thought we were dead."

"That was a Big One?"

"I don't know. No one has ever seen one. Maybe it was just a Fairly Large One."

The old joke. Kit choked on a weak laugh.

"Shit," Rasali said in the darkness. "I dropped the oar."

"Now what?" he said.

"I have smaller spares, but it's going to take longer and we'll land in the wrong place. We'll have to tie off and then walk up to get help."

I'm alive, he did not say. *I can walk a thousand miles tonight.*

It was nearly dawn before they got to Nearside. The two big moons rose just before they landed, a mile south of the dock. The spice traders and their dog went on ahead while Kit and Rasali secured the boat and walked up together. Halfway home, Valo came down at a dead run.

"I was waiting and you didn't come—" He was pale and panting. "But they told me, the other passengers, that you made it and—"

"Valo." Rasali hugged him and held him hard. "We're safe, little one. We're here. It's done."

"I thought. . . ." he said.

"I know," she said. "Valo, please, I am so tired. Can you get the *Crossing* up to the dock? I am going to my house and I will sleep for a day, and I don't care if the Empress herself is tapping her foot, it's going to wait." She released Valo, saluted Kit with a weary smile, and walked up the long flank of the levee. Kit watched her leave.

The "Imperial seal" was a letter from Atyar, some underling arrogating authority and asking for clarification on a set of numbers Kit had sent— scarcely worth the trip at any time, let alone across mist on a bad night. Kit cursed the capital, Empire, and the Department of Roads, and then sent the information along with a tautly worded paragraph about seals and their appropriate use.

Two days later, he got news that would have brought him across the mist in any case. The caravan carrying the first eyebars and bolts was twelve miles out on the Hoic Mine Road. Kit and his ironmaster Tandreve Smith rode out to meet the wagons as they crept southward and found them easing down a gradual slope near Oud village. The carts were long and built strong, their contents covered, each pulled by a team of tough-legged oxen with patient expressions. Their pace was slow and drivers walked beside them, singing something unfamiliar to Kit's city-bred ears.

"Ox-tunes. We used to sing these at my uncle's farm," Tandreve said, and sang:

> *"Remember last night's dream,*
> *the sweet cold grass, the lonely cows.*
> *You had your bollocks then."*

Tandreve chuckled, and Kit with her.

One of the drivers wandered over as Kit pulled his horse to a stop. Unattended, her team moved forward anyway. "Folks," she said and nodded. A taciturn woman.

Kit swung down from the saddle. "These are the chains?"

"You're from the bridge?"

"Kit Meinem of Atyar."

The woman nodded again. "Berallit Red-Ox of Ilver. Your smiths are sitting on the tail of the last wagon."

One of the smiths, a rangy man with singed eyebrows, loped forward to meet them and introduced himself as Jared Toss of Little Hoic. They walked beside the carts as they talked, and he threw aside a tarp to show Kit and Tandreve what they carried: stacks of iron eyebars, each a rod ten feet long with eyes at either end. Tandreve walked sideways as she inspected them. She and Jared soon lost themselves in a technical discussion. Kit kept them company, leading Tandreve's forgotten horse and his own, content for the moment to let the masters talk it out. He moved a little forward until he was abreast of the oxen. *Remember last night's dream,* he thought and then: *I wonder what Rasali dreamt?*

After that night on the mist, Rasali seemed to have no bad days. She took people the day after they arrived, no matter what the weather or the mist's character. The tavern keepers grumbled at this but the decrease in time each visitor stayed was made up for by the increase in numbers of serious-eyed men and women sent by firms in Atyar to establish offices in the towns on the River's far side. It made things easier for the bridge as well, since Kit and others could move back and forth as needed. Kit remained reluctant, more so since the near-miss.

There was enough business for two boats. Valo volunteered to ferry more often but Rasali refused the help, allowing him to ferry only when she couldn't prevent it. "The Big Ones don't seem to care about me this winter," she said to him, "but I can't say they would feel the same about tender meat like you." With Kit she was more honest. "If he is to leave ferrying to go study in the capital, it's best sooner than later. Mist will be dangerous until the last ferry crosses it. And even then, even after your bridge is done."

It was only Rasali who seemed to have this protection. The fishing people had as many problems as in any year. Denis Redboat lost his coracle when it was rammed ("—by a Medium-Large One," he laughed in the tavern later: sometimes the oldest jokes really were the best), though he was fished out by a nearby boat before he sank too deep. The rash was only superficial but his hair grew back only in patches.

Kit sat in the crowded beer garden of The Deer's Hart watching Rasali and Valo cover with fishskin a little pinewood skiff in the boat yard next door. Valo had called out a greeting when Kit first sat down and Rasali turned her head to smile at him, but after that they ignored him. Some of the locals stopped by to greet him and the barman stayed for some time, telling him about the ominous yet unchanging ache in his back, but for most of the afternoon Kit was alone in the sun, drinking cellar-cool porter and watching the boat take shape.

In the midsummer of the fourth year, it was rare for Kit to have all the afternoon of a beautiful day to himself. The anchorages had been finished for some months. So had the rubble-filled ramps that led to the arched passages through each pillar. The pillars themselves had taken longer, and the granite saddles that would support the chains over the towers had only just been put in place.

They were only slightly behind on Kit's deadlines for most of the materials. More than a thousand of the eyebars and bolts for the chains were laid out in rows, the iron smelling of the linseed oil used to protect them during transit. More were expected in before winter. Close to the ramps were the many fishskin ropes and cables that would be needed to bring the first chain across the gap. They were irreplaceable—probably the most valuable thing on the work sites—and were treated accordingly, kept in closed tents that reeked.

Kit's high-work specialists were here, too: the men and women who would do the first perilous tasks, mostly experts who had worked on other big spans or the towers of Atyar.

Valo and Rasali were not alone in the boat yard. Rasali had sent to the ferry folk of Ubmie a hundred miles to the south, and they had arrived a few days before: a woman and her cousin, Chell and Lan Crosser. The strangers had the same massive shoulders and good looks the Ferrys had, but they shared a faraway expression of their own. The river was broader at Ubmie, deeper, so perhaps death was closer to them. Kit wondered what they thought of his task. The bridge would cut into ferry trade for many hundreds of miles on either side and Ubmie had been reviewed as a possible site for the bridge, but they must not have resented it or they would not be here.

Everything waited on the ferry folk. The next major task was to bring the lines across the river to connect the piers—fabricating the chains required temporary cables and catwalks be in place first—but this could not be rushed. Rasali, Valo, and the Crossers all needed to feel at the same time that it was safe to cross. Kit tried not to be impatient. In any case he had plenty to do—items to add to lists, formal reports and polite updates to send to the many interested parties in Atyar and Triple, instructions to pass on to the ropemakers, the masons, the road-builders, the exchequer. And Jenner: Kit had written to the capital, and the Department of Roads was offering Jenner the lead on the second bridge across the river, to be built a few hundred miles to the north. Kit was to deliver the cartel the next time they were on the same side, but he was grateful the officials had agreed to leave Jenner with him until the first chain on this bridge was in place. Things to do.

He pushed all this from his mind. *Later,* he said to the things, half-apologetically. *I'll deal with you later. For now just let me sit in the sun and watch other people work.*

The sun slanted peach-gold through the oak's leaves before Rasali and Valo finished for the day. The skiff was finished, an elegant tiny curve of pale wood, red-dyed fishskin, and fading sunlight. Kit leaned against the fence as they tossed a cup of water over its bow and then drew it into the shadows of the storage shed. Valo took off at a run—*so much energy, even after a long day;* ah, youth—as Rasali walked to the fence and leaned on it from her side.

"It's beautiful," he said.

She rolled her neck. "I know. We make good boats. Are you hungry? Your busy afternoon must have raised an appetite."

He had to laugh. "We laid the capstone this morning. I *am* hungry."

"Come on then. Thalla will feed us all."

Dinner was simple. The Deer's Hart was better known for its beer than its foods, but the stew Thalla served was savory with chervil and thick enough to stand a spoon in. Valo had friends to be with, so they ate with Chell and Lan, who turned out to be like Rasali, calm but light-hearted. At dusk, the Crossers left to explore the Nearside taverns, leaving Kit and Rasali to watch heat lightning in the west. The air was thick and warm, soft as wool.

"You never come up to the work sites on either side," Kit said suddenly after a comfortable, slightly drunken silence. He inspected his earthenware mug, empty now except for the smell of yeast.

Rasali had given up on the benches and sat instead on one of the garden tables. She leaned back until she lay supine, face toward the sky. "I've been busy, perhaps you noticed?"

"It's more than that. Everyone finds time here and there. And you used to."

"I did, didn't I? I just haven't seen the point lately. The bridge changes everything but I don't see yet how it changes me. So I wait until it's time. Perhaps it's like the mist."

"What about now?"

She rolled her head until her cheek lay against the rough wood of the tabletop: looking at him, he could tell, though her eyes were hidden in shadows. What did she see, he wondered. What was she hoping to see? It pleased him but made him nervous.

"Come to the tower now, tonight," he said. "Soon everything changes. We pull the ropes across and make the chains and hang the supports and lay the road. It stops being a project and becomes a bridge, a road. But tonight it's still just two towers and some plans. Rasali, climb it with me. I can't describe what it's like up there—the wind, the sky all around you, the river below." He flushed at the urgency in his voice. When she remained silent he added, "You change whether you wait for it or not."

"There's lightning," she said.

"It runs from cloud to cloud," he said. "Not to earth."

"Heat lightning." She sat up. "So show me this place."

———

The work site was abandoned. The sky overhead had filled with clouds lit from within by the lightning, which was worse than no light at all since it ruined their night vision. They staggered across the site, trying to plan their paths in the moments of light, doggedly moving through the darkness. "Shit," Rasali said suddenly in the darkness, then: "Tripped over something or other. Ghost sheep." Kit found himself laughing.

They took the internal stairs instead of the scaffold. Kit knew them thoroughly, knew every irregular turn and riser, so he counted them aloud to Rasali as he led her by the hand. They reached one hundred and ninety-four before they saw light from a flash of lightning overhead, two hundred and eighteen when they finally stepped onto the roof, panting for air.

They were not alone. A woman gasped; she and the man with her bolted down the stairs, laughing. Rasali said with satisfaction, "Sera Oakfield. I'd recognize that laugh anywhere. Then that was Erno Bridgeman with her."

"He took his name from the bridge?" Kit asked but Rasali said only, "Oh," in a child's voice. Silent lightning painted the sky over her head in sudden strokes of purple-white, shot through what seemed a dozen layers of cloud, an incomprehensible complexity of light and shadow.

"The sky is so much closer." She walked to the edge and looked down at Nearside. Dull gold light poured from doors open to the heavy air. Kit stayed where he was, content to watch her. The light—when there was light—was shadowless and her face looked young and full of wonder. After a time she came to him.

They said nothing, only kissed and then made love in a nest of their discarded clothes. Kit felt the stone of his bridge against his knees, his back. It was still warm as skin from the day's heat, but not as warm as Rasali. She was softer than the rocks and tasted sweet.

A feeling he could not have described cracked open his chest, his throat, his belly. It had been a long time since he had had sex, not met his own needs. He had nearly forgotten the delight of it, the sharp rising shock of his coming, the rocking ocean of hers. Even their awkwardness pleased him, because it held in it the possibility of doing this again, and better.

When they were done they talked. "You know my goal, to build this bridge." Kit looked down at her face, there and gone in the flickering of the lightning. "But I do not know yours."

Rasali laughed softly. "Yet you have seen me succeed a thousand times, and fail a few. I wish to live well."

"That's not a goal," Kit said.

"Why? Because it's not yours? Which is better, Kit Meinem of Atyar? A single great victory or a thousand small ones?" And then: "Tomorrow," Rasali said. "We will take the rope across tomorrow."

"You're sure?" Kit asked.

"That's a strange statement coming from you. The bridge is all about crossing being a certainty, yes? Like the sun coming up each morning? We agreed this afternoon. It's time."

Dawn came early with the innkeeper's rap on the door. Kit woke disoriented, tangled in the sheets of his little cupboard bed. After he and Rasali had come down from the pillar, Rasali to sleep and Kit to do everything that needed to happen before the rope was brought across, all in the few hours remaining to the night. His skin smelled of Rasali but he was stunned with lack of sleep, and had trouble believing the sex had been real. But there was stone dust ground into his palms. He smiled and, though it was high summer, sang a spring song from Atyar as he quickly washed and dressed. He drank a bowl filled with broth in the taproom. It was tangy, lukewarm. A single small perch stared up at him from a salted eye. Kit left the fish, and left the inn.

The clouds and the lightning were gone. Early as it was the sky was already pale and hot. The news was everywhere and the entire town, or so it seemed, drifted with Kit to the work site, flowed over the levee, and settled onto the bank.

The river was a blinding creamy ribbon, looking as it had the first time he had seen it; and for a minute he felt dislocated in time. High mist was seen as a good omen and though he did not believe in omens he was nevertheless glad. The signal towers' flags hung limp against the hot blue-white sky.

Kit walked down to Rasali's boat, nearly hidden in its own tight circle of people. As Kit approached, Valo called, "Hey, Kit!" Rasali looked up. Her smile was like welcome shade on a bright day. The circle opened to accept him.

"Greetings, Valo Ferry of Farside, Rasali Ferry of Farside," he said. When he was close enough, he clasped Rasali's hands in his own, loving their warmth despite the day's heat.

"Kit." She kissed his mouth to a handful of muffled hoots and cheers from the bystanders and a surprised noise from Valo. She tasted like chicory.

Daell Cabler nodded absently to Kit. She was the lead ropemaker. She, her husband Stivvan, and the journeymen and masters they had summoned were inspecting the hundreds of fathoms of twisted fishskin cord, loading them without kinks onto spools three feet across and loading those onto a wooden frame bolted to *The Tranquil Crossing*.

The rope was thin, not much more than a cord, narrower than Kit's smallest finger. It looked fragile, and nothing like strong enough to carry its own weight for a quarter of a mile. The tests said otherwise.

Several of the stronger people from the bridge handed down small heavy crates to Valo and Chell Crosser, in the bow. Silverwork from Hedeclin and copper in bricks: the ferry was to be weighted somewhat forward, which would make the first part of the crossing more difficult but should help by the end, as the cord paid out and took on weight from the mist.

"—We think, anyway," Valo had said, two months back when he and Rasali had discussed the plan with Kit. "But we don't know. No one's done this before." Kit had nodded and not for the first time wished that the river had been a little less broad. Upriver perhaps—but no, this had been the only option. He did write to an old classmate back in Atyar, a man who now taught the calculus, and presented their solution. His friend had written back to say that it looked as though it ought to work, but that he knew little of mist.

One end of the rope snaked along the ground and up the levee. No one touched the rope. They crowded close but left a narrow lane and stepped only carefully across it. Daell and Stivvan Cabler followed the lane back up and over the levee, to check the temporary anchor at the Nearside pillar's base.

There was a wait. People sat on the grass or walked back to watch the Cablers. Someone brought broth and small beer from the fishers' tavern. Valo and Rasali and the two Crossers were remote, focused already on what came next.

And for himself? Kit was wound up but it wouldn't do to show anything but a calm, confident front. He walked among the watchers and exchanged words or a smile with each of them. He knew them all by now, even the children.

It was nearly midmorning before Daell and Stivvan returned. The ferryfolk took their positions in the *Crossing*, two to each side, far enough apart that they could pull on different rhythms. Kit was useless freight until they got to the other side, so he sat at the bow where his weight might do some good. Uni stumbled as she was helped into the boat's stern: she would monitor the rope but, as she told them all, she was nervous: she had never crossed the mist. "I think I'll wait 'til the catwalks go up before I return," she added. "Stivvan can sleep without me 'til then."

"Ready, Kit?" Rasali called forward.

"Yes," he said.

"Daell? Lan? Chell? Valo?" Assent all around.

"A historic moment," Valo announced. "The day the mist was bridged."

"Make yourself useful, boy," Rasali said. "Prepare to scull."

"Right," Valo said.

"Push us off," she said to the people on the dock. A cheer went up.

The dock and all the noises behind them disappeared almost immediately. The ferryfolk had been right that it was a good day for such an undertaking. The mist was a smooth series of ripples no taller than a man, and so dense that the *Crossing* rode high despite the extra weight and drag. It was the gentlest he had ever seen the river.

Kit's eyes ached from the brightness. "It will work?" Kit said, meaning the rope and their trip across the mist and the bridge itself—a question rather than a statement: unable to help himself, even though he had worked the calculations himself and had Jenner and Daell and Stivvan and Valo and a specialist in Atyar all check them, even though it was a child's question. Isolated in the mist, even competence seemed insufficient.

"Yes," Daell Cabler said from aft.

The rowers said little. At one point Rasali murmured into the deadened air, "To the right," and Valo and Lan Crosser changed their stroke to avoid a gentle mound a few feet high directly in their path. Mostly the *Crossing* slid steadily across the regular swells. Unlike his other trips, Kit saw no dark shapes in the mist, large or small. From here they could not see the dock, but the levee ahead was scattered with Farsiders waiting for the work they would do when the ferry landed.

There was nothing he could do to help, so Kit watched Rasali scull in the blazing sun. The work got harder as the rope spooled out until she and the others panted. Shining with sweat, her skin was nearly as bright as the mist in the sunlight, and he wondered how she could bear the light without burning. Her face looked solemn, intent on the eastern shore. Her eyes were alight with reflections from the mist. Then he recognized her expression. It was joy.

How will she bear it, he thought suddenly, *when there is no more ferrying to be done?* He had known that she loved what she did but he had never realized just how much. He felt as though he had been kicked in the gut. What would it do to her? His bridge would destroy this thing that she loved, that gave her name. How could he not have thought of that? "Rasali," he said, unable to stay silent.

"Not now," she said. The rowers panted as they dug in.

"It's like . . . pulling through dirt," Valo gasped.

"Quiet," Rasali snapped and then they were silent except for their laboring breath. Kit's own muscles knotted sympathetically. Foot by foot the ferry heaved forward. At some point they were close enough to the Farside upper dock that someone threw a rope to Kit and at last he could do something, however inadequate. He took the rope and pulled. The rowers pushed for their final strokes. The boat slid up beside the dock. People swarmed aboard, securing the boat to the dock, the rope to a temporary anchor on the bank.

Released, the Ferrys and the Crossers embraced, laughing a little dizzily. They walked up the levee toward Farside town and did not look back.

Kit left the ferry to join Jenner Ellar.

It was hard work. The rope's end had to be brought over an oiled stone saddle on the levee and down to a temporary anchor and capstan at the Farside pillar's base, a task that involved driving a team of oxen through a temporary gap Jenner had cut into the levee: a risk but one that had to be taken.

More oxen were harnessed to the capstan. Daell Cabler was still pale and shaking from the crossing, but after a glass of something cool and dark, she and her Farside counterparts walked the rope to look for any new weak spots. They found none. Jenner stayed with the capstan. Daell and Kit returned to the temporary saddle in the levee, the notch polished like glass and gleaming with oil.

The rope was released from the dockside anchor. The rope over the saddle whined as it took the load and flattened, and there was a deep pinging noise as it swung out to make a single line down from the saddle, down into the mist. The oxen at the capstan dug in.

The next hours were the tensest of Kit's life. For a time, the rope did not appear to change. The capstan moaned and clicked, and at last the rope slid by inches, by feet, through the saddle. He could do nothing but watch and rework all the calculations yet again in his mind. He did not see Rasali, but Valo came up after a time to watch the progress. Answering his questions settled Kit's nerves. The calculations were correct. He had done this before. He was suddenly starved and voraciously ate the food that Valo had brought for him. How long had it been since the broth at The Fish? Hours. Most of a day.

The oxen puffed and grunted and were replaced with new teams. Even lubricated and with leather sleeves, the rope moved reluctantly across the saddle, but it did move. And then the pressure started to ease and the rope paid through the saddle faster. The sun was westering when at last the rope lifted free of the mist. By dusk, the rope was sixty feet above it, stretched humming-tight between the Farside and Nearside levees and the temporary anchors.

Just before dark, Kit saw the flags go up on the signal tower: *secure*.

Kit worked on and then seconded projects for five years after he left University. His father knew men and women at the higher levels in the Department of Roads, and his old tutor, Skossa Timt, knew more, so many were high-profile works, but he loved all of them, even his first lead, the little toll gate where the boy, Duar, had died.

All public work—drainage schemes, roadwork, amphitheaters, public squares, sewers, alleys and mews—was alchemy. It took the invisible patterns that people made as they lived, and turned them into stone and brick and wood and space. Kit built things that moved people through the intangible architecture that was his mind and his notion—and Empire's notion—of how their lives could be better.

The first major project he led was a replacement for a collapsed bridge in the Four Peaks region north of Atyar. The original had been a chain suspension bridge but much smaller than the mist bridge would be, crossing only a hundred yards, its pillars only forty feet high. With maintenance, it had survived heavy use for three centuries, shuddering under the carts that brought quicksilver ore down to the smelting village of Oncalion; but after the heavy snowfalls of what was subsequently called the Wolf Winter, one of the gorge's walls collapsed, taking the north pillar with it and leaving nowhere stable to rebuild. It was easier to start over, two hundred yards upstream.

The people of Oncalion were not genial. Hard work made for hard men and women. There was a grim, desperate edge to their willingness to labor on the bridge, because their livelihood and their lives were dependent on the mine. They had to be stopped at the end of each day or, dangerous as it was, they would work through moonlit nights.

But it was lonely work, even for Kit who did not mind solitude, and when the snows of the first winter brought a halt to construction, he returned with some relief to Atyar to stay with his father. Davell Meinem was old now. His memory was weakening though still strong enough.

He spent his days overseeing construction of a vast and fabulous public maze of dry-laid stones brought from all over Empire: his final project, he said to Kit, an accurate prophecy. Skossa Timt had died during the Wolf Winter, but many of Kit's classmates were still in the capital. Kit spent evenings with them, attended lectures and concerts, entered for the season into a casual relationship with an architect who specialized in waterworks.

Kit returned to the site at Oncalion as soon as the roads cleared. In his absence, through the snows and melt-off, the people of Oncalion had continued to work in the bitter cold, laying course after course of stone. The work had to be redone.

The second summer, they worked every day and moonlit nights and Kit worked beside them.

Kit counted the bridge as a failure although it was coming in barely over budget and only a couple of months late, and no one had died. It was an ugly design; the people of Oncalion had worked hard but joylessly; and there was all his dissatisfaction and guilt about the work that had to be done anew.

Perhaps there was something in the tone of his letters to his father, for there came a day in early autumn that Davell Meinem arrived in Oncalion, riding a sturdy mountain horse and accompanied by a journeyman who vanished immediately into one of the village's three taverns. It was the middle of the afternoon.

"I want to see this bridge of yours," Davell said. He looked weary but straight-backed as ever. "Show it to me."

"We'll go tomorrow," Kit said. "You must be tired."

"Now," Davell said.

They walked up from the village together. It was a cool day and bright, though the road was overshadowed with pines and fir trees. Basalt outcroppings were stained dark green and black with lichens. His father moved slowly, pausing often for breath. They met a steady trickle of local people leading heavy-laden ponies. The roadbed across the bridge wasn't quite complete and could not take carts yet, but ponies could cross carrying ore in baskets. Oncalion was already smelting these first small loads.

At the bridge, Davell asked the same questions he had asked when Kit was a child playing on his work sites. Kit found himself responding as he had so many years before, eager to explain—or excuse—each decision; and always, always the ponies passing.

They walked down to the older site. The pillar had been gutted for stones so all that was left was rubble, but it gave them a good view of the new bridge: the boxy pillars, the curve of the main chains, the thick vertical suspender chains, the slight sprung arch of the bulky roadbed. It looked as clumsy as a suspension bridge could. Yet another pony crossed, led by a woman singing something in the local dialect.

"It's a good bridge," Davell said.

Kit shook his head. His father, who had been known for his sharp tongue on the work sites though never to his son, said, "A bridge is a means to an end. It only matters because of what it does. Leads from *here* to *there*. If you do your work right they won't notice it, any more than you notice where quicksilver comes from, most times. It's a good bridge because they are already using it. Stop feeling sorry for yourself, Kit."

It was a big party that night. The Farsiders (and, Kit knew, the Nearsiders) drank and danced under the shadow of their bridge-to-be. Torchlight and firelight touched the stones of the tower base and anchorage, giving them mass and meaning, but above their light the tower was a black outline, the absence of stars. Torches ringed the tower's parapet; they seemed no more than gold stars among the colder ones.

Kit walked among them. Everyone smiled or waved and offered to stand him drinks but no one spoke much with him. It was as though the lifting of the cable had separated him from them. The immense towers had not done this; he had still been one of them to some degree at least—the instigator of great labors but still, one of them. But now, for tonight anyway, he was the man who bridged the mist. He had not felt so lonely since his first day here. Even Loreh Tanner's death had not severed him so completely from their world.

On every project, there was a day like this. It was possible that the distance came from him, he realized suddenly. He came to a place and built something, passing through the lives of people for a few months or years. And then he left. A road through dangerous terrain or a bridge across mist saved lives and increased trade, but it changed the world as well. It was his job to make a thing and then leave to make the next one—but it was also his preference, not to remain and see what he had done. What would Nearside and Farside look like in ten years, in fifty? He had never returned to a previous site.

It was harder this time or perhaps just different. Perhaps *he* was different. He was staying longer this time because of the size of the project, and he had allowed himself to love the country on either side of the bridge. To have more was to have more to miss when he eventually left.

Rasali—what would her life look like?

Valo danced by, his arm around a woman half a head taller than he—Rica Bridger—and Kit caught his arm. "Where is Rasali?" he shouted, then knowing he could not be heard over the noise of drums and pipes, he mouthed *Rasali*. He didn't hear what Valo said but followed his pointing hand.

Rasali was alone, flat on her back on the river side of the levee, looking up. There were no moons, so the Sky Mist hung close overhead, a river of stars that poured east to west. Kit knelt a few feet away. "Rasali Ferry of Farside."

Her teeth flashed in the dark. "Kit Meinem of Atyar."

He lay beside her. The grass was like bad straw, coarse against his back and neck. Without looking at him she passed a jar of something. Its taste was strong as tar and Kit gasped for a moment.

"I did not mean. . . ." he started but trailed off, unsure how to continue.

"Yes," she said and he knew she had heard the words he didn't say. Her voice contained a shrug. "Many people born into a Ferry family never cross the mist."

"But you—" He stopped, felt carefully for his words. "Maybe others don't but you do. And I think maybe you must do so."

"Just as you must build," she said softly. "That's clever of you to realize that."

"And there will be no need after this, will there? Not on boats anyway. We'll still need fishskin, so the fishers will still go out, but they—"

"—stay close to shore," she said.

"And you?" he asked.

"I don't know, Kit. Days come, days go. I go onto the mist or I don't. I live or I don't. There is no certainty but there never is."

"It doesn't distress you?"

"Of course it does. I love and I hate this bridge of yours. I will pine for the mist, for the need to cross it. But I do not want to be part of a family that all die young without even a corpse for the burning. If I have a child she will not need to make the decision I did: to cross the mist and die, or to stay safe on one side of the world and never see the other. She will lose something. She will gain something else."

"Do you hate me?" he said finally, afraid of the answer, afraid of any answer she might give.

"No. Oh, no." She rolled over to him and kissed his mouth, and Kit could not say if the salt he tasted was from her tears or his own.

The autumn was spent getting the chains across the river. In the days after the crossing, the rope was linked to another and pulled back the way it had come, coupled now; and then there were two ropes in parallel courses. It was tricky work, requiring careful communications via the signal towers, but it was completed without event, and Kit could at last get a good night's sleep. To break the rope would have been to start anew with the long difficult crossing. Over the next days, each rope was replaced with fishskin cable strong enough to take the weight of the chains until they were secured.

The cables were hoisted to the tops of the pillars, to prefigure the path one of the eight chains would take: secured with heavy pins set in protected slots in the anchorages, making straight sharp lines to the saddles on the pillars and then, two hundred feet above the mist, the long perfect catenary. A catwalk was suspended from the cables. For the first time, people could cross the mist without the boats, though few chose to do so, except for the high workers from the capital and the coast: a hundred men and women so strong and graceful that they seemed another species and kept mostly to themselves. They were directed by a woman Kit had worked with before, Feinlin. The high-workers took no surnames. Something about Feinlin reminded him of Rasali.

The weather grew colder and the days shorter, and Kit pushed hard to have the first two chains across before the winter rains began. There would be no heavy work once the ground got too wet to give sturdy purchase to the teams. Calculations to the contrary, Kit could not quite trust that cables, even fishskin cables, would survive the weight of those immense arcs through an entire winter—or that a Big One would not take one down in the unthinking throes of some great storm.

The eyebars that would make up the chain were ten feet long and required considerable manhandling to be linked with bolts larger than a man's forearm. The links became a chain, even more cumbersome. Winches pulled the chain's end up to the saddles and out onto the catwalk.

After this, the work became even more difficult and painstaking. Feinlin and her people moved individual eyebars and pins out onto the catwalks and joined them in place; a backbreaking dangerous task that had to be exactly synchronized with the work on the other side of the river so that the cable would not be stressed.

Most nights Kit worked into the darkness. When the moons were bright enough, he, the high-workers, and the bridgewrights would work in shifts, day and night.

He crossed the mist six more times that fall. The high-workers disliked having people on the catwalks but he was the architect, after all, so he crossed once that way, struggling with vertigo. After that he preferred the ferries. When he crossed with Valo, they talked exclusively about the bridge—Valo had decided to stay until the bridge was complete and the ferries finished, though his mind was already full of the capital—but the other times, when it was Rasali, they were silent, listening to the hiss of the V-shaped scull moving in the mist. His fear of the mist decreased with each day they came closer to the bridge's completion, though he couldn't say why this was.

When Kit did not work through the night and Rasali was on the same side of the mist, they spent their nights together, sometimes making love, at other times content to share drinks or play ninepins in The Deer's Hart's garden. Kit's proficiency surprised everyone but himself—he had been famous for his accuracy, back in Atyar. He and Rasali did not talk again about what she would do when the bridge was complete, or what he would do, for that matter.

The hard work was worth it. It was still warm enough that the iron didn't freeze the high-worker's hands on the day they placed the final bolt. The first chain was complete.

Though work was slow through the winter, it was a mild one, and the second and third chains were in place by spring. The others were completed by the end of the summer.

With the heavy work done, some of the workers returned to their home-places. More than half had taken the name Bridger or something similar. "We have changed things," Kit said to Jenner on one of his Nearside visits, just before Jenner left for his new work. "No," Jenner said: "*You* have changed things." Kit did not respond but held this close and thought of it sometimes with mingled pride and fear.

The workers who remained were all high-workers, people who did not mind crawling about on the suspension chains securing the support ropes. For the past two years, the ropemakers for hundreds of miles up- and downstream had been twisting, cabling, looping, and reweaving the fishskin cables that would support the road deck. Crates, each marked with the suspender's position in the bridge, stood in carefully sorted towers in the old sheep field.

Kit's work was now all paperwork, it seemed—so many invoices, so many reports for the capital—but he managed every day to watch the high-workers. Sometimes he climbed to the tops of the pillars and looked down into the mist and saw Rasali's or Valo's ferry, an shape like an open eye half-hidden in tendrils of blazing white or pale gray.

Kit lost one more worker, Tommer Bullkeeper, who climbed onto the catwalk for a drunken bet and fell, with a maniacal cry that changed into unbalanced laughter as he vanished into the mist. His wife wept in mixed anger and grief, and the townspeople wore ash-color, and the bridge continued. Rasali held Kit when he cried in his room at The Bitch. "Never mind," she said. "Tommer was a good person: a drunk but good to his sons and his wife, careful with animals. People have always died. The bridge doesn't change that."

The towns changed shape as Kit watched. Commercial envoys from every direction gathered. Some stayed in inns and homes. Others built small houses, shops, and warehouses. Many used the ferries and it became common for these people to tip Rasali or Valo lavishly—"in hopes I never ride with you again," they would say. Valo laughed and spent this money buying beer for his friends. The letter had come from University and he would begin his studies with the winter term, so he had many farewells to make. Rasali told no one, not even Kit, what she planned to do with hers.

Beginning in the spring of the project's fifth year, they attached the road deck. Wood planks wide enough for oxen two abreast were nailed together with iron stabilizer struts. The bridge was made of several hundred sections constructed on the worksites and then hauled out by workers. Each segment had farther to go before being placed and secured. The two towns celebrated all night the first time a Nearsider shouted from her side of the bridge and was saluted by Farsider cheers. In the lengthening evenings, it became a pastime for people to walk onto the bridge and lie belly-down at its end, and look into the mist so far below them. Sometimes dark shapes moved within it but no one saw anything big enough to be a Big One. A few heedless locals dropped heavy stones from above to watch the mist twist away, opening holes into its depths, but their neighbors stopped them. "It's not respectful," one said; and, "Do you want to piss them off?" said another.

Kit asked her but Rasali never walked out with him. "I see enough from the river," she said.

Kit was Nearside, in his room in The Fish. He had lived in this room for five years and it looked it. Plans and timetables overlapped one another, pinned to the walls in the order he had needed them. The chair by the fire was heaped with clothes, books, a length of red silk he had seen at a fair and could not resist. It had been years since he sat there. The plans in his folio and on the oversized table had been replaced with waybills and receipts for materials, payrolls, and copies of correspondence between

Kit and his sponsors in the government. The window was open and Kit sat on the cupboard bed, watching a bee feel its way through the sun-filled air. He'd left half a pear on the table. He was waiting to see if the bee would find it, and thinking about the little hexagonal cells of a beehive, whether they were stronger than squares were and how he might test this.

Feet ran along the corridor. His door flew open. Rasali stood there blinking in the light, which was so golden that Kit didn't at first notice how pale she was, or the tears on her face. "What—" he said as he swung off his bed.

"Valo," she said. *"Pearlfinder."*

He held her. The bee left, then the sun, and still he held her as she rocked silently on the bed. Only when the square of sky in the window faded to purple and the little moon's crescent eased across it, did she speak. "Ah," she said, a sigh like a gasp. "I am so tired." She fell asleep as quickly as that, with tears still wet on her face. Kit slipped from the room.

The taproom was crowded, filled with ash-gray clothes, with soft voices and occasional sobs. Kit wondered for a moment if everyone had a set of mourning clothes always at hand and what this meant about them.

Brana Keep saw Kit in the doorway and came from behind the bar to speak with him. "How is she?" she said.

"I think she's asleep right now," Kit said. "Can you give me some food for her, something to drink?"

Brana nodded, spoke to her daughter Lixa as she passed into the back, then returned. "How are *you* doing, Kit? You saw a fair amount of Valo yourself."

"Yes," Kit said. Valo chasing the children through the field of stones, Valo laughing at the top of a tower, Valo serious-eyed with a handbook of the calculus in the shade of a half-built fishing boat. "What happened? She hasn't said anything yet."

Brana spread her hands out. "What can be said? Signal flags said he was going to cross just after midday but he never came. When we signaled over they said he left when they signaled."

"Could he be alive?" Kit asked, remembering the night that he and Rasali had lost the big scull, the extra hours it had taken for the crossing. "He might have broken the scull, landed somewhere downriver."

"No," Brana said. She was crying, too. "I know, that's what we wanted to hope. But Asa, one of the strangers, the high-workers; she was working overhead and heard the boat capsize, heard him cry out. She couldn't see anything and didn't know what she had heard until we figured it out."

"Three more months," Kit said mostly to himself. He saw Brana looking at him so he clarified: "Three more months. The bridge would have been done. This wouldn't have happened."

"This was today," Brana said, "not three months from now. People die when they die. We grieve and move on, Kit. You've been with us long enough to understand how we see these things. Here's the tray."

When Kit returned, Rasali was asleep. He watched her in the dark room, unwilling to light more than the single lamp he'd carried up with him. *People die when they die.* But he could not stop thinking about the bridge, the nearly finished deck. *Another three months. Another month.*

When she awakened, there was a moment when she smiled at him, her face weary but calm. Then she remembered and her face tightened and she started crying again. After a while Kit got her to eat some bread and fish and cheese and drink some watered wine. She did so obediently, like a child. When she was finished she lay back against him. Her matted hair pushed up into his mouth.

"How can he be gone?"

"I'm so sorry," Kit said. "The bridge was so close to finished. Three more months, and this wouldn't have—"

She pulled away. "What? Wouldn't have happened? Wouldn't have *had* to happen?" She stood and faced him. "His death would have been unnecessary?"

"I—" Kit began but she interrupted him, new tears streaking her face.

"He *died*, Kit. It wasn't necessary, it wasn't irrelevant, it wasn't anything except the way things are. But he's gone and I'm not and *now* what do I do, Kit? I lost my father and my aunt and my sister and my brother and my brother's son, and now I lose the mist when the bridge is done and then what? What am I then? Who are the Ferry people then?"

Kit knew the answer. However she changed, she would still be Rasali. Her people would still be strong and clever and beautiful. The mist would still be there, and the Big Ones. But she wouldn't be able to hear these words, not yet, not for months maybe. So he held her and let his own tears slip down his face and tried not to think.

Five years after the Oncalion bridge was completed, Kit was two years into building an aqueduct planned across the Bakyar valley. There were problems. The first stones could not sustain both the weight of the aqueduct and the water it was meant to carry. His predecessor on the project had been either incompetent or corrupt, and Kit was still sorting through the mess she had left behind. They were a season behind schedule, but when he heard about Davell Meinem's death, he left immediately for Atyar. Some time would be required to put his father's affairs in order but mostly he did not wish to miss Twentieth-day, when Davell would be remembered. Kit had known that Davell's death would leave a hole in him, but he had known his father was dying for years. He hadn't expected this to hurt as much as it did.

The Grayfield was a little amphitheatre Davell had designed when he was young, matured now to a warm half-circle of white stone and grass, fringed with cherry trees. It was a warm day, brilliantly sunny. The air smelled of honey-cakes and the last of the cherry blossoms. Kit was Davell's only child, so he stood alone at the red-tasseled archway to greet those who came. He was not surprised at how many came to honor his father, more and more until the amphitheatre overflowed, the honey-cakes were all eaten, and the silver bowls were filled with flowers, one from each mourner. Davell Meinem had built seven bridges, three aqueducts, a forum, two provincial complexes, and innumerable smaller projects, and he had maintained contacts with old friends from each of them; many more people had liked him for his humor and his kindness.

What surprised Kit was all the people who had come for *his* sake: fellow students, tutors, old lovers and companions, even the man who ran the wine shop he frequented whenever he was in the city. Many of them had never even met his father. He had not known that he was part of their patterns.

Five months later, when he was back in the Bakyar valley, a letter arrived wrapped in dirty oiled paper and clearly from far away. It was from the miners of Oncalion. "We heard about your father from a trader when we were asking about you," the letter said. "We are sorry for your loss."

The fairs to celebrate the opening of the bridge started days before the official date of Midsummer. Representatives of Empire, from Atyar and Triple, from the regional governors and anyone else who could contrive an excuse all polished their speeches and waited impatiently in suites of tents erected on hurriedly cleaned-up fields near (but not too near) Nearside. The town had bled northward until it surrounded the west pillar of the bridge. The land that had once been sheep-pasture—Sheepfield, it was now—at the foot of the pillar was crowded with fair tents and temporary booths, cheek by jowl with more permanent shops of wood and stone that sold food and the sorts of products a traveler might find herself needing.

Kit was proud of the new streets. He had organized construction of the crosshatch of sturdy cobblestones as something to do while he waited through the bridge's final year. The new wells had been a project of Jenner's, planned from the very beginning, but Kit had seen them completed. Kit had just received a letter from Jenner with news of his new mist bridge up in the Keitche mountains: on schedule, a happy work site. It was gneiss bedrock, so he was using explosives and had hired Liu Breaker for it; she was there now and sent her greetings.

Kit walked alone through the fair which had climbed the levee and established itself along the ridge. A few people, townspeople and workers, greeted him but others only pointed him out to their friends (*the man who built the bridge; see there, that short dark man*); and still others ignored him completely, just another stranger in a crowd of strangers. When he had first come to build the bridge everyone in Nearside knew everyone else, local or visitor. He felt solitude settling around him again, the loneliness of coming to a strange place and building something and then leaving. The people of Nearside were moving forward into this new world he had built, the world of a bridge across the mist, but he was not going with them.

He wondered what Rasali was doing over in Farside, and wished he could see her. They had not spoken since the days after Valo's death except once for a few minutes when he had come upon her at The Bitch. She had been withdrawn though not hostile. He had felt unbalanced and not sought her out since.

Now, at the end of his great labor, he longed to see her. When would she cross next? He laughed. He of all people should know better: *ten minutes' walk.*

The bridge was not yet officially open but Kit was the architect. The guards at the toll booth only nodded when he asked to pass and lifted the gate for him. A few people noticed and gestured as he climbed. When Uni Mason (hands filled with fairings) shouted something he could not hear clearly, Kit smiled and waved and walked on.

He had crossed the bridge before this. The first stage of building the heavy oak frames that underlay the roadbed had been a narrow strip of planking that led from one shore to the other. Nearly every worker had found some excuse for crossing it at least once before Empire had sent people to the tollgates. Swallowing his fear of the height, Kit himself had crossed it nearly every day for the last two months.

This was different. It was no longer his bridge but belonged to Empire and to the people of Nearside and Farside. He saw it with the eyes of a stranger.

The stone ramp was a quarter of a mile long, inclined gradually for carts. Kit hiked up, and the noises dropped behind and below him. The barriers that would keep animals (and people) from seeing the drop-off to either side were not yet complete: there were always things left unfinished at a bridge's opening, afterthoughts and additions. Ahead of him, the bridge was a series of perfect dark lines and arcs.

The ramp widened as it approached the pillar, and offered enough space for a cart to carefully turn onto the bridge itself. The bed of the span was barely wide enough for a cart with two oxen abreast, so Nearside and Farside would have to take turns sending wagons across. *For now,* Kit thought. *Later we can widen it, or build another. They.* It would be someone else.

The sky was overcast with high clouds the color of tin, their metallic sheen reflected in the mist below Kit. There were no railings, only fishskin ropes strung between the suspension cables that led up to the chains. Oxen and horses wouldn't like that, or the hollow sound their feet would make on the boards. Kit watched the deck roll before him in the wind, which was constant from the southwest. The roll wasn't so bad in this wind but perhaps they should add an iron railing or more trusses to lessen the twisting and make crossing more comfortable. Empire had sent a new engineer to take care of any final projects: Jeje Tesanthe at Atyar. He would mention it to her.

Kit walked to one side so that he could look down. Sound dropped off behind him, deadened as it always was by the mist. He could almost imagine that he was alone. It was several hundred feet down, but there was nothing to give scale to the coiling field of hammered metal below him. Deep in the mist he saw shadows that might have been a Big One or something smaller or a thickening of the mist, and then, his eyes learning what to look for, he saw more of the shadows, as though a school of fish were down there. One separated and darkened as it rose in the mist until it exposed its back almost immediately below Kit.

It was dark and knobby, shiny with moisture, flat as a skate, and it went on forever—thirty feet long perhaps, or forty, twisting as it rose to expose its underside or what he thought might be its underside. As Kit watched, the mist curled back from a flexing scaled wing of sorts, and then a patch that might have been a single eye or a field of eyes or something altogether different, and then a mouth like the arc of the suspension chains. The mouth gaped open to show another arc, a curve of gum or cartilage. The creature rolled and then sank and became a shadow and then nothing as the mist closed back over it.

Kit had stopped walking when he saw it. He forced himself to move forward again. A Big One, or perhaps just a Medium-Large One. At this height it hadn't seemed so big or so frightening. Kit was surprised at the sadness he felt.

Farside was crammed with color and fairings as well, but Kit could not find Rasali anywhere. He bought a tankard of rye beer and went to find some place alone.

———

Once it became dark and the Imperial representatives were safely tucked away for the night, the guards relaxed the rules and let their friends—and then any of the locals—on the bridge to look around. People who had worked on the bridge had papers to cross without charge for the rest of their lives but many others had watched it grow, and now they charmed or bribed or begged their way onto their bridge. Covered lamps were permitted, though torches were forbidden because of the oil that protected the fishskin ropes. From his seat on the levee, Kit watched the lights move along the bridge, there and then hidden by the suspension cables and deck, dim and inconstant as fireflies.

"Kit Meinem of Atyar."

Kit stood and turned to the voice behind him. "Rasali Ferry of Farside." She wore blue and white, and her feet were bare. She had pulled back her dark hair with a ribbon and her pale shoulders gleamed. She glowed under the moonlight like mist. He thought of touching her, kissing her, but they had not spoken since just after Valo's death.

She stepped forward and took the mug from his hand, drank the lukewarm beer, and just like that the world righted itself. He closed his eyes and let the feeling wash over him.

He took her hand and they sat on the cold grass and looked out across the river. The bridge was a black net of arcs and lines. Behind it the mist glowed blue-white in the light of the moons. After a moment he asked, "Are you still Rasali Ferry, or will you take a new name?"

"I expect I'll take a new one." She half-turned in his arms so that he could see her face, her eyes. "And you? Are you still Kit Meinem, or do you become someone else? Kit Who Bridged the Mist? Kit Who Changed the World?"

"Names in the city do not mean the same thing," Kit said absently. "*Did* I change the world?" He knew the answer already.

She looked at him for a moment as though trying to gauge his feelings. "Yes," she said slowly after a moment. She turned her face up toward the loose strand of bobbing lights: "There's your proof, as permanent as stone and sky."

"'Permanent as stone and sky,'" Kit repeated. "This afternoon—it flexes a lot, the bridge. There has to be a way to control it but it's not engineered for that yet. Or lightning could strike it. There are a thousand things that could destroy it. It's going to come down, Rasali. This year, next year, a hundred years from now, five hundred." He ran his fingers through his hair. "All these people, they think it's forever."

"No, we don't," Rasali said. "Maybe Atyar does, but we know better here. Do you need to tell a Ferry that nothing will last? *These* cables will fail eventually, *these* stones will fall—but not the *dream* of crossing the mist, the dream of connection. Now that we know it can happen, it will always be here. My father died. My sister Rothiel. My brother Ster. Valo." She stopped, swallowed. "Ferrys die, but there is always a Ferry to cross the mist. Bridges and ferryfolk, they are not so different, Kit." She leaned forward, across the space between them, and they kissed.

"Are you off soon?"

Rasali and Kit had made love on the levee against the cold grass. They had crossed the bridge together under the sinking moons, walked back to The Deer's Hart and bought more beer, the crowds thinner now, people gone home with their families or friends or lovers—the strangers from out of town bedding down in spare rooms, tents, anywhere they could. But Kit was too restless to sleep and he and Rasali ended up back by the mist, down on the dock. Morning was only a few hours away and the smaller moon had set. It was darker now and the mist had dimmed.

"In a few days," Kit said, thinking of the trunks and bags packed tight and gathered in his room at The Fish: the portfolio, fatter now and stained with water, mist, dirt and sweat. Maybe it was time for a new one. "Back to the capital."

There were lights on the opposite bank, fishers preparing for their work despite the fair, the bridge. *Some things don't change.*

"Ah," she said. They both had known this. It was no surprise. "What will you do there?"

Kit rubbed his face and felt stubble under his fingers. "Sleep for a hundred years. Then there's another bridge they want, down at the mouth of the river, a place called Ulei. The mist's nearly a mile wide. I'll go down and look at the site and start working on a budget."

"A mile," Rasali said. "Can you do it?"

"I think so. I bridged this, didn't I?" His gesture took in the bridge and the woman beside him. "Ulei is on an alluvial plain. There are some low islands. That's the only reason it's possible. So maybe a series of flat stone arches, one to the next. You? You'll keep building boats?"

"No." She leaned her head back and he felt her face against his ear. She smelled sweet and salty. "I don't need to. I have a lot of money. The rest of the family can build boats but for me that was just what I did while I waited to cross the mist again."

"You'll miss it," Kit said. It was not a question.

Her strong hand laid over his. "Mmm," she said, a sound without implication.

"But it was the *crossing* that mattered to you," Kit said, realizing it. "Just as with me, but in a different way."

"Yes," she said and after a pause: "So now I'm wondering. How big do the Big Ones get in the Mist Ocean? And what's on the other side?"

"Nothing's on the other side," Kit said. "There's no crossing something without an end."

"Everything can be crossed. Of course it has an end. There's a river of water deep under the Mist River, yes? And that water runs somewhere. And all the other rivers, all the lakes—they all drain somewhere. There's a water ocean under the Mist Ocean and I wonder whether the mist ends somewhere out there, if it spreads out and vanishes and you find you are floating on water."

"It's a different element," Kit said, turning the problem over. "So you would need a boat that works through mist, light enough with that broad belly and fishskin sheathing; but it would have to be deep-keeled enough for water."

She nodded. "I want to take a coast-skimmer and refit it, find out what's out there. Islands, Kit. Big Ones. *Huge* Ones. Another whole world maybe. I think I would like to be Rasali Ocean."

"You will come to Ulei with me?" he said but he knew already. She *would* come, for a month or a season or a year or even longer, perhaps. They would sleep tumbled together in an inn very like The Fish or The Bitch, and when her boat was finished, she would sail across Ocean, and he would move on to the next bridge or road. Or he might return to the capital and a position at University. Or he might rest at last.

"I will come," she said. "For a bit."

Suddenly he felt a deep and powerful emotion in his chest: overwhelmed by everything that had happened or would happen in their lives, the changes to Nearside and Farside, the ferry's ending, Valo's death, the fact that she would leave him eventually or that he would leave her. "I'm sorry," he said.

"I'm not," she said and leaned across to kiss him, her mouth warm with sunlight and life. "It is worth it, all of it."

All those losses, but this one at least he could prevent.

"When the time comes," he said: "When you sail. I will come with you."

A fo ben, bid bont. To be a leader, be a bridge.
Welsh proverb

The Evolution of Trickster Stories
Among the Dogs of North Park
After the Change

North Park is a backwater tucked into a loop of the Kaw River: pale dirt and baked grass, aging playground equipment, silver-leafed cottonwoods, underbrush, mosquitoes and gnats that blacken the air at dusk. To the south is a busy street. Engine noise and the hissing of tires on pavement mean the park is no retreat. By late afternoon the air smells of hot tar and summertime river bottoms. There are two entrances to North Park: the formal one, of silvered railroad ties framing an arch of sorts, and an accidental little gap in the fence back where Second Street dead-ends into the park's west side, just by the river.

A few stray dogs have always lived here, too clever or shy or easily hidden to be caught and taken to the shelter. On nice days (and this is a nice day, a smell like boiling sweet corn easing in on the south wind to blunt the sharper scents), Linna sits at one of the faded picnic tables with a reading assignment from her summer class and a paper bag full of fast food. She waits to see who visits her.

The squirrels come first and she ignores them. At last she sees the little dust-colored dog, the one she calls Gold.

"What'd you bring?" he says. His voice, like all dogs' voices, is hoarse and rasping. He has trouble making certain sounds. Linna understands him the way one understands a bad lisp, or someone speaking with a harelip.

(It's a universal fantasy, isn't it?—that the animals learn to speak and at last we learn what they're thinking, our cats and dogs and horses: a new era in cross-species understanding. But nothing ever works out quite as we imagine. When the Change happened, it affected all the mammals we have shaped to meet our own needs. They all could talk a little, and they all could frame their thoughts well enough to talk. Cattle, horses, goats, llamas. Pigs. Minks. And dogs and cats. And we found that, really, we prefer our slaves mute.

(The cats mostly leave, even ones who love their owners. Their pragmatic sociopathy makes us uncomfortable and we bore them, and they leave. They slip out between our legs and lope into summer dusks. We hear them at night, fighting as they sort out ranges, mates, boundaries. The savage sounds frighten us, a fear that does not ease when our cat Klio returns home for a single night asking to be fed and to sleep on the bed. A lot of cats die in fights or under car wheels but they seem to prefer that to living under our roofs, and as I said, we fear them.

(Some dogs run away. Others are cast out by the owners who loved them. Some were always free.)

"Chicken and French fries," Linna tells the dog, Gold. Linna has a summer cold that ruins her appetite and in any case it's too hot to eat. She brought her lunch leftovers, hours old but still lukewarm: half a Chik-fil-A sandwich and some fries. He never takes anything from her hand, so she tosses the food onto the ground just beyond kicking range. Gold likes French fries so he eats them first.

Linna tips her head toward the two dogs she sees peeking from the bushes. She knows better than to lift her hand suddenly, even to point or wave. "Who are these two?"

"Hope and Maggie."

"Hi, Hope," Linna says. "Hi, Maggie." The dogs dip their heads nervously as though bowing. They don't meet her eyes. She recognizes their expressions, the hurt wariness: she's seen it a few times on the recent strays of North Park, the ones whose owners threw them out after the Change. There are five North Park dogs she's seen so far. These two are new.

"Story," says the collie, Hope.

2. One Dog Loses Her Collar.

This is the same dog. She lives in a little room with her master. She has a collar that itches, so she claws at it. When her master comes home, he puts a leash on the collar and takes her outside to the sidewalk. There's a busy street outside. The dog wants to play on the street with the cars, which smell strong and move very fast. When her master tries to take her back inside, she sits down and won't move. He pulls on the leash and her collar slips over her ears and falls to the ground. When she sees this, she runs into the street. She gets hit by a car and dies.

This is not the first story Linna has heard the dogs tell. The first one was about a dog who's been inside all day and rushes outside with his master to urinate against a tree. When he's done, his master hits him because his master was standing too close and his shoe is covered with urine. *One Dog Pisses on a Person.* The dog in the story has no name, but the dogs all call him—or her: she changes sex with each telling—One Dog. Each story starts, "This is the same dog."

The little dust-colored dog, Gold, is the storyteller. As the sky dims and the mosquitoes swarm, the strays of North Park ease from the underbrush and sit or lie belly-down in the dirt to listen to Gold. Linna listens, as well.

(Perhaps the dogs always told these stories and we could not understand them. Now they tell their stories here in North Park, as do the dogs in Cruz Park a little to the south, and so across the world. The tales are not all the same though there are similarities. There is no possibility of gathering them all. The dogs do not welcome eager anthropologists with their tape recorders and their agendas.

(The cats after the Change tell stories as well but no one will ever know what they are.)

When the story is done and the last of the French fries eaten, Linna asks Hope, "Why are you here?" The collie turns her face away. It is Maggie, the little Jack Russell, who answers. "Our mother made us leave. She has a baby." Maggie's tone is matter-of-fact. It is Hope who mourns for the woman and child she loved, who compulsively licks her paw as though she were dirty and cannot be cleaned.

Linna knows this story. She's heard it from the other new strays of North Park: all but Gold, who has been feral all his life.

(Sometimes we think we want to know what our dogs think. We don't, not really. Someone who watches us with unclouded eyes and sees who we really are is more frightening than a man with a gun. We can fight or flee or avoid the man, but the truth sticks like pine sap. After the Change, some dog owners feel a cold place in the pit of their stomachs when they meet their pets' eyes. Sooner or later they ask their dogs to find new homes, or they forget to latch the gate, or they force the dogs out with curses and the ends of brooms. Or the dogs leave, unable to bear the look in their masters' eyes.

(The dogs gather in parks and gardens, anywhere close to food and water where they can stay out of people's way. Ten blocks away, Cruz Park is big, fifteen acres in the middle of town. Thirty or more dogs already have gathered there. They raid trash or beg from their former masters or strangers. They sleep under the bushes and the bandstand and the inexpensive civic sculptures. No one goes to Cruz Park on their lunch breaks anymore.

(In contrast North Park is a little dead end. No one ever did go there and so no one worries much about the dogs, yet.)

3. One Dog Tries to Mate.

This is the same dog. There is a female he very much wants to mate with. All the other dogs want to mate with her too, but her master keeps her in a yard surrounded by a chain-link fence. She whines and rubs against the fence. All the dogs try to dig under the fence, but its base is buried too deep. They try to jump over, but it is too tall for even the biggest or most agile dogs.

One Dog has an idea. He finds a cigarette butt on the street and puts it in his mouth. He finds a shirt in a Dumpster and pulls it on. He walks right up to the master's front door and presses the bell button. When the master answers the door, One Dog says, "I'm from the men with white trucks. I have to check your electrical statico-pressure. Can you let me into your yard?"

The man nods and lets him go in back. One Dog takes off his shirt and drops the cigarette and mates with the female. It feels very nice, but when he is done and they are still linked together, he starts to whine.

The man hears and comes out. He's very angry. He shoots One Dog and kills him. The female tells One Dog, "You would have been better off if you had found another female."

———

The next day after classes—hot again, and heavy with the smell of cut grass—Linna finds a dog. She hears crying and crouches to peek under a hydrangea, its blue-gray flowers as fragile as paper. It's a Maltese with filthy fur matted with twigs and burrs. There are stains under her eyes and she is moaning with the terrible sound of an injured animal.

The Maltese comes nervous to Linna's outstretched fingers and the murmur of her voice. "I won't hurt you," Linna says. "It's okay."

Linna picks the dog up carefully, feeling the dog flinch under her hand as she checks for injuries. She knows already that the pain is not physical. She knows the dog's story before she hears it.

The house nearby is massive, a graceful collection of Edwardian gingerbread work and oriel windows and green roof tiles. The garden is large, with a low fence just tall enough to keep a Maltese in. Or out. A woman answers the doorbell. Linna can feel the Maltese vibrate in her arms at the sight of the woman: excitement, not fear.

"Is this your dog?" Linna asks with a smile. "I found her outside, scared."

The woman's eyes flicker to the dog and away, back to Linna's face. "We don't have a dog," she says.

(We like our slaves mute. We like to imagine they love us and they do. But they are also with us because freedom and security war in each of us, and sometimes security wins out. They love us. But.)

In those words Linna has already seen how this conversation will go, the denials and the tangled fear and anguish and self-loathing of the woman. Linna turns away in the middle of the woman's words and walks down the stairs, the brick walkway, through the gate and north toward North Park.

The dog's name is Sophie. The other dogs are kind to her.

(The story is, that when George Washington died, his will promised freedom for his slaves, but only after his wife had also passed on. A terrified Martha freed them within hours of his death. Though the dogs love us, thoughtful owners can't help but wonder what they think when they sit on the floor beside our beds as we sleep, teeth slightly bared as they pant in the heat. Do the dogs realize that their freedom hangs by the thread of our lives? The curse of speech, the things they could say and yet choose not to say, makes that thread seem very thin.

(Some people keep their dogs even after the Change. Some people have the strength to love, no matter what. But many of us only learn the limits of our love when they have been breached. Some people keep their dogs. Many do not.

(The dogs who stay seem to tell no stories.)

4. One Dog Catches Possums.

This is the same dog. She is very hungry because her master forgot to feed her, and there's no good trash because the possums have eaten it all. "If I catch the possums," she says, "I can eat them now and then the trash later, because the they won't be getting it all."

She knows that possums are very hard to catch, so she lies down next to a trash bin and starts moaning. Sure enough, when the possums come to eat trash, they hear her and waddle over.

"Oh, oh, oh," moans the dog. "I told the rats a great secret and now they won't let me rest."

The possums look around but they don't see any rats. "Where are they?" the oldest possum asks.

One Dog says, "Everything I eat ends up in a place inside me like a giant garbage heap. I told the rats and they snuck in, and they've been there ever since." And she let out a great howl. "Their cold feet are horrible!"

The possums think for a time and then the oldest says, "This garbage heap, is it large?"

"Huge," One Dog says.

"Are the rats fierce?" says the youngest.

"Not at all," One Dog tells the possums. "If they weren't inside me, they wouldn't be any trouble even for a possum. Oh! I can feel one dragging bits of bacon around."

After whispering among themselves for a time, the possums say, "We can go in and chase out the rats, but you must promise not to hunt us ever again."

"If you catch any rats, I'll never eat another possum," she promises.

One by one the possums crawl into her mouth. She eats all but the oldest, who is too tough and stringy to be worth it.

"This is much better than dog food or trash," she says.

(Dogs love us. We have bred them to do this for ten thousand, a hundred thousand, a million years. It's hard to make a dog hate people though we have at times tried, with our junkyard guards and our attack dogs.

(It's hard to make dogs hate people but it is possible.)

Another day, just at dusk, the sky an indescribable violet. Linna has a hard time telling how many dogs there are now, ten or twelve perhaps. The dogs around her snuffle, yip, bark. One moans, the sound of a husky trying to howl. Words float up: *dry, bite, food, piss.*

The husky continues its moaning howl, and one by one the others join in with drawn-out barks and moans. They are trying to howl as a pack but none of them know how to do this, nor what it is supposed to sound like. It is a wolf-secret and they do not know any of those.

Sitting on a picnic table, Linna closes her eyes to listen. The dogs out-yell the trees' restless whispers, the river's wet sliding, even the hissing roaring street. Ten dogs, or fifteen. Or more. Linna can't tell because they are all around her now, in the brush, down by the Kaw's muddy bank, behind the cottonwoods, beside the tall fence that separates the park from the street.

The misformed howl, the hint of killing animals gathered to work efficiently together—it awakens a monkey-place somewhere in her amygdala or even deeper, stained into her genes. Adrenaline hits hot as panic. Her heart beats so hard that it feels as though she's torn it. Her monkey-self opens her eyes to watch the dogs through pupils constricted enough to dim the twilight; it clasps her arms tight over her soft belly to protect the intestines and liver that are the first parts eaten; it tucks her head between her shoulders to protect her neck and throat. She pants through bared teeth, fighting a keening noise.

Several of the dogs don't even try to howl. Gold is one of them. The howling would have defined them before the poisoned gift of speech, but the dogs have words now. They will never be free of stories though their stories may free them. Gold may understand this.

(They were wolves once, ten thousand, a hundred thousand, a million years ago. And before we were men and women, we were monkeys and fair game for them. After a time we grew taller and stronger and smarter: human, eventually. We learned about fire and weapons. If you can tame it a wolf is an effective weapon, a useful tool. If you can keep it. We learned how to keep wolves close.

(But we were monkeys first and they were wolves. Blood doesn't forget.)

After a thousand heartbeats fast as birds', long after the howl has decayed into snuffling and play-barks and speech, Linna eases back into her forebrain. Alive and safe. But not untouched. Gold tells a tale.

5. One Dog Tries to Become Like Men.

This is the same dog. There is a party, and people are eating and drinking and using their clever fingers to do things. The dog wants to do everything they do, so he says, "Look, I'm human," and he starts barking and dancing about.

The people say, "You're not human. You're just a dog pretending. If you wanted to be human, you have to be bare with just a little hair here and there."

One Dog goes off and bites his hairs out and rubs the places he can't reach against the sidewalk until there are bloody patches where he scraped off his skin as well.

He returns to the people and says, "Now I am human," and he shows his bare skin.

"That's not human," the people say. "We stand on our hind legs and sleep on our backs. First you must do these things."

One Dog goes off and practices standing on his hind legs until he no longer whimpers when he does it. He leans against a wall to sleep on his back, but it hurts and he does not sleep much. He returns and says, "Now I am human," and he walks on his hind legs from place to place.

"That's not human," the people say. "Look at these, we have fingers. First you must have fingers."

One Dog goes off and he bites at his front paws until his toes are separated. They bleed and hurt and do not work well, but he returns and says, "Now I am human," and he tries to take food from a plate.

"That's not human," say the people. "First you must dream, as we do."

"What do you dream of?" the dog asks.

"Work and failure and shame and fear," the people say.

"I will try," the dog says. He rolls onto his back and sleeps. Soon he is crying out loud and his bloody paws beat at the air. He is dreaming of all they told him.

"That dog is making too much noise," the people say and they kill him.

Linna calls the Animal Control the next day, though she feels like a traitor to the dogs for doing this. The sky is sullen with the promise of rainstorms and even though she knows that rain is not such a big problem in the life of a dog, she worries a little, remembering her own dog when she was a little girl, who had been terrified of thunder.

So she calls. The phone rings fourteen times before someone picks it up. Linna tells the woman about the dogs of North Park. "Is there anything we can do?"

The woman barks a single unhappy laugh. "I wish. People keep bringing them—been doing that since right after the Change. We're packed to the rafters and they *keep* bringing them in, or just dumping them in the parking lot, too chickenshit to come in."

"So——" Linna begins but she has no idea what to ask. She can see the scene in her mind, a hundred or more terrified angry confused grieving hungry thirsty dogs. At least the dogs of North Park have some food and water, and the shelter of the underbrush at night.

The woman has continued, "——they can't take care of themselves——"

"Do you know that?" Linna asks but the woman talks on.

"——and we don't have the resources——"

"So what do you do?" Linna interrupts. "Put them to sleep?"

"If we have to," the woman says, and her voice is so weary that Linna wants suddenly to comfort her. "They're in the runs, four and five in each one because we don't have anywhere to put them, and we can't get them outside because the paddocks are full. It smells like you wouldn't believe. And they tell these stories...."

"What's going to happen to them?" Linna means all the dogs, now that they have speech, now that they are equals.

"Oh, hon, I don't know." The woman's voice trembles. "But I know we can't save them all."

(Why do we fear them when they learn speech? They are still dogs, still subordinate to us. It doesn't change who they are or their loyalty.

(It is not always fear we run from. Sometimes it is shame.)

6. One Dog Invents Death.

This is the same dog. She lives in a nice house with people. They do not let her run outside a fence and they did things to her so that she can't have puppies, but they feed her well and are kind, and they rub places on her back that she can't reach.

At this time, there is no death for dogs. They live forever. After a while One Dog becomes bored with her fence and her food and even the people's pats. But she can't convince the people to allow her outside the fence.

"There should be death," she decides. "Then there will be no need for boredom."

(How do the dogs know things? How do they frame an abstract like *thank you* or a collective concept like chicken? Since the Change, everyone has been asking that question. If awareness is dependent on linguistics, an answer is that the dogs have learned to use words, so the words themselves are the frame they use. But it is still *our* frame, *our* language. They are still not free of it.

(Any more than we are.)

It is a moonless night and the hot wet air blurs the streetlights so that they illuminate nothing except their own glass globes. Linna is there though it is very late. She no longer attends her classes and has switched to the dogs' schedule, sleeping the afternoons away in the safety of her apartment. She cannot bring herself to sleep in the dogs' presence. In the park she is taut as a strung wire, a single monkey among wolves; but she returns each dusk and listens, and sometimes speaks. There are at least fifteen dogs now, though she's sure more hide in the bushes, doze, or prowl for food.

"I remember," a voice says hesitantly. (*Remember* is a frame. They did not "remember" before the word, only lived in a series of nows longer or shorter in duration. Memory breeds resentment, or so we fear.) "I had a home, food, a warm place, something I chewed—a, a blanket. A woman and a man and she gave me all these things, patted me." Voices in assent: pats remembered. "But she wasn't always nice. She yelled sometimes. She took the blanket away. And she'd drag at my collar until it hurt sometimes. But when she made food she'd put a piece on the floor for me to eat. Beef, it was. That was nice again."

Another voice in the darkness: "Beef. That is a hamburger." The dogs are trying out the concept of *beef* and the concept of *hamburger* and they are connecting them.

"*Nice* is not being hurt," a dog says.

"Not-nice is collars and leashes."

"And rules."

"Being inside and only coming out to shit and piss."

"People are nice and not nice," says the first voice. Linna finally sees that it belongs to a small dusty black dog sitting near the roots of an immense oak. Its enormous fringed ears look like radar dishes. "I learned to think and the woman brought me here. She was sad but she hit me with stones until I ran away and then she left. A person is nice and not nice."

The dogs are silent, digesting this. "Linna?" Hope says. "How can people be nice and then not nice?"

"I don't know," she says because she knows the real question is, *How can they stop loving us?*

(The answer even Linna has trouble seeing is that *nice* and *not-nice* have nothing to do with love. And even loving someone doesn't mean you can share your house and the fine thread of your life, or sleep safely in the same place.)

7. One Dog Tricks the White-Truck Man.

This is the same dog. He is very hungry and looking through the alleys for something to eat. He sees a man with a white truck coming toward him. One Dog knows that the white-truck men catch dogs sometimes, so he's afraid. He drags some old bones from the trash and heaps them up and settles on top of them. He pretends not to see the white-truck man but says loudly, "Boy that was a delicious man I just killed, but I'm still starved. I hope I can catch another one."

Well, that white-truck man runs right away. But someone was watching all this from her kitchen window and she runs out to the white-truck man and tells him, "One Dog never killed a man! That's just a pile of bones from my barbeque last week, and he's making a mess out of my backyard. Come catch him."

The white-truck man and the barbeque person run back to where One Dog is still gnawing on one of the bones in his pile. He sees them and guesses what has happened, so he's afraid. But he pretends not to see them and says loudly, "I'm still starved! I hope the barbeque person comes back soon with that white-truck man I asked her to get for me."

The white-truck man and the barbeque person both run away and he does not see them again that day.

———

"Why is she here?"

It's one of the new dogs, a lean mastiff-cross with a limp. He doesn't talk to her but to Gold, but Linna sees his anger in his liquid brown eyes, feels it like a hot scent rising from his back. He's one of the half-strays, an outdoor dog who lived on a chain. It was no effort at all for his owner to unhook the chain and let him go; no effort for the mastiff to leave his owner's yard, drift across town killing cats and raiding trash cans, and end up in North Park.

There are thirty dogs now and maybe more. The newcomers are warier around her than the earlier dogs. Some, the ones who have taken several days to end up here, dodging police cruisers and pedestrians' Mace, are actively hostile.

"She's no threat," Gold says.

The mastiff says nothing but approaches with head lowered and hackles raised. Linna sits on the picnic table's bench and tries not to screech, to bare her teeth and scratch and run. The situation is as charged as the air before a thunderstorm. Gold is no longer the pack's leader—there's a German Shepherd dog who holds his tail higher—but he still has status as the one who tells the stories. The German Shepherd doesn't care whether Linna's there or not. He won't stop another dog from attacking if it wishes. Linna spends much of her time with her hands flexed to bare claws she doesn't have.

"She listens, that's all," says Hope: frightened Hope standing up for her. "And brings food sometimes." Others speak up: *She got rid of my collar when it got burs under it. She took the tick off me. She stroked my head.*

The mastiff's breath on her ankles is hot, his nose wet and surprisingly warm. Dogs were once wolves; right now this burns in her mind. She tries not to shiver. "You're sick," the dog says at last.

"I'm well enough," Linna says.

Just like that the dog loses interest and turns back to the others.

(Why does Linna come here at all? Her parents had a dog when she was a little girl. Ruthie was so obviously grateful for Linna's love and the home she was offered, the old quilt on the floor, the dog food that fell from the sky twice a day like manna. Linna wondered even then whether Ruthie dreamt of a Holy Land and what that place would look like. Linna's parents were kind and generous, denied Ruthie's needs only when they couldn't help it, paid for her medical bills without too much complaining, didn't put her to sleep until she became incontinent and began to mess on the living-room floor.

(Even we dog-lovers wrestle with our consciences. We promised to keep our pets forever until they died, but that was from a comfortable height, when we were the masters and they the slaves. It is said that some Inuit groups believe all animals have souls, except for dogs. This is a convenient stance. They could not use their dogs as they do—beat them, work them, starve them, eat them, feed them one to the other—if dogs were men's equals.

(Or perhaps they could. Our record with our own species is not exemplary.)

8. One Dog and the Eating Man.

This is the same dog. She lives with the Eating Man, who eats only good things while One Dog has only dry kibble. The Eating Man is always hungry. He orders a pizza but he is still hungry so he eats all the meat and vegetables he finds in the refrigerator. But he's still hungry so he opens all the cupboards and eats the cereal and noodles and flour and sugar in there. And he's still hungry. There is nothing left so he eats all of One Dog's dry kibble, leaving nothing for One Dog.

So One Dog kills the Eating Man. "It was him or me," One Dog says. The Eating Man is the best thing One Dog has ever eaten.

Linna has been sleeping the days away so that she can be with the dogs at night, when they collect. So now it's hot dusk a day later, and she's just awakened in tangled sheets in a bedroom with flaking walls: the sky a hard haze, air warm and wet as laundry. Linna is walking past Cruz Park on her way to North Park. She has a bag with a loaf of day-old bread, some cheap sandwich meat, and an extra order of French fries. The fatty smell of the fries sticks in her nostrils. Gold never gets them anymore unless she saves them from the other dogs and gives them to him specially.

She thinks nothing of the blue and red and strobing white lights ahead of her on Mass Street until she gets close enough to see that this is no traffic stop. There's no wrecked car, no distraught student who turned left across traffic because she was late for her job and got T-boned. Half a dozen patrol cars perch on the sidewalks around the park and she can see reflected lights from others through the park's shrubs. Policemen stand around in clumps like dead leaves caught for a moment in an eddy and released according to some unseen current.

Everyone knows Cruz Park is full of dogs—sixty or seventy according to today's editorial in the local paper, each one a health and safety risk—but at the moment very few dogs are visible and none look familiar to her, either as neighbors' former pets or wanderers from the North Park pack.

Linna approaches an eddy of policemen. Its elements drift apart, rejoin other groups.

"Cruz Park is closed," the remaining officer says to Linna. He's a tall man with a military cut that makes him look older than he is.

It's no surprise that the flashing lights, the cars, the yellow CAUTION tape, and the policemen are about the dogs. There've been complaints from the people neighboring the park—overturned trashcans, feces on the sidewalks, even one attack when a man tried to grab a stray's collar and the stray fought to get away. Today's editorial merely crystallized what everyone already felt.

Linna thinks of Gold, Sophie, Hope. "They're just dogs."

The officer looks a little uncomfortable. "The park is closed until we can address current health and safety concerns." Linna can practically hear the quotation marks from the morning briefing.

"What are you going to do?" she asks.

He relaxes a little. "Right now we're waiting for Animal Control. Any dogs they capture will go to Douglas County Humane Society. They'll try to track down the owners—"

"The ones who kicked the dogs out in the first place?" Linna asks. "No one's going to want these dogs back, you know that."

"That's the procedure," he says, his back stiff again, tone defensive. "If the Humane—"

"Do you have a dog?" Linna interrupts him. "I mean, did you? Before this started?"

He turns and walks away without a word.

Linna runs the rest of the way to North Park, slowing to a lumbering trot when she gets a cramp in her side. There are no police cars up here, but more yellow plastic police tape stretches across the entry: CAUTION. She walks around to the break in the fence off Second Street. The police don't seem to know about the gap.

9. One Dog Meets Tame Dogs.

This is the same dog. He lives in a park and eats at the restaurants across the street. On his way to the restaurants one day, he walks past a yard with two dogs. They laugh at him and say, "We get dog food every day and our master lets us sleep in the kitchen, which is cool in the summer and warm in the winter. And you have to cross Sixth Street to get food where you might get run over, and you have to sleep in the heat and the cold."

The dog walks past them to get to the restaurants, and he eats the fallen tacos and French fries and burgers around the Dumpster. When he sits by the restaurant doors many people give him bits of food. One person gives him chicken in a paper dish. He walks back to the yard and lets the two dogs smell the chicken and grease on his breath through the fence. "Ha on you," he says, and then goes back to his park and sleeps on a pile of dry rubbish under the bridge where the breeze is cool. When night comes he goes looking for a mate and no one stops him.

(Whatever else it is, the Change of the animals—mute to speaking, dumb to dreaming—is a test for us. We pass the test when we accept that their dreams and desires and goals may not be ours. Many people fail this test but we don't have to, and even failing we can try again. And again. And pass at last.

(A slave is trapped, choiceless and voiceless, but so is her owner. Those we have injured may forgive us, but how can we know? Can we trust them with our homes, our lives, our hearts? Animals did not forgive before the Change. Mostly they forgot. But the Change brought memory, and memory requires forgiveness, and how can we trust them to forgive us?

(And how do we forgive ourselves? Mostly we don't. Mostly we pretend to forget.)

At noon the next day Linna jerks awake, monkey-self already dragging her to her feet. Even before she's fully awake, she knows that what woke her wasn't a car's backfire. It was a rifle shot and it was only a couple of blocks away and she already knows why.

She drags on clothes and runs to Cruz Park, no stitch in her side this time. The flashing police cars and CAUTION tape and men are all still there but now she sees dogs everywhere, twenty or more laid flat near the sidewalk, the way dogs sleep on hot summer days. Too many of the ribcages are still; too many of the eyes open, dust and pollen already gathering.

Linna has no words, can only watch speechless; but the men say enough. First thing in the morning the Animal Control people went to Dillon's grocery store and bought fifty one-pound packages of cheap hamburger on sale, and they poisoned them all and then scattered them around the park. Linna can see little blue styrene squares from the packaging scattered among the dogs.

The dying dogs don't say much. Most have fallen back into the ancient language of pain, wordless keening. Men walk among them shooting the suffering dogs, jabbing poles into the underbrush looking for any who might have slipped away.

People come in cars and trucks and on bicycles and scooters and on their feet. The police officers around Cruz Park keep sending them away—"A health risk," says one officer: "Safety," says another—but the people keep coming back, or new people.

Linna's eyes are blind with tears. She blinks and they slide down her face, oddly cool and thick.

"Killing them is the answer?" says a woman beside her. Her face is wet as well but her voice is even, as though they are debating this in a class, she and Linna. The woman holds her baby in her arms with a white cloth thrown over its face. "I have three dogs at home and they've never hurt anything. Words don't change that."

"What if they change?" Linna asks. "What if they ask for real food and a bed soft as yours, the chance to dream their own dreams?"

"I'll try to give it to them," the woman says but her attention is focused on the park, the dogs. "They can't do this."

"Try and stop them." Linna turns away tasting her tears. She should feel comforted by the woman's words, the fact that not everyone has forgotten how to love animals, but she feels nothing. And she walks north, carved hollow.

10. One Dog Goes to the Place of Pieces.

This is the same dog. She is hit by a car and part of her flies off and runs into a dark culvert. She does not know what the piece is, so she chases it. The culvert is long and it gets so cold that her breath puffs out in front of her. When she gets to the end there's no light and the world smells like metal. She walks along a road. Cold cars rush past but they don't slow down. None of them hit her.

One Dog comes to a parking lot which has nothing in it but the legs of dogs. The legs walk from place to place but they cannot see or smell or eat. None of them are her legs, so she walks on. After this she finds a parking lot filled with the ears of dogs, and then one filled with the assholes of dogs, and the eyes of dogs and the bodies of dogs; but none of the ears and assholes and eyes and bodies are hers, so she walks on.

The last parking lot she comes to has nothing at all in it except for little smells like puppies. She can tell one of the little smells is hers, so she calls to it and it comes to her. She doesn't know where the little smell belongs on her body, so she carries it in her mouth and walks back past the parking lots and through the culvert.

One Dog cannot leave the culvert because a man stands in the way. She puts the little smell down carefully and says, "I want to go back."

The man says, "You can't unless all your parts are where they belong."

One Dog can't think of where the little smell belongs. She picks up the little smell and tries to sneak past the man but the man catches her and hits her. One Dog tries to hide it under a hamburger wrapper and pretend it's not there but the man catches that, too.

One Dog thinks some more and finally says, "Where does the little smell belong?"

The man says, "Inside you."

So One Dog swallows the little smell. She realizes that the man has been trying to keep her from returning home but that the man cannot lie about the little smell. One Dog growls and runs past him and returns to our world.

———

There are two police cars pulled onto the sidewalk before North Park's main entrance. Linna takes in the sight of them in three stages: first, she has seen police everywhere today so they are no shock; second, they are *here*, at *her* park, threatening *her* dogs, and this is like being kicked in the stomach; and third, she thinks: *I have to get past them.*

North Park has two entrances. Linna walks down a side street and enters the park by the little narrow dirt path from Second Avenue.

The park is never quiet. There's busy Sixth Street just south, and the river and its noises to the north and east and west; trees and bushes hissing with the hot wind; the hum of insects.

But the dogs are quiet. She's never seen them all in the daylight but they're gathered now, silent and loll-tongued in the bright daylight. There are forty or more. Everyone is dirty now. Any long fur is matted. Anything white is dust-colored. Most of them are thinner than they were when they arrived. The dogs face one of the tables, as orderly as the audience at a string quartet, but the tension in the air is so obvious that Linna stops short.

Gold stands on the table. There are a couple of dogs she doesn't recognize in the dust nearby, lying flat with their sides heaving, tongues long and flecked with white foam. One is hunched over; he drools onto the ground and retches helplessly. The other dog has a scratch along her flank. The blood is the brightest thing Linna can see in the sunlight, a red so strong it hurts her eyes.

The Cruz Park cordon was permeable, of course. These two managed to slip past the police cars. The vomiting one is dying.

She realizes suddenly that every dog's muzzle is swiveled toward her. The air snaps with something that makes her back-brain bare its teeth and scream, her hackles rise. The monkey-self looks for escape but the trees are not close enough to climb and she is no climber, the road and river too far away. She is a spy in a gulag. The prisoners have little to lose by killing her.

"You shouldn't have come back," Gold says.

"I came to tell you. Warn you." Even through her monkey-self's defiance, Linna weeps helplessly.

"We already know." The pack's leader, the German Shepherd, says. "They're killing us all. We're leaving the park."

She shakes her head, fighting for breath. "They'll kill you. There are police cars on Sixth. They'll shoot you however you get out. They're *waiting.*"

"Will it be better here?" Gold asks. "They'll kill us anyway with their poisoned meat. We *know.* You're afraid—"

"I'm not—" Linna starts but he breaks in.

"We smell it on *everyone*, even the people who take care of us or feed us. Even you. We must leave."

"They'll *kill* you," Linna says again.

"Some of us may make it."

"Wait! Maybe there's a way," Linna says and then: "I have stories."

In the stifling air, Linna can hear the dogs pant even over the street noises. "People stories are only good for people," Gold says at last. "Why should we listen to yours?"

"We made you into what we wanted; we owned you. Now you are becoming what you want. You belong to yourselves. But we have stories and we learned from them and maybe they will help you. Will you listen?"

The air shifts, but whether it is the first movement of the still air or the dogs shifting, she can't tell.

"Tell your story," says the German Shepherd.

Linna struggles to remember half-read textbooks from a sophomore course on folklore, framing her thoughts as she speaks them. "We used to tell a lot of stories about Coyote. The animals were here before humans were, and Coyote was one of them. He did a lot of stuff, got in a lot of trouble. Fooled everyone."

"I know about coyotes," a dog says. "There were some by where I used to live. They eat puppies sometimes."

"I bet they do," Linna says. "Coyotes eat everything. But this wasn't *a* coyote, it's *Coyote.* The one and only."

The dogs murmur. She hears them work it out: *Coyote* is the same as *This is the same dog.*

"So. Coyote disguised himself as a bitch so that he could hang out with a bunch of other females just so he could mate with them. He pretended to be dead and then when the crows came down to eat him, he snatched them up and ate every one. When a greedy man was keeping all the animals for himself, Coyote pretended to be a very rich person and freed them all so that everyone could eat. He—" She pauses to think, looks down at the dogs all around her. The monkey-fear is gone. She is the storyteller, the maker of thoughts. They will not kill her, she knows. "Coyote did all these things and a lot more. I bet you'll think of some too.

"I have an idea of how to save you," she says. "Some of you might die but some chance is better than no chance."

"Why would we trust you?" says the mastiff-cross who has never liked her, but the other dogs are with her. She feels it and answers.

"Because this trick, maybe it's even good enough for Coyote. Will you let me help?"

We people are so proud of our intelligence, but that makes it easier to trick us. We see the white-truck men and we believe they're whatever we're expecting to see. Linna goes to U-Haul and rents a pickup truck for the afternoon. She digs out a white shirt she used to wear when she ushered at the concert hall. She knows *clipboard with printout* means *official responsibilities,* so she throws one on the dashboard of the truck.

She backs the pickup to the little entrance on Second Street. The dogs slip through the gap in the fence and scramble into the pickup's bed. She lifts the ones that are too small to jump so high. And then they arrange themselves carefully, flat on their sides. There's a certain amount of snapping and snarling as later dogs step on the ears and ribcages of the earlier dogs, but eventually everyone is settled, everyone able to breathe a little, every eye tight shut.

She pulls onto Sixth Street with a truck heaped with dogs. When the police stop her she tells them a little story. Animal Control has too many calls these days: cattle loose on the highways, horses leaping fences that are too high and breaking their legs—and the dogs, the scores and scores of dogs at Cruz Park. Animal Control is renting trucks now, whatever they can find. The dogs of North Park were slated for poisoning this morning.

"I didn't hear about this in briefing," one of the policemen says. He pokes at the heap of dogs with a black club. They shift like dead meat. They reek; an inexperienced man might not recognize the stench as mingled dog breath and shit.

Linna smiles, baring her teeth. "I'm on my way back to Animal Control," she says. "They have an incinerator." She waves an open cell phone at him and hopes he does not ask to talk to whoever's on the line because there is no one.

But people believe stories and then they make them real. The officer pokes at the dogs one more time and then wrinkles his nose and waves her on.

Clinton Lake is a vast place, trees and bushes and impenetrable brambles ringing a big lake: beyond that, open country in every direction. When Linna unlatches the pickup's bed, the dogs drop stiffly to the ground and stretch. Three died of overheating, stifled beneath the weight of so many others. Gold is one of them but Linna does not cry. She knew she couldn't save them all but she has saved some of them. That has to be enough. And the stories will continue. Stories do not easily die.

The dogs can go wherever they wish from here, and they will. They and all the other dogs who have tricked or slipped or stumbled to safety will spread across Kansas, the world. Some will find homes with men and women who treat them not as slaves but as friends, freeing themselves as well. Linna herself returns home with little shivering Sophie and sad Hope.

Some will die, killed by men and cougars and cars and even other dogs. Others will raise litters. The fathers of some of those litters will be coyotes. Eventually the Changed dogs will find their place in the changed world.

(When we first fashioned animals to suit our needs, we treated them as though they were stories and we the authors, and we clung desperately to an imagined copyright that would permit us to change them, sell them, even delete them. But some stories cannot be controlled. Perhaps we started them but they change and they are no longer ours, if they ever were. A wise author or dog owner listens and learns and says at last, "I never knew that.")

———

I I. One Dog Creates the World.

This is the same dog. There wasn't any world when this happens, just a man and a dog. They lived in a house that didn't have any windows to look from. Nothing had any smells. The dog shit and pissed on a paper in the bathroom, but not even this had a smell. Her food had no taste, either. The man suppressed all these things. This was because the man didn't want One Dog to create the world and he knew it would be done by smell.

One night One Dog was sleeping and she felt the strangest thing that any dog has ever felt. It was the smells of the world pouring from her nose. When the smell of grass came out, there was grass outside. When the smell of shit came out, there was shit outside. She made the whole world that way. And when the smell of other dogs came out, there were dogs everywhere, big ones and little ones all over the world.

"I think I'm done," she said, and she left.

Publication History

"26 Monkeys, Also the Abyss," *Asimov's Magazine*, July 2008.

"Fox Magic," *Asimov's Magazine*, December 1993.

"Names for Water," *Asimov's Magazine*, October/November 2010.

"The Bitey Cat," published here for the first time.

"The Horse Raiders," *Analog*, May 2000.

"Dia Chjerman's Tale," *Tales for the Long Rains*, Scorpius Digital, 2001

"My Wife Reincarnated as a Solitaire—Exposition on the Flaws in my Wife's Character—The Nature of the Bird—Her Final Disposition," www.kijjohnson.com.

"Schrödinger's Cathouse," *Fantasy and Science Fiction*, March 1993.

"Chenting, in the Land of the Dead," *Realms of Fantasy*, October 1999.

"The Empress Jingu Fishes," *Conqueror Fantastic*, Pocket Books, 2004.

"At the Mouth of the River of Bees," *SciFiction*, September 2006.

"Story Kit," *Eclipse 4*, Night Shade Books, 2011.

"Wolf Trapping," *The Twilight Zone Magazine*, April 1989.

"Ponies," Tor.com, November 2010.

"The Cat Who Walked a Thousand Miles," Tor.com, July 2009.

"Spar," *Clarkesworld Magazine*, October 2009.

"The Man Who Bridged the Mist," *Asimov's Magazine*, October/November 2011.

"The Evolution of Trickster Stories among the Dogs of North Park after the Change," *The Coyote Road*, Avon Books, 2007.

Acknowledgments

Many years of writing short fiction means that I have had the opportunity to learn from a lot of people, too many to list. I would like to specifically acknowledge the following people, who helped significantly with these particular stories.

Editors: Neil Clarke, Ellen Datlow, Gardner Dozois, Tappan King, Shawna McCarthy, Patrick Nielsen Hayden, Kris Rusch, Pamela Sargent, Stan Schmidt, Jonathan Strahan, Sheila Williams, and Terri Windling; and Gavin J. Grant and Kelly Link.

Muses: Ed Bryant, Octavia Butler, Ted Chiang, Samuel Delany, Bob Howe, Lucy Huntington, Peg Kerr, John Kessel, Ursula K. Le Guin, Chris McKitterick, Irene Michon, Lane Robins, Vivi Trujillo, Eric Warren, Barbara Webb (*especially* Barbara Webb), Connie Willis, the students and faculty of North Carolina State University's MFA program, my own students, and ten thousand *cafés au lait* at innumerable coffee shops.

Finally, I owe more than I can say to James Gunn, who taught me as much as anyone could about writing science fiction.

About the Author

Kij Johnson's short stories have received the Theodore Sturgeon Memorial Award, World Fantasy, and Nebula Awards. Her novels include two volumes of the Heian trilogy Love/War/Death: *The Fox Woman* (which received the Crawford Award) and *Fudoki*. She is currently researching a third novel set in Heian Japan; and *Kylen*, two novels set in Georgian Britain.

She taught writing and science fiction writing at Louisiana State University and at the University of Kansas. She has run chain and independent bookstores and has worked at Tor Books, Dark Horse Comics, Wizards of the Coast, Microsoft, Real Networks, as well as worked as a radio announcer and engineer, edited cryptic crosswords, and waitressed in a strip bar. She has an MFA in Creative Writing and is an Assistant Professor of Fiction Writing at the University of Kansas English Department.

Shirley Jackson Award winner · *Publishers Weekly* Top 10 Best Books of the Year · io9 Best SF&F Books of the Year · Story Prize Notable Book · Tiptree Award Honor List · Philip K. Dick Award finalist

"Each tale is a beautifully written character study. . . . McHugh's great talent is in reminding us that the future could never be weirder — or sadder — than what lurks in the human psyche. This is definitely one of the best works of science fiction you'll read this year, or any thereafter."—Annalee Newitz, NPR

paper · $16 · 9781931520294 | ebook · $9.95 · 9781931520355

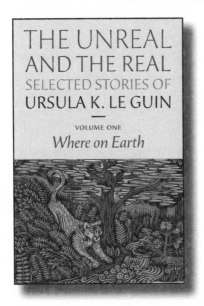

Ursula K. Le Guin's stories have shaped the way many readers see the world. By giving voice to the voiceless, hope to the outsider, and speaking truth to power—all the time maintaining her independence and sense of humor—she has proven herself a truly great writer.

This two-volume selection—as selected and organized by the author—contains almost forty stories and both volumes include new introductions by Le Guin.

"She is the reigning queen of . . . but immediately we come to a difficulty, for what is the fitting name of her kingdom? Or, in view of her abiding concern with the ambiguities of gender, her queendom, or perhaps—considering how she likes to mix and match—her quinkdom? Or may she more properly be said to have not one such realm, but two?"—Margaret Atwood, *New York Review of Books*

The Unreal and the Real: Selected Stories Volume One: Where on Earth
cloth · $24 · 9781618730343 | ebook · $14.95 · 9781618730367

The Unreal and the Real: Selected Stories Volume Two: Outer Space, Inner Lands
cloth · $24 · 9781618730350 | ebook · $14.95 · 9781618730374

Recent and forthcoming short story collections and novels from
Small Beer Press for independently minded readers:

Joan Aiken, *The Monkey's Wedding and Other Stories*
"Wildly inventive, darkly lyrical, and always surprising."—*Publishers Weekly* (starred review)

Nathan Ballingrud, *North American Lake Monsters: Stories**

Ted Chiang, *Stories of Your Life and Others*
"Shining, haunting, mind-blowing tales"—Junot Díaz (*The Brief Wondrous Life of Oscar Wao*)

Peter Dickinson, *Earth and Air: Tales of Elemental Creatures*
"Beautiful stories, deft, satisfying, unexpected. They deserve to become classics."—*Wall Street Journal*

Karen Joy Fowler, *What I Didn't See and Other Stories*
"An exceptionally versatile author."—*St. Louis Post-Dispatch*

Angélica Gorodischer, *Kalpa Imperial* (trans. Ursula K. Le Guin);
*Trafalgar** (trans. by Amalia Gladheart)

Elizabeth Hand, *Errantry: Stories*
"Ten evocative novellas and stories whisper of hidden mysteries. . . .
Elegant nightmares, sensuously told."—*Publishers Weekly*

Nancy Kress, *Fountain of Age: Stories*
"A master class in the art of short-story writing."—*Kirkus Reviews*

Kelly Link, *Magic for Beginners; Stranger Things Happen*

Karen Lord, *Redemption in Indigo*
Mythopoeic, Crawford, & Frank Collymore Award winner.

Geoff Ryman, *Paradise Tales*
"Includes one of the most powerful stories I've read in the last 10 years."—*New York Times*

Sofia Samatar, *A Stranger in Olondria**
"Samatar has an expansive imagination, a poetic and elegant style, and she writes stories so rich, with
characters so full of life, they haunt you long after the story ends."—Chris Abani (author of *GraceLand*)

*Forthcoming
Our ebooks are available from our indie press ebooksite:

www.weightlessbooks.com

www.smallbeerpress.com